Congratualtions to Lori Morgan,
***HOLT Medallion winner for* Indigo Moon!**

LESSON IN EQUALITY

From his vest pocket, he withdrew her necklace. Heart pounding, she watched him bring it to his nose as if struck by some redolence. Her eyes lifted to his. "Tell me, Miss *Nobody,* what is a twenty-dollar gold eagle worth in the currency you were trading that night? The soft intensity in his voice stilled her breath.

She scraped the tip of her tongue across her bottom lip. "Surely you're still not under the misnomer that I am a . . ." The indelicate word stuck to the roof of her dry mouth.

In the light that streamed in from the French doors, his strength seemed even more pronounced as he braced his palms on either side of her. "A what?" he prodded.

She had the distinct impression that her innocence mattered little in his opinion of her.

Her blood boiled with his pretension. Ha! The big tough marshal. He meant to intimidate her. Lacey wrapped her fists in his collar. He didn't know her mettle. She'd give him a lesson in equality. "Is this what you wanted that night instead, Mister Marshal?" She planted her lips on his.

The contact stabbed at her, starting somewhere in her lower extremities and radiating out like a melding prism of light. His mouth was hot and moist, shaping to hers, nothing like she expected. Lord. Her heart was beating too hard. Heat stirred in her loins. And at once, she knew her mistake. Dear Lord, did she ever.

Other *Leisure* books by Lori Morgan
INDIGO MOON

Lori Morgan

Autumn Star

LEISURE BOOKS NEW YORK CITY

A LEISURE BOOK®

July 2001

Published by

Dorchester Publishing Co., Inc.
276 Fifth Avenue
New York, NY 10001

Cover art by John Ennis
www.ennisart.com

ISBN 0-8439-4892-2

Printed in the United States of America.

For my nephews Keith and Brian Herring.
Two young men with big dreams, remarkable talent and awesome fortitude that comes naturally from being born and raised in Alaska. You guys are the best!

With great affection and much thanks to Cheri Smolich & Joyce Koehl for your support and five years of continuous encouragement.

To Donna Key and her two beautiful daughters, Lindsey and Lacy, the first Autumn Star.

And finally to my good friend Liz Krejcik aka Elizabeth Rose, our Windy City resident Greek Goddess. RT *was a blast!*

Autumn Star

Chapter One

San Francisco
August 1873

Outside on the street, the noise of the crowd grew louder. Clad in nothing but dark denims and a pair of leather boots, Morgan Caine lifted the frilly edge of black lace that encased the window. He stared dispassionately at the chaos below, hesitating only an instant before his gaze rose past rows of clapboard gray houses that stair-stepped down the hill. A rolling fog bank crept in from the coast. Soon it would be dusk. Gambling halls and whores would not lack for rowdy patrons tonight.

Gunshots sounded as men fired into the air. Out of professional habit, Morgan sided away from the glass. Buggies and horses packed the street. Drunken pedestrians ambled out of saloons and houses, venturing even from the hill to catch a glimpse of the scaffold where four ropes hung listlessly in the still air.

Waiting.

A man's death shouldn't be made into a public spectacle,

even for killers such as those who would soon be led from the jailhouse, who deserved no more than a rough hemp of rope around their neck to end their worthless existence.

Anger clenched his fists as he tried not to remember the sister he'd buried a few months before or that these men were only a handful of the gang he still hunted.

Behind him the slight movement of the raven-haired beauty crawling out of bed, whispered in the silence. She was beginning to get impatient. He'd dismissed her earlier to look out the window. To find some pleasure in the moment. Now, he wondered why he'd come to her at all. He'd needed . . . He'd needed what? Comfort? Feminine libations to ease his anger? A gentle touch?

His mouth lifted into a grin. Such sentiment amused him. It was not in his character to be soft; not when it could easily get him killed. At thirty-two, he'd already outlived the life expectancy of a man in his occupation.

Her arms wrapped around his waist, her familiar body, warm and pliant. His shirt lay on the floor beside the bed. Her breath fluttered against his back like the wings of a butterfly. "You're so far away. I hope that smile is for me, John Caine."

"I told you not to call me that," he said flatly, looking at her in the glass past his own unshaven reflection.

"You needn't get so testy," she said, pouting. "I like it. That's what all the papers call you."

The name was part of a past he'd buried long ago. It infuriated him that the *Examiner* could learn so much about him in a matter of weeks, then print it.

His muscles tensed as her fingers fanned across his belly to his breeches. The sky had grown darker. The room colder. The cloying scent of her perfume surrounded him. "You are so angry." Her lips trailed along his back. "Are you still thinking about the trial? You won."

Her words eager, her breath was hot against his skin, and a surge of repugnance filled him. "I've won nothing," he whispered.

"Then you're still going after those other men who—"

"Cat—" he warned, his voice intentionally sharp. Caitlyn

Madigan always had a way of prying. "I didn't come here to talk business. That was our agreement."

"Brett Lawton's men will find you first and kill you."

Studying her face, he grinned. "Do I detect a hint of glee, Caitlyn?"

"Maybe." She flicked idly at his arm and flounced away. His gaze followed her naked derriere. Confident of his bold regard, she turned and placed her hands on her hips. "Perhaps I will clap when someone finally outdraws the indomitable John Morgan Caine."

Christ! She could act like such a bitch.

Even so, Caitlyn possessed an irresistible lure, making the occasional tryst quite pleasant—the devil fly with his good sense. Still, something nagged at him about her behavior. Though her theatrics weren't out of character, Caitlyn wasn't the clingy type. It was almost as if she had some other reason that she wanted him to stay.

Out of habit that came from years of being a lawman, Morgan's glance circled the shadows around the quaint Victorian parlor. Caitlyn was doing rather nicely for herself in the short time since she'd arrived in San Francisco for the trail. At least he never felt compelled to worry about her welfare. He turned and watched the street, letting the sounds of the night fill his head.

His gaze settled absently on a carriage trying to push past the crowd. It listed drunkenly to one side, its front wheel lodged in one of the many holes that pocked the muddy street. He leaned an arm against the glass.

In the maelstrom of people and horses, his fleeting glimpse came to rest on a face framed in the carriage window. Golden light from inside the coach cast her profile in luminous relief, drawing his attention. Redolent of sunshine, she was out of place in the motley surroundings of charcoal mist and mud. Her purity contrasted sharply with the darkness hovering over his life. The ugliness. She didn't belong in a place like this.

Captivated by the ethereal vision, Morgan pressed closer to the window. Then suddenly her gaze lifted, and he knew the instant she found him in the shadows behind the dirt-streaked glass. His breath stopped. Flaxen hair curled astray around a face made beautiful by a full curving mouth. He could feel the intensity of her gaze. And he didn't breathe.

A second later the window flap dropped back in place—and she vanished. Curiously bereft, his eyes lingered where her face had been, before he realized that he was staring.

He dropped the curtain edge and stared at the lace fisted in his hand. Caitlyn slipped her palms up the length of his chest to tangle in the crisp, dark hair just below his neck. For the first time since she'd touched him, he was conscious now of her willing body. He wrapped his hands in her hair and traced his mouth down the arch of her neck, letting his hunger overtake him. A small catlike sigh quaked from her mouth.

"Don't go to the hanging."

He didn't want to hear any more of her talk.

She pressed against him, sprinkling kisses across his shoulders. "I want to be with you. We're good together. We know where we stand with each other. No promises."

He could hear her small gasps of pleasure as he backed her toward the wall, his hands sliding over her breasts and down the curve of her waist. Her mouth found solace against his chest, nibbling and caressing the resilient muscles that moved in response to the heat of her touch. Gripping his arms, she nuzzled against his neck. "Morgan," she groaned. "I've . . . missed you."

"Caitlyn"—his words were a harsh rumble in his chest—"you talk too damn much." They struck the wall solidly—her back pressed firmly against the small feminine swirls curling in and out of the silk wallpaper.

"You're still a bastard, Morgan Caine." Her movements became more frenzied. "I don't know why I bother with you at all."

She pushed his pants down past his hips, her hand wrapping around him. He barely heard her moan above his own response. He was so hard it ached. The rest of the world could go to hell. He needed her—the release she would provide.

"Kiss me, Morgan," she commanded.

She lifted her face, stretching herself to kiss him, but he buried his mouth against her hair, pressing his cheek against her temple. His hands dropped to her bottom, and bracing her against his knee, he lifted her until her legs wrapped around his waist. He slid inside her warmth, gliding, until she swallowed all of him.

She cried out, hanging against him as he moved back and forth, increasing the tempo with every ragged breath, each thrust deeper until he heard her breath break in quick, short gasps. She flung her head back, her hips grinding faster and faster. He felt her hands glide across his shoulders and tunnel into his hair, her cries turning into sweet agony.

The brass corner of a trunk dug into his knee. With a low growl, he shifted, and dropped with her onto the bed. The carnal need for sexual release swelled through him, numbing the noise outside, his emotions and memories. He thrust inside her, seeking repletion. But the deep-down loneliness never went away.

Never.

No doubt, somewhere in the world, the sun blazed down on glorious rooftops, but not in San Francisco. A light mist filled the air. Earlier it had rained.

And Lacey Ashton had loved every wet drop of it. The way it tasted on her lips. Like home.

Home. The simple notion was as elusive as the breeze. No one wanted her. Not as a wife. Not as a daughter.

Lacey shifted uneasily in her seat. The rocking lull of the carriage was reminiscent of the past months spent aboard ships, sailing from England, stuffed in cramped living quarters that turned her into a veritable harpy. A renewed hint of seasickness weakened her resolve as the taxi lurched in the mud like a sick snail. Lacey squelched the panic to throw open the door and leap outside. A little mud between the toes never hurt anyone.

Instead, she gazed back at the second-story window waiting for the elusive figure to appear again. Her pulse quickened, compelling her to inch aside the leather flap a little more. Awareness permeated her reserve. A man had been behind that glass looking at her.

Gunshots froze her. The carriage swayed as the crowd outside jostled past. The door swung open and a square-built man wearing a Prince Albert coat and beaver hat filled the doorway.

The driver stomped the mud from his boots. "We ain't goin' no farther, ma'am," he informed her. "I'll have to let you out here."

Horrified at the prospect of being abandoned in bedlam, she glanced outside at the chaos. Her hand went to the choker around her neck. The necklace had been Aunt Clare's last gift to her before she died. "But you can't. There are no inns around here."

"There's a hangin', miss. Down the street. You'll be lucky to find a place to stay at all tonight. Maybe you should have stayed down at the wharf."

"My packet to Portland doesn't arrive until tomorrow. The purser's office would only keep my trunks."

"I'm sorry, miss."

Once outside, Lacey gripped her carpetbag to her chest and looked around her. Bullet hole–ridden buildings lined the planked walkway now fragmented and crumbling with age. Horse-drawn wagons were mired in mud. Wild-looking men with long hair and unkempt beards fired their guns into the sky, their insane actions measuring every unsavory attribute she'd come to expect from American men.

The crowd bumped and jostled her, throwing her against the driver. He set her upright. "The trial's been in all the papers," he said as if in explanation to his brethrens' crude behavior. "Some lawman brought this bloody bunch hundreds of miles down from the territory alone. Brett Lawton hisself. Part of the Lawton gang. They were wanted from here to Montana Territory. A year ago they stole a hundred thousand in gold from the Feds."

"They're hanging four men for stealing from your government?"

"No, ma'am." He laughed. "They're hangin' 'em I suppose because they killed seven people here last year."

She frowned in disgust. Murder a few people, no one blinks an eye. Steal gold, the fickle Americans are in love. Only a Yank would elevate an outlaw to fame of such heroic proportions.

"Why would a man risk his life to bring murderers so far away?"

"Guess the marshal didn't want to wait months for a circuit judge to hear their case. Too dangerous for any jail that would try to hold this bunch. If you want some entertainment, go find yourself a seat someplace."

With that, he trotted off. A hanging indeed. The very idea repulsed her. She was a lady, not some barbarian.

Someone bumped her, and she stumbled, catching herself on the carriage wheel. The horse swished its tail, and she took a step backward. Fixing her gaze on the monstrous creature, Lacey slapped the mud off her gloves and tried to remember her determination to like her new homeland. But this untamed frontier offended her in a way that England, with its sterile class structure and customs, never did. Somehow, she had a feeling that executing a curtsy would only get her shot in the backside. She should have been honing her skills with knives, not needlework.

Straightening, she forced the starch back in her spine. Put simply, she had nowhere else in the world to go. This was a sink-or-swim situation. And frankly, Lacey was convinced that after the events of this past year she knew how to swim better than most.

She cheered herself with the notion that nothing could get any worse. Tomorrow, she would be leaving for Portland to meet her father. His by-blow daughter was a lady, even if he hadn't seen her in thirteen years to confirm anything else about her life.

Brushing the untidy wrinkles from her indigo silk skirt, she pulled the edge of her sleeve to shield the annoying heart-shaped birthmark that marred her shoulder. Her bodice stretched taut across a bosom that had matured considerably in the past three years, but being one step from the poorhouse after her aunt Clare died, purchasing something as frivolous as a new evening dress was out of the question.

Stepping onto the boardwalk, Lacey stole one last unsure glance at the window behind her before the crowd suddenly swept her up and took her along in its midst. Half the size of most of the men around her, she could barely see past their bulky, smelly shoulders. If she fell, she was certain they'd trample her.

Seeking purchase on solid ground, Lacey struggled at an angle to get across the busy street. A bump from the side knocked her bonnet off. Her coifed hair came loose. She cried out, attempting to snag the precious hairpins before they followed the way of her bonnet. A lamppost appeared before her. Latching on, she held herself taut, almost losing her carpetbag in the press of people.

Packed like cattle, the crowd roared, craning their necks to view something. After a while everything seemed to quiet. A low buzz of anticipation pervaded the area. Lacey turned her head, and a glance over her shoulder made her gasp. A wooden gallows stood like a decapitated dragon at the center of a pebbled square where three roads merged in front of a large brick courthouse. Four men wearing hoods, their hands bound behind them were dragged in full view out of the building to the top of the platform. Another man dressed in a black judge's cloak walked up and down the line of prisoners. Finally, he lowered a rope around the first man's neck. Lacey swallowed. Her throat tightened.

A firm believer in Jehovah's commandments, she abhorred violence and the kind of men who used it. Even a civilized murder was still a murder. She couldn't even bear to hurt a mouse. She loved kittens and puppies. At home she'd cared for a simple vegetable garden and spent her time with her elderly aunt, a vicar's daughter, who'd been like a mother to her, who'd died peacefully in her sleep less than a year ago.

Nothing in Lacey's young life had ever prepared her for anything like this. The crowd grew silent. Mesmerized, she watched as the hideous rope was placed over the last man's head and cinched tightly. The man fought violently, only to be cuffed into silence. Lacey flinched. Her heart beat a fierce tattoo against her ribs. Someone coughed from his perch on the roof above her. A preacher spoke to each of the condemned then turned and read something to the crowd. A beautiful verse from Psalms.

Lacey could hear the water lapping at the shores of the bay. Somewhere a brass bell tolled six o'clock, its hollow clang a saddened sound in the sudden emptiness. Then the shaft on the gallows opened, and four men dropped to their deaths.

Their necks snapped. Like the sound of an English acorn beneath her boot. A woman beside her fainted.

Gripping the gaslight pole, Lacey watched it all.

Suddenly she thought of England. Of green hills and civilization. Untainted raindrops. Soirées and laughter. And knew a grim realization that her life as she'd known it was over.

Chapter Two

Fumbling with the few coins left in her small reticule, Lacey lifted her awed gaze up the monolith building that suddenly appeared in her path. Like an oasis rising from its dingy surroundings, the Chateau Hotel towered five stories before disappearing into the languorous fog bank hovering over this wretched city. A lead crystal roof stretched over an inner atrium filled with exotic plants.

The smell of cheese bisque and hot bread permeated her senses. Mentally, Lacey began to add up the money she had left. Night had already descended on the city, and she was no closer to finding the dock in this fog than when she'd started out hours ago.

Her carpetbag and what few belongings she'd taken with her for tonight were gone: stolen by six street roughs who'd dared accost her in full view of at least a dozen pedestrians. She hadn't eaten or drunk anything since dawn when her steamer docked. She hadn't slept in almost thirty-six hours. She'd watched four men hang. Her body ached. Her senses were ravaged. Lord. A hot burn built behind her eyes. She was scared.

Stopping her fingers from fidgeting with her choker, she reassembled her courage. This was no time to feel sorry for herself. She had to find her way back to the docks to board her packet to Portland in the morning. But first she had to eat. If another establishment refused her entry, she would bloody well scream. Or throw a rock through its window, or even hit someone. Let them toss her in jail. At least she would have a place to sleep and something to eat for the night.

Inside, the doorman was engaged with a pretty-faced blonde and didn't see Lacey enter. Moving quietly in the shadows, Lacey followed the cobblestone path toward the sound of excited voices, hoping to find the restaurant that was baking such delicious bread.

Rounding a corner beside a miniature waterfall, she came to an abrupt halt. Her jaw dropped at the magnificence that opened before her. The clanking of coins and rolling dice blended with the raucous sound of excited gamblers. Roulette wheels clicked in cadence to her pulse.

It was a foreign world. A complete contrast to her sheltered existence. Decadent. The girl she was could disappear inside such a place. Never to be found.

Mesmerized by the spectral brilliance of the crystal chandelier hanging suspended over the hall, Lacey floated into the giant, smoke-filled gaming hall looking at everything. She'd heard of places such as this. Gentlemen's clubs were what people called them in England. Only this one looked to allow women.

A black-clad server passed, and no one noticed when Lacey plucked a glass of champagne off the silver platter carried high above his head. The champagne was served in French Baccarat crystal. She eagerly drank, and boldly plucked a second glass off a tray as another waiter passed into the gambling hall.

After her fourth glass of champagne, her senses wavered between the tin-panny music and the voices of the gamblers drifting like disembodied spirits about her head.

Lacey stayed in the shadows. Everyone was in a festive mood. Watching the crowded room over the rim of her fluted glass, she felt out of place. The familiar disconcerting sentiment that seemed to dog her heels no matter the occasion. But no one leaped forward to throw her out. No one even noticed her presence.

Reassured by their lack of interest, she relaxed enough to look around her. Curtained beneath the wings of a monstrous stone-carved cupid, the crowded salon invited her attention. A waterfall chandelier cast a shimmering glow over the plush red-and-gold velvet decor dominating the salon, making the ridiculous cupid indiscreetly inviting to the gaze.

The heady scent of tobacco filled Lacey's head. A mahogany bar stretched the length of the room. Her gaze fell on a basket of shelled cashews at the far end of the spacious bar. Her heart leaped.

Food.

She stumbled slightly as she pressed through the crowd, her eyes on the basket. Once at the bar, Lacey devoured handfuls of nuts. Lord, she closed her eyes. They were still warm. Shoving more into her reticule, she giggled at the absurd tableau. The ever so proper Lacey Ashton had resorted to stealing nuts from a gambling hall. What would Aunt Clare think?

It took her a moment to realize the din of voices around her had fallen away in silence.

"A little outta yer territory, ain't yuh, Marshal?"

The low, gruff voice startled Lacey upright. Her attention converged on the broad back of a man slouched against the bar.

"The marshal's been testifying at the Lawton trial," a buckskin-clad, old-timer grunted, letting his insolent gaze go over the tall stranger who slapped two coins on the bar. "Big hero. Brought 'em all the way down from Washington territory hisself just fer us to hang."

"Hell," the unkempt man nearest Lacey said, snickering, "a man would rightly sell his ma fer the bounty on that man's head. Ain't nothin' noble 'bout that."

"Gressett, you fool," the barkeep hissed.

"Bug out, Skinny!"

"That's no cow-town sheriff you're bullyin', Sam."

"The jasper's name is Caine." The man named Sam Gressett spat a wad of tobacco juice at the offending one's boot. "Morgan Caine. A former sheriff in these parts. Ain't that so, Marshal?"

"I don't want no killin's, Sam," Skinny interceded.

Gressett's horse-faced countenance whipped around on the lanky barkeep. "Shut yer yap, Skinny. If I wanted yer advice, I'da asked."

Lacey glanced toward the marshal. Tall, with compelling features made dark by a growth of black stubble, he had the look of someone who spent a great deal of his time outdoors. Lacey strained slightly away from the bar, registering the dark hair brushing the collar of his blue chambray shirt. Her wide-eyed gaze dropped past the flash of silver on his black leather vest, to the walnut-handled gun strapped to his lean hips. Her eyes shifted over all of him, noting immediately his casual stance. He ignored them.

The jittery barkeep slapped a glass and bottle of rye on the bar. "Ain't Caine I'm worried about," he grumbled, swiping up the coins in front of the tall marshal before walking away.

Lacey's gaze followed the man called Skinny, then stopped abruptly on the marshal's reflection in the gold-veined mirror stretching the length of the wall. Fascinated by long, tapered fingers that cradled the drink, she watched him bring the glass slowly to the light as if savoring the amber liquid. The mirror reflected only a shade of his somber expression. Beneath the brim of his battered low-brim hat, his eyes were a startling clear blue. They were the sharp eyes of a hunter, predatory eyes—and they were looking directly at her!

Mortified to be caught staring, Lacey watched the whiskey glass lower abruptly to the bar. He turned to look at her as if he knew her, and their eyes met directly. Lacey tore her gaze from his, but not before she felt an odd, indefinable tremor jolt her insides. Her reaction to this stranger stunned her as much as being caught gaping.

"Lookie here what I found," the man beside her murmured, his shrewd, assessing glance hesitating on her reflection before turning to face her fully.

Sam Gressett closed the short distance between them. "Seen my gold, did yuh, girlie? Well, yuh come to the right place to be entertained."

Lacey's gaze sided to the pile of gold dust on the bar. Her eyes shifted back to Gressett in astonishment. With brown uncombed hair, soiled clothes, and twin gun belts slung from his hips, the man's demeanor was a dire contradiction to the wealth he so carelessly flaunted.

"Excuse me, sir?" Her English lilt was blatantly out of place. The guffaws that followed alarmed her.

"Hear that, Sam?" Old Buckskin slapped him on the back. "She called yuh, sir. That must mean she likes ya."

More snickers erupted.

"And what's wrong with that? Aye, the lady knows *quantity* when she sees it, don't yuh, love?" he mimicked, demolishing her accent. The man was a half-wit.

"You see, I'm new to port—"

"This is yer first time, is it?" The laughter grew bolder.

"—and don't wish to be accosted." She watched the buckskin-clad man cut off her escape.

Gressett rudely appraised her curves. "Did yuh hear that boys? I'm 'costing the whore. Maybe she thinks she's worth more 'an my gold here."

"Maybe she just don't like ya, Sam." His partner smirked.

Speechless, she looked around. Gruff, unshaven creatures were watching her with the savage interest of vultures. The marshal stood with his elbows braced against the bar, his head bowed. Tightly laced fingers cradled an empty glass of whiskey. She was out of her element here, and no amount of expensive champagne could dilute the dread that suddenly knotted her stomach.

Gressett snaked his bulky arm around her waist. "Maybe yuh think Caine's got something I ain't."

"Let go of me, you stinking jackass."

Gressett laughed. "Not really so *toity-hoity,* are ya? Sorta makes us have something in common after all, don't it?"

"Leave her alone."

Lacey registered a stranger's voice. She could barely breathe against her tightly cinched corset. Gressett's grip slackened. "Shut up, Caine. This here filly's mine. I seen her first."

The marshal's head turned. "I said leave her alone."

Gressett shoved Lacey into Buckskin's arms. "Or what?

You'll hunt me down like yuh did Lawton fer what he did to that breed sister of yers?"

An unnatural hush rippled down the bar. Morgan Caine radiated danger as he straightened to his full height.

"Did I bring up bad memories, Marshal?"

"How about you go to hell, Gressett."

Sam swaggered forward. "Maybe ya'd care to fight me fer the whore." He spit into his hands, wiping them with confident ease down the front of his soiled shirt. "Winner take all? 'Less yer afraid to do anything without that gun strapped to yer side. How are yuh with yer fists, Caine?"

Morgan Caine hit him.

The blow caught Gressett full on the jaw, knocking him off his feet and into the crowd, which couldn't move fast enough to get out of the way. He smashed against the bar, sending drinks in every direction, before his lumbering mass hit the floor. Nothing more threatening than a groan issued forth from his bloody mouth as he lay sprawled at Lacey's feet.

A pair of black, hand-tooled boots suddenly came into focus. She pulled her bleary gaze over well-formed, black-clad thighs, past the shine of a silver badge, to the stark-blue eyes of Morgan Caine. Then he turned the full import of his gaze on old Buckskin.

The man hastily set Lacey upright. "Now, Marshal. We was just funnin' with the gal. See?" He patted her shoulders as if she needed a good polishing. "Not a scratch. She's all yers." Without another word, he expeditiously retreated.

Lacey didn't find the marshal's defense of her reassuring; nothing about this tall man was reassuring. She experienced a flutter of panic while her muddled brain struggled for somewhere to go.

"Lady, maybe they operate by different rules where you come from, but in this thirst parlor you best learn to play the game, or get out and make a living doing something else. I don't make it a habit of interfering with the business of any establishment."

"I'm not a . . ." She swallowed the atrocious word. "I'm *certainly* not a—"

"A lady?" he said helpfully.

"Oh!" She'd had it up to her earlobes with Yank hospitality. Furiously she tried to kick him in the shin, and missed, hitting Gressett in the ribs instead. A muffled groan permeated her horrified ears, rendering her speechless.

"I'm sure he didn't feel it." A hint of amusement laced his western drawl.

Morgan Caine was proving to be no more civil than his uncouth brethren. He was a ruffian, the very same manner of man who flaunted his prowess like a trophy of manhood. The wretched gun draped around his narrow hips proved that much.

"Get out of my way, Mr. . . . Marshal." Her facade of independence vanquished by reality, she whirled in a flurry of outdated silk and panic. Parting a throng of gaping bystanders, she stumbled through the gambling hall. Even in her pitifully inebriated state, his outrageous accusation burned. Was every man so dense? By the time she reached the lobby, the world had dropped into a tailspin.

Lord. She caught her balance on the door as it opened for her by an attentive uniformed employee. She was going to be sick.

Then suddenly there were strong hands at her back, squiring her outside into fresh air, past waiting carriages and curiosity seekers. Only the strength of the grip around her waist and shoulders kept her from falling flat on her face.

"Breathe deeply," the voice beckoned.

She complied, sucking in huge gulps of air. Some of the dizziness abated. She pressed the heel of her hand against her forehead and groaned miserably, her head lolling against the rock-hard warmth of the stranger who fostered her balance. The scent of sandalwood and leather permeated the dreadful nausea. Her heart jolted. She registered the feel of something pressing against her head, something metal. A badge!

Her dignity already trampled, Lacey swung around, ready to defend her corroded honor, but her skirts, with a lifelike will of their own, wrapped around Marshal Caine's legs, hauling her flush against him. She stumbled sideways in his arms, smacking against the boot of one of the carriages lining the cobblestone walk. Then in a final caricature of humiliation, his hat tumbled off his head, knocking her squarely on the bridge of her nose. Two pairs of eyes followed its descent as it hit the ground, tottering precariously to a halt beside a nasty-smelling puddle.

His shoulder muscles bunched beneath her fingertips as he turned his head and looked directly in her eyes. On closer inspection, Lacey realized his eyes were a lighter shade of blue. They swept her face, then impatiently settled on her arms, draped around his neck.

"You can let me go now, sweetheart. People are watching."

People *were* watching. Aghast, Lacey untangled herself from his arms, only to be caught short when she realized her hair was knotted in his cuffs. He was a bloody magnet. Before he could reach around her and unhook the flaxen tangles from their merciless grip on his clothing, she yanked herself free. The sound of rending cloth answered her painful summons.

The man brusquely set her back on her heels. "Christ, lady," he said in some astonishment, impatiently rolling up his ripped sleeve. "You're going to ruin me."

Lacey wobbled slightly. "Before or after you ruin me?"

His hands hesitated mid-motion. "You've done a fair job of that all on your own."

Lacey blinked. Suddenly, her taciturn reserve vanished. She'd spent years in England cultivating skills to be a lady, only to spend her first night in America lost on the streets of this ungodly city, a witness to a sordid hanging, and mistaken for a prostitute by every man she'd met thus far that night. The irony was too much.

"Do I amuse you?" he asked.

"Yes." Her mouth snapped shut. "I mean, not you, exactly, per se," she rushed to clarify. She was babbling. *Lord.* She rubbed her temples.

The marshal's brows lowered. "How much have you had to drink?"

"Not much. At least I don't think it was much. You see, I came here after these despicable brats stole my bag. I would have done so earlier, eat that is," she explained because he looked dreadfully confused or bored. It was hard to tell which with the shadow from the streetlight across his face. "Except

I saw four men hanged today. I couldn't get out of the crowd . . ." Faltering, she swallowed.

Her dress proved a frail barrier to the press of his muscular body. She could feel the heat of his masculinity all the way to the souls of her sore feet. But it was her own shocking response to his presence that stole her train of thought and left her mumbling like some imbecile. That and the fact that she hadn't talked to a single human being who gave a leaping fig about her since landing on America's footsteps.

"Heaven knows I've managed to lose everything else to-night."

"It could be worse. At least you still have your clothes—"

Lacey placed her fingers on his lips. "Shh," she cautioned. "Every time I say something like that, it gets worse."

Her body almost touched his. His height forced her to tilt her head back to meet his eyes. A strange awareness tingled through her fingertips, and she could feel the heat of his breath, taste his scent. Slowly, she dropped her hand and stepped away.

"When was the last time you had a decent meal?" he quietly asked.

"Honestly, I haven't had a decent meal in months." Ship food could hardly be considered decent fare. Lacey didn't know why any of this should matter to a complete stranger or why she felt compelled to explain anything. She eyed the gun hanging at his hip and remembered he'd been none too kind to her inside. He was probably a killer to boot.

"Look, I'm sure you have other things to do, make arrests, shoot someone, do whatever it is marshals do. I wouldn't want to take you from your business."

"You're very considerate. But you've already taken me away from my business." His eyes yielded less patience as they raked her from head to toe. A faint musical jingle pre-ceded his movements. Spurs.

"What are you doing?"

He stalked her backward. "Isn't one brawl over you enough?"

"What do you want?"

His eyes never wavered from hers. "I'm asking myself that very same question as we speak."

Lacey bumped against a gaslight pole. The world danced a terrific circle around her head. "Don't you dare take another step."

"I dare a lot." His gaze slipped over her breasts. Then he bent to retrieve his hat. "I won you, remember?"

Setting her spine rigidly against the wooden post, her chin lifted as she sought to gather her scattered composure and properly redress his comment. The very notion was absurd. But the words never formed past the horrible things he was doing to her sluggish mind.

He gave her an appraising glance. "How old are you anyway? Seventeen? Eighteen?"

This man's observation miffed her. She was twenty. A woman full-grown. Not a child. "I'm old enough to do as I please."

"And this pleases you?" He looked around him then slapped his hat against his thigh. "Don't you have a father someplace?"

The mention of her father brought her chin up. "Not one who cares what I do."

"He should be shot."

"No doubt in this country that would be an easy task to accomplish."

The hard edge of his expression vanished, as he seemed to reassess her. "I see you've recovered enough to find your sense of humor." He settled his hat back on his head. "So, what do they call you?"

"Nobody." Her heart raced. "I mean . . . I'm nobody, really."

"Then, Miss *Nobody*"—with lazy expertise, he slipped his hand beneath the weight of her hair—"tonight, I'm taking you off the streets."

His fingers brushed her neck. Mayhem catapulted her senses to the moon. She lost herself beneath the sensuous warmth of his touch. And Lacey, who had only been kissed once in her life, closed her eyes, wondering if his mouth would taste as good as it looked.

Nothing happened. No sparks or fire. No glorious melding

of mouths. Slowly, she opened her eyes, and she met the amusement in his.

"The clasp should be fixed," he offered after a moment.

Her eyes dropped to his hand. He held out her blue choker.

"Are you always so eager to be kissed?"

With a gasp, Lacey snatched the precious memento and held it to her chest. His eyes were laughing at her as if she were a silly schoolgirl. And why shouldn't he laugh? He was probably used to women acting like dolts around him. She'd never behaved like a hoyden before. Something was definitely wrong with her.

"Thank you," she said quietly. "I wouldn't want to lose this."

"Come on."

"Wait," she said. "Where are you taking me?"

He pulled back to stare down at her. "You need something to eat. And by the look of you, you can't afford this place."

She glanced down at her dress. What was it about her that made everyone say that? Her dress was not inexpensive. "Do federal marshals make so much money then that they can afford this place?"

He yanked down the brim of his hat and glared at her. "Are you hungry or not?"

Her heart leaped at the prospect of food. "What if I told you I wasn't a prostitute but just some innocent bystander here?"

"I'd take you to jail and track down whoever is responsible for leaving you out here."

"Then I'll relieve your mind of that notion, Mr. Marshal. I'm an orphan." Lord, if he somehow found her father and told him what had happened here—her heart stopped—she'd die a thousand deaths from humiliation. Her father would have more reason to hate her. "An older orphan, of course," she remedied for good measure in case he suddenly got it in his head to drop her off at some goodwill mission. She had a steamer to catch in the morning.

"If you want to eat then follow me."

She hurried after him as he walked away from the hotel. He was either too arrogant to think that she wouldn't follow, or he didn't care. No matter, she wasn't so brainless as to let him out of her sight. Nor was she worried that he would harm her. He was a lawman after all, even if he was an uncouth Yankee.

"Did you really bring those four men down from Washington Territory by yourself?"

He didn't answer.

"Do you live here in San Francisco?"

"No."

"Where do you live?"

"Christ, lady. Are you the inquisition?"

How many people even knew what the inquisition was? He was a curiosity. A ruffian who toted a gun, knocked men brainless with one swing of his fist, and read history books.

Fingering the blue satin choker, she surveyed him. He was taller than most men and walked with the ease of one who was comfortable with the night, no matter how dark the shadows. And there was something in his eyes when he looked at her that went directly to the point. A woman could get lost in that deep, blue gaze and forget to breathe. Indefinitely.

She hurried her pace. "I've never been a charity case before."

"Miss Nobody"—he stopped to hail a conveyance—"I've never been known to be charitable."

Chapter Three

"Why not?"

Morgan turned his attention from the main taproom where the serving girl had just disappeared. Miss Nobody hadn't quit her chatter since he'd found her. A plate stacked with fried chicken, corn, and potatoes steamed in a halo around her flushed face. Tendrils of flaxen hair curled around her pink cheeks. She'd already devoured half of the food and one glass of milk.

"Well?" She regarded him with wide eyes, sea green in the amber-tinted light. "Why aren't you considered charitable?" she queried again, biting into a hot biscuit. A row of pearly teeth nibbled on the hot delicacy sloughed in butter. "If you saw someone on the street starving, wouldn't you give him food?"

It took Morgan a moment to focus on her words as he tried to figure out exactly what she was talking about now. They'd been at the restaurant an hour. "No," he finally said.

"Why not?"

"A man can figure out how to make his own way. Or he isn't a man."

She speared a potato and plopped it in her mouth. "Maybe

he doesn't care if he's considered a man. Maybe he's just hungry."

"How long did you say you've been in America?"

"Fifteen hours."

Again, he came close to asking who she was and what in hell's name she was doing plying her body on the streets of San Francisco. Or even if she was a whore. "Are you always so trusting of strangers?"

"Is that badge real?" she asked without a pause in her meal.

Morgan almost smiled. "Real enough."

"Then I trust you. Do you play poker, Mr. Marshal? Well, I do," she said before he could answer. "I play whist and backgammon, too, but I play poker the best. My aunt was a teetotaler, but she knew how to gamble with cards. I used to watch her face."

Curious as to where this new string of conversation was leading, he relaxed in the chair and waited for her to get to the point. The girl certainly wasn't dull.

"Playing poker has taught me to read things about people." Waving her fork in a circle, she continued, "Like behind that poker face you wear is another man entirely."

"Is that so?"

"One that you don't let out to play very often. One that would help a starving man on the street."

"Christ." He rolled his eyes and sat up. "Where did you say you were from?"

"England," she cheerfully informed him. "A little village on the coast of Dover. I . . . ran away."

His eyes narrowed. The hell she did. "You crossed the Atlantic alone?"

"Actually," she perked, "I signed on as a companion to an elderly matron. Her son hired me, you see." Finishing the biscuit, she seemed to gather her thoughts. "When we arrived in New York, my companion ran off with another man she'd met on the steamer. Mind you she was sixty years old. One could hardly fault her energy here. And she did leave me the cabin we were supposed to share on the ship to Panama. I crossed the Isthmus alone, with the other passengers of course. That's why I ran out of money. My connecting packet in Panama, the one that was supposed to bring me here sank, and I had to stay an extra week. I was fortunate to get out of that place alive," she said quietly. It was the first crack in her stoic veneer that he'd seen all evening. Her fork scraped the plate as she pushed the last potato around. "I intend to pay you back," she suddenly replied to the silence. "I promise."

Her eyes lifted and seemed to swallow him in their liquid-green depths. Something inside Morgan kicked. He could drown in that gaze if he wasn't careful. "Why didn't you just take the train out here?"

"Oh, no." She shook her head vehemently. "I'd heard about Indians and dreadful train bandits. A girl would hardly be safe."

He laughed. This from a woman who'd practically sailed the world alone. She looked miffed that he should laugh at her.

"It's hardly as bad as all that," he said.

"I've read plenty on the subject of frontier travel and would beg to differ."

The serving girl returned with a hot dish of bread pudding and set it down along with another glass of cold milk. Morgan thanked her, and watched her a little longer than he should have as she walked away, her red skirts twitching invitingly.

"She's been eyeing you all night." Miss Nobody replied, following his gaze. "Do you think she's pretty?"

"She has her charm."

The girl snorted before returning to dessert. "It's just like a man to look only at the wrapping and not the whole package."

Morgan sipped his beer and gave the green-eyed beauty his full attention. Frankly, he'd as soon unwrap the package sitting in front of him. She possessed the shiny allure of soft satin. Even the silly outdated dress did nothing to hinder her seductiveness. Indeed, she appeared more vulnerable for the fashion faux pas, in a city that lived and breathed opulence.

"You know what I think?" she said.

Finishing the milk, she licked the white mustache from her upper lip with an unladylike zeal that oddly appealed to him. His gaze followed the pink tip of her tongue before he could stop himself from staring. Gritting his teeth, he took solace in a draught of beer.

"Somehow I have the feeling you're going to tell me whether I want to hear it or not."

"I think you're attracted to women you can't form attachments to. No commitments. That's why you ogle anyone who looks eager to get cozy with you."

With an oath, he abruptly sprawled back in his chair and crossed his arms.

"Men are such notional creatures. Frankly, it's a wonder any of you live to enjoy old age."

"Do you always talk this much?"

"Are you adverse to conversation?"

"Only when the person doing the talking has to stop just to breathe."

She set down her milk glass. "Do you have other family?"

"Christ, lady—"

"Well, do you?"

Her gaze probed his; then as if sensing that she'd treaded on private ground, she lowered her head and fidgeted with the pudding.

"You knew that awful man, Gressett, didn't you?"

Surrendering his impatience, Morgan set down his beer. He let his gaze run the length of the cozy dining room, taking in the other diners, the simple pine furnishings, and the small fire crackling in the fireplace across the room, seeing the good things here that made a home.

"Sam Gressett is wanted in Washington Territory for murder," he finally replied.

The girl almost spewed the pudding she'd just eaten. Her gaze slowly lifted. "That's what you were doing tonight? Following him?"

"He's part of the Lawton gang that hanged today." Morgan studied the moist ring on the table left by the glass of beer. "He's not the man I'm after though."

"I see."

Her voice was contemplative. Her silence respectful. He looked up to find her watching him. "I'm sorry," she said. "I shouldn't have pried."

He leaned his elbows on the table. "I have an uncle and friends that are as close to a family as I've ever had," he said.

Not that it was her business, but something about her made him say things. Personal things.

"You must love them very much. They're very lucky," she replied.

He frowned, expecting another one of her philosophical observations about his life. But she left her thoughts unsaid. Perhaps because the waif had no one at all.

After dinner, Morgan didn't return to The Chateau. Instead, he did something he never did. He hired a taxi and headed to the boardinghouse where he stayed, far away from the filthy hellhole of the city. The girl fell asleep almost the instant she climbed into the taxi. Her head rested in his lap, her profile open to his gaze. The vision of the girl in the carriage that afternoon gathered in his thoughts. She was the one he'd seen. The one he couldn't get out of his head.

The idea of putting her back on the street, or that she would have nowhere else to go when she awakened in the morning sent a surge of discord through him. Perhaps because he saw in her face an innocence he'd never had. An optimism, he couldn't begin to understand. She was lucky to have survived the night on these streets at all. On the other hand, he didn't want to be saddled with her either, and he began to wonder what the hell possessed him to take her with him at all.

Absently, he touched the flaxen hair that spilled over his lap and down his legs. Light from the lamp inside the carriage washed the silken strands in gold. The pale curves of her breasts told him she was no child. A man could find pleasure from a body like hers.

Gritting his teeth, he put his hands anywhere but near her. His other arm was numb from holding it aloft on the back of the narrow seat rim. His left thigh cramped from want of shifting. Still, he didn't move.

Her reticule lay on the cracked leather seat across from him. Someone had gone to great lengths to make the thing pretty, stitching blue and white love knots throughout. He'd already rifled the contents looking for some hint as to her identity, and discovered only a cache of nuts, four neatly folded greenbacks, and a small dainty vile of something that smelled suspiciously like summer-ripened raspberries. The fresh scent fit her. It was something his sister might have worn. . . .

Morgan had had enough. Abruptly, he shifted, nearly dropping the girl to the floor. "All right, Miss Nobody." He set her up. Her sleepy-eyed gaze fell on him. Facets of amber light touched her green eyes. She groaned, then tried to lie back down. He caught her. "No you don't. I'm not carrying you upstairs."

Annoyance filtered through his guard, and as the conveyance began to slow, he realized that he hadn't even considered the logistics of where he'd be sleeping tonight once he gave her his bed.

"Is it morning, yet?" she asked.

"Not hardly."

This boardinghouse was closer to the coast, away from the activity in the city. The residents were mostly families with children he hoped were asleep. The carriage stopped. Throwing open the door, he stepped out. The girl lay down again to sleep. He eyed her disheveled form severely. She was probably feeling the last effects of the alcohol she'd consumed. That or she was severely oxygen deprived from the corset she wore. Or merely exhausted by the looks of the shadows beneath her eyes. He paid the driver, then pulled Miss Nobody out of the conveyance.

The main room was filled with a dozen people, mostly men drinking around tables. He was hardly in a position to explain why he was carrying a half-unconscious waif to his room. Christ, he'd never live this one down.

He made it to his room without being stopped by the landlady. The girl's blond head rested securely on his shoulder. She should be more afraid of him. How many men's rooms had she visited in her lifetime?

"You're making me seasick," he heard her mumble.

"Not in this room, you better not."

With the kick of his heel, he slammed the door behind him, and lowered her to the floor. Her hands braced his chest as she caught her balance. The top of her head barely touched his collar, making her appear like fragile porcelain. Her hair shielded her face but not the slight tremble in her hands.

"You'll have to put up here for the night."

He watched her gaze go around the room. A strange awareness crept through him as her eyes touched his personal possessions, before settling on the brass bed. Lifting her face, she met his gaze.

"You don't have to worry that I'll compromise you," she reassured him, her words less than confident now as she tried to sound flippant. "You see, I could never like a man who carries a gun for a living."

"I'm not worried, sweet." He disengaged her grip from his vest. "I won't be joining you in bed."

Her relief was so apparent he almost laughed. Out of self-preservation, he turned toward the door.

"Where will you sleep?"

"Don't worry about it."

"Mr. Caine." Her quiet voice stopped him. The silence stretched between them as he held her gaze, and felt like an awkward schoolboy in the throes of his first crush. She smelled of raspberries and summer flowers and a past he didn't want to remember.

"Thank you," she finally said.

"Don't mistake me for being kind, Miss Nobody." He resettled his hat on his head. "I'm not."

Her smile trembled. "There's that poker face again. But I won't tell anyone, I promise."

His eyes narrowed. Without another word, he left the room.

Out in the hallway, Morgan glared at the door, still bemused at her nerve. Lifting a cheroot from inside his vest, he clamped it between his teeth. He bent and lit a wooden match against the scuffed heel of his boot. The cheroot flamed to life. An instant of insanity prevailed as he considered going back inside. Taking what he'd paid for this night.

Grimly, Morgan curbed an oath. Discretion wisely steered him down the back hallway to the lobby. It was good that he'd never see the girl again. He wouldn't want to start liking her. Tomorrow he'd arrange with his landlady that the girl be taken to the Christian charity mission north of the city where she'd be safe. Maybe have a chance at a decent life. Something he'd really never given his sister. If he had, maybe she'd still be alive today.

* * *

Lacey leaned with her ear pressed to the door listening to the muffled sounds of Morgan's retreat. A knot tightened in her stomach. Opening the door a crack, she peeked into the hallway just in time to see his imposing form disappear around the corner. The sound of spurs followed his descent to the lobby. She inhaled the masculine tang of tobacco mixed subtly with sandalwood.

"This is bloody swell." She slammed the door and swung her gaze across the brass bedstead. The starburst quilt remained crumpled as if he'd just crawled out of bed. His physical presence filled every crevice of her prim Victorian imagination and touched her in places she was sure would send her to perdition.

Lacey opened all the drawers in the room, which were mostly empty. She flung open the wardrobe doors. The vague scent of sandalwood permeated her senses.

Kneading her temples, she closed her eyes. If only she could rub the man from her head as easily as she did the ache. The very idea of being remotely attracted to a total stranger scandalized her, especially since she found American men so unappealing. Indeed, men in general behaved boorishly and, in England, she'd grown exhausted, fending off eager swains who considered her easy pickings because she lived alone with an ailing aunt.

She snapped her head up. So, why hadn't Morgan kissed her?

Didn't he think she was pretty? He'd certainly looked his fill at that frumpy serving girl, who did all but bare her bouncing bosoms for him when she leaned down to serve dinner.

A leather fringe jacket hung on a nail inside. What little clothes he possessed were folded neatly inside, and without conscious thought, she touched his pants, a vest, and shirts. The essence of sweet tobacco caressed her senses. He certainly didn't lack for expensive tastes. Cuban tobacco in any form wasn't cheap.

Her gaze suddenly caught something shiny. Her hand stilled. "Lord!" she gasped, lifting the edge of a shirt.

Two twenty-dollar gold pieces!

She scooped up the precious wealth then hastily dropped it back between the shirts as if burned. Her pulse thumped, and she fingered the shiny gold coins. A groan of frustration sounded. She was completely and utterly broke.

Lacey stepped away from the wardrobe. She shouldn't have gone through his things. It was wrong.

But what if her father wasn't waiting for her in Portland?

Picking up the gold pieces, she held them to her. She'd never stolen a farthing in her life. How could she pay back the marshal's kindness by stealing from him? She had nothing to exchange.

Except . . .

Her necklace had a small teardrop diamond. Surely, it was worth forty dollars. So, this wasn't exactly like stealing. Was it?

Lacey chewed her lip. Fingering the necklace, she felt an enormous weight settle over her. The choker held an emotional value that was priceless.

But she needed the money.

Removing her aunt's choker from her pocket, Lacey carefully set it down in place of the twenty-dollar gold coins.

Sandalwood permeated her senses. Fingering a black shirtsleeve, she brought it to her cheek. Morgan Caine didn't seem the type of man to cross. The fact that he was a federal marshal aided in her trepidation. Hadn't she just seen four men hanged today?

Reluctantly, Lacey put one coin back.

Closing the doors, she found a ceramic pitcher and basin of fresh water on the commode, then climbed into bed. Morgan's scent was everywhere. On the pillows and blankets. In her dreams.

Especially in her dreams. His presence radiated through her like heat in winter.

Near dawn, a distant ferry whistle sounded through the walls, and she came awake with a start. Outside, she could hear the ocean.

Lord! She sat straight up in bed. After enduring every probable catastrophe, she'd ended up near the docks. Right back where she'd started.

Lacey leaned against the starboard rail as the *Gambling Lady* banked into the Willamette River overlooking Portland. She gripped the starboard rail, her nervousness tempered by the small thread of anticipation crawling around in her head.

Above her, seagulls circled, their shrill cries piercing against the bright glare reflecting off the water. She held her crumpled bouquet, a gift she'd bought for her father's wife before leaving San Francisco. The colorful petals swirled like rare butterflies chasing the tangy breeze sweeping off the water.

For all of her blustering, she was surprised by the little girl inside who indeed needed to be wanted. She'd missed her father.

She remembered her terrifying flight with her father from Virginia to England as if it were yesterday. Her whole world, as insignificant as it was, had toppled. Suddenly, she was seven years old again, standing beside her aunt, weeping for a man who had been her very world. A man, who had abandoned her for thirteen years, in a strange world, bereft of a child's understanding, with nothing more than a photo and a tattered doll to remind her of his passing.

Again, she'd been brought full circle, restrained by circumstances beyond her control.

She could barely breathe with the lump in her throat. "I can do this," she said, determined to put the past behind her. All of it!

Lacey took perverse pleasure in her resolve to stand in the chilling wind as penance for her idiocy in San Francisco. The persistent headache she'd suffered the last few days—a grievous lesson on the ills of drinking—was finally subsiding. But not the memories that refused to leave her head. The tableau always ended with the vision of one man whose blue eyes could melt an ice cap. Good sense argued that Morgan Caine was best forgotten and now, for the first time in three days, something else grabbed her thoughts. She had a whole new life to find here. A family.

Lacey lifted her chin and untied the fluffy pink bow of her bonnet. The wind snatched the pins from her hair, whipping it behind her like one of the many colorful banners flapping from the lance-like bowsprit. She relished the sense of freedom, and as her gaze soared toward the mountains in the distance, the blue eyes in her memory became the warm summer sky. All around her, the shadows of giant Douglas firs and northern hemlocks eclipsed bright green rolling hills. In a sweeping emerald vista, bright green rolling hills promised space and freedom. She ached to touch such beauty. To have it fill the emptiness inside. To belong.

She'd never belonged anywhere before. Not to Virginia where she'd been born. Not even to her precious England.

Lifting on her toes, Lacey searched the crowded docks for her father. What would he look like after all these years?

Overhead, another noisy steam-driven blast from the stack bellowed their approach. Passengers began to line the rails. Beneath her slippered feet, the engines trembled in cadence to the giant paddle wheels churning through the white-capped water as the steamer settled against the wharf.

A modern town of obvious prosperity, Portland City looked in the midst of an economic boom. Huge warehouses inhabited the riverbank for miles. Everyone seemed in such a hurry to be somewhere else. With the news of gold in the Northwest Territory and Alaska, she'd read that Portland was the stop-and-shop port of the West, the last jump off before no-man's-land. Lacey had heard the talk and wondered about people who could leave their life in search of gold and riches, and the-dreams-come-true that were supposed to follow. Her father had been such a gambler.

And in a way, so was she.

"Your bags, ma'am," a porter said.

Lacey turned and thanked him as he led her down the ramp into the crowd. He deposited her two trunks in a neat stack beside the cobbled curb. She tipped him with her last coin.

Lacey eagerly looked around her. After an hour, the crowd had thinned. Beside her, a small one-horse taxi waited for the arrival of the next ferry.

"Oh, Daddy," she whispered, "where are you?"

She sat on her trunks, hands clasped around the silly flower bouquet. Naught but naked stems survived her worried handling.

She continued to search the faces of the men who remained. But when the dock had emptied of passengers, Lacey was all that was left of the hustle surrounding the steamboat's arrival.

Chapter Four

Maybe her father hadn't received the telegram from New York or the one she'd sent from San Francisco.

Or maybe nothing had changed, and she'd been a fool to think that he'd want to see her after all these years. After all, it had been her decision to come here. Her need. Not his.

Coming to her feet, Lacey finally tossed the silly flowers away. She would find a way to make it on her own.

"Lacey?" A man's voice wheeled her around. He stood behind her, his suit slightly crumpled, his leathery hands kneading the brim of the bowler hat. "Lacey Ashton?"

She gawked.

Unable to move, Lacey clasped her hands in front of her to still their trembling. After all the years and the rehearsed speeches, every breath, every word stuck in her throat.

She was amazed how little her father's image had changed from the mental picture she'd carried with her. A shock of blond hair still covered his head, hiding a receding hairline. His prominent nose suggested a past fight or two, and an expressive mouth gave way to a handsome smile. His eyes were a light hazel-brown, like the color of meadow grass.

"Lordy, Lacey, you're all grown up." Her father's awkward embrace deterred her unconscious retreat. She felt him stiffen, and he dropped his arms as if suddenly unsure of their purpose. "When I received your wire from San Francisco, I couldn't believe it." He clasped his arms in front of him. "Just . . . look at you. Clare raised you to be a genuine lady."

"Clare was very good to me."

"I'm sorry about Clare," he said quietly.

A jerky nod was her only answer. At any moment, she was afraid the silly tears that clamored behind her eyes would fall.

Wild shouts snapped Lacey around. Driven by a brawny-shouldered man, a noisy buckboard careened down the street. A tow-headed youth waved his hat and yelled like a crazed banshee. People abruptly stopped, staring aghast as the wagon bore down the street in a terrific noise of jangling harnesses, blazing gunshot, and a cracking whip. Lacey jumped back out of harm's way as the vehicle came to a protesting halt directly in front of them.

"My men are gathered at the loading docks crating supplies for our trip back to the territory," her father said. "I came as soon as I heard your packet had arrived."

"We did like ya told us, Pa," the youth breathlessly piped in. "Did we give you enough time. Huh, Pa? Did we?"

Lacey stared at the boy. This would be her stepbrother, the one so frequently mentioned in all of her father's correspondence. There was pride in her father's expression as he nodded to the freckle-faced youth wriggling beside him. "This is my stepson, Joshua."

Her father elbowed his giant of a friend who watched the proceedings with amusement. "Didn't I tell you she'd be a perfect beauty? A real lady. Every man in the territory will be after this one," he boasted as if that was the only thing he cared about, as if thirteen years didn't stand empty between them.

"Ma would be here but she had to stay home 'cause she's gonna have a baby," Joshua said.

Lacey's gaze lifted to her father. But before she could understand the strange knot of foreboding in her heart, the boy dashed forward to hug Lacey. "I'm glad to make your acquaintance," he burst out, his skinny arms wrapping around her. "I never had a sister before."

"I . . ."

Lacey felt a sudden helpless rush of love. Lord. But she needed to feel wanted by someone. This further assault on her emotions left her tongue-tied, a unique experience for someone who prided herself on her verbal prowess.

The big man beside her father stepped forward and extending his large hand boomed a noisy introduction. "The name's Jack, ma'am. Jack Kipp. Friend to the family. We're neighbors."

Lacey had never seen a man Jack's size. At least five inches over six feet, with bushy blond hair, a full beard, and dancing hazel eyes, his apparent easygoing nature contrasted sharply with his intimidating appearance. As American custom dictated, she shook the proffered hand.

Joshua laughed at her reticence. "Don't worry none about Jack. He may look mean as a grizzly, but he's not so bad."

Jack's bearded face split into an amiable grin. "Not unless they talk as much as you do, Josh. Then I can get downright ornery." Swinging the boy up into the back of the wagon, he walked around the taxi to load her baggage onto the buckboard.

Struggling with her wayward thoughts, Lacey's gaze flickered uneasily over her father. "Are you ready?" he asked.

"Don't worry none about your comfort, Miss Lacey," Joshua reassured her. With the sweep of his arm, he indicated the lumpy blanket at his thigh. "Fit for a queen."

A vague odor, reminiscent of a stable, drifted in the air. Lacey grinned. She already liked this new brother of hers.

"We'll be leaving for Kingston in a few days." Her father handed her into the wagon. "The trip will take us two months, so we need to get started as soon as possible. Jack's nephew wired that he should be arriving day after tomorrow."

"Yea, he's the best," Joshua piped in.

"We'll be starting our trip north as soon he gets here." Colin slapped the reins, and the horses jolted forward, nearly toppling Lacey backward off the seat.

For the first time in days, blue eyes didn't haunt her

thoughts. Lacey took in the sight of her new family, felt a yearning grow deep inside, and knew she'd find a way to make things work. She could finally forget Morgan Caine and get on with her life.

"Pa said when we get to Waylen Springs we can buy you a horse."

Lacey stood beside Joshua staring at a brown swayback creature with hairy legs. They'd stopped at the corral again today to view the newest acquisitions to the stable. Joshua's favorite pastime. He rocked back on his heels. Scrubbed and dressed in his pressed white shirt and suspender britches, he continued to counsel her on the many virtues of horse ownership.

From the first day, he'd stolen her affection. A dusting of freckles and two very handsome dimples, which showed often in his animated conversations, brought forth a certain charm that Lacey found irresistible. There wasn't an inch of Portland they hadn't explored, nor a candy shop they hadn't sampled.

Lacey gazed at the picturesque mountain ridge in the distance. Not a single cloud marred the view. She stopped her hand from going to her neck. A habit she had to break since she no longer had her necklace. She loosened the ribbons on her bonnet.

"Lacey." Joshua's impatience brought her focus back to the horse. The creature was practically dead. "What do you think?"

"I think that you don't have an eye for horseflesh, Joshua."

"Not for me, Lacey."

"Josh, how many ways from sundown do I have to tell you. I don't ride horses. Come on. We're late for lunch."

She moved aside as an elderly matron carrying a parcel of bags hurried by, her high-heeled shoes clicking on the boardwalk. A wagon rattled past stirring dust. Lacey fluffed her skirt, one of two calico dresses she owned. This one was blue. Her favorite color. It belonged to her scrupulously researched frontier wardrobe. She'd made it herself on the ship from England.

Josh followed her down the street and into the hotel. "We can get a little horse."

"Big or little, horses don't like me. A simple relationship actually, built on a mutual lack of trust."

"What's not to trust?" he called, running after her.

"Their teeth for one thing. And somehow I never mastered the art of staying on a crazed, bucking horse. Besides, they're animals."

"You're in the West now, Lacey. Animals are everywhere."

The debate continued past curious patrons, to the extravagantly set table in the dining room where lunch was already being served. Her father and Jack Kipp sat with two other men. The table rattled precariously in their haste to stand. Lacey recognized both men from previous meals and smiled in polite greeting. The Western male didn't adhere to any logical fashion, and these two with their mismatched denims and red flannel shirts were no exception.

Joshua presented her to the seat beside her father. She met her father's gaze and smiled. His uneasiness mirrored her own.

"What's this about horses?" Colin asked. It was one of the few times since she'd arrived three days ago that he directed conversation directly at her.

Roasted turkey basted in sage went around the table, followed by potatoes, peas, and fresh bread.

"Lacey's chicken a' horses, Pa."

Everyone stopped eating and looked at her as if she'd grown a horn between her eyes. "What's wrong with that?" she asked.

"She was thrown from a horse when she was younger." Her father seemed compelled to explain. But he knew she'd almost broken her neck. She was in bed for a month. . . .

"You shoulda got right back on," Josh insisted, unsympathetic. He slapped butter all over his biscuit. "You're all ruined now."

Jack Kipp eyed Lacey. "Out here you'll learn a good horse is worth more than the salt of most men."

"You might enjoy a gentle Arabian, Lacey," her father suggested. "We can purchase a side saddle."

"Well, I never seen a dumber thing!"

"Joshua," Jack admonished.

"That's how ladies back east and in England ride," her father said.

This lady business was really beginning to annoy her. She met her father's assessing gaze. For all his adoration, he'd never once since she arrived sat down with her for an earnest talk. Or he'd know more about her. They had thirteen years between them and issues to settle. He was a stranger. Like this town and this country. She wanted to please him but not enough to risk life and limb just to ride a silly horse.

Before she could comment, the attention at the table shifted to the meal. And just like that, the topic changed.

For the next thirty minutes, Lacey ate and listened to the men discuss the wagon train, their route, and the loads each of the wagons carried. Many families from Kingston sent in orders for goods that her father would be bringing back. The topic of Indians and renegades took over. Lacey sipped her tea. This world leaped from the pages of a dime-store novel.

Her mouth went dry at the thought. She felt betrayed by her nervous fear. Disappointed that she wasn't more western-wise. Someone who knew the ropes so to speak. Her father might brag about her being a lady, but she'd seen the way he let Joshua help him while she was left to lounge away the last three days in her room.

"The sheriff at Waylen Springs thinks part of Brett Lawton's gang has regrouped near that town of his," the silver-haired cowboy named Caleb replied to something Jack said.

Intercepting the flickering grimace on her father's face at the mention of Lawton's name, Lacey realized she'd heard that name before.

"If the rest of our men weren't already waitin' on us there, I'd suggest stayin' a sight clear of that whole area," the rangy carrottop sitting next to her father added. Lacey remembered he went by the appropriate name Red.

"I say, let the marshal handle 'em." Joshua's eagerness at the prospect was apparent. "Corralling polecats is easy for him."

A vague impression filled her mind, further eroding her appetite. Setting the cup of tea back in its china saucer, her glance registered the tall man framed in the doorway talking to their server. The man filled out the jacket of his black broadcloth suit with a familiar air of authority.

Her hand stilled.

Responding to the woman at his elbow, his lopsided grin flashed white against his dark visage. Lacey couldn't hear the words exchanged, but the woman pointed in their direction. With casual grace, he tipped his hat and straightened. Lacey's heart sped up then skipped. It couldn't be! Not here! Not now!

Lord, it *was* Morgan Caine!

Taking no notice of the feminine regard of half a dozen women in the dining room, he moved toward the table with the casual gait of a wolf. His coat opened, and Lacey's gaze took in the walnut-handled peacemaker hanging at his hips. Her eyes swung to the vest he wore beneath the jacket, and a groan stuck in her throat. The silver badge flashed in the dour light filtering through the lace curtains, mocking her with a morbid sense of impending doom.

Her first panicked thought was that he'd tracked her to Portland. She'd heard of men hanged for stealing a horse. What was the penalty out here for stealing gold from a federal marshal?

Sitting back abruptly, Lacey hit her father's glass of wine and sent the ruby liquid spilling over the tabletop. Her pulse throbbing, she snatched a napkin from her lap and tried to catch the thin rivulet of red wine. Too late, she realized, as the wine flowed onto the front of her dress. She leaped up. Her chair tipped, and in the stunned silence that greeted Morgan Caine's arrival, it hit the ground with a loud, obnoxious thud.

Lacey looked across the chasm of startled faces, directly into Morgan's clear blue eyes. Recognition flickered in their depths, and she was jarred by the intensity in that piercing gaze. Apprehension overwhelmed her—and something else—something that made her weak in the knees.

"Marshal Caine!" He barely pulled his gaze from her face, before Joshua grabbed his arm and directed him the rest of the way to the table. "We thought you'd never get here."

"I wondered that a time or two myself, Josh."

The deep, familiar voice washed over Lacey, evoking every scintillating detail of him she thought to forget. Her eyes closed. Her pulse thundered. It was truly the smallest of worlds, and Lacey decided in that moment of insight, that she was doomed.

"You've been gone a long time, Marshal Caine," Josh said.

"The boy just about grew up in your absence, nephew." Jack took Morgan's outstretched hand in a strong grip.

"The trial took longer than planned."

"I take it everything went off with no surprises?" Lacey heard her father ask. "You didn't say anything in your telegram."

Red had straightened her chair, and she found herself braced against its spindled back. Morgan's sobering glance offered her no comfort.

"You know San Francisco," he said mildly. "The place is full of surprises where you least expect them."

Nodding in her direction, her father's gaze encompassed her. "Morgan, this is my daughter, Lacey. She's come all the way from England to be with us," he announced as if no one in all of Portland knew that fact about her. "Lacey, this is Jack's nephew. If you've picked up a paper in the last day or so, you've heard of him already."

Morgan removed his black brimmed hat, and thick, dark hair fell in waves over his brow. Acknowledging her with what could barely pass as a civil nod, he looked pointedly at the spilled mess. "I've heard white wine does wonders for a red-wine stain, Miss Ashton." He must think her a habitual lush. "Are you in need of assistance?"

"I'm sure someone of your *prominence* has more important matters to deal with than me, Marshal."

"Nonsense," he countered, his smooth voice less than reassuring. "*Nobody* would consider it less than my duty . . . Miss Ashton."

"Appearances can actually be deceiving, Mr. Caine."

"I have on occasion discovered that to be the case," he agreed.

"Sometimes it could even be a simple misunderstanding. Nothing that a little explanation here or there wouldn't clear up." Lacey's mind scrambled for something else to say. A bluff. Anything to gain control. Morgan Caine looked just irritated enough beneath that staid facade to reveal every reputation-shattering detail she'd shared with him in San Francisco.

"Have you ever played poker, Miss Ashton?" He looked her in the eyes. "Well don't," he said before she could respond. "You'd lose."

His meaning clear, Lacey's stomach pulled taut. Clearly, a tactful retreat was preferable to total annihilation.

Lacey shifted her attention to her father. He was staring at her. They all were.

Humbled by their obvious loyalty to Morgan, and her own sense that she'd just lost something special here, Lacey felt the sting of tears. "If you'll excuse me, I have to change. Please don't hold up dessert."

A week ago, she would have argued the merits of seeking her place in her father's world. Now she feared losing that chance completely. The blue-eyed man of her dreams had the power to ruin her life.

Snapping the belt tight on her bulky purple robe, Lacey paced the carpet in her room waiting for the maid to bring water for a bath. Her stained dress draped over her bed as if lying in a traitorous swoon. She rolled her eyes at the very idea. Even wearing a flannel nightshirt that she'd made for the arduous Atlantic crossing, she shivered with foreboding. Her throbbing heart had as much to do with Morgan's sudden arrival as it did with trepidation over what he would do to her now. Even if Mr. Caine had come to her aid in San Francisco, he wouldn't forgive her theft. Not when he'd been so kind.

The swish of her bright pink slippers on the carpet marked her pacing. Daddy had sent her these childish slippers a few years ago, thinking perhaps that she was still eight years old. Remembering her father now didn't help matters. How could she ever tell him about that night with Morgan in San Francisco? Being mistaken for a strumpet, stealing money, spending the night in Morgan's bed. It didn't matter that she'd slept alone, she'd been dreaming about him, and that had to count against her somehow. She'd be ruined, and she hadn't even been in America a week!

Lacey twisted her hair into a bun and shoved pins into her hair. She felt suffocated, as if someone had just dropped her down a well and nailed the lid shut.

A knock sounded on the door.

Finally. Her water. "It's open," she called.

Tilting over, she wrapped a red checkered scarf around her hair to prevent it from getting wet with her bath.

After what seemed like a hesitation, the door clicked open. "Put it over by the porch doors," she instructed. One end of the scarf drooped over her face. Her nose was sunburned from that day's excursion.

Walking to the dresser, she yanked out a drawer and withdrew her face balm. When no one entered the room, she turned, and her heart slammed in her chest.

"You!"

Leaning negligently, with his hand braced against the doorframe, his suit coat open to the vest and badge beneath, Morgan let his gaze linger first on her unorthodox slippers. His eyes hesitated on the thick purple robe to finally settle with insulting amusement on the red scarf that bound her hair. Lacey still clutched the jar of white balm.

One dark brow raised. "Why do I get the feeling I made a huge mistake in San Francisco?"

She placed the balm down on her dresser. "Is that such a novelty, Mr. Caine?"

"Is your father aware of our little escapade?" His crisp inquiry jolted her. "I need to know."

"You shouldn't be seen out there."

His brows arched in interest. "Are you inviting me in?"

With a sharp intake of breath, Lacey narrowed her eyes on him. "Don't be absurd. I only meant that this is my room, and you are out of place being here. If someone should see you . . . it would not bode well," she finished lamely, flushing beneath his bold regard.

"Indeed?" His eyes dropped to her mouth, and Lacey's entire being flooded with sensations, the foremost being panic.

"Don't you think it's a little late to be worrying about your reputation?"

She moved to slam the door in his face. Morgan planted a booted foot strategically in the way.

He leveled her with cobalt eyes. "I'm not convinced by this little act. Either invite me in or answer my question. Does your father know about our meeting in San Francisco?"

"Go away, Mr. Caine."

He drove her back into the room. With a kick of his boot, the door slammed shut, and Lacey found herself wedged between Morgan Caine and the porch doors both impenetrable objects of doom.

"The least you owe me are some answers, Miss Ashton."

He smelled pleasantly of soap. She snatched the robe together. "If I'd told you who I was when we were in San Francisco, you would have taken me to the magistrate and hunted down my father. You said so yourself. As long as you thought I was a prostitute, I was safe."

"Now that logic goes right over my head."

"Are you calling me illogical?"

"I've known Colin and your stepmother for many years. I don't want to be put into the middle of something that would require me to explain my version, as to what I was doing with his perfect daughter at the The Chateau. Or why I was carrying her to my room afterward."

"Oh yes, the brave marshal. My reluctant knight. Did I not thank you in the proper manner for risking your life on my behalf? Shall I fall down and grovel on your boots, good sir?" Her gaze dropped impertinently to his boots. "They do rather look in need of a good spit 'n shine," she lied. They looked as impeccable as the rest of him, Lacey irritably thought. He was too close. And she was possessed with utter madness to splay her palms across his chest.

From his vest pocket, he withdrew her necklace. Heart pounding, she watched him bring it to his nose as if struck by some redolence. Her eyes lifted to his. "Tell me Miss *Nobody,* what is a twenty-dollar gold eagle worth in the currency you were trading that night?" The soft intensity in his voice stilled her breath.

She scraped the tip of her tongue across her bottom lip. "Surely you're still not under the misnomer that I am a . . ." The indelicate word stuck to the roof of her dry mouth.

In the light that streamed in from the French doors, his strength seemed even more pronounced as he braced his palms on either side of her. "A what?" he prodded.

She had the distinct impression that her innocence mattered little in his opinion of her.

"Miss Ashton, The Chateau is famous for its French courtesans. What were you doing in that place?"

"You wouldn't believe me."

"Try me."

"I was . . . hungry."

Dark brows gathered over beautiful blue eyes. "Your performance was at least worth dinner, sweetheart." He shoved her precious necklace back into his vest pocket.

Her blood boiled with his pretension. Ha! The big, tough marshal. He meant to intimidate her. But hadn't Aunt Clare lectured her more than once that an upper hand was worth two in the bush? Or was that a bird in hand . . . ?

Lacey wrapped her fists in his collar. He didn't know her mettle. She'd give him a lesson in equality. "Is this what you wanted that night instead, Mr. Marshal?" She planted her lips on his.

The contact stabbed at her, starting somewhere in her lower extremities and radiating out like a melting prism of light. His mouth was hot and moist, shaping to hers, nothing like she expected. Lord. Her heart was beating too hard. Heat stirred in her loins. And at once, she knew her mistake. Dear Lord, did she ever.

He'd mocked her plight, insulted her priceless necklace, and now he'd made a farce of her control in the five breathless seconds of melding her lips to his.

Morgan pulled back, but only an astonished hesitation separated them. His breath was warm against her mouth. Temperate compared to the heat in his eyes. Then he took her face between his palms and his mouth descended upon hers.

This kiss was no chaste imitation of the one she'd given him. She could not still the kick of her heart or the jolt that rippled through the core of her being. His tongue plied her lips, beckoning them to flower beneath his hot, velvet touch. And lost beneath the sensuous assault, Lacey lifted on her toes to better grasp the strange and wondrous sensations as he plundered her mouth. He buried his grip beneath the scarf, pulling it from her head. Pins dropped to the floor and her hair tumbled in a molten wave to her hips. His arm lowered down her spine, a caressing whisper against her skin that measured the wild race of her desire. Then a deep growl threaded through the haze of her consciousness.

Helpless to stop him from pulling away, she met his gaze and drank in the echo of incredulity that mirrored her own. His mouth was so close to hers she could melt in the heat surrounding her. Her knees felt shaky. Like soft baked dough that had yet to take the shape of legs.

Her voice was little more than a wobbly sigh. "I think Clare underrated this kissing business."

His arms dropped, and the distance between them suddenly tripled. "You're dangerous, lady."

She tipped her chin a nervous notch and confronted his gaze. Reaching into his vest pocket, he carelessly flipped her a second twenty-dollar gold coin. The mate of the one she'd pirated.

"What's this?"

"I'd say you earned it, sweetheart."

She stopped him as he swung open the door. "You know what I think?"

He braced an elbow on the door. "I'm sure I'm going to hear."

"You're annoyed to discover that I'm not one of your soiled doves from the gaming dens of San Francisco. That you might actually form an attachment to someone who is normal."

Morgan threw up his hands. Her robe hung open. "Lady"—he raked his gaze over her flannel nightshirt and frilly, pink slippers—"you have a strange notion about a lot of things. There's nothing normal about you." He left her gaping at his broad back.

"That's a pathetic apology, but I'll accept it anyway," she called. "Buffoon!" She slammed the door.

The arrogant oaf! Her gaze dropped to the gold coin still warm in her hand. What kind of country was this that a lawman could accost a woman in her room? That a kiss would be worth forty dollars?

Morgan sliced a glare at the offending portal. The vague scent of raspberries drifted over him—the redolence of Lacey Ashton. He'd smelled it on her in San Francisco, in her hair, on her skin. He hadn't realized just how much of her he remembered.

Who the hell was he kidding? She'd been entrenched in his head since the moment he had the misfortune of laying eyes on her in that carriage—framed within a halo of golden light—like some celestial presence. An angel.

He almost laughed at the absurdity. Lacey Ashton was about as pure as celestial pond water.

Nothing could have prepared him to see her today. His first reaction had been to see her throttled for weaseling her way to Portland, plying her trade on any unsuspecting mark, who illogically happened to be his friends. Discovering she was Ashton's daughter nearly dropped him in his boots. She'd caught him by surprise on all fronts.

And Morgan was not a man caught by anything. It was an insult to his instincts as a lawman.

He didn't trust her, he realized, turning away. Colin and Lorraine Ashton didn't need anymore heartache in their lives.

Morgan entered the dining room, his focus now on the boisterous group settled around the center table, disrupting the quiet flow of conversation in the restaurant. His hat remained on the back of the spindle-backed chair where he'd left it. Joshua looked up and grinned around a gooey mouthful of berry pie as he approached.

"Settled in?" Colin eyed him expectantly.

Morgan sat in Lacey's vacated spot aware that everyone seemed to be watching him expectantly. The spilled wine was now gone, and the soiled setting replaced with fresh linen. "I've decided not to stay in this hotel," he said, shifting his gaze to Caleb and Red. "I'll bunk with the men at the boardinghouse on Main. I'd just as soon not find myself too comfortable."

"Then that boardinghouse is the place fer you," Caleb reassured him. "A real bona fide stable of discomfort. Fleas an' all."

Colin leaned into the table. "No one would fault you if you did something for yourself every now and then, Morgan." Gratitude laced Colin's voice, sobering Morgan as nothing else could.

He was uncomfortable with gratitude. It tipped the balance of a relationship, dug beneath his skin with a sense of ill-placed permanence. He liked his aloneness. It was his price for remaining sane in a world that struggled beneath a thin veneer of civilization.

"Your telegram didn't say much," Colin prompted.

"I didn't attend the hanging."

Colin glanced uneasily at Joshua as if suddenly remembering the boy's presence. "Still, you went beyond your responsibilities."

As a federal marshal it was within Morgan's right to transport his prisoners to any jurisdiction holding a federal warrant on them. California was as far away from Washington Territory as he could go.

"How about sharing some pie with us and taking a load off," Jack offered, "maybe socializing a little."

Joshua handed Morgan a plate of pie. "It's really good."

"But not nearly so delicious as Lacey can probably make." Jack seemed to watch him curiously before turning to Colin. "Any woman who can't ride a horse is bound to be a good cook at least."

Morgan tugged at his necktie and tried to imagine Lacey Ashton having talent for anything else—but the obvious—which he wished he wasn't acquainted with. Morgan dismissed the thought and settled himself over his pie. Raspberry.

"Why don't you give me the rest, Josh," he said after the first bite. "I wouldn't want to see it wasted on these mongrels."

"By crackedy!" Caleb snorted. "Ain't been with us an hour an' he already insults us."

"Been hobnobbing with outlaws for so long he's lost his manners," Red declared in a similar fashion.

"Marshals don't need no manners."

"*Any* manners, son," Colin corrected.

"Pa even agrees."

"So, nephew." Jack's eyes glimmered. "Now that you've discussed what all of us have waited to hear about your business in San Francisco, why don't you tell us the rest?"

Taking Jack's full measure, Morgan's grip on his fork tightened before he realized everyone was watching him. Leave it to his uncle to be a pain in the ass and get away with it. Managing a suspiciously lame response about the dregs of city life, he shifted his attention back to the pie. The devil fly with responsibility.

Morgan knew the complications involved if he said the wrong thing. He wasn't in the market for a wife. Especially one with frilly silks and bonnets. A genuine, bona fide lady. One who would wilt at the slightest hardship. Faint at the sight of blood. Who didn't know a French cathouse from the back end of a horse. Colin's daughter was good for only one thing. And he didn't need a wife for that.

No. Morgan was staying the hell away from Lacey Ashton.

Chapter Five

"She makes a regular trip out here every morning." Jack set his Spencer rifle against the whitewashed fence separating the knoll from the riverbank. "Brings Colin and Josh lunch."

Morgan eyed his uncle from beneath the brim of his hat. Above him, seagulls circled the wharf. "Good morning to you, too."

"She's Colin's daughter, Morgan."

"Don't you think I know that?"

"She didn't come down for breakfast this morning. And here you are taking a midmorning stroll. Do you want to tell me what's going on between you two?"

Morgan leaned against the fence and lit a cheroot. His gaze narrowed, shifting beyond Lacey to the water lapping at the ridge.

His first reaction when he'd seen the streak of yellow flying past the boardinghouse that morning was to step outside and look behind Lacey to see what devil rode her heels. Aside from the curious glances following her harried progress down the street, she was not being chased. He wondered if Colin's daughter was predisposed to strange behavior. When she disappeared down a side street, he decided to follow on a notion. Expecting to learn some dark insight into her character, Morgan followed her to the docks where her father worked. A score of men were loading crates and barrels onto the ferry that would take them up river. Clearly, she was attempting to be useful. But what could she do? She didn't even know how to hitch a wagon. He watched as she moved away from her father to the riverbank.

The breeze caught the silken drift of her hair in a waterfall of light. She turned away to clutch the fence and stared off across the river, the wind pulling at her skirts. Her expression possessed a yearning for freedom. He recognized that look, because he'd felt it more times than he cared to remember.

Morgan tossed the cheroot to the ground. He wasn't prone to tenderness, but evidently, he wasn't immune to an occasional weak lapse of sentimentality, either. The idea irritated him.

"Why didn't Colin tell us his daughter wasn't a kid. The way he went on about her you'd think she was ten years old."

"Colin has her figured all wrong," Jack said, watching her. "She's a scrapper, that one is. You'll see."

Morgan snorted. "She's a bullet shy of a loaded gun."

Jack chuckled. "Your telegram caught us by surprise."

"Maybe I just needed some company, Jack."

His uncle knew him well enough not to pursue the subject. Morgan now wished he'd bypassed Portland completely. Gone straight on to Waylen Springs as he'd originally planned.

"Are you traveling with the wagon train?" Jack asked.

"Only as far as Waylen Springs. I have a job to finish."

Leather creaked as Jack crossed his big arms and observed Morgan from beneath bushy brows. "Lawton didn't work alone," he replied. "You wait around long enough, and they'll find you. Or anyone else you care about."

"Does Lacey know who Joshua's real father is?"

"Colin hasn't told her anything." Jack looked away and finally said what Morgan had already read in his hazel eyes. "Brett Lawton is gone now. You brought him in when no one else could."

"It's not finished."

"I loved Shannon, too, Morgan. She was my sister's flesh. You can't continue to blame yourself for her death, or her life. She chose her own way. As stubbornly as you always chose yours."

"Christ, Jack. She was barely nineteen years old. You didn't have to bury her. You didn't see . . . she deserves justice for what those men did to her. I can never forget it."

Morgan remembered the nights alone, where no other man save the Creator himself stood between him and the killers he'd brought down through the territory to hang. With single-minded purpose, he'd driven them past hunger and exhaustion. Until the end of a rope looked more inviting than facing another night on the trail.

In bringing Brett Lawton in to hang, Morgan had served notice to the entire Lawton gang. Hunting down the rest of his sister's killers would be his final act as territorial marshal before he moved on. He had to escape before roots took hold and buried him in this country that had killed his family. He'd lived here too long.

An earsplitting whistle announced the arrival of another steamer chugging into the bay. Stark white, with tiered decks and French doors that opened onto the second level from the great staterooms, it invited his full attention. People lined the decks for docking.

Fumbling absently in his vest pocket, Morgan ran his thumb against the satin edge of Lacey's choker, and watched as she wended a path through the crowd of passengers disembarking from the steamer. His attention riveted on the swing of her bustle, then eased up the length of her silken hair, until all he could see was that pert blond head bobbing in and out of the crowd. By the time she reemerged at the edge of the pier, his was not the only gaze trained on her progress across the docks. Abruptly, Morgan shoved the choker back in his pocket. He started to push away from the fence when he registered the man shouldering off the corner of the livery as Lacey passed.

Wearing a tanned buffalo-hide coat with fringe on the sleeves, he was a huge man, unkempt with a scraggily growth of beard and a belly hanging over pants that were too tight.

Even without seeing the man's misshapen purple nose, Morgan recognized him.

What the hell was Sam Gressett doing in Portland?

Lifting his Spencer rifle, Jack took his stance beside Morgan. "That no-account never travels alone. Do you see who he is with?"

Morgan was already gone.

Lacey heard commotion behind her. At first glance, nothing registered beyond the surging crowd pressing in on her. And she turned her gaze back to the shop window. Harnesses, a plow, and an assortment of men's denim breeches decorated the alcove behind the glass. This world was nothing like the one she'd left. Living in the simple English countryside, where the worst crime committed last year was the theft of an outhouse, had not prepared her for the reality of living on the frontier. A long exhale withered past her lips as she turned to peruse the next window. What she needed was a goal in life. Something she could work toward that would give her a sense of purpose. To this end, she'd been thinking about teaching.

The sun beat down on her back. In contrast to Lacey's mood, that morning had bloomed gloriously. Her hand lingered on her neck, and out of nowhere the memory of Morgan's kiss melted through her.

Lacey stiffened. She'd reframed her opinion of him in something a little less gilded. Something in wood, which fit his personality.

Still, other memories beckoned and despite herself, she couldn't entirely forget San Francisco.

Horses loped past, and she turned to look at the street. The tin-panny music of a crowded saloon trickled out the bat-wing doors she'd just passed. She started to turn back when her gaze slammed into the man standing negligently beneath the sloping overhang.

Her heart stopped.

"Hello, princess."

Gressett!

Mulling the old cigar stub in his mouth, the look on his face bore no illusion about her safety at that moment.

Hiking her skirt, Lacey raced across the street. People scattered out of her way. By the turmoil behind her, she knew Gressett gave chase. She ran past the smelly mud around the stables, ducking onto another street. Her skirt snagged on a wooden crate that toppled over onto a pile of rubble. Lacey's heart squeezed in a rush. She yanked at the cloth. Sam Gressett rounded the corner. The scream died in her throat as he slammed into her, knocking her against the side of the building.

Regaining his balance, Gressett's eyes sharpened on her. "If it ain't Miss Toity Hoity." He chuckled, planting a beefy hand against the wall behind her, blocking her escape.

The air stank of garbage and rotten fish, and fighting for breath, Lacey sucked it all in. Her other hand inched blindly down the wooden slats at her back, seeking a weapon. "You lay one finger on me, and you'll be sorry."

He laid a finger against her shoulder, jabbing her. "And whose gonna stop me?" Gressett laughed. "You?"

The knee smashing into his groin doubled him over, but the board that cracked across the center of his forehead sent him stumbling backward over the pile of crater. With a bellow of rage, Gressett hit the ground like a ponderous elephant. A foul string of curses followed, and Lacey beamed him again. Ignoring the splinters slicing into her hand, she hurdled the chunk of wood at him.

"Yes, me!" She kicked him in the shin.

An arm snaked out, yanking her backward against the solid wall of a man's chest. She flailed her fists. She couldn't breathe. Her lungs wouldn't expand past her corset.

"Lacey . . . for Christ's sake—"

Morgan's voice broke over her. The brace of his forearm beneath her breasts kept her from dropping to her knees. Against her back, she felt the tandem beat of his heart.

"I want that imbecile arrested for assaulting me."

"I ain't done nothin'. She's the one that assaulted me."

"You are such a liar."

Morgan's shocked gaze traveled over her as the realization dawned that she was responsible for Gressett's condition. From somewhere behind her, Jack laughed.

"By criminy, she just beat the hell out of Gressett."

His face mottled, Gressett looked like a grizzly just tricked from the honeycomb. Morgan placed himself between Lacey and Gressett.

"Get up, Gressett."

"Now," Lacey added, brandishing her fist.

Morgan pulled her back. The press of her fingers stirred the hairs on his arm. That it should dominate his thoughts at this crucial moment made him scowl. His fingers curled around hers to dislodge her grip. "For Christ's sake, Lacey."

She emitted a low groan. Morgan took her hand, turning her palm upward. Two nasty splinters were embedded in her palm.

And his eyes narrowed.

Gressett climbed to his feet. Without a stiff drink of rye to bolster his courage, the man availed himself of a new disposition. "Aw, Marshal, I was just having me some fun." He smirked, hooking his right thumb over his gun belt in a state of readiness. After all, we both know she owes me fer that night in San Francisco. I paid fer her fair."

Lacey's indignant cry warned Morgan a moment before she attempted to push past. Jack snatched her back out of the way.

"My gold was gone, Marshal, when I came to. And she weren't nowhere around."

"If I were you, Gressett, I'd leave town while you're standing enough to sit a horse."

Lacey's gasp ground through Morgan. But he couldn't look at her. She wouldn't understand that there was more at stake here than her honor.

All the bluster gone from his arrogant swagger, Gressett glowered at Jack, then shifted his attention back to Morgan. And for one second, as rage seemed to consume him, his hand inched down toward his gun. The crowd grew quiet. Expectant.

"Do it, Gressett, and I'll kill you where you stand," Morgan's voice rippled over the silence.

Gressett's narrowed gaze pierced Morgan with hate. "All right, Marshal. I can tell when I ain't wanted." He swaggered backward onto the boardwalk in front of the millinery. "I'll be seein' yuh 'round. And you, my pretty whore"—he gestured rudely to Lacey—"still owe me."

Lacey launched past Jack. "You can't just let him go."

Morgan caught her, swinging her around into his arms. "Not now, Lacey." He pinned her back against his chest, attempting to subdue her fury.

"You have to arrest him."

He didn't see her hand. Only felt his gun sliding from his holster. With a violent oath, he seized Lacey's wrist . . . and the gun went off.

The bullet whistled over Gressett's head, shattering a street lamp. Shards of glass rained all over him. Gressett stumbled off the walk onto the street, his eyes wide with disbelief as he wiped the twin trickles of blood from his neck. Lifting his head, he stared incredulously as Morgan wrestled the gun from Lacey's grip.

He opened his mouth to protest when Jack stepped between them, rifle in hand. "Go, Gressett. Before I finish what the girl started."

This time Gressett didn't hesitate. He pivoted his bulk and ran.

Wrenching the gun away with enough force to snap her wrist, Morgan ignored Lacey's cry. He felt his own fury; the way one feels the power of lightning just before it strikes. If her life had ever been imperiled, he knew with certainty, it was now. He spun her around to face him . . . and stared into sea-green eyes, gloriously bright with unshed tears.

The tangled fall of her hair swept into her flushed face, and she shoved it back. Her teeth were set as if the effort would control the faint quiver in her jaw as she stared up at him. "You just let him go, Morgan. Just like that."

She looked stricken. In her innocence and determination to see justice rendered, he knew she hadn't fully recognized her violence. "Has it occurred to you that Sam Gressett was here for another purpose than to ruin your day? That there are other ways to cap this problem? That maybe I know more about my job than you do?" Morgan gripped her chin firmly. "You draw a gun out here on these streets, you better be prepared to kill . . . or die, Miss Ashton."

Morgan heard the commotion in the street behind him, but his eyes never wavered from Lacey's ashen face. A wagon and horsemen bore down on them. He looked over his shoulder to see Colin riding up, his windblown hair disheveled, his expression filled with worry.

Before Colin could assess the situation, Morgan scooped Lacey off the street and stalked past her father, cutting him off.

Lacey struggled, her own fury sparked anew by Morgan's coarse treatment—as if *she* were the guilty one.

"Let me go!"

Morgan's abuse infuriated her. He carried her to the buckboard and tossed her in as if she weighed no more than a sack of feed. The momentum carried her backward, and she landed with an indignant thud on her backside.

"How could you?"

Morgan stalked past Colin to his horse milling on a hitching post in front of the boardinghouse. Lacey scrambled to stand. Struggling for balance against the sway of the wagon, she gripped the sides and glared through a screen of tangled hair as Morgan stepped into the stirrups of the big zebra dun and swung the horse around to face her father. "I suggest you take your spoiled daughter back to the hotel before she causes any more trouble. And whatever you do, don't let her get close to a gun."

Lacey gasped in outrage. "You traitor!"

He rode away. The skittish horses shifted their feet nervously. Lacey tried to balance in the wagon. Shoving the hair out of her face, she realized that a sizable crowd had gathered.

The shock of their presence drew her up indignantly. Only Jack seemed amused by the turn of events. She could hear him chuckling as he gathered the reins of his own horse and stepped into the saddle.

People swarmed around her father, like bees to honey, recounting the just-transpired event, as if it were some contest to be the first in its telling.

"Don't be too hard on the girl," Jack said, his horse prancing sideways. "Morgan's full of saddle burrs because your girl got the drop on him." He gave a wide-toothed grin and something like appreciation crossed his face. "But I suggest you teach her to shoot—so next time, she won't miss."

He rode away, and Lacey knew she'd be forever grateful to Jack for his support.

Someone in the crowd coughed. Red, the tall, lanky cowboy she'd eaten lunch with all week, jumped into the wagon and released the brake. Colin nudged his horse beside Lacey, and her heart jolted with sudden fear. He looked stunned, perhaps because she wasn't the perfect angel he'd expected. His attention shifted to her ruined dress.

"Are you all right?"

Tears betrayed her. "No, I'm not all right. That Gressett person should have been arrested."

"Lord, Lacey. You have no idea who these people are."

She lifted her chin. "And whose fault is that, Father?"

Colin clenched his jaw then kneed his horse and bolted off down the street. The thunder of a dozen horsemen followed his exit. Lacey barely caught her balance as Red swung the wagon around and set the horses running down the street behind them toward the hotel.

What would happen now?

Lacey remained in church long after the service ended. The sun spilled through the stained-glass windows above the pulpit, painting a nebulous echo of sainted images over the empty island of pews. A wedge of scarlet pressed against her lap and embraced the frayed prayer book clutched in her hands.

The object of the congregation's curiosity and gossip, she had endured their stares all morning. She'd never been a scandal before. It rankled her that even her father seemed to pass judgment over her. After all, the villain in this situation was that no-account Gressett.

Lacey welcomed the silence after the droning of the minister. Especially after she'd failed to ignore the tall, forbidding figure seated in front of her all morning. Her glance had strayed more than once to the wide shoulders and strong line of Morgan's handsome profile throughout the long service. She'd heard him sing, amazed that his was the voice that stood out in the large congregation. Somehow, it didn't fit the stoic demeanor of the hardened lawman.

Then nothing about Morgan Caine made sense. He was a confusing mixture of man. Indeed, he was a low-down hypocrite to his profession. That he had been kind to her in San Francisco was a fluke. Obviously, the man has a soft spot for prostitutes.

Her eyes fell on the back door.

Freedom beckoned. Freedom from her thoughts of Morgan and from the predicament she'd gotten herself into yesterday. Fire heated her veins. She was finished taking everything lying down.

Tucking her prayer book in her pocket, she stood.

"I wouldn't, if I were you." The deep voice spun her around.

Garbed in his white silk shirt and black broadcloth suit that barely tamed the muscled length of his body, Morgan was braced negligently in the doorway of the church, his arms crossed over his chest. The reckless slant of his hat shadowed his eyes, preventing her from gaining full view of his face. But the firm line of his chiseled mouth was set resolutely.

Lacey didn't pretend to hide her errant thoughts of escape. "Is it a crime to want to have a few moments of peace?" she challenged with false nonchalance, less than optimistic that he would grant her succor as he stalked into the sanctuary of the church.

"The moment's all yours once you get back to the hotel. Until then you'll do as you're told."

"Another order?"

"Take it as you wish. I don't have time for this today."

"I give you credit, sir." Lacey tilted her chin and smiled prettily, her feet pumping in double time to his sure movements as he propelled her toward the door. "You make a far better jailer than you do a marshal. Maybe you should trade occupations."

Morgan released her so suddenly she almost stumbled. "Anybody ever tell you, you talk too damn much?"

"Anybody ever tell you, you swear too much?"

In the dimmest region of her mind, Lacey thought she glimpsed a flicker in his eyes.

"Not lately, no," he said.

She crossed her arms. "Me neither."

He didn't seem to know what to say to her. Then his gaze dropped to her injured hand, and his expression changed. Lifting it, he inspected the bandage with an almost tender touch.

"What happened yesterday?"

"My dress snagged on a junk pile," she said, puzzled by the change in his manner. "When Gressett caught me . . ." She hesitated. Morgan's sober visage intensified the reckless urge to part with some of her own fastidiousness. "Shall I demonstrate my mode of self-defense, sir? It is a most effective maneuver on bullish men. That is, when I haven't imbibed too much to see straight enough to take care of myself."

Morgan dropped her hand. "I wasn't aware young English ladies were acquainted with the skill to fight so . . . efficiently."

"I'm a Yank," she said proudly, "and a Yank of a little means in a class society is prime fodder for any sweet-talking dandy who thinks he has a right to own you. Do you have any idea what it's like not to fit in, Mr. Caine?"

Though his sapphire eyes remained hooded, Lacey got the vague feeling he knew exactly the stigma attached to such rejection.

"You don't fit in here either, Miss Ashton," Morgan said suddenly, cutting short her charitable thoughts. "You're better off going back where you came from."

"To be exact, I'm *from* Virginia, Mr. Caine. And if you want me to leave—discuss that option with Father. I'm sure he's all ears where you're concerned." She whirled away, abandoning Morgan to the sanctum of the church.

Once outside, the crisp beauty of the summer day enveloped her like a gentle embrace. She welcomed the warmth. Hesitating at the top of the stairs, her eyes strayed to the faraway hills. The invigorating breeze flowed through her hair and washed over her face. She caught the vague scent of wildflowers. Not for the first time did Lacey discover a growing respect for this untamed frontier.

Morgan was wrong, she thought, settling her bonnet on her head. She may lack knowledge of the land, but she did not lack the grit to fit in. If yesterday's events accomplished anything, they lent determination to her decision to stay.

"Anytime now, Lacey," the object of her thoughts interrupted, prodding her with his towering presence, "you're dallying again."

Lacey meticulously fluffed the ribbon of her bonnet, refusing to be rushed.

"For Christ's sake," Morgan snapped, "winter will be here at this rate."

"Such blasphemy, Mr. Caine. And on holy ground, too," she piously stated. Grabbing handfuls of her skirt, Lacey started down the stairs—and stopped.

All eyes on her dropped. With the exception of her father and Joshua, who were standing at the bottom of the stairs, his men hastily turned away, clearly embarrassed to be caught gawking.

Muttering something inane, Morgan gripped Lacey's elbow, helpfully conducting her down the rest of the stairs where he then delivered her to her father.

"Your daughter, Colin." Morgan tipped his hat at her with a considerable flourish, needling Lacey's temper.

Forcing her eyes from his tall form as he walked away, Lacey politely returned her father's greeting while giving Joshua a hug.

"Lacey, it's time we talk," Colin quietly said.

She followed him to the edge of the boardwalk, and for a moment, hope squeezed her belly.

"You are aware that tomorrow we're leaving here." He plopped a change purse in her hand. "This is yours."

By the feel of it, it contained a lot of money. Lacey panicked as she imagined he was getting ready to give her the boot, as her aunt Clare would so aptly describe the process of getting rid of unwanted guests. "What is this for?" she dared to ask.

"I know nothing about women's apparel," he said.

"I don't understand."

"You can't sit in a wagon with an outfit like—" He wagged his finger at the bright sunshine-yellow poplin dress she was wearing.

"What's wrong with my clothes?"

"Lacey, it's not just your dresses." He was flustered and not for the first time annoyed with her. "Do you have to argue with me?"

Morgan, who was sitting on his horse and watching the proceedings, slid from the saddle with animalistic grace that set Lacey on edge. He looked just in the mood to throttle her for something.

If only she understood what that something was.

Propping one leg on the boardwalk, he negligently rested his elbow on his knee. The walk where she was standing was at least ten inches off the street, and she looked directly into his eyes. Eyes as beautiful as the warm summer sky.

Only they were more like the downwind zephyr of a winter's storm. "Miss Ashton," he formally addressed her, "your father is politely trying to tell you . . ."

She intercepted his glance to her father. Whatever it was between them, Morgan obviously possessed the qualifications to handle this matter. She waited for him to continue, curious to find out what could possibly turn a grown man like Colin Ashton to mush.

"Get rid of the corset."

"I beg your pardon?"

"And all this other fashionable, feminine useless attire." He pointed rudely to her bustle. "We are not going on a Sunday outing through the park."

A slow burn traveled to the roots of her hair. Delicate issues were not bantered about in such a cavalier fashion, and with a man no less. She glared at her father who was directing Joshua to the horses. He was a coward for not telling her this himself.

She turned back to Morgan. "I'll choose my own wardrobe without your help." Her hushed whisper was not filled with the outrage she had every right to express, but with a reckless urge to bait the arrogant man. "And what manner of undergarments I choose to wear may interest you, but that, too, will be my decision. I'll not be bullied by you any more than I will by the likes of Sam Gressett who happens to still be roaming around free, thanks to you."

"Don't mistake me, Lacey," he warned, a dangerous note underlying his words. "You can't breathe in that corset and as long as you wear it, it's a danger to you. I'll personally cut it off you myself if I find you wearing one on the trail."

"I'll just bet you would, and enjoy it, too," she whispered. "A very capable man you are with the ladies."

"I'm capable of doing just about anything, sweetheart," he whispered silkily, "but if I ever put my hands on you again, it won't be the sweet sound of violins you'll hear this time."

"Were there violins, Mr. Caine?"

Morgan's mouth drew slowly into a grin, his teeth flashing white. Lacey's heart thumped, nearly unbalancing her fortitude. "I'm sure it would prove interesting to find out."

"Hah!" she tapped his chest. "You lost all future chances there, Sir Marshal."

Morgan gave his hat a yank. He turned and mounted his horse. Draping his forearm across the saddle horn, he leaned over to speak, his words clearly meant for her father. "Jack still hasn't returned with news of Gressett. I recommend keeping an escort on your daughter." His blue eyes drilled her as he spoke. "For obvious reasons, it's safer that way for everyone."

"Caleb, you and Will, don't let her out of your sight," Colin snapped to the two able-bodied cowboys standing near the hitching post beside the buggy. They turned away, looking hassled at the prospect of having to spend the remainder of the day following her around.

Their displeasure didn't nearly compare to hers.

To Lacey's credit, she remained calm. Dismissing Morgan, she turned stiffly to the other guilty party in this charade. Her father. "Fine. I'll go shopping as you wish. May Joshua come along?"

"No, Lacey."

"Aw, Pa!" Joshua complained.

"No, Josh. Shopping isn't for boys." He gave the boy a stern glance, silencing any further protest. Helping Joshua mount the horse, he stepped lithely into the saddle behind the boy.

Her father still cut a dashing figure, and as Lacey watched him, loneliness crowded her like nothing she'd felt before.

Then her lids dropped over her eyes, and she picked absently at a thread on her skirt. She preferred her anger.

"Enjoy your shopping trip," her father said. He looked over at the two men assigned to guard her. "See that you don't lose her."

He swung his horse around and took off in a distance-eating canter. The others followed in a thundering cloud of dust. Gripping back on the reins to restrain his agitated horse, Morgan was the last to leave. Beneath his wide-brimmed hat, his gaze lifted past her to the two men standing unhappily beside the buggy. Then he swung his horse around and galloped off after the others.

If he sought to defeat her, he'd failed.

Lacey Ashton was not so easily defeated. Not by her father—and certainly not by Morgan Caine.

She turned. Like a naughty Cheshire cat, who just cornered two mice, Lacey looked at her captive bodyguards . . . and smiled.

Chapter Six

Four hours later, Jack found Lacey in the dining room of the hotel enjoying a cup of English tea. Knowing that she had outfoxed all the wily hounds, Lacey allowed herself the satisfaction of a smug grin as he approached.

Losing her guards had been a matter of strategic brilliance. After wending her way for hours through Portland's finest shops, Lacey had stopped at a French boutique filled with titillating and blushing female types, where no self-respecting gentleman would be caught dead. As anticipated, her flustered guards abandoned her in the store, to wait outside, leaving her to escape out the back door.

Walking to the Feedloft, she then purchased the necessary items for her trip before meandering through the back alleys to her hotel. Removing her cumbersome bustle, she'd hidden beneath her bed with a good book in hand, evading capture when the search party arrived in town to look for her.

Lacey had just congratulated herself on a successful campaign when Jack lumbered into the dining room. "Would you like to take a seat?" she invited.

For a moment, as he stared down at her, Lacey almost lost

her courage. Finally, as if sensing the cause already lost, he removed his fur cap and accepted the proffered chair. Dressed in a heavy buckskin coat with fringed neck and sleeves that creaked when he crossed his arms, Jack stretched out his legs and regarded her dolefully.

"Your father is very worried about you."

She shrugged unrepentantly. "I've been here in the hotel."

Jack shook his head and a slow grin replaced the thin line of disapproval on his face. "You pulled a fast one on old Caleb, and you bein' just a slip of a girl, Caleb's reputation is forever ruined. Poor Will just lost point to Foley for the trip home. Believe you me, it's no small insult to go from point to drag, especially between those two boys who would argue the proper side to butter bread."

Lacey sipped her tea, trying unsuccessfully to shrug off the guilt.

"You've ruined their chaste opinion of women forever."

"Maybe I did them a favor."

"You cured them of their misconceptions, I'm sure." Looking at the fat coin purse beside Lacey, Jack cocked a bushy brow in surprise. "Did you find everything you wanted?"

"I didn't need much. Besides"—her fingers tightened around her cup—"I'm not ready to be indebted to my father any more than I have to be."

Shaking his blond head in resignation, Jack's hazel eyes sparkled with their usual mirth. "You're a lot of trouble. Colin had you pegged all wrong from the start."

"Is that so?"

"You're no ring-tailed dove that's fer sure."

Jack Kipp was nothing like his arrogant nephew. Lacey liked Jack and his easygoing nature. Setting down her cup, she leaned on her elbows and looked intently across the table at him.

"Tell me, Mr. Kipp, is it true what I heard about you? That you're a legend?"

He made a rude sound and leaned on his elbows, mirroring Lacey's own casual mannerism. "Everyone has a long memory here in the West—sometimes it's all they've got. You can't take it serious."

"You were an army scout," she prompted, "and a hero in five Indian campaigns. You were the one who finally found your sister's son after six years of captivity with the Indians. You brought your nephew out of the mountains, along with eight other survivors. I would say that's something."

"Has Joshua been filling your head full of this stuff?"

Lacey lifted the newspaper in her lap. "This is last week's paper from San Francisco. I found it in the lobby on my way down earlier. Being the *infamous* Marshal Caine's uncle has brought you a certain amount of notoriety. He and his sister were part of the group you brought out of captivity."

"That happened a long time ago, Lacey. It's a cryin' shame a man's past has to be someone else's business."

It was all the comment Jack would make on the subject. Just as well, Lacey thought as she set the paper down. She didn't dare allow sentiment to interfere with her opinion of Morgan Caine. Even old wounds from the past couldn't justify his boorish behavior.

Jack seemed to read her mind. "Morgan don't cotton much to patience, Miss Ashton. He wasn't raised to it. If he seems rough, he usually has good reason."

"Yesterday . . ." She hesitated, drawing in a ragged breath in an effort to hold back the tears that suddenly seemed to surface. "Yesterday, what that man, what Sam Gressett said, it wasn't true."

"I know."

"I can't deny my responsibility for what happened in San Francisco. But I never took his gold. I'm not what he called me." Lacey suddenly glanced up at him. "You know?"

"Even before Morgan explained what happened in San Francisco, none of us in this whole outfit believed any of it."

Her heart sank. "Morgan . . . explained?"

"He said Gressett was drunk and accosted you." Jack eyed her keenly. "That's all he said."

Fighting to control the depth of her shock, Lacey remained speechless. Morgan didn't betray her.

"No one ever doubted your integrity, Lacey."

All day she'd been nursing her anger at everyone. She regarded Jack bleakly. "I didn't know."

"Imagine how surprised we all were when Morgan told us he'd met you in San Francisco." Lacey didn't think he looked very surprised. "Your father wasn't pleased that he would keep the incident to himself."

Remembering Morgan's stern warning when he'd come to her room that first day in Portland, Lacey felt a surge of guilt. "I should have said something. I hope Mr. Caine wasn't blamed."

"I wouldn't worry too much on his account. That man walks on water when it comes to your father."

The revelation annoyed Lacey and made her feel even more like an outsider than she already was. Morgan Caine was a bloody paragon. Even in this, he managed to come out shining like polished brass.

She knew she was being emotional. Even jealous of his relationship with her father. But she couldn't help it. She sniffed, and from deep in her chest, a sob wracked her body. Maybe it was because she didn't want to feel gratitude toward Morgan. Or because the past couple of weeks had worn her thin, and she was just tired of the constant wall of defense she had to build daily. The tears flowed. Letting her cry in peace, Jack didn't waste time on patronizing sentiment.

After awhile, Lacey picked up her napkin. Dabbing at her eyes, she gave Jack a tentative smile. "Are you married, Mr. Kipp?"

"Is this a proposal, Miss Ashton?"

Her mood brightened. "It's just that you should be," she said, blotting at her nose. "You'd make a good father."

Jack's bearded countenance split into an amiable grin. Evidently, no one in all his life had ever accused him of having the makings of a good father.

A disturbance in the lobby drew their attention, and Lacey glanced up to see her father, hat in hand, stumble through the doorway to the dining room. His gaze strafed the room, stopping on her. Something twisted itself deep inside her.

"Well, Miss Ashton, this is my cue to leave."

"I take it I've been under guard."

"Lock and key." He grinned. "Wouldn't do my hero nature any good to lose you the way old Caleb did." He picked up his beaver hat. When Colin reached the table, he stood.

Colin had not taken his eyes off Lacey. "You've been crying."

"It's all right, Daddy. We were just talking."

Colin looked at Jack. Relief seemed to wash over him. "Yes, I can see how Jack would have that effect on a woman." Jack laughed and turned to go, stopping as Colin put a hand on his arm. "Everyone returned to the boat. Tell them . . ." He gave Lacey a meaningful glance. "Tell them I won't be back for a while. I need to spend some time with my daughter."

Jack looked from her father to Lacey and grinned. "Good day, Miss Ashton."

Colin watched him leave, but Lacey's eyes were on her father. "That's a good man." He turned, encompassing her with his gaze. "May I?" He indicated the seat Jack had just vacated.

At her nod, he sat.

And suddenly years of questions vanished through the cracks in her composure. Silence stretched between them. Longing resurfaced. She had a need to reach out and touch this man. She wanted her father back. Not this shadow of a man she once adored.

"I thought you left on the steamer that went out at two," he said. "I knew that if you had, I would never have forgiven myself."

Lacey dabbed at her eyes, hastily seeking to collect herself. "Where would I have gone, Daddy?"

He acknowledged the change purse at her elbow. "You could have bought your way back to New York with that."

"I have no desire to go to New York, or back to England for that matter." And it was the truth. She didn't want to leave. Ever.

The realization shocked her.

Colin averted his eyes and looked away as if the momentary reprise would help him regain his thoughts. "I've acted like a—" he flushed. "We have a lot of catching up to do," he amended. "Something I should have done the very first day you stepped off the steamboat from San Francisco. But I was too much of a coward to face you with my own failings. You were quite angry with me when you got here."

Lacey dropped her gaze, fumbling with the frayed edges of the bandage on her hand. Anger was not the emotion that characterized her feelings that day. Terror more aptly described her state of mind: terror of the new world she faced. Of failure. Of him.

He continued. "I didn't know who I expected to greet that day. I only know it wasn't you. You were all grown up. A part of me was lost with that realization, because I knew that I'd missed out on your whole life. Clare," he said suddenly, "was she good to you? She gave you my letters?"

"I still have them all."

Colin hesitated. "I don't know what got into me yesterday. I acted like a fool about everything."

"Oh, Daddy," she said with a sigh, relieved that they weren't going to hash over the fiasco with Gressett again. But Lacey's mood sobered. "Why didn't you save the estate in England when it was obviously in your means to do so? It was your home, too." The subject was a sore one and vexed her much with unanswered questions.

His expression shadowed. "Didn't Clare ever tell you?"

Dread filled her. "Tell me what?"

"It was her decision, not mine."

Lacey sank back into her chair. "I don't understand."

"Clare knew you weren't happy in England. You belonged here."

"But did you want me here?"

"That was never the problem, Lacey."

She sat up. "Then what was the problem? What was so horrible that you took me to England and left me there for thirteen years?"

He looked at her intently. Faint lines deepened his face. "Times were dangerous, Lacey, for both of us. A war loomed in this country."

She shook her head. "It was more than that."

He wrapped his fingers around her palm. "When we reach Kingston . . . I promise, we'll talk. This is a matter for our whole family to discuss. Please, I don't know what else to say."

How about, I love you? I've missed you?

But already raw from the fierce emotions raging through her, she acquiesced. In the lobby, a clock chimed five times. The mingled aroma of bread and roasting chicken percolated into the dining room from the kitchen. Her stomach grumbled.

Colin scraped his chair away from the table. "I know a place around the corner that serves the best beef steak in Portland." He traced the rough edge of his knuckles over the contour of her cheek, like a gentle whisper, expressing in kindness what he did not say aloud. "If you're not embarrassed to be seen in public with a grubby old man, would you like to go?"

She looked into his shining eyes and accepted his arm. "Grubby old man, indeed."

"We're leaving for Waylen Springs in the morning," he said. "You'll move to a room on the steamer tonight. Joshua misses you."

Lacey felt herself thaw. "Is his mother anything like him?" she asked, anticipation over the idea of her new family washing over her.

"Actually, Lorraine's very much like you. I practically had to hog-tie her to keep her in Kingston until after the baby is born. She wanted to meet you that much."

He opened the front door of the lobby, and Lacey stepped outside into the pedestrian traffic.

"I talked to Morgan," he said. "Seems he's concerned that he might have injured your sensibilities this morning at church."

Like the cat ruffling the canary's feathers. "Is he now?"

"So what is your opinion of the good marshal?"

The offhanded statement was too quaint to be casual. "Not nearly so high as yours, Daddy."

Her father's paragon may have won the battle today, but the war wasn't lost. She was about to mount a second charge.

Lacey awakened to the humming vibrations of the steamboat's boiler engines. In a few days, they would reach Waylen Springs, where the stock animals and huge canvas-covered wagons waited to be loaded for the overland journey to Kingston. She stretched in languid catlike grace and opened her eyes.

Her room was bathed in a depressing gray. Throwing back the covers, she came up on her knees to look out the window above her head. The steamer sloshed downriver at a cautious pace. Walled in on both sides by enormous mist-shrouded cliffs, Lacey caught glimpses of sheer granite walls barely visible in the murky drizzle swallowing the river. The scenery would have been spectacular on a sunny day.

The door thundered beneath the weight of someone's fist, nearly sending her out of her skin. "Lacey," Joshua called.

Lacey crawled out of the bunk and opened the door.

"I've been waiting for you to get up." Fixing a fastidious eye on Lacey's quarters, Josh ducked past her. "*I* don't have a room like this," he complained, hopping onto her bunk to look out the window.

"You've had a rough time of it, have you?"

Jumping off the bed, he landed with a muffled thud onto the throw carpet. "I have to sleep in a hammock that rocks enough to make a person green. I don't know how Marshal Caine and Jack do it, and still be able to walk and talk straight in the morning."

The mention of Morgan's name drew Lacey up. Her gaze swung to the sturdy black trunk on the floor beside the armoire. Anticipation fluttered in her stomach.

"Now, I'm not complaining—"

"Of course not," she said, nudging him back out the door.

"I just don't like boats is all."

"Sort of the way I feel about horses, I'm sure."

"It's not the same." Joshua looked as if he were preparing to launch into his usual long-winded tirade on the merits of horseback riding.

"Out. I have to get dressed. And don't come back, either," she added, edging the door closed behind him. "This may take awhile."

Joshua latched on to the doorway like a cocklebur to stockings. "I'm glad you're not in trouble anymore." He grinned. "I should have been with you when you escaped from Caleb.

He was steamin' like the big smokestack on this boat when he got back."

It was obvious her brother didn't share her remorse over the matter. Peeling his fingers from the doorframe, Lacey infused her voice with as much authority as she could summon. "Good-bye, Joshua."

She forced the door closed in his face.

"Someone like you . . . it would take no time to learn to ride a horse," he yelled through the closed portal.

"No horses," she called back.

Going straight to the chest, Lacey flung open the lid. The clothes she bought yesterday were still neatly wrapped the way she left them. Tearing open the bundles, she carefully set out everything on her bed. Then she stood back and gazed down at her new traveling wardrobe with nothing short of awe.

It occurred to her suddenly that she didn't know the least thing about men's paraphernalia.

Lacey stripped off her nightdress. Turning to her toilette, she washed herself and braided her long hair, wrapping it around her head so it would stay hidden beneath the felt hat she'd bought. Tugging on her flimsy undergarments, she shoved her arms into the sleeves of a red flannel shirt and buttoned it up the front to her collarbone. On second thought, she released the top two buttons. A pair of boys' denim pants followed. Wriggling them up to her waist, Lacey tucked the shirt in, working diligently to close the rigid steel fastenings above the crotch. She picked up the flattened hat and kneading it back into shape, tugged it firmly down on her head. The boots, her father had had custom-made for her as a surprise, sat polished in the corner of the room. She pulled them over her stockinged feet, stomping them on solid. Her attire complete, Lacey ran a hand down the shape of her leg, testing the fit. The material hugged the curve of her hips.

Nobody could complain about frilly, feminine trappings now.

Aunt Clare would have died of shock.

Lacey straightened. With the hard-edged determination of one about to embark on a mission of war, she marched out of her room.

Breakfast was being served when Lacey strolled into the dining room. She recognized most everyone scattered across the long bench tables. It seemed that the steamer belonged solely to the large group from Kingston. Lacey pinpointed her mark.

Conversing with Jack beside the salon window overlooking the river, Morgan was a daunting figure. Wearing dark trail clothes, he looked more the outlaw brigand than the paladin who had on more than one occasion put himself between her and danger. Lacey drew her breath in swiftly. She didn't dare feel burdened by gratitude.

Yanking her hat lower over her eyes, she marched forward.

As Lacey walked past the tables, the low drone in the dining hall died behind her. Joshua, who was sitting next to her father looked up, and Lacey saw his mouth drop, his disbelief mirroring the look of shock on her father's face as he choked on a piece of toast.

Morgan turned idly from his conversation. Blue eyes met hers over the rim of his coffee cup. The hand gripping the metal cup froze, then slowly lowered to the table beside him. Over the wild drumming in her ears, Jack's deep, resonating chuckle was the only sound heard in the tomblike silence as she cornered her quarry.

Hands splayed on her hips, Lacey lifted her chin. Morgan was too tall for her to stare down, but she attempted the feat anyway. "I thought since you made a public case of my apparel yesterday, Mr. Caine, you should be the first to inspect my attire before I attempted to tackle the rigors of the trail."

A dark brow arched in response.

"I took great care as you suggested buying clothing void of all feminine frills and frippery. And you should find everything to your . . . specification."

"Everything, Miss Ashton?" he drawled.

The gauntlet had been thrown.

Her eyes flared in challenge. Palms out, Lacey brashly opened her arms for his inspection. "If you doubt my honesty, you can certainly check for yourself. Should I pass out on the trail, I would hate for you to strip me naked for no cause."

Whether Morgan thought she had the guts or not, Lacey

didn't miss the faint glimmer of incredulity in his eyes. Tension filled the turbulent space between them like the current of a hot monsoon wind sucking the breath from her. Morgan Caine was not a man overburdened by the restrictions of a conscience, and Lacey wasn't entirely confident he wouldn't publicly frisk her just for spite.

"Well?" she boldly asserted, struggling to remain aloof.

His gaze dropped to the shiny tips of her handcrafted boots and with agonizing slowness raised over every inch of her to finally level on her face. A less hearty opponent might have crumbled.

"Don't tempt me, Miss Ashton."

"And I thought you were a man above temptation."

"I'm not above calling your bluff."

Lacey was sure the fiery pride she'd nursed all yesterday glittered in her eyes. Her hands again went to her hips. "I don't bluff, Mr. Caine," she stated emphatically. She *wanted* him to test her. To touch her; so she could have the pleasure of slugging him.

"You know, Morgan," Jack broke in, studying Lacey's attire with more interest than was warranted, considering he was older than her father. "She doesn't look to be bluffin'."

Morgan still fixed his gaze on hers. A rakish lock of dark hair swept his tanned brow. Lacey steeled herself against the annoying knot of discomfort crippling her defenses.

"First smart thing I've actually seen a woman wear in these parts for a long time," Jack continued, voicing his approval to the obvious irritation of Morgan. "You'll do all right, Miss Ashton. A sweet thing like you. Why you got more brass than most men I know."

"That's very good, Jack. You encourage her anymore, and she'll be running around in her skivvies."

"Lacey?" Her father's voice startled her. "What are you doing?"

"I had some business to attend to before breakfast."

Colin eyed her warily. "I see," he said, settling his gaze on Morgan. "Does this have something to do with yesterday?"

"It has everything to do with yesterday, Father. After all, Mr. Caine seemed to have my welfare in mind when he so *privately* instructed me on the necessities of a proper wardrobe. I thought it only just to grant him my appreciation for his . . . kindness."

"These are the clothes you bought?"

Her father's amused tone drew Lacey up. "As instructed," she pronounced, daring any one of them to start an argument with her for flaunting propriety. "Besides," she added, running a hand down the curve of her hip. "I like these clothes. I could really get use to this new feel."

Morgan muttered something profane, but before Lacey could respond to the unorthodox language he continued to use while in her presence, her father interrupted. "This is my fault. I apologize for any misunderstanding." He ran a hand through his sandy hair. "I heard what Morgan said, and I don't think he meant any harm."

Her eyes cut upward to spear Morgan. Obviously, her father was under the erroneous assumption his paragon could do no wrong. Morgan's mouth quirked slightly as he watched her with speculative eyes. "You heard everything, Father? Then you would know that the message was most clear. Wasn't it, Mr. Caine?"

"Your aptitude for following instructions shows great promise, Miss Ashton," he answered, his voice uncommonly pleasant. Then he caught her chin gently in his hand, and she was staring into those arresting eyes. "But don't try my patience again." Something in his cobalt gaze warned Lacey that she wouldn't relish the consequences.

With a less-than-gentle rap to her nose, he dismissed her, leaving her gaping at his back as he walked away.

Somehow in the last moment of her strategically planned battle, he'd snatched the wind from her sails.

Jack watched him go, scratching his whiskers. Joshua broke the awkward silence. "Jiminy! I never seen Marshal Caine so calm unless he was gonna shoot someone."

Lacey frowned at her brother. "Is that so?"

"Son—" Jack shook his grizzled head, studying Lacey with interest. "That marshal is about as fearsome as a tiger cub when it comes to your sister." Chuckling to himself, he followed Morgan's straight path out of the dining hall.

"Can you just answer one question for me, daughter?"

Aware of the serious tone in her father's voice, Lacey turned.

"How did Clare survive all those years?"

"Are you angry?" she quietly asked.

Her father looked at her with something akin to pride, and she felt warm all over. "No," he said, glancing to the doorway where Morgan had stopped to talk to Caleb. "But *he* is."

"Does that bother you?"

His eyes widened. "Bother me?" He laughed, dispelling her concern. "Why it delights me to no end."

This was not the answer she expected. Her wary gaze flickered to the doorway, now empty, wondering why everyone seemed to take such pleasure in Morgan's discomfiture.

Reaching Waylen Springs should have been the end to Lacey's confinement. Restricted to the safety of the boat, she and Joshua stood on the deck of the steamer watching as the cargo was removed to the wagons that would finally take them overland to Kingston.

Morgan was the only one who had business to do in town.

Lacey moved within the shadows of the second deck overhang to watch as Joshua pounced on the unsuspecting marshal. Her brother, who had patiently lain in wait for Morgan to arrive topside, was far more daring than she was in their mutual quest to get off the boat.

As usual, Morgan was irritatingly impossible to ignore. The rugged buckskin jacket he wore hugged the wide curve of his shoulders and opened to a faded blue cavalry-style shirt that emphasized the color in his eyes. Feeling harassed with a sudden case of indigestion, Lacey leaned against the balustrade, content to allow Joshua to deal with all of the negotiations.

Her gaze ambled past the men unloading the crates to a group of riders approaching from the west end of town. The rough outfit appeared to be the other half of Colin's men. Lacey's attention settled absently on the dark-clad figure separating from the group. As equally impressive as the sleek black Arabian he rode, he was dressed in clean black cords with the customary colt hanging at his hip, white shirt, and black ankle-length duster. He seemed out of place among the stock and trail hands gathering on the docks. Lacey followed his progress across the docks as he brought his horse to a prancing halt in front of the wagon where her father was working.

Colin's animated greeting carried back to her over the noises surrounding the dock. Lacey piqued when she heard her name, but before she could eavesdrop, they both turned suddenly, trapping her in their gaze. In a moment, it registered that the man had moved past her father and was coming aboard.

"Seems you have an admirer." Morgan's rough voice startled her. "Your father's foreman," he said, acknowledging the stranger.

Lacey met Morgan's gaze. "You don't like him, I take it."

"It doesn't matter what I think. He works for your father."

For once, whatever plagued Morgan wasn't her fault.

Then her father was calling her. Lacey stepped out of the shadows to greet the new visitor. His good looks stunned her. With dark, compelling eyes and hair the color of night, he could surely coax a smile from a rock. Lacey imagined a fair share of women swooned daily at the sight of this devil. The stranger's midnight eyes flared with interest at her approach.

"Lacey," her father said. "I want you to meet Jared Coyle."

With great resplendence, the stranger bowed over her hand, catching her completely off guard. "I have to admit, you were not what I was expecting." His eyes entailed every inch of her in one hungry sweep. "You're no prim English lass."

Lacey stared in fascination as he brought her hand to his mouth. She could not conceal her years of training and dipped automatically, catching herself before she completed a full curtsy. "In truth, Mr. Coyle, I'm not English." She smiled, removing her fingers from his grip. "I was born in Virginia."

"Ah, that explains it, I'm sure. The clothes, I mean. We Americans tend to be more practical in matters of fashion."

Her father seemed amused. "Jared is also from Virginia."

"Where beauty abounds," her father's foreman elaborated.

Lacey thought the sound emanating from behind her resembled a groan. She shifted uneasily, jolting when she stepped full on Morgan's boot. Her gaze sliced to his, only to feel assaulted as he patiently removed her from his arms. Morgan always managed to make her feel like a child.

"Welcome back, Caine," Jared said, acknowledging Morgan with a cool gaze. "I've brought tidings from home for you."

"How's everyone doing?" Colin asked.

"Waiting anxiously for your return," Jared said. "Your missus is doing well. She's moved in with my sister until you get back, or until the baby arrives, whichever comes first. And my sister sends the marshal here . . . all her love."

"Jolene owns the town general store," Colin informed Lacey. The news was strangely disconcerting. "Jared here is her younger brother. He arrived for a visit about a year ago and stayed. He manages my range . . . which reminds me," Colin said, slapping his hands in relish.

"He's a beaut, Colin," Jared said, grinning. "Nothing like him in the whole territory."

"Cattle," Morgan supplied for Lacey's benefit. "Colin and Jack furnish beef for almost every mining camp and army outpost in British Columbia. Your dad just purchased a prized Hereford bull all the way from Wyoming Territory."

"Been trying to get Morgan to join our operation for some time," Colin added. "He even has a nice homestead in the mountains. Great summer pasture."

"I didn't know you'd built a house up there, Caine." Jared suddenly looked interested.

"Is there a reason why you should?"

"I think we're keeping Morgan from his job," Colin said suddenly. "He's got work to do, the same as us."

"Pa!" Josh grabbed Colin's arm. "Lacey and me wanna go to town with Marshal Caine."

Colin looked askance at Morgan. Joshua turned his saucer eyes back on Morgan. "Please, Marshal Caine. Like I said, we'll be no trouble." He elbowed Lacey in the ribs. "Isn't that so, sis?"

"That'll be the day." Morgan's skeptical glance encased her with equal interest. Stripping off his buckskin jacket, he placed it on her shoulders. Immediately the warmth and man-scent of him penetrated the mist as his jacket enveloped her.

Tugging her hat down over her eyes, Morgan pinned her with his gaze. "Whatever you do, don't talk to anyone."

"Is this truly necessary?"

"It is if you want to go with me," Morgan said flatly.

Her father added, "Sam Gressett is still unaccounted for, Lacey."

Irritated that she should be forever held accountable for that man's bullish crimes, Lacey frowned.

"Sam Gressett is here?" Jared asked.

"The same troublemaking son of a bitch as always," Colin replied. "Lacey tried to shoot him after he insulted her a few days back."

Eyeing Lacey, Jared delivered a slow whistle. "Remind me to be ever the gentleman around this one."

Morgan's dark brow lifted. "You need reminding?"

"Go." Colin waved them all on.

Josh pulled her after Morgan. "Told you he'd let us go," he whispered conspiratorially. "You owe me two bits."

Trying to ignore the warm scent of the man who had worn the jacket, Lacey struggled with the sleeves. She was getting tired of the protective attitude that made her a virtual prisoner in a land of beauty and open space that should have been free to all. She wondered if a woman alone in this territory ever stood a chance at survival.

Chapter Seven

Lacey and Joshua ran to keep up with Morgan's long-legged stride. The crowd jostled them from all directions. By the time they reached the street corner, Lacey lost sight of Morgan. Frustrated, she stared around her. Cowboys and dockworkers—coming and going in and out of saloons and other various establishments that lined the waterfront—moved along the narrow wood-planked boardwalk.

A short, beefy man beside her darted across the street. Lacey started to follow when a heavy-handed grip on her shoulder yanked her back just as a large beer wagon barreled around the corner. Muddy water drenched her. Her outraged protests were squandered beneath the din of thundering hooves as the team of horses raced past without even slowing.

"For God's sake, Lacey." She barely heard Morgan's harsh reprimand behind her. "Get that hat out of your eyes so you can see."

Still gaping in shock, Lacey surged forward with the crowd. Morgan's hand, now braced against her back, pushed her along. She tried to look around for Joshua and only hoped that he had the good sense to be following safely behind Morgan.

Just when Lacey thought she'd scream in frustration, Morgan turned onto a quiet street.

Releasing her breath in an exasperated sigh, Lacey reached over her shoulder and unhooked Morgan's grip from her jacket. She was finished with his prodding.

"Mr. Caine—" She snatched herself from his grasp. She paused to spit the grit out of her mouth. "You pull my hat down so I'm blind, then yell at me because I can't see. You prod me about . . . and look at me—" She glared at her muddied sleeves, swiping at the dirt. She was a mess, and it was Morgan's fault. "Why are you always in such a blood-awful hurry?"

Silence . . .

Incredulous that Morgan should say nothing in his defense, Lacey pulled her eyes from the mud-caked sleeves and glared up at him. Only to find him staring down at her, his mouth twitching suspiciously in an abortive attempt not to smile.

No. Smile would be an understatement. He was on the verge of laughing—at her! Beside him, Joshua could barely contain himself, and they both suddenly plunged into a fit of laughter.

Instantly, Morgan changed, so dramatically, that Lacey could only gawk at the transformation. Gone was the hardness that etched his face. He was incredibly handsome. His laugher was deep and rich, like the voice she'd heard in church. For one astounding moment, Lacey forgot he was laughing at her. Or that he had plodded her impatiently about and treated her rudely. She forgot that she was wet, covered in mud, and irate.

She forgot everything!

Pleasure fluttered in the pit of her stomach, and she struggled with desires that tested every bad opinion she'd ever formed about him. Lacey wondered suddenly what it would be like to have this man look at her with respect, or with half the warmth she saw him share with Joshua. But he didn't share that same camaraderie with her; he only laughed at her because she looked like an urchin.

Lacey tipped her chin and made a chiding face. "Are you finished?" she asked, having suffered their amusement long enough.

Morgan eyed her speculatively. They'd both recovered sufficiently to consider her in a more sober manner. Completely remorseless, Morgan untied the red handkerchief from around his neck and diligently wiped at her face. "That should teach you to be in such a hurry to cross the street." His blue eyes sparkled as he leisurely studied her wretched state. There was no severity in his voice, and his ministrations were surprisingly gentle. "Especially on rainy days such as this."

"Thank you for the advice," Lacey managed, averting her gaze from his penetrating blue eyes. She felt resentment that he should affect her so thoroughly with merely a kind look.

"You're welcome, Miss Ashton." Settling his attention on Joshua, his mouth crooked into a smile. "Two bits, huh?" he casually inquired of the youth.

Joshua nearly choked. Morgan glanced back at Lacey. Again, Lacey experienced that dizzy feeling of displacement that left her suspended somewhere between the moon and the stars.

"Ye of so little faith," he said magnanimously, dabbing at her nose. "I'd have done it for a lot less."

"I'll keep that in mind next time." Jerking the bandanna from Morgan's hand, she was aghast that her hands were trembling.

Lacey yanked the hat off her head and snapped it against her leg, splattering mud and grit. Then shoving the limp thing back down over her hair, she surveyed the damage to Morgan's buckskin.

"I guess we don't have to worry about no disguise now," Josh observed.

"Don't count on it," Morgan said.

Lacey settled her hands on her hips and endeavored to redress the issue properly. "I'm tired of this cloak-and-dagger act. I should be able to wear what I want. I'm not interested in what people think."

Morgan's handsome features hinted at amusement. "It takes some time. It would be the same for . . ." He turned to frankly consider Joshua. "Joshua here. What if he were to decide to walk about in public wearing a dress?"

"Marshal Caine!" Joshua's eyes bulged.

Lacey glanced between the two in dismay. "It's not the same thing, and you know it."

Morgan's brows shot up. "Why not?"

Lacey suspected his stubborn resistance was not bent on any ideals he possessed. She couldn't understand why he should be so disagreeable on the matter.

"Am I interrupting?" The husky voice cut Lacey's reply short.

They all turned at once.

Astride the saddle of a magnificent Appaloosa, a beautiful woman watched them, her dark eyes alight with a mischievous sparkle. "Howdy, Morgan."

Morgan shoved his hat back off his forehead. "If it isn't the sweet-tempered Caitlyn Madigan." His easy manner astounded Lacey. "So you decided to return." The sound of his boot steps on the weathered boardwalk boasted his casual gait. As tall as he was, he looked directly into the woman's eyes.

Her impish raven curls fell around her lovely face in tousled disarray. "Without you, San Francisco lacked . . . excitement. I was told you'd probably be in town sometime today."

"Your brother never could keep anything from you."

"He said you'd be here on business. You work much too hard, Morgan."

He shot a sideways glance in Lacey's direction. "Some days are certainly more trying than others."

"He also said you recommended him for the job of deputy marshal."

"I did."

"Heaven knows this territory needs more law, what with the horrible rumors circulating about that wretched Lawton gang."

Morgan leveled his gaze at Caitlyn. "Since when have you ever worried about anything?"

Caitlyn assumed a mien of injury. "Morgan, you're so cruel."

"And selfish, narrow-minded, and arrogant," he added for flavor. "You leave my character in verbal cinders every time I see you."

"That's because you deserve it." Caitlyn draped her arms shamelessly around Morgan's neck and pulled herself off the saddle "I'd like to make everything up to you, tonight," she said, lingering within his strong arms even after he lowered her to the ground. "I'll make it worth your while, Marshal. I always do, don't I?"

Confused by the strange emotions that forced her to look away, Lacey kicked at a pebble. The excitement of a few moments ago gave way to a hollow feeling.

Morgan set her away from him. "I'm not alone, Cat."

Looking past him, Caitlyn sighed. "And what crime have these children committed to be in your custody?"

Lacey squelched the urge to protest the undignified observation. Children, indeed. Clearly amused by the insult, Morgan proceeded with the introductions.

Josh grimaced when Caitlyn fluffed his hair. "You've grown since I saw you last."

Morgan's eyes gleamed into Lacey's. "And this is Lacey Ashton. Lacey is Joshua's sister," he offered, clearly anticipating Caitlyn's reaction once he revealed it was a woman hiding beneath the layer of grime.

Caitlyn's jaw dropped. Refusing to be intimidated by the woman's scrutiny, Lacey stared back.

"So, you're Colin Ashton's daughter." The woman's sweet conjecture bristled over Lacey. "You're certainly no prim English lass. I heard . . . well it doesn't really matter what I heard."

Lacey realized it was the second time that day someone had voiced those exact words. The sentiment left her curiously violated.

Something in Morgan's expression changed. "I had no idea Miss Ashton would inspire such far-reaching interest."

"Why, Morgan, her father is very well-known. It's only natural that his daughter would arouse curiosity. Especially after the wild rumors that she tried to kill a man in Portland. But she's just a child. Who would believe such a thing?"

Morgan raised a brow. "Definitely not you."

Caitlyn strode to his side. "Must you always be so principled?"

"I have business with your brother, Cat."

"I wouldn't dare stand in the way of your duties, Morgan."

She shifted her sultry gaze on Lacey. "Do be a doll, honey." Caitlyn punctuated her words with a lovely smile. "Walk with Sandiford, will you?"

Before Lacey could respond, Caitlyn thrust the reins of the horse into her hand, leaving her to stare dumbly at the beast.

"I'd like to go on ahead with Morgan. You understand, don't you, dear?"

No, she didn't understand and a contentious voice bade Lacey to throw the reins back in the woman's face. But Morgan grabbed Caitlyn's arm, his expression carefully shuttered as he turned her swiftly away.

Behind Lacey, Joshua stirred. "It's all right. Horses only bite if they don't like you."

Lacey dragged her gaze from Morgan's back and measured the beast morosely.

"He hasn't bitten you. So I think you're safe."

Lacey was just in the mood to bite the creature in return if he dared show his teeth. She cut her eyes back up the street and intercepted Morgan's glance. He was probably reassuring himself that she wasn't going to run off the horse. The way Caitlyn oozed over him was disgusting. Warily, Lacey followed.

At first, Lacey tried ignoring the couple by dividing her attention between the quaint scenery and Joshua's generous conversation. But whatever her attempt to tarry, it was too fast for Morgan's pace. He was not letting her lag, and she soon found herself marching the horse at their heels.

In a flurry of impatience, Caitlyn finally drew around, nearly elbowing the hapless Sandiford in the nose. "Don't you have someplace else you can be?"

Lacey rounded her eyes. "At the moment?"

Caitlyn snatched the reins out of Lacey's hands. Lacey caught a quick flash of humor in Morgan's expression a moment before he shouldered between them to lift Caitlyn back in the saddle.

He *would* consider the whole episode amusing. Glancing away as Morgan's capable hands settled around Caitlyn's tiny waist, Lacey backed up, her mind whirling in a million different directions. None of them pleasant.

"Try to stay out of trouble, Caitlyn," she heard Morgan say.

Caitlyn's gaze lifted past Morgan to settle on Lacey. "Perhaps I should give you that warning, honey." She blew Morgan a kiss. "At least until tonight." The horse reared in a graceful arc, sending clods of dirt high into the air. Leaping the watering trough, the stallion thundered away.

"She always was a show-off," Joshua grumbled, unimpressed as horse and rider disappeared down the street.

Morgan turned and lifted his eyes to the sheriff's sign creaking in the breeze, then his penetrating gaze dropped to her.

For a heartbeat, her breath caught, but whatever she glimpsed, vanished as his attention shifted to consider Joshua. "Do you think the two of you can stay out of trouble while I go inside?"

Lacey swept past Morgan to find solace on the bench in front of the sheriff's office. "It'll be hard, but we'll do our very best, sir." She arched her brows. "I even promise I won't try to shoot anyone."

Morgan stepped in front of her, presenting her with a full view of his imposing presence. His teeth flashed white against his stubbled jaw. "A wise decision, sweetheart." He tapped her on the nose. "As I said before. Your aptitude for learning shows promise." He walked past her into the office.

"Take your time," she called after him.

"Yea," Joshua piped in, plopping down beside Lacey, "I don't wanna go back to no stupid boat."

When the door closed soundly behind Morgan, Lacey felt the gloomy mist settle upon her almost at once. Young maples lined the street, stretching hopelessly toward the bleak sky. Somewhere a dog barked. Having tasted the sweet yearnings of fancy, Lacey was loath to relinquish her heart back to its natural state. Something had happened to her earlier. Something wonderful and exciting. And like a bird testing its wings for the first time, she felt the urge to soar. To find such wonder and discover its loss all in one day was an act of cruelty! She could barely contain the stabbing disappointment.

Jolene. Now Caitlyn. Morgan seemed to have female companionship stuffed at both ends of the territory. Lacey was insane to consider him worthy of her heart. "Who is Jolene?"

"Jolene's real nice . . . for a female. A lot nicer than her brother," Joshua added, surprising Lacey with his disdain. "She owns the general store in Kingston. Her husband used to be one of Marshal Caine's deputies. He got killed in a shoot-out. The marshal, he's kinda taken care of her since. He's like that, you know."

Lacey crossed her arms against her chest. The buckskin creaked with her movement practically advertising her agitation. "Have you known Mr. Caine long?"

"Since we lived in California. Ma took Shannon to live with us."

"Shannon?"

His youthful visage sobered. "She was Marshal Caine's sister. The Lawton gang . . . they killed her."

A horrible memory squirmed through her head, like a living thing. What Sam Gressett had said in San Francisco, about Morgan tracking down Lawton for murdering his sister. With sudden clarity, Lacey remembered the bleak fury in Morgan's eyes and understood.

"She never did no one any harm, either," Joshua said to the ground. "People would call her breed. They wouldn't let her go to school. Sometimes they would throw rocks at her. And spit. They had no cause to be so mean. Ma said they were ignor . . ."

"Ignorant?" Lacey quietly supplied.

He nodded. "She was thirteen when I first met her, and Ma said she needed a mother so she could learn to be a lady. Ma was once a fine lady in Virginia. Marshal Caine wouldn't let Shannon come live with us at first, but when Ma sets her cap on somethin', a body has the good sense not to argue."

That explained Morgan's loyalty to her father. But it didn't explain her father's fealty to Morgan. Something else had happened.

"How did you end up in Washington Territory?"

"Don't know. The marshal, he's from around these parts, but I don't know why Pa wanted to come. We never lived any place for long. Except now. Pa said we're never moving again."

He suddenly jumped up. Lacey realized he was chasing a

butterfly. "If you catch one, it means something good is going to happen to you." He took a breathless swipe at the hapless creature. "It's an Indian custom. Shannon told me about it. But you can't hurt it," he qualified. "That's bad luck."

Her spirits lifted as she watched Joshua's energetic efforts, and slowly her attention shifted to the bright fluttering creature he chased.

Leaning against the desk in the main office, Morgan was talking to Sheriff Madigan in the other room, when movement outside drew him to the window. Swinging a vigilant glance along the street, he looked back at Lacey and Joshua kneeling at the edge of the boardwalk. Caitlyn's visit left him with a heightened protectiveness over his two charges. Yet, he couldn't pin any reason to his uneasiness.

Nor could he understand his own mind. He was about to turn down an invitation to visit Cat tonight.

Lacey shifted, granting him a glimpse of her shapely derriere. Morgan raised an arm and braced it against the glass. He found himself riveted to her lissome movements. She was bent over something in her hands and, though the brim of her floppy hat hid her magnificent eyes, it did not conceal the soft contour of her cheek. Then she lifted her head, and her generous mouth curved into a smile. Stretching out her arms, she opened her hands. Morgan could hear her laughter as an orange butterfly gracefully fluttered skyward.

He'd never heard Lacey laugh. The gentle sound of it rippled through him, jerking him back to reality.

Christ! What was he thinking? But before he could rationalize why he was staring at Colin's daughter like some unseasoned tinhorn, Sheriff Madigan came back into the office. His arms were laden with the latest memos and wanted posters detailing the territorial problems that had occurred during Morgan's absence.

Morgan turned and settled his gaze on Madigan, who was watching him curiously. "You're as irritating as that sister of yours."

Madigan dropped the load on his desk. "I suppose I am." Lighting the long nine between his lips, he looked out the window before shifting to reconsider Morgan with interest. "Cat came in here and found out you were coming to town. I hope she wasn't a nuisance."

"Caitlyn has a mind of her own, Jim. She always has."

"When the news about the trial in San Francisco broke across the wires, she leaped the first stage to California. I was worried about her down there, alone."

Determined not to dampen Jim Madigan's opinion about his less-than-sainted sister, Morgan merely shrugged. "Caitlyn can handle herself and a few others besides."

"Except you, I reckon. She never could get a handle on you. I was hoping she'd come back married."

Morgan regarded his friend accusingly. It never ceased to amaze him that even after five years, Jim Madigan still found the tenacity to bleat about love like a ram being led to slaughter. Even if Morgan had made it abundantly clear in the past that he had no desire to be twisted in the romantic machinations of the heart.

Obviously refusing to be dissuaded by Morgan's apparent lack of interest to talk, Madigan made himself comfortable on the edge of the desk. "I hear Sam Gressett made an appearance in Portland."

"I let him get away from me. Twice."

"Maybe you were sidetracked."

Morgan looked up from thumbing through the wanted posters.

Madigan straightened. "Three men came in earlier representing the Bodie assay office from up your way. They were asking questions about Ashton's wagon train north . . . and they gave me this." He handed Morgan an official-looking document.

Without opening the missive, Morgan knew what it was. He glared at Madigan.

An assay office dealt in cash and gold exchange, and the paper in his hand was a federal mandate of protection. It would be his job to see that the Bodie money arrived at its destination.

Damn! He had a job to do, and it *wasn't* coddling a wealthy mining company rich enough to police its own shipment.

"I'm not even traveling with the wagon train."

"You are now."

Morgan pushed away from the window. "This is bullshit. Every outlaw in the territory will be down Colin's throat if this should get out." He flagged the paper before him. "Has anybody else seen this?"

"It's only come through this office."

Morgan crushed the missive and tossed it in the garbage.

The soft mewling purr of a kitten drew him around. Staring into the shadows of the next room, he wondered if he had just imagined the sound. "Kittens." Madigan answered Morgan's questioning look. "Their mother didn't make it through some hazing by the town roughs. She left three kittens. I've been trying to keep them alive."

Morgan walked to the doorway of the other room. Three tiny black kittens lay curled on a blanket. He looked back over his shoulder at Madigan—all hundred and seventy solid pounds of him.

"What can I say?" Madigan shrugged. "I'm a softy." He shouldered past Morgan to view the kittens. "Can I interest you in one of these babies? The little furballs would make a nice pet for someone inclined to care for them."

Morgan raised a lofty brow.

Hell no, he didn't want a cat!

Chapter Eight

"You've practiced for more than a week. Go ahead and try it, Lacey."

She squirmed on the hard bench, listening to her father's last-minute instructions on driving a wagon. She stared dismally at the pockmarked road wending through the flat countryside. Heat waves shimmered like a glassy veil on the brown horizon.

"A long pull on this line, and he goes left. That's the direction we're headed."

"East."

"North."

Sucking in her breath, she straightened. It seemed the whole line of twenty wagons plodded breathlessly behind them waiting for her to take the reins. And the day seemed to grow even hotter. She pulled at her damp shirt, willing for a hint of a breeze to touch her moist skin or a sudden downpour to wash her in a lake.

"Take the cat off her lap, Josh."

Lacey's heart leaped. "And be nice to her—"

"Yea," Red said, laughing. Holding the reins of a brown

splotched horse, he trotted his gelding on her left. "Caine still ain't lived this one down."

From beneath his tan hat brim, her father peered at Red. "You keep that up, and you'll find yourself on the bad side of ornery."

Red laughed harder. Picking up the tiny kitten with one hand, Lacey rubbed her cheek in its fur. No precious bauble could have meant more. But she'd learned from experience that Morgan did just fine defending himself without her help.

"Remember, the front mule on the left is your lead." Her father lay the reins across her gloved palms.

The mule went left on her bold command, and she suddenly perked.

Joshua poked his head between them on the seat. "She'll be ridin' a horse yet." He laughed, clearly at ease offering unwelcome humor to the situation. She wanted to elbow him in the nose.

"Relax your grip, Lacey," her father said.

She slapped the reins and edged the mules right. Rattling the lines, she made them go faster. She wiggled in newfound excitement.

"It's not so hard, is it?" Jared rode his shiny black stallion on her father's right. With his hat cocked at a jaunty angle, he smiled at her with his devil-may-care grin.

She wondered if Morgan watched her. And what he thought of her efforts. But he hadn't so much as spoken a word to her since he'd given her the kitten in Waylen Springs, and taken harassment for the gesture. Not like Jared, who'd made his intentions clear that very first day on the steamer.

The wagon suddenly hit a rut. Stifling a groan, Lacey didn't know which could be worse, traveling on an ill-tempered horse, or the wagon.

"Remember, anyone who can force her way into Cook's domain to help him prepare meals for this lot can beat driving this wagon."

Her heart swelled at the recognition of pride on her father's face. Taking Joshua with him, her father climbed onto the horse Red towed. Everyone except her cat abandoned her on the wagon.

"Besides, I got four bits resting on this," Joshua said. "You *have* to do it."

Lacey noted the sparkle in Jared's eyes, and her glance swung suspiciously on Red. "Why do I smell something afoot?"

Red grinned. "We're trying to decide which side a' the fence we're going to put our money on. You or those mules."

"A wager, Miss Ashton," Jared informed her. "The men are putting odds on your success today."

Lacey glared at her father. "Oh, really?"

"Hell, yes, ma'am." Red's huge grin left her slack-jawed. "We haven't had an opportunity like this since we put down bets on you escapin' Caleb."

"You made a wager on that?"

"Why, of course."

"I didn't have anything to do with that," her father said.

She felt sorely used. The very idea. "So who won?"

"Marshal Caine, of course." Red laughed. "He was convinced you were going to pull a fast one, so he followed you hisself. That's why Jack was waitin' at the hotel when you finally came outta hiding."

She spit dust out of her mouth as they rode off.

"Liniment is the worst god-awful smelling stuff I've ever endured on my person." Lacey wrinkled her nose.

"They don't look so bad." Joshua looked down at her hands and grimaced. "But I suppose on a girl, they'd hurt."

Lacey refrained from grinning at his white-lipped remark. Even through her leather gloves, her hands had taken abuse today. And they did hurt like the blazes. She rubbed liniment liberally onto her palms and the backs of her feet. The blisters from her boots had mostly healed. But the newer ones on her hands would take longer.

With Joshua's help, Lacey finished hanging clothes on a makeshift line strung between two gaunt trees beside her wagon, then plopped down on a boulder still holding heat from that day. Night had descended in a halo of indigo twilight that embraced the open prairie. Rain scented the air.

In camp, Caleb struck up the fiddle, and most of the men

joined him around the central campfire as they did every night since leaving Waylen Springs. They drank corn whiskey from a jug, and mostly did a lot of swearing over cards. Lacey didn't see the harm in joining them but her father told her the men couldn't be men with a lady around.

She hadn't seen Morgan since dinner hours before. But then he rarely joined the social activities that followed dinner. Jared was on watch. Idly tracing a weed clump with the toe of her boot, she watched Joshua lay the last of his breeches over the clothesline.

"So, are you going to let me teach you to dance tonight?"

"Ah, that's girl stuff, Lacey." Joshua grimaced. "Go ask Pa."

She'd already asked. And Jack also. Not even Jared could waltz. "All the lords and ladies in England dance. You'll have fun. No one has to see us."

"I ain't a lord, Lacey. And I ain't never plannin' on bein' one neither. Not if I have to dance like a girl."

Joshua ran off and left her sitting alone. She kicked at the clump of grass. A streak of black pounced on the grass and attacked her boot. "Look at you." She scooped up the kitten and playfully lifted her high in her hands. "You're all dusty, you bad girl."

Though Morgan had suffered much good-natured prodding because of it, he'd not been remiss in seeing her supplied with the necessary items to nurse her kitten. And so during the past few weeks, she'd watched the kitten grow more robust. "Not that I won't let you inside the wagon to sleep, mind you." Golden eyes blinked back at her. "I've developed a fondness for rocks and dirt that I never had before."

The sound of an approaching horse pulled her around. Against the low-lying clouds, lightning flickered somewhere over the prairie. She could not still the leap of her pulse. On the other side of camp, Morgan reined in sharply. With a single tug of his gloved hand, he swung the horse around. Even from this distance, she could see the way his dark hat settled low over his face. A brief flash of white greeted her father as Morgan slid from the saddle.

Laughter burst from around the fire. Caleb started playing a foot-stomping polka.

Tucking the kitten to her chest, Lacey slid past the other wagons. A few minutes later, she found Morgan alone near the makeshift corral, bent over the back hoof of his horse. His hat tilted when she approached.

A growth of beard darkened his jaw, and his dusty black shirt, a little too tight for his wide shoulders, was unbuttoned at the top, revealing a worn red kerchief tied at his neck. His eyes moved over the jacket she wore. Enjoying its warmth at night when it was cooler, she'd been compelled to keep it since Waylen Springs. At least that's the reason she gave herself. If Morgan resented the theft of his coat, he didn't tell her.

He looked around him as if to ascertain that she'd come alone. "What are you doing over here, Lacey?"

"Are you a troll, Mr. Caine? That you can't say hello?"

Morgan's features grew impatient. He went back to work on the horse. When he didn't reply, she cheerfully added, "Besides, most everyone is kicking up their heels by the fire. I thought I'd come over to visit. I brought Shadow." She held out the kitten but he didn't look up. "She's not such a scrawny thing anymore."

Lacey watched his hands. He plucked a rock from the horse's shoe. She noticed he always wore gloves. Lightning flashed in the distant clouds. "Is that what you named her?" he finally asked.

"Actually, my father named her. She follows me everywhere. And she's quite a little chatterbox." Sprinkling kisses between the kitten's tiny ears, she cooed, "Aren't you, sweetie? She's already devoured half the tins of milk you bought. And she loves fish."

She lifted her gaze, and froze. Bracing an elbow on his knee, Morgan watched her. It surprised her to see his mouth quirked at the corners. It was as close to a smile as she'd seen all week from a man who kept his own company to the point of being unsociable.

Her silly hands trembled. "Thank you for the kitten." She

forced out a lighthearted smile. "She's been a wonderful companion."

Their eyes seemed to hold before he broke off. "You're welcome, Lacey."

She stepped around the horse to better see him as he made his way to the front hoof. A lizard scurried away and disappeared in the rocks. She shivered. Three nights ago, Jared had come to visit and killed a rattlesnake near her father's bedroll. The incident had made Lacey appreciate the fact that she slept in the wagon with Joshua. "So, where is it that you go at night?"

He scraped the horse's shoe. "I look around."

"All by yourself?"

"All by myself, sweet."

"For what?"

"Anything out of the ordinary."

"Goodness, Morgan. Everything is out of the ordinary here. How do you tell what's normal and what's not?"

He lifted his chin and gave her an exasperated look. Finally, he stood. The heady scent of cheroot smoke and soap surrounded him like an implacable masculine aura.

"I just can," he said.

Recklessly, she traced the star on his vest. "Is that what makes you such a good lawman? Because you just can?"

He removed her hand from his chest and put the horse between them.

"Honestly, Morgan. You're such a prig." She laughed. "It's not as if you interest me in *that* way. Well, maybe a little in that way. After all, you did kiss me in Portland. And now we have a kitten."

He tilted his hat back on his head. "One thing naturally leading to the other, of course."

"Of course." She smiled. "So you see, that's why I came over."

"Because of the cat?"

"To ask you to dance."

Morgan laid his arms across the saddle and stared at her. Inexplicably emboldened, she leaned closer to those gloved hands curled loosely into his palm. "Unless you can't dance.

I've learned that such a feat is not easily accomplished by the American male."

She anticipated a curt rebuff but instead met the brilliant blue in his eyes. Caleb's music seemed to float around them like the breeze and the scent of sage.

Morgan suddenly stepped around the horse. With a start of surprise, her eyes chased upwards to his. Her breath grew shallow. His boots were dusty and added to his uncivilized height.

Carefully, he took the kitten from her hands and tucked it in her coat pocket. Their clothes touched, an intimate whisper broken only by the call of a lonely whippoorwill. Taking one of her hands in his larger gloved one, he slipped the other beneath her jacket and laid his palm lightly on her waist just beneath her breast.

"Caleb's playing 'Golden Slippers,' " he said quietly.

The hot whisper of his words caressed her cheek, and she looked up into his face made more devastatingly handsome by the glow of campfire. Then he swept her around the clearing, as if she wore the finest gown of blue silk, as if he'd spent his life in ballrooms hobnobbing with aristocracy. Caleb's fiddle framed the rhythm of their steps. Morgan led her among clumps of grass and boulders and a thousand imaginary candles. Distant thunder rolled over the plains. She moved breathlessly in his strong arms, floating in a sky so velvety black, she reached out and touched the stars.

Her eyes opened to the sight of him watching her.

"Believe it or not, Miss Ashton, we western folks aren't entirely ignorant." His breath was warm against her temple. "Some of us even know how to read and write our name."

"Are . . . you an educated man then?"

"When I was seventeen, Jack took me back east, where I was schooled in the ways of a gentleman. Unfortunately, my grandfather and I didn't share the same point of view on life."

"That doesn't surprise me."

"That I should be educated?" A glimmer of humor laced his voice. "Or that I disagreed with my grandfather's benign view of life."

"Neither." Her palm dampened his coarse shirt. She was aware of the smooth ripple of muscle beneath her hand. "It doesn't surprise me that you would have trouble suffering through eastern pragmatism. I could just see you in your snug breeches and cravat, smoking cigars and drinking brandy, ever the polished gentleman," she lilted in her most priggish English accent. "How very dull." Morgan's quiet laughter made her feel as if she'd just moved a mountain.

"You are acquainted with stuffy types, I presume."

"I was Miss Prim and Proper. I could drink a cup of tea with perfection." She extended her pinkie in demonstration. "I learned to curtsy with grace, play the piano, and to behave as a proper lady should. Not that it really mattered to anyone but my aunt." She glanced at the broken nails on her once manicured hands. "What would Clare say if she saw me now?"

"After the way you drove that wagon today, she'd probably congratulate you. Liniment and all."

Lacey looked up at him seeking the strange approval she heard in his voice. That smile, the one that affected her down to the tips of her toes, touched his mouth. Her breathing came too fast. His blue eyes dark beneath his hat brim, were shadowed by more than firelight.

He was distant, and dark, and dangerous beyond her ken. He made her feel things. Hot, powerful things that burned like a slow-growing ember through her veins.

After a moment, she realized the music had stopped. Mortified, she pressed her hands to her face and stepped out of his arms.

"The party sounds over." His deep voice oddly strained, he laid the kitten in her arms. The night filled with the whirring of insects and the sound of her mewing kitten. "Good night, Lacey."

She fled his powerful presence, utterly confused by what, if anything, had just happened between them. At the wagons, she slowed.

A glance over her shoulder found Morgan watching her still.

The next two days were hotter than Hades's ass. Following the unshod pony tracks he'd picked up that morning, Morgan reined in his mount at the farthest edge of the first copse of green trees he'd seen in more than a week. Studying the ground, he frowned.

The wagon train had been following those same tracks for almost three days. Morgan narrowed his eyes on the horizon. Even as he finally glimpsed the ragged mountain peaks, he knew they were still days out of Spokane, maybe more if the river ran high and they couldn't cross at Sarasota Falls. Then after that, another week or two before they reached Kingston.

Nearer to the plodding wagon train, antelope scattered across the sage-dotted plain. The thunder of horses signaled the departure of the hunting party.

He took off his hat and wiped his brow with his sleeve. Dragging his glasses out of the saddlebags, he quartered the landscape then cut his gaze up the long line of plodding wagons. He stopped on Lacey's wagon. Red sat beside her. Since Joshua had taken to riding, her father had placed her with the perfect companion. Hardly older than herself, Red's outlook on life was as cheery as sunlight on a spring day. The two got along famously.

The wagon hit a rut, throwing Lacey forward. She grabbed the back of her seat, holding on to her cat. Morgan felt a queer jolt inside. But the leap of his pulse had little to do with the heat or the fact that she'd been mooning over him since he'd waltzed her around the glade a few nights ago.

Lacey's gentle humility touched him. She coddled his gift as if it were a treasure of gold he'd given her, instead of a sickly cat. He had not expected the extent of her warmth or her determination. On the contrary, he'd underestimated her totally, but then he'd been doing that consistently since he'd met her.

What did she see in him anyway? Again, he straddled the sharp edge of his patience. She was no different than any other woman he'd ever known except that she was more trouble and younger. He neither welcomed nor understood the effect she was having over him.

Dimly, he perceived that his glasses were still fixed on Lacey's face and that she was looking back at him.

Neither of them moved.

Suddenly, he had the strangest sensation of being watched.

It rippled down his spine in a shiver, and he lowered the glasses.

He didn't see the approaching rider.

Skidding the stallion to a halt directly in front of him, Jared marked his arrival with a bout of showy maneuvering that left Morgan struggling to retain control of his mount. The horse stomped in a circle, sidestepping Jared's spirited black.

Morgan brought his horse around, and his furious gaze fixed on Jared's face. "What the hell was that for?"

"Your wagon to Bodie is showing signs of throwing its back wheel bearing. Colin wants to know if it'll make it to Sarasota Falls."

"Aren't you supposed to be on point, Jared?"

Jared's jaw clenched as he gave Morgan a considering look; then his penetrating gaze fell on Lacey in the distance. "Isn't she a little too green for your tastes, Caine? I imagine Colin will have something to say if you try to fu—"

Morgan grabbed his shirt collar. "Back off, Jared."

"Or what? You'll arrest me?"

"One day you're going to step over the line, Jared, just far enough to smash into my fist. Jolene be damned."

Morgan swung his mount away. Gritting his teeth against Jared's laughter, he followed the pony tracks until they joined up with the hunting party. And mysteriously disappeared.

An hour after sunset, Morgan returned with the hunting party. A flash of lightning from an approaching storm seared the sky, preceding their arrival into camp by only a few minutes. Three antelope were removed from the packhorses and carefully tendered over to the cook, who would make piecemeal of them in a matter of hours. Dinner had already been served, and the small group sat down to devour what remained of the black beans and corn bread.

Morgan looked around. With the exception of the men standing guard, no one else seemed to be present in the camp.

"Where is everybody?" Jack asked first, turning to look in the direction the cook curtly waved.

"The river?" Caleb inquired. All eyes settled with interest on the man who wielded the butcher knife.

"The salmon are running thick as fleas on old Caleb here. Red took Ashton's daughter to learn her a few pointers 'bout fishin'."

"Oh yea?" Jack grinned. "That should prove interesting."

"That's what they all said," the old cook snorted. "Doesn't seem right to be poking fun at the kid the way they do."

"If I didn't know better, Whitey, I'd think you'd taken a shine to the girl yourself." His eyes narrowed thoughtfully. "Come to think of it, you look mighty spruced up tonight. I haven't seen your hair combed so pretty like since you went to church last year."

The cook sniffed and turned away. "So what if I have? She's no snobby lady, the way I thought she'd be. And being the only woman . . . why she ain't complained. Not a word."

"She cooks a sight better 'an you, too." Caleb tossed the tin-plate down. He stood. The scattered sound of dull metallic clinks followed as other plates thudded to the ground.

"Where yuh going?" Whitey asked, clearly surprised to see everyone rising swiftly.

"To see the fun." Old man Grundy, a jowl-faced rancher, grinned. "Odds are if she can handle those fish the way she handled ol' Caleb and Will here, she'll catch her a big one!"

Jack looked over at Whitey. "There's worse things for a girl to learn than fishing. Might come in handy someday."

"There ain't even enough moon to see by," the cook yelled after them as they hurried off. "Fools," he muttered and turned back. "Hope she catches one. It'll serve them coyotes right."

Only Morgan was left tending quietly to his meal, and Whitey glanced at him with interest. "Not curious yerself, huh?"

"Seems to me the camp is deserted enough." Morgan wiped the last of his beans up with his corn bread.

"Seen tracks, did you?" Whitey picked up a sanding block and, with quick, even strokes, honed the blade of the butcher knife, as he prepared to get to work on the antelope. "Do you think it's Lawton's old gang out there?"

Morgan set his plate down. His gaze narrowed on the non-descript wagon in the middle of camp. With the exception of a few men, nobody knew the contents of that wagon, and the missive had not left Sheriff Madigan's office.

Whitey turned to dip the knife in a bucket of soapy water at his feet. "No one's gonna find us easy pickins, Marshal."

"His men are murderers, Whitey. If you have what they want, they'll kill you if you get in their way."

"Seems to me then, we ain't got nothin' to worry about from a buncha scheming polecats," he said, his voice muffled by the stoop.

Morgan helped Whitey rope the antelope between the thick branches of a cottonwood. Lightning illuminated the camp in sporadic intervals. The sweet scent of rain mingled with wood smoke. Then the sky let loose with icy sheets of water. Men were running back. After a while no one else came over the incline.

By the time Morgan finished stringing the antelope, the brunt of the storm had swept over them toward the east, leaving behind the hint of blue moonlight through a broken band of black sky.

Lacey's wagon remained unoccupied.

Morgan reached the ledge overlooking the riverbank and drew up under the dead branches of an aged pine. He recognized Colin on the sandbank, and Red's gangly form in a dark slicker casting his line and yelling instructions. He identified Joshua, but it took him a moment to realize the fourth person on the sandbar was Lacey. Her laughter drifted to him on the currents of the breeze.

Rain dripped from his hat brim and he thumbed it back on his head so he could see. For a long time, he did nothing but stare.

Morgan recalled the way she'd made him laugh in Waylen Springs, and again when they'd danced, not that it endeared him to her. But for those brief moments, her presence gave him more life than he'd felt in years. And it had been sweeter than anything he'd ever known. Not since he was a kid, and life stretched beyond him forever, had he behaved with such foolishness.

The bittersweet emotions jerked him back to the present. Had he ever been a kid? Had there ever been a time in his life when self-preservation was something as simple as making it to dinner on time? He couldn't remember that, either.

A renegade tribe of Cayuse had ended his childhood. And the boy he'd been had become a man who believed in nothing but a prevailing sense that justice would somehow find a way to conquer evil.

But vengeance did not nourish the soul, and for the first time in his life, Morgan couldn't shake his solitude.

Clearly, the group was having a lot of fun. He hadn't the slightest idea what to do with himself: to stay on the hill watching, like some kid with his nose pressed against the glass of the candy store, or venture down and join them.

Or leave.

Almost against his will, Morgan started down the hill when movement at the river's edge stopped him. Fixing Jared with an unblinking stare, Morgan's mouth twisted cynically. It shouldn't have surprised him to find Jared present. The man had put his stamp all over Lacey the very first day out of Waylen Springs. And she seemed to accept Jared's possessive interest in her with little complaint.

But then women rarely did complain. Evidently, Colin's daughter wasn't immune to his slick southern charm, either.

Shadowed by the night, Morgan turned and walked away.

Chapter Nine

Lacey caught her salmon, pursuing her quest even while her father and Red napped on the riverbank in complete oblivion to her success. It was left to Jared to net the fish, which he managed with the same helpful enthusiasm he displayed when he carried her back to camp after the heel on her boot broke.

The sight of all of them returning to camp like beleaguered heroes roused such a disconcerting fuss that Lacey blushed crimson in Jared's arms. She'd practically fled to her wagon.

For three days afterward, caged between the unknown and her own confusion, Lacey remained bleakly secluded. What was wrong with her?

The world had been snatched from beneath her feet, leaving her displaced. She should appreciate Jared's attention. Worse, she knew her lack of enthusiasm was not due to propriety.

Lacey inhaled the invigorating scent of pine. Even as she'd finally begun to catch glimpses of the ragged mountain peaks, she despaired of ever seeing a beautiful towering pine again. Purple flowering vines, made silver in the moonlight, surrounded the glen, and Lacey lifted her eyes, following their heavenly ascent through the wispy branches of blue spruce.

For the hundredth time, her gaze shifted to the ledge above the glen, where her father had set the guard. The sound of rushing water was almost deafening.

She skirted the campfire as she stepped around her father and Jack, who pored over a map talking about the river crossing tomorrow. Joshua lounged next to Jack. Her kitten was nowhere.

Negotiating the boulder-strewn pathway, Lacey stepped into the narrow clearing beside the forbidding pool, nearly black in the moonlight. Dread surged through her. It would be impossible to hear her kitten over the sound of the nearby falls.

Lacey stopped abruptly as the red-gold ember of a cheroot flared to life in the shadows, then dimmed. A man was sitting with his back against a tree, one wrist dangling over a knee. He held a mostly empty whiskey bottle.

"Is there something you want, Miss Ashton?" The deep voice resonated against her. Moonlight fell in dappled patches through the branches of the tree, and Morgan's face came into view.

Lacey closed the short distance separating them until Morgan was forced to tilt his face to look up at her. It occurred to her that she'd never seen him from this lofty vantage point. His dark hair, still moist from a bath, lay across his brow in a roguishly disheveled manner. Clean-shaven, the contour of his jaw clearly visible, he was so beautiful, Lacey's breath caught.

A gust of wind tossed the branches of the trees, and the dappled pattern shifted. Morgan's damp shirt was unbuttoned, and Lacey could not pull her eyes from his bare chest. His muscles rippled with strength. The kind that came from living hard to survive.

Plagued with a childish curiosity to test the warmth of his skin, she averted her gaze from his chest and slammed back into the full force of his penetrating stare. "Are you finished?" he said roughly.

Lacey's chin shot up at his tone. "Maybe."

"Maybe?"

"I'm looking for my—" His arm dropped to reveal the black bundle of fur curled in his lap.

"I thought it was a big rodent at first. Almost shot it."

Lacey noted the gentle way he stroked the kitten, a dubious contradiction to the harshness of his words. When she sat beside him, she could almost hear the impatient intake of his breath.

He ground the cheroot roughly into the dirt beside him. "You shouldn't be here."

"Why not?"

"Because I said so."

She reached out to stroke her sleeping kitten when Morgan caught her wrist, snapping her eyes back to his. His grip gentled.

Then his eyes dropped to her lips for a breath-stopping moment. "What is it you want, Lacey?" He let loose her hand.

"Father mentioned that you grew up around this area," she rattled, for wont of anything else to fill the space between them. "Did you live out here with your parents?"

Morgan set the bottle of whiskey down and leaned his head against the tree.

"I presume you did have parents?"

"They were missionaries," he said, finally conceding to her inquiry. "When I was eight, we came out west to convert the so-called savages and save their souls."

The son of a preacher. The prodigal son had wandered far from his father's chosen path.

"What happened?"

"His scalp was a prized trophy, treated with deference by those who raided the mission and murdered him. A blasted irony for one who was so hated in life, to be revered in death."

"I'm sorry . . ."

Morgan's eyes focused on her. "Don't be," he said dryly. "The brave who killed him didn't live long after that."

Lacey perched her chin on her knees and wondered why she wasn't appalled by the insinuation that he had committed murder at such a tender age. Her gaze dropped to his hands. They moved in gentle strokes over the kitten; perhaps because the indelible mark made by his years in captivity had not torn away his core. There was an inherent gentleness in his soul, even if he didn't see it himself.

"How long were you a captive?"

Lacey saw his eyes pass over the scars on his wrists that were usually covered by his gloves. She couldn't bear to ask how such scars came to be.

"It took Jack five years to find my mother and me. Part of the tribe had split and went north trying to escape the reservation only to find the one up here."

"Did you ever try to leave?"

Morgan stared out into the darkness. "I couldn't leave my mother. Later, she became the wife of the new chief. A good man. She had twins by him. The younger girl died. My sister Shannon was always a survivor, even from the beginning." He held her gaze as if to determine censure. Then he let his head fall back against the tree. "She would have been twenty last month."

Clearly, Morgan loved his sister. Riveted to the play of shadows crisscrossing his face, Lacey could not look away. He angled his head, and she watched the corner of his mouth lift, as if a sudden memory tamed his mood. "She also had a penchant for mischief. Maybe it's a trait of women in general."

"Maybe it's a reaction to your arrogance," Lacey said sweetly. "After all, some women *can* think for themselves. It's called intelligence."

He seemed unaffected by her barb. "Or defiance."

"More like enlightened. Witty."

"Like you?" A primitive thrill shot through her as his eyes locked on hers. "Another endearing trait, perhaps?"

"Do you wish to argue my intelligence then?" Even to her own ears, her voice sounded shockingly coy. "In which language would you like to proceed, sir?"

Morgan raised a brow. "Do I detect a boast?"

"I speak three languages."

"So do I, sweetheart. How about we begin in native Cayuse?"

Lacey laughed. He certainly had her there. She looked into his handsome face and stirred restlessly. "Oh, Morgan." The words rushed out suddenly in her zeal. "I want to find my place here. The way my father has . . . the way you have. I would love to learn Cayuse."

His mouth grew rigid. "You have a little girl's vision, Lacey."

She heard the condescension in his voice, felt it all the way to her bones. His words paralyzed her. Is that what he thought of her? Childish? "But don't you see?" She looked into his dark eyes and felt her helplessness turn to determination. "I know what this place can be. A person can make a life here. A home. I'm going to be something. A teacher."

"Life isn't that simple, not even in fairy tales."

"You're cynical," she said, jarred by his lack of hope.

"And you're too young to know any better."

"I'm twenty. Most women my age are married and have children."

"Is that what you want? To marry and have children?"

"If I found the right man." He grunted his disapproval, and she peered at him intently. "You don't believe in marriage?"

"What goes on between a man and a woman doesn't require marriage." The kitten jumped out of his lap.

"And I suppose you would know all about that?"

"Enough to know you're in way over your head right now."

He started to get up. Impulsively, Lacey reached out to stop him. "Please—"

Morgan moved swiftly. He pulled her against his chest. His hot breath filled her senses with the taste of whiskey. "Please, what?"

"Don't . . . go."

His eyes smoldered ominously in the moonlight before dropping to her lips. She felt his power as he drove her backward into the soft ground. Felt the blood dancing in her veins, heating her skin.

"You're too bold for your own good, Lacey."

Then his mouth slanted across hers.

The contact shattered Lacey's control. She opened her mouth to his probing tongue and, swallowing his throttled groan, returned the intimate caress by some innate sense. Halting at first. Then reckless and consuming. The heady taste of whiskey grazed her senses and feasted on nerve endings so raw they tingled. Abandoning her grip on his arms, she tangled her fingers in the wavy silk of his hair. His hand spanned her rib cage and covered her breast. Excitement blossomed in her body. It rippled through her, turning her blood to fire, tumbling her into a swirling vortex as she yielded to the luxury of Morgan's plundering kiss.

He dismantled her slowly. Piece by precious piece. Her hands splayed his chest, savoring the intensity of his hardened flesh. His heart thudded against her palm. Her blood hummed.

His mouth dipped to the curve of her neck. Her head fell back as his lips moved over her breast. "Oh, Morgan . . ." Nothing mattered but the tender violence of his assault. "What are you doing to me?"

The soft-spoken entreaty seemed to shatter the spell. Morgan stiffened. The word uttered against her throat was recognizable only in its tone as he tore himself from her.

Lacey blinked. Sensuous emotions still rippled through her, unwinding in wondrous confusion. She sat up, her disheveled hair falling around her face. Morgan was on his feet, one hand braced against the tree.

"Christ, Lacey," he grimaced, tearing his fingers through his hair. "Get up before you make me do something I'll regret." A dire look of warning penetrated her befuddled senses. "*Now,* Lacey."

Any hint of softness in his expression had vanished. He offered no helping hand, but seemed to pull away, wanting nothing more to do with her. With trembling hands, she buttoned her shirt. She had not impressed him, but humiliated herself instead.

Reaching for her kitten, as it sat back watching her with wide-eyed interest, Lacey struggled to her feet only to find her knees wobbly beneath her. The breeze whipped around Morgan's body and through her hair. Her unschooled passions left her bereft of any control or knowledge as to how to follow properly where her heart was wont to lead. She wanted to say something—anything—to bring the gentleness back to his face.

"I don't have room in my life for your kind of trouble, Lacey," Morgan snapped, deftly fastening the buttons on his shirt. He shoved the shirt into the waistband of his breeches. "You don't know what you're doing. Colin is my friend, for Christ's sake. He trusts me."

She heard his disapproving tone.

Was that what this was about? His loyalty to her father?

Morgan's piercing glance drove into her. "Tonight . . . you were available, Lacey. Nothing more." He bent to retrieve the bottle of whiskey. "Do you understand?" She couldn't seem to pull herself together enough to say anything. "Stay away from me. I mean it." He snatched his rifle up and with catlike strides, walked past her toward the path and out of the glade.

Too stunned to follow, Lacey stared after him in amazement. She wanted to disabuse him of the notion that she should be accountable to her father, but his furious rebuke silenced her. She could have waltzed naked on his chest, and he still wouldn't have touched her!

Straightening, she wrapped her arms around her kitten, annoyed that she was perilously close to tears; then the moon went behind a cloud, plunging Lacey into sudden darkness. The night closed around her. And suddenly she felt her skin prickle, as if unseen eyes were watching her. Swinging her gaze slowly over the thick wall of trees, she took a step toward the path. Then scurried after Morgan.

He was waiting for her just beyond the wall of purple vines, his easy strength lending her protection. He'd not left her.

His gaze encompassed her before he looked behind her into the shadows. Had he seen her run? Like a child, afraid of her own shadow. Rankled that she should feel so safe in his presence, she lifted her chin. Without a word, she swept past him.

The trail was steep, and Lacey had to watch her step to keep from stumbling up the hill. She could feel Morgan's impatience behind her. Let him be annoyed. She'd done nothing wrong. Nothing except fall recklessly and foolishly in love with him.

The awful realization didn't stop her in her tracks. She'd known the night he'd waltzed with her. And without a doubt tonight when he kissed her.

Her fingers clenched around the kitten. She wasn't without some pride. Hurrying her pace, she fled up the hill.

Morgan left her once they got to the camp. Later as she yanked her clothes off the line beside her wagon, her searching gaze found him among the men gathered around the horses. He was talking to Jack.

"Don't you worry none 'bout the marshal, ma'am." Red

came out of the shadows and tossed his bedroll down below her wagon where he usually slept. "He can take care of his-self."

She stiffened. "No doubt he's had a lot of experience."

"I suppose he has at that. He'll know whether it'll be safe to make the crossing tomorrow or if we have to go farther north. It's been raining a lot in those hills."

Lacey watched Morgan mount up. Shifting his rifle to the other gloved hand, he swung the horse away, disappearing like a wraith into the night. He was gone.

Just like that.

And he hadn't even looked back.

Lacey opened her eyes. Twisting on her side, she leaned on an elbow to open the back flap of the wagon. Above her, stars gleamed against a black sky. Only the movement of the night watch gave clue of another's presence in the whole world. She was jumping at shadows. Hearing things. Irritated, Lacey dropped the canvas flap in place.

She called to her kitten, but there was no response. Testing the darkness, she found Joshua sleeping soundly. She edged around him for her cat—and her fingers contacted something human.

A hand lanced out of the darkness smothering her scream and spinning her backward. Colliding with a hard, naked chest, she flung out her arms only to find herself in a fierce breath-robbing chokehold. A hint of a whisper caressed her cheek.

"It is not my wish to see you hurt, White Hair."

Lord, he would kill her! She grappled for anything to use as a weapon. Her hand enclosed her crumpled boot. She swung her arm, sending the hard-edged sole against something solid. An audible *thwack* accompanied a string of profanities that stretched the bounds of at least three languages. He pushed her flat onto her belly, straddling her back.

"Open your mouth," the voice bade. And she did—to scream, but found a rag stuffed in it before a single sound came out.

He bound the rag with a strip of cloth. His long, coarse hair rubbed across her face. "You are a lot of trouble." He secured her wrists with what felt like a bandanna. "Maybe your father will be happy to have you taken off his hands."

Lacey heard Joshua's whimper. Outside, the voices of the guard disrupted the silence of the camp. Had they been discovered? Her heart constricted in her throat. Where was Red?

This savage must have done something horrible to him. Red would never have slept through the noise in the wagon.

"We are supposed to come for you and the boy," the masculine voice returned to her ear.

Who? Lacey's frustrated response was muffled behind the gag.

"If they take you, Lawton's men will ransom you for the cash on this wagon train. Tell your father . . . and no one else. You are not safe here in this camp. If you stay, you will not live, White Hair."

Then the pressure on her back was abruptly gone. Too stunned to blink, Lacey didn't move until she felt the tug of Joshua's hand.

"Lacey," he whispered, "are you all right?"

Outside a sudden shout raised the alarm, and shots volleyed off into the darkness. Lacey saw the flare of an erupting fire as the wagon beside her exploded into flames, followed by yelling and more gunshots. Watching demonic shadows of the fire dance on the canvas of their wagon, Lacey struggled to loosen her bonds. Joshua crawled behind her to untie the one on her mouth. Her throat burned.

As quickly as it began, the fire was out. Men's shouts filled the night. Then she heard her father's voice, and the wagon flap was thrown wide revealing his face against the campfire-light behind him.

"Lacey? Joshua?"

"She's tied up, Pa!"

Beside her father, Jack stretched into the wagon and pulled her out. His worried gaze encompassed her before his big hands went to work untying her. In a few seconds, Lacey was free and in her father's embrace.

He tipped her throat. "My God, Lacey."

Numbly, she looked at the soot-covered faces around her, stopping abruptly on Red's bruised face.

"I'm sorry. He was on me before I knew what happened."

"It was an Injun, Pa! He was going to take us."

"Like hell!" Caleb spat.

A nervous murmur rose. "They'll slaughter us—"

"Bullshit!" Colin spat. "Now get back to your wagons, all of you, before they catch the lot of us here lollygagging."

"This doesn't make sense," Jack said when they were alone.

Lacey finally found her voice. "They want the cash on this wagon train." She followed her father's gaze. Six men stood around the covered wagon in the center of camp, rifles perched uneasily in their hands as they watched the proceedings with wary interest.

Colin stared up at Jack. "No one knows about that money—"

"Daddy, they knew," she whispered, wondering where she found the strength to talk. Her neck hurt. She told him the rest of what the Indian had said. "He said the Lawton gang was behind this."

Even in the dim firelight, Lacey saw her father pale.

"Brett Lawton is dead," Jack whispered.

"Hell, don't you think I know that? When Morgan gets back I want to see him." He turned to Lacey. "For now we're moving you both."

"Wait." Lacey whirled away from him. She wanted her kitten. The need was irrational and childish. She had not been hurt; yet, her nerves were giving way, scratching at the edges of control.

Frantically, Lacey dug through her wagon on her hands and knees—and stopped. The blood drained from her face. Her kitten lay motionless in the front corner beside its box.

Lacey touched it. It was cold and stiff. The kitten had died hours ago. Long before the Indian came to her. Numbly, she plucked at the leafy stem near its food, staring at it in horror. Nightshade.

Her anguished cry brought her father running. Gathering the tiny thing protectively in her arms, she crawled from the wagon, sheltering the kitten as she'd done for the past weeks. Its death was the final barrier.

Lacey felt the hot burn of tears. There was nothing to hold back the tide of emotions as the events of the whole desolate night crashed in at once, and everything crumbled beneath her. The dismal feeling that she'd somehow failed everyone swept against her, and she turned away from them all . . . directly into Morgan's arms.

He had appeared out of the night. Her voice broke over his name.

"I'm sorry." She wept, and with the lifeless kitten clutched against her, she pressed into the solid warmth of his body. "I . . . don't mean to cry."

"Christ, Lacey. What happened—"

He took the kitten and laid it aside. She shook her head, burying her face against him, sobbing irrationally. Didn't he understand? Their kitten was dead. His arms wrapped around her, chasing the pain away. The cold metal of his badge pressed into her cheek—and brought forth the memory of another time. Once before out of the darkness, Morgan had come to her aid, and even as a stranger had protected her and made her feel safe.

"Shh," he whispered, prying the poisonous leaves from her fist.

He was like granite, anchored solidly to the world, and she held on to him as if her very life depended on that grip.

Maybe it did, she realized as she harnessed his strength.

Maybe it always had. Even if he didn't know it.

A few hours before dawn, Morgan and a select few gathered around a small fire away from the main camp. The last thing he wanted to do was listen to Colin's harebrained scheme. He wanted to hunt the bastard who'd hurt Lacey.

Morgan looked at her now. Eyes closed, bunched beneath his jacket, she was leaning against the rock at her father's feet. Joshua slept with his head in her lap.

"It's the only way, Morgan," Colin said. "You have to get them out of here. You and Jack can take them up the river."

"This is madness, Colin."

"Is it?" Colin demanded.

"Caine's right," Jared replied. "Taking Joshua and Lacey from this camp opens them up to attack. It's too dangerous."

Morgan met Jared's glare across the firelight. The dark eyes watched him intently. Since when had he and Jared ever agreed?

"No one will know they're gone," Colin furiously countered. "Don't you understand? The wagons won't make it across the river. You said so yourself, Morgan. We'll be on this road for another few weeks, at least, skirting this river until we find a place where we can ford. Tonight we had an Indian walk into this camp beneath the very nose of our guards . . ." His voice trailed. "Lacey and Joshua are in danger here. You must get them away."

Morgan looked over at Jack who was sitting on a rock with his head bent in his hands. What manner of man did Colin think he was that he could be trusted to protect his daughter; that he had the power to guard her life and that of Joshua's?

Somewhere he heard Colin talking. "You can take the Old Smith mining trail to the river. We have good solid canoes with us. They can make the trip. In five days, you'll reach Meadow Pass. From there, you can borrow horses from the Burton place and be in Kingston inside a few days."

"My responsibility is with this wagon train, Colin," Morgan said slowly, as if to remind himself that his job went beyond personal favors, no matter how close that friend was, or what the reasons were. "You're asking me to walk away from here."

"Hell, that money is as safe as it's going to be—and it won't matter anyway, if those men get their hands on . . ." Colin let the heavy silence hang. Clearly, he was on the verge of breaking.

"You and Jack know the territory," Colin pleaded. "I would trust their lives with no other."

"*I'll* do it," Jared furiously retorted. "You want them out of camp so bad, I'll get them to Kingston."

"Jared, you don't know this country. Morgan grew up here."

Jared's gaze swept over Morgan. "How could any of us forget Caine's trials with the savages? We've all heard the story."

Morgan met Jared's eyes.

"We'll do it," Jack interrupted, and bent a stare on Morgan. "Caleb's canoes can make the trip."

Jared swore beneath his breath. "And if you run into an ambush?"

"No one will know," Colin said.

"We can take Caleb and Red," Jack said. "They're both good with a gun. And no one can out track, Caleb."

"When you reach Kingston, you can enlist the aid of Major Simcoe at Fort Okanogan," Colin added. "Explain the situation. Tell him about the Indians who've gone renegade. He'll consider it his problem. Morgan"—Colin's eyes ripped a hole right through him—"for God's sake, you've got to do this."

Furious, Morgan looked away—and directly into Lacey's eyes. She was watching him, her wide, luminous gaze flickering with the firelight. Sometime in the past few minutes, she had awakened. His gut twisted with a life of its own. Perhaps it was the edge of fear that knifed through him at seeing her harmed; or that he ached more burying that damn cat of hers than he ever did over any man's grave. Her trust was like a beacon. Her vulnerability, a magnet. He couldn't pull his eyes away.

All at once, he remembered the way she felt in his arms, and his nerves roiled in a hot cauldron of trouble. He didn't like the distraction she caused. He didn't like the fact that she was Colin's daughter and just downright dangerous to the balance of that friendship. Worse, her presence made him careless. She could get him killed.

"Morgan," Jack said.

Against his will, he lifted his head, the dark hat tipping up as his eyes came to rest on Jack. Morgan realized Jack read his thoughts—all of his thoughts—and recognized the fine line he now straddled.

Morgan wanted nothing to do with any of them. Lacey least of all. Colin was mad to think she would be any safer with him.

"I'll go with Jack," Jared shot back.

Morgan's gaze shifted to Jared and saw in the banked fires of his eyes a spark of something dangerous. Morgan stood, his spurs scraping the ground. "I'll be ready to leave within the hour."

He strode away before he had time to regret his decision completely.

Chapter Ten

Mingling with an occasional sprig of sagebrush or Canadian thistles, scraggly pines rooted in the sparse soil above the sloping riverbank. Listening to the quiet splash of paddles against the water, Morgan felt like an insignificant spec in the midst of this untamed country, his passing no more than a whisper in time.

Shannon had loved it here, spending months living in these hills with the Indian tribe that was also her family. He listened to the breeze curl through the pines rooted in solitude on the cliffs above him. It was as if the world had gone on to heal itself without him.

Lacey moaned in her sleep and settled against the buckskin jacket rolled up at his feet. Dark lashes fanned against her pale cheeks. He heard the quick intake of her breath. But whatever nightmare had awakened her vanished when her eyes snapped open. She rose on her elbow, her disheveled hair tumbling around her flushed face. Her eyes were like a hot sunbeam on his skin.

"I shouldn't have slept."

"This is not a contest of strength, Lacey. Quit trying to be something you're not."

He felt the heat of her gaze intensify, and part of him knew she didn't deserve the comment. He was conscious of the shape of her lips—the way they'd molded to his when he'd kissed her last night, fool that he'd been. Hell, better to walk through fire than touch that mouth again. Gritting his teeth, he forced himself to look away.

He didn't want to like her.

Hell, he didn't even want to be talking to her.

Gauging the position of the sun, he knew they needed rest. Already his shoulders ached from paddling. Morgan looked over at Jack and Caleb in the second canoe. The big man still looked game, but not his companion. In front of Morgan, Red also showed signs of strain.

"Morgan?"

He squinted down at Lacey beneath the shadowed brim of his hat.

"Don't you ever want to run away from the violence and hatred?"

The kind of peace Lacey shared with the world was an illusion he gave up long ago. Yet, he had an urge to shelter her from his reality. "It's not something I think about."

"How do you do it? Not think about it, I mean?"

"I do what I do, Lacey. If I have to think about it, I'll make a mistake. You don't live long in my business making mistakes."

"I was so frightened last night," she whispered, looking away. "I didn't mean to make such a fool of myself about everything."

"I'm sorry about your cat, Lacey."

The sun reflected in her eyes. He could sense her mulling over something else. "I think she was poisoned."

The thought had crossed his mind last night when he'd taken the crushed nightshade from her hands. He'd been surprised to find the leaves in her wagon, then realized the plants grew in abundance around the glade. "The kitten didn't have sense enough not to eat the leaves, Lacey. They probably blew in, or came in attached to the bottom of your pants. It wasn't anyone's fault."

Tears crystallized in her eyes, but with a firm tilt of her chin, they seemed to vanish. "Thank you for doing your best to care for Joshua and me. I know this isn't a job you volunteered to do."

His arms moved the paddle, stretching more than they had before. He found solace in the clipped movement as the canoe continued to glide soundlessly over the water. His thoughts were on her words and on her eyes and the way she had of getting inside a man.

"Morgan?"

He noticed for the first time that she was holding his watch. She'd flipped the lid and was looking at the photo inside.

He must have dropped it getting in the canoe. The impulse to snatch the watch from her prevented him from hearing the question at first.

"Is she?" Her gaze lifted. "Your sister, I mean?"

Morgan's grip on the paddles tightened. "She was seventeen when that was taken."

"She was very beautiful. This Brett Lawton person was a part of what happened to her, wasn't he?"

Morgan went cold inside. "Christ, Lacey. You talk too much."

"What does he have to do with my father?"

Morgan didn't like her scrutiny. Evidently, her father had told her nothing, or she wouldn't be asking him. "Whatever it was between Brett Lawton and your father . . . it's over now, Lacey."

"No, it's not." She snapped the watch shut. "It's not over for him, any more than it is over for you. Even in death. This Brett Lawton haunts you both."

Lacey earned a glare for her insight. The fact that it was true rendered his response obsolete. She had no idea.

Morgan could not close his eyes at night and not see his sister's blood, remember the smell of her death or forget that Brett Lawton had been responsible. His sister's life was worth more than the price Lawton had paid. Shannon deserved justice against everyone who had been there that day. It was all

Morgan could give her. But he could not hunt her killers while Lacey and Joshua remained in his care.

Morgan quit the conversation and said nothing more.

Finally, Lacey laid her head back on the jacket. Tucking one hand beneath her cheek, she dropped the other on his knee. The unexpected gesture jolted him. His jaw squared. But before Morgan could respond, she turned away from him.

The watch on his leg was all that remained of her touch.

He jealously watched Morpheus claim her again.

Lacey sat with Joshua and listened to the quiet conversation between the men as they discussed their course. Twice they had to ford a waterfall. At midday, they edged the canoes into a small alcove protected on three sides by large boulders and a sparse cropping of scraggly pine. There they ate and rested before nightfall found them camped near a huge lava cliff basin that skirted the twisting river on both sides. They built no fire in the darkness, and they ate the rest of Lacey's salmon, which Whitey had smoked.

Long after everyone went to sleep, Lacey remained beside the river, dangling her feet in the chilly waters. The pale light of the moon cast a chalky glow over the rugged landscape, and she listened to the restless wind prowling the treetops. Unseen from the talus overhang, she knew Morgan kept watch over the camp. She could feel his eyes on her now, their touch radiating through her.

Suddenly Lacey smiled.

Surely her mind had snapped. No sane person would find her position anything but horrid under the circumstances. They were in the middle of nowhere, fording a dangerous river, escaping a band of outlaws—and then all at once she was remembering the look in Morgan's eyes that afternoon. Somewhere between his irritation and impatience, he watched her with eyes that stirred her blood. The same look she'd seen on his face last night when he'd kissed her.

She hadn't permitted herself to dwell on that kiss all day, and the very thought now rekindled the fire inside her. She should be terrified of him. Rational thought warned her against him. Yet, she was drawn to him with every fiber in her being.

A part of her cringed at her own boldness. Another braver part vowed to make him see her as his equal. No matter the years that separated them. No matter that she was nothing to him but an awkward English girl swallowed up by her own inexperience. Beneath his cold facade, she'd glimpsed a spark of something alive. An emotion that stirred him when she was around. His denial of its existence didn't make it any less visible. She had only to make *him* see it.

Determinedly, she set her heart on its course. She'd known all along that it was the right one.

Lacey looked into the sky, now bright with stars. Would the dark give way to light? she wondered.

Will you let me in, Morgan Caine?

Morgan watched the sun rise. Building a fire, he was less worried about being seen in the daylight than getting a good meal in their bellies. Around him, the others awakened. For all the world, it was as if nothing more significant than the approaching weather was on anyone's mind. He listened absently to Caleb and Jack bantering in casual morning chitchat while they repacked the canoes. Red and Joshua skimmed rocks down by the river's edge near the copse of trees where Lacey had disappeared earlier with her bar of fruity soap.

For the second time, as Morgan knelt beside the fire working on breakfast, he glanced toward the spot where he'd last seen Lacey.

"It smells good," she said brightly from behind him.

Surprised by the stealth of her approach, he twisted around to face her. Framed in the morning glow of sunshine, her male attire made her alluring in ways no fashionable dress ever could.

Approval flared in his thoughts before he snatched it back and retreated behind a wall of self-control. She seemed quite cheerful, and Morgan had the impression he was the cause of her amusement.

"I never thought to see you cooking," she avowed. "Somehow it doesn't fit the image I have of you."

He quirked a brow. His boots creaked as he adjusted his position. "And how is that?"

"I imagine such duplicity relates to women wearing pants and men wearing dresses. Some people have definite opinions about those gender-related things."

Morgan managed to suppress a grin as he turned to move the pan on the fire. "I suppose out here, one has to adapt."

"Precisely. That's exactly what I said before."

"So how long has it taken for you to dream that one up?"

"Not long," she said, shrugging. "I saw you over here, looking so . . . sweet, kneading that dough. I thought I should come over and offer you my support."

"My opinion of women in men's attire remains unchanged, Lacey. However," he amended lightly, raking her with his eyes, "it's not for reasons you might think."

"Then explain your reasoning."

"Lacey, if you haven't figured it out by now, it won't do any good for me to explain."

Appearing to consider his words, she finally shrugged. "It must be a man's thinking, then." Sitting across from him, she made a great show of adjusting herself to the hard ground then lifted bright probing-green eyes to his.

Wary, Morgan poured himself a cup of coffee. A quick glance over the rim found Lacey still watching him with curious interest. "I would offer you some, but I know how you feel about coffee."

"I don't remember saying anything about that."

She hadn't, he realized. He just knew. As he knew her favorite color was blue, she couldn't ride a horse, and she liked hot tea, sunsets, and long walks.

He realized he knew a lot about her.

Annoyed with himself, Morgan took a deep swallow of coffee.

"Have you ever been in love, Mr. Caine?" Lacey asked so suddenly, he barely pulled the cup from his mouth before he choked.

Coffee dribbled over his pants, nearly unseating him as he tried to dodge the simmering brew. His head snapped up with the intention to glower at her, but when his eyes met hers, he saw only serenity. She was waiting politely for him to answer.

"No," he said firmly.

"Do you ever want to be married?"

"Not hardly."

"Don't you ever get lonely?"

"Not when I have such stimulating conversation as yours to keep me company."

Unabashed, Lacey forged on. "Marriage can't be that bad," she challenged, obviously ignorant of the concept. "And you're not so young anymore. So, why haven't you set your sights on someone? Surely there must be *someone* who interests you."

Giving up the effort to drink his coffee, Morgan prudently set it down out of the way. "I have little patience for the gentler things in life. Especially a young wife."

"What about an older one?"

"Anyone."

"Then you don't answer to anyone now?"

"No, I don't."

Lacey climbed to her feet. "Well," she pronounced, brushing the pine needles and dust from her backside. "That answers *that!*"

Morgan followed the movement of her hands down her thighs. "And what exactly is *that?*"

Her eyes raised and caught his gaze. "Obviously you haven't found the right woman, yet."

"And why should that matter to you, Miss Ashton?"

Her bright laughter astounded him. "It matters to me a great deal, *Mr.* Caine. And to you also, I imagine."

Morgan's dark brow lifted as he measured this green-eyed elf with caution.

"You see, I know you're alone . . . a lot. I also know that no one person can truly live to the exclusion of the rest of the world. Even you. And . . ." she continued with great aplomb. "I haven't forgotten the way you kissed me the other night. I don't think you have either. Though, you do a fine job at pretending it never happened. Now, I don't know a lot about kissing—I have to admit it's not an area I've studied—but I do think it impossible for a man to kiss the way you did without feeling *something.*"

Morgan came slowly to his feet. What did she think to

prove, waltzing over and telling him his own mind?

With a saucy tilt of her head, she smiled up at him. "Oh, I know what you told me. But I'm a big girl, Morgan. You *might* notice that sometime."

Hell, he couldn't keep it out of his mind.

Dismissing him, Lacey walked away. Briefly admiring the swing of her hips, Morgan watched her go, before he remembered himself and frowned. Lacey was too impudent for her own good.

He dropped his attention to the meal at hand, noting unhappily the blackened edges of his biscuits. Breakfast had suffered as much abuse as he had.

Delegated to Jack's canoe, Lacey sat happily wedged between Jack and Caleb, content to have people to converse with, now that she was feeling chipper again. Jack and Caleb proved to be fascinating companions, and Lacey soon found herself laughing as the two related a legion of stories that kept her in stitches. For a while she dismissed Morgan's mood, but as the hours crept by, even the clouds overhead grew ominously turbulent.

It was near dusk when Lacey noticed Morgan watching the cliffs. With increasing regularity, his pace in the other canoe had slowed. Finally, he stopped paddling and removed a pair of army field glasses from his pack. He methodically began to scan the cliffs. Lacey spied his buckskin jacket on the floor at Joshua's feet, over her other things, and had an urge to ask her brother to toss it to her. Without the warmth of the sun, she shivered in the breeze.

Up ahead, the river dipped, narrowing into a horseshoe bend. She glimpsed white water on the fast-moving surface and realized a waterfall was near. She wondered if Morgan was scouting for a campsite. The canoes drifted and began to catch on the current.

"What do you think?" Jack called over to him.

"Doesn't feel right," Morgan yelled back.

Something in the tone of his voice warned Lacey that it was not the approaching violence of the river making him edgy.

Jack's gaze settled keenly on the cliffs. Thunder grumbled.

And like a bolt of lightning, something shattered the lip of the canoe beside Caleb. The canoe tottered precariously. Jack cursed, and in front of Lacey, Caleb struggled to bring his rifle to bear when another bullet slapped against the soft bark of the canoe.

The canoe flipped so fast, Lacey barely felt the warning tilt before she smashed into the frigid surface of the water and went under. Groping frantically, she tried to claw her way back, but the tug of the current sucked at her legs, sweeping her away.

All around her, the swirling barrage of white water gradually deafened the roar in her ears. Her lungs began to burn. Struggling against the weight of her sodden pants and boots, she crawled blindly upward toward the open air, found it, and gasped in a precious breath.

Caught in the rush that pushed her along, the overturned canoe raced beside her. She flung her arms over it, fighting the grip of the undertow as it refused to relinquish its hold on her. Water frothed against her face whipping her around the rocks jutting precariously out of the river. Determinedly, she angled herself toward shore. The realization that she was about to come up on a waterfall lent strength to her purpose.

Lunging away from the canoe, Lacey scrabbled across the slick surface of a rock, grasping for a perch, anything she could hold. Torrents of water sloshed over her head. Using all her strength, she managed to hang on. In the distance, she could still hear the staccato of rifle fire. Purpose drove her to move. She opened her eyes—and blinked up into Morgan's worried face.

Even while Lacey's heart climbed, nothing but a pitiful squeak came out of her mouth, testament to the amount of water washing over her.

The muscles straining on his neck, Morgan leaned precariously over the edge of the bank. "Grab on!" he yelled over the roaring of the water. Lacey slapped out for his extended hand—and missed. Her grip on the rock slipped. "Grab on, dammit," he yelled again.

Furious that he should be so angry with her, as if she wasn't doing her best, she flung her arm harder and felt a moment's elation when his fingers grappled over hers.

Then her grip on the slimy rock broke, snatching her from Morgan's hold. The racing current swept her away, and Lacey was swallowed again by the roaring water. The roaring grew louder.

The waterfall!

Terror rendered Lacey calm. She could only hope the drop wouldn't be a big one.

Morgan's heart raced against his ribs. Powerless to reach Lacey, he sprang back to his feet. Oblivious to the crevices and fallen trees that could break his leg, he raced along the rocky bank.

He caught a glimpse of blond hair disappearing over the falls. He knew her biggest threat wasn't the drop. As waterfalls go, this one was considered uninspiring. The danger lay in breaking her neck on the rocks below.

Morgan slid his way down the leaf-strewn hill, sloping steeply against the river's edge. Leaping to his feet, he reached the bottom at a full run. His harried gaze scanned the river beneath the falls.

Christ, why didn't she swim toward his canoe the same as Jack and Caleb? His mouth felt like a wad of cotton.

Then he saw her. She was on her knees crawling out of the shallow water to his right toward shore. Morgan sloshed through the river, reaching her with the haste of a waterlogged turtle. Wrapping his arms around her waist, he lifted her easily. In a tangle of arms and legs, he crumbled with her to the ground, barely able to relinquish his hold to test for broken bones. Relief for her safety made him weak.

She was sobbing. Hell, she couldn't help it. Look at the state *he* was in. He eased her over onto her back, and his hands stilled their careful ministrations. Behind a mess of tangled hair, her animated gaze found his. It took him a stunned moment to realize that it wasn't weeping he heard.

Lacey Ashton was choking on laughter!

She'd just been shot at, washed down a river, and dumped

over a waterfall. Her tenacity stunned him. More so because he never would have believed it of her.

Morgan felt his expression shadowed in disbelief, and he sat back on his heels. "I take it you're all right?"

"Did you see that?" she coughed out.

"I saw," he said blandly, hardly able to keep his voice steady.

"I went over the falls . . . I went over the bloody falls!"

"You're hysterical."

"Of course I'm hysterical." She laughed and reached her hand up to touch his face. The irresistible glint of humor in her eyes flashed back at him. Morgan did not pull away. "You'd be hysterical, too, if you had drowned, and in your dying breath, God pulled you from the waters of Charon."

Ignoring her emotional musings, he assessed her frankly. "Are you hurt anywhere?" He felt her fingers drift across his jaw, and he gently disengaged them.

"I'm hurt everywhere." She cheerfully proceeded to display the cuts that marred her forearms as if they were battle wounds deserving of the iron cross. She smiled up at him, her disheveled beauty so beguiling that Morgan remained speechless. "I shan't be able to walk for a month. You'll have to carry me everywhere."

"You look like a drowned squirrel," he said gently, pulling her to her feet. "I don't carry squirrels."

Morgan allowed a moment's respite as she leaned into him. His arms wrapped her to him. The smell of raspberry drifted over him, and he remembered she'd packed the scrap of soap in her shirt pocket when they left that morning. Surprisingly, her coveted piece of treasure was still there.

"Perhaps if I combed my hair, you'd find me more inspiring."

Morgan's hands came up to cup her face, testing her soft skin beneath the gentle stroke of a callused thumb. "You scared the hell out of me, Lacey." He felt the slight tremble of her body and knew she wasn't completely unaffected by her ordeal.

Morgan's hand splayed over the graceful contour of her

cheek, crawling into her hair. A tight sensation curled through him.

The wet clothes molded against her, revealing every curve and crevice inviting his touch. His gaze lingered on the heart-shaped birthmark just below her collarbone before traveling down the flannel shirt pressed against palm-sized breasts. The heat of her seeped into him, drawing out a response that would make him into a reprobate should he persist in holding her. Then he was looking into her eyes, and the tender yearning in her luminous gaze came perilously close to breaching his control. Her generous lips fell open, and suddenly he was remembering the velvet touch of her mouth against his. The taste of her kisses on his tongue.

Her innocence was a potent mix of heady desire—and disaster.

Colin's gently raised daughter could seduce old man winter himself with the soft promise of that mouth. If only the little fool knew how close to peril she was. But Morgan didn't delude himself about her innocence or the brand of trouble that came with betraying a good friend. Colin trusted him to protect his daughter, not debauch her.

Morgan untangled himself from her arms. "We need to get back to the others." His voice was hard. He'd never felt the noble restrictions of a conscience before. It weighed like an anchor around his neck. "Someone has been taking pot shots at us. We have to get out of here," he said gruffly.

His whole body suddenly went rigid. Before Lacey could bat an eye or gasp, Morgan drew his gun.

Lacey had never actually *seen* a real Indian—the fabled savage that was the scourge of the West and the source of unending speculation and gossip. Not twenty feet away, sitting on an Appaloosa was the formidable foe of such Western lore.

Wearing a red bandanna on his head, his long, black hair trailing behind to his waist, he was a menacing figure, tall and lithe, his chest bare beneath an open, faded blue cavalry vest. A muscular arm encircled Joshua, who was pale as winter. Black eyes stared down at them. Lacey noted the rifle resting across the crook of the man's elbow shift slightly.

"We are at an impasse," the Indian said in perfect English.

Lacey stiffened. She knew that voice.

"And that surprises you?" Morgan's voice remained calm.

Lacey stared up the barrel of the gun pointed directly at Morgan's chest and would have done anything at that moment to defuse the situation. Her heartbeat ticked off the seconds.

The Indian's obsidian gaze glittered on Morgan. "I suggest you put down your gun before my men shoot you."

Summoning all her strength to act—to do anything but stand helpless, Lacey flung herself against Morgan. "Please!" She wrapped her arms tightly around his. His muscles coiled with something akin to shock. "Please don't do anything foolish," she pleaded, her voice muffled against his chest. "He's the man who came into my wagon at the camp . . . he's dangerous."

"Lacey . . ." he rasped, but she sensed gentleness behind the harshness of his voice.

"He'll kill you, Morgan . . . please, I couldn't bear it." The strength of his heart tattooed against her ear, and suddenly his arms tightened around her with a possessiveness that stunned her.

"Christ, Lacey . . ."

She felt the whisper of his words as he touched his lips to her hair. "Hawk isn't going to kill me."

The words registered. But not the sentiment. Slowly, she lifted her face. Morgan's shadowed gaze seemed oddly caressing. And uncertain. She eased her clamp on him.

Morgan had called the Indian by his name.

She only partially understood the sudden fierce anger that grabbed her as his words settled in. Aghast, she stared at him, then whirled to face the nefarious *Hawk*: the man who dared trespass in her wagon, choke her, threaten her, and cause all manner of chaos.

"I should shoot you myself," she snapped in a fine show of temper. "After what you did to me and Joshua, you should be . . ." *Drawn and quartered, horsewhipped.* She could think of a dozen tortures but everything seemed too harsh. After all, he did come to warn her, not harm her. "You should be ashamed," she finished lamely. "Why didn't you just approach in the normal manner and talk to us?"

Hawk's expression remained unrepentant, but his eyes seemed to take on a new light. Lacey could see he was curious about her.

The Indian suddenly grinned, lifting a questioning brow as he shifted his dark eyes back to Morgan. Strong white teeth shone against the dark planes of his handsome face. "And be shot between the eyes for my effort?"

"Nothing less than you deserve," Morgan replied in a tight voice.

The corners of Hawk's mouth lifted as he peered down at Morgan. "I tried to warn you earlier. But you were both . . . busy."

"I should have known those were your damn tracks I've been following. You're the only man I've ever known who could disappear."

Hawk smiled. "You're losing your touch, John Caine."

Lacey knew she was staring back at them in outrage. Her mind whirled like a dervish out of control. Morgan may not have known it was Hawk that night, but he had no cause to allow her to think he was in danger a few moments ago, causing her to believe the worst. She wanted to hit him for making her suffer even one instant of panic on his behalf. She suppressed a shiver. Feeling a bewildering combination of embarrassment and confusion, she distanced herself from Morgan.

Hawk lowered Joshua from the horse and slid off behind him. Joshua ran over to Lacey, and she welcomed him into her arms, grateful for the distraction while she gathered her composure.

"Jack and the others are still up there," Joshua burst out, pointing past the falls. "They're getting the horses that belonged to the men who tried to ambush us. There's Injuns all over."

"Who shot at us on the river, Hawk?" Lacey heard Morgan ask.

"Brett Lawton's men were waiting for you. I have been sent to find the boy . . ." The Indian's voice trailed off as his dark eyes casually raked Lacey. "And her. But that one is too much trouble for gold. I think I'll let you keep her."

"She's not *mine* to keep, Hawk." Was she imagining? Or was Morgan's voice colder now. "She's Colin Ashton's daughter."

Hawk's assessing gaze was carefully blank. "You'll come with me back to the village. And since you have no claim on the girl, John Caine, she can ride with me. The boy will go with you."

Hawk's words froze Lacey. Her eyes swung to Morgan. If she expected some sort of protest, it didn't come.

Morgan kept his gaze averted from hers. His stance became more deliberate. "Aren't you going to be missed by your esteemed comrades?" he asked Hawk.

"I will probably earn a bullet for my generosity, but I don't have a choice." Hawk grunted. "You only have one canoe left and no supplies. It is fortunate I came upon you when I did."

Morgan walked forward. "Lucky for us," he said flatly.

"I have discovered that you are not well-liked."

"Damn right—" Morgan's fist whipped out, smashing into the Indian's jaw. Hawk stumbled backward, but only a few steps before he lithely regained his balance. "In the circles you run, I'm not surprised." Morgan's voice was angry. "Why I even trust you, I'll never know."

Nursing his mouth, Hawk glared back but remained silent.

"That's for being careless with Lacey the other night. And something to think about while she's riding with you."

Hawk's considering gaze shifted to Lacey. Absently testing his jaw, his attention edged back to Morgan. "Does she have other clothes to change into?" Amusement peppered his query. "I would hate to be blamed if she should catch her death."

"Her things are in the canoe." Morgan's gaze swept the turbulent sky overhead. "Though I doubt it will matter. It looks like rain."

Lacey glared between both men. "I'll not be subjected to either of you. I can just learn to ride my own horse."

"Like hell." Morgan turned on her. "We don't have time to coddle you while you try to prove something. You'll ride with Hawk. Now go."

Lacey swung her gaze back to Hawk. Her fear of him had lessened in comparison to her anger at Morgan.

"And Lacey." A thread of warning polished Morgan's voice. She looked into eyes that were now unfathomable. "Don't ever step between me and another man's gun. Do you understand?"

His statement intensified her humiliation. He was making it clear he didn't appreciate interference, even if it was a moment of lunacy that had prompted her foolish heroics.

Under a dying sky, the thunder grumbled again, and huge drops of rain began to pelt the earth.

Lacey refused to be intimidated by either man. "I'll ride with Hawk." Squaring her shoulders, she pampered Morgan with a smile, relenting only because it suited her to do so.

Chapter Eleven

Morgan sat beneath the makeshift shelter, out of the drizzle and away from the main activity around the campfire. Chafing against the impulse to join the social camaraderie, he propped himself against the trunk of a dead pine and meticulously cleaned his guns. The charred bones of a roasted rabbit eaten at dinner sizzled in the fire that warmed his soggy feet and dried his clothes. Beside him, Jack finished the last of his own dinner and returned to his Spencer, picking up where he'd left off earlier, trying to salvage the aged rifle that was all but ruined from when he'd plunged into the river.

They both listened absently to the animated conversation beneath the cluster of trees where the rest of their group warmed themselves. For the past hour Hawk had been entertaining Lacey and Joshua, teaching them to speak bits and pieces of colorful phrases in native Cayuse. They both responded to the task with enthusiasm. Caleb and Red merely listened, but the expression on their faces betrayed their amusement. Like Morgan and Jack, they both spoke Hawk's language enough to recognize the words being bantered about.

Jack chuckled. Light glinted off the brass casing in his hand as he held it up for inspection. "Do you think she knows what she's saying?"

Morgan looked at Lacey. Not only did she know but she clearly enjoyed the use of Hawk's native profanity. "She knows."

"Her lady's sensibilities should be scandalized."

"Since when has Lacey acted like a lady?"

Jack lifted a considerable brow and turned his full attention on Morgan. "Since when have you cared? I was under the impression you didn't like the conventional lady. Too much trouble, you always said. Too dependent. Helpless."

"Lacey *is* helpless. She doesn't know the wrong end of a horse from a hole in the ground. She's pampered by a bunch of bewhiskered nursemaids who do her every bidding. She doesn't belong here."

"She's as wild as a turpentined cat," Jack disagreed. "She doesn't belong anywhere else. I think the problem with you is you can't get a rein on yourself when she's around."

"The problem with you, *Uncle* Jack, is you think too much." Morgan climbed to his feet. "I'm going for a walk."

Feeling damnably uncertain of himself at the moment, Morgan stalked away, his long-legged strides taking him deeper into the shadows of the night. The darkness suited him.

It complimented his mood.

He still hadn't recovered completely from the river debacle. A part of him remained troubled over Lacey's foolish act when she'd thrown herself between him and her perceived threat of danger. The dawning realization that she'd been willing to die for him still stunned him. That she would be dead had Hawk intended to use his rifle left him feeling sick. And now she sat laughing and swearing as if the world were a candy-coated apple for the taking.

Lacey didn't possess his jaded view of life, and for a moment, Morgan yearned for a taste of her world. Her stability. Her dreams.

But what did Lacey really know? She lived in a fantasy of castles in the clouds and fairy tales. She believed in love and happy endings. Her naiveté intrigued and dismayed him.

More than anything, it irritated him. What did Lacey know

of reality? Of evil or death? He was damned sick of her constant cheer.

Morgan stopped and glared around him, annoyed that he'd walked a great distance without even knowing where the hell he was. Tomorrow he couldn't be so foolish. They'd be on the reservation, and he'd likely get an arrow in his back by some malcontent Indian buck. Which suddenly brought Hawk to mind and the vagaries of fate that threw them together again.

Hawk's appearance today perplexed Morgan. The last time he'd seen the big renegade had been the day they'd buried Shannon. They'd very nearly killed each other and might have if Colin hadn't interceded.

Once they'd been the very best of friends. Raised together under Chief Black Raven's protection, they'd religiously spent their reckless youth besting the other in some manner of competition. But when Morgan's mother died, Black Raven didn't live long afterward. Morgan took his sister and left the camp. Jack found them at a homesteader's cabin and brought them out of the mountains.

Five years ago, Morgan returned as a territorial marshal, and found his way back to the village—back to Shannon's roots. Then one day Hawk returned from a stint in the army, blowing back into his life. He'd gone outlaw and carried a substantial price on his head. Morgan carried a badge and served justice.

Neither of them had taken their direction in life with any intent or purpose. Both were skilled with guns and lethal in a fight. Only Morgan drew a line, where Hawk did not.

Then like a mountain storm, Shannon stepped between them. Shannon and her penchant for making wrong decisions, her impulsiveness and stubbornness. Hawk should have known better, fought harder against the romantic wiles of a stubborn young girl. Instead, by loving her, he'd ultimately destroyed her.

The past year had tempered Morgan's anger. Though deeply buried, the bond forged long ago in blood and loyalty still lay between him and Hawk like an invisible lifeline. Morgan had felt it beside the river. Felt its power, and momentarily followed its lead.

But some things could never be reconciled.

Morgan returned to camp. Hawk and Lacey still chatted by the fire. After a moment of taut silence following his entrance, Morgan's gaze swept the tree-shrouded boundary encircling the camp. Two braves stood guard beyond the shadows. Everyone else sought sanctuary in their blankets, their bodies littering the ground like cigar-shaped cocoons.

Morgan's gaze shifted back to Lacey then settled on Hawk. Tempering his annoyance over their apparent chumminess, he walked the short distance to his bedroll. Using a saddle for a pillow, Morgan tilted his hat over his eyes and promptly went to sleep.

It seemed he'd just dozed when the gentle strums of a quaint melody penetrated the cobbled recesses in Morgan's head. He opened his eyes. A morning mist hovered over the ground. Dawn had yet to break. Morgan's gaze stretched the short distance to focus on Lacey's empty bedroll. Neither was Hawk in his. But that didn't surprise him. Hawk never slept past dawn. Lacey did. Were they together?

Jolting awake, Morgan climbed to his feet. His gun belt still snugly fastened on his hips, he detailed every inch of camp with the sweep of his vigilant gaze. At first, the familiar sound of laughter didn't register. When it did, fury accompanied recognition. Stopping at the edge of the glen near the watering creek, Morgan discreetly pushed aside the weeping branches of an aged willow.

Lacey was alone, rendering him motionless beneath a barrage of conflicting emotions. He had expected . . . he didn't finish the thought. Instead, he berated his idiocy and remained transfixed.

Her petite form barely visible, Lacey stood among an assemblage of hobbled horses gathered near the water's edge. They appeared to be studying her with curiosity; evidently pleased as they mulled over something she'd just fed them.

Her attention turned to the palomino nudging her shoulder. "Aren't you an eager one?" he heard her nervously chide, then watched as she swept a currycomb gently over the mare's coarse golden mane.

She began to sing a ditty. He watched the gentle sweep of

her fine-boned hand, his senses so attuned to her voice, he was only vaguely aware of the stir of leaves in the morning breeze or that a hint of blush began to tinge the sky. Everything about Lacey was arousing. The fact that she couldn't sing made her more endearing. His jaw clenched in utter disbelief.

Christ! He was so damn hard, he ached.

"You naughty girl," she said, giggling, when the horse butted her pocket. She withdrew a handful of sugar, presenting it to the eager mare that lapped it up with relish. "Don't tell anyone I raided Hawk's precious supplies," she conspired, "even if it is stolen contraband from the wagon train."

Morgan's presence drew the attention of the horses.

Lacey turned abruptly. "Morgan!"

She palmed her pant leg, discreetly wiping it clean of evidence. Amusement tinged his mood, and he found himself drawn into the clearing. "I didn't mean to interrupt."

"You haven't, truly." She reached an unsteady hand up to sweep the wisps of hair from her face. "I thought to . . ."

"Spoil Hawk's horses?" he prompted. "He'll appreciate it."

She laughed, looking back at her equine audience. "I've been having a wonderful time. I didn't know horses could be so nice."

"You do have a way of taming beasts."

Had he meant himself? Peering down at her, he thought he saw her wondering that very question.

"Since I don't know their names, those two are Eenie and Meenie"—she pointed out a paint gelding and a bay mare—"Miney, and Moe are over there by the creek. This one"—she caressed the palomino—"I haven't named her yet. Isn't she beautiful?"

Morgan stood mesmerized, savoring the play of light on Lacey's face, a moment before he discerned that she was talking about the horse. He took the currycomb from her grasp and proceeded to finish combing the mare where she'd left off.

"There's a special way to do this," he instructed, trying to get a grasp on himself. "What you really need is a dandy brush. I use the currycomb mostly to pick the grit out of the brush."

Lacey sidled up beside him apparently observing his lesson with interest. He ignored the warmth that crept through him. She was small compared to him. The top of her head barely reached his shoulder.

"You know a lot about horses," she said.

"You don't survive long out here without one. Caring for them is essential."

Lacey seemed to consider this. "I've decided that if I'm to make a go of it out here, I'll need to learn to ride. Maybe Hawk could show me."

Her words, and the trust she seemed to have developed for Hawk irritated him. "He'd be quite happy to instruct you, then sit back and watch you break your neck. This isn't the time to learn to ride on your own, Lacey. Mountain trails are notorious for being hard on novice riders."

If his negative sentiment discouraged her, she didn't let it show. "Why does Hawk call you John Caine?"

Morgan turned to face her, and her chin tilted to meet his eyes. "It's my name."

"I don't understand."

"I was named after my father. Hawk used to live with the tribes near the mission where we lived. He knew my father and developed an attachment to him. When my father was killed, I buried the name with him. But Hawk refused to relinquish the title. Morgan is my middle name. Hawk and I used to get in fights over his refusal to call me anything other than John Caine. As you can see, I lost."

Lacey ran a finger along the side of the horse's belly, tracing, yet never touching Morgan's hand. Her gaze shifted past his shoulder toward the pastel-tinted sky. "I don't think I'll ever get used to the beauty of the sunrise in this place."

"It's still early. Both of us should be in bed."

Lacey's large eyes moved over his. "Why, Morgan Caine." Her finger trailed from the horse to his shirtfront. "I'm shocked."

Her sassy confidence knocked him flat. "It isn't a proposition if that's what you're wanting." Lacey stiffened, and he grabbed her. "And it will never be a proposal either."

"Let me go."

He was forced to rearrange his hold on her until he had her pressed flush against him. He had a point to prove, and he'd damn well prove it now that she'd provoked him. "Why?" he drawled, noting with satisfaction the color in her face and the way her pupils expanded to darken her eyes. "Because you can't stand the heat of a verbal sparring match you're too naive to have started in the first place?"

"Because . . . you're obviously *safer* someplace else," she pronounced, tilting her chin away from him.

Morgan grappled with the realization that Lacey was just about more than he could handle. "I'm as *safe* as dry grass in September anywhere within ten miles of you."

Her gaze swung back to his. "What's that supposed to mean?"

With an effort, he set her away from him. "Think about it, sweetheart, before you light any more sparks. You wouldn't like the consequences, and neither would I."

"I told you once before, Morgan Caine, I'm a big girl."

"You're not my type, Lacey."

"What is your type? A French strumpet? A soiled . . . bird?"

"Dove, Lacey. Soiled dove." He rolled the words slowly. "And you're about as provincial as they come. I owe Colin and Lorraine more than my life for what they did for Shannon. They took her in and raised her like she was their own. I would never betray their trust. That kiss the other night was a mistake. I was drunk." Lacey's normal measure of pluck vanished. "You need someone who can sweep you off your feet, dress you in fancy clothes, and marry you. Maybe even take you back to Portland or San Francisco so you can live in comfort."

"Don't tell me what I need, Mr. Caine."

"This is my world." He swept his arm around him. "It's hard and cruel. The land gives no more quarter than the men who scratch a life from it. Out here, there's a fine line between right and wrong, and every day I walk that line. I hunt men for a living. I've killed men. And I'll continue to do so with little or no regret."

"Morgan . . ."

Lacey splayed her fingers across his jaw in a gentle grip more powerful than a band of steel. Her compelling gaze probed his with tenderness, tearing away part of his insides.

Restraint battled with the thing unraveling inside Morgan, awakening sensations he had no business feeling. He looked into her eyes. They were wide and searching, more beautiful than the stars. She was heaven in a world bereft of dreams. He was falling for a girl who didn't have sense enough to stay away from him. Who nursed kittens and lost souls. A girl who looked at the world and saw hope and passion, who was naive enough to believe in dreams and optimistic enough to convince him they might just truly exist.

Her childlike faith unbalanced him.

At any moment, he was going to kiss her.

With teeth-gritting frustration, Morgan pulled her hands away from his face. "I don't want what you have to offer, Lacey."

"I think you do."

His eyes narrowed, and she took a startled step backward. Like a stalking panther, he was on her, dragging her forward. His strength easily overpowered her resistance. "You want to know what a woman really means to a man? Have you ever felt a man's need or drive?"

He pressed her hand against his arousal. She lifted shock-filled eyes to his. She looked etched in stone.

"Lady, this is what a man is. What he thinks about when he's around a woman who has the face of an angel and a body like yours. You don't know me, Lacey. I'm not your childish fantasy. You're playing with a fire you can't put out."

"Maybe I like fire." Her whisper broke over his fury.

Morgan was incredulous. He flung her hand away from him.

"Can you deny there's something strong between us?" She pressed him back against the horse.

There *was* something between them, and Morgan knew it. The little vixen drew him to her like a moth to flame. He could devour her. Destroy her innocence. It was in him to toss her flat on her back and make love to her by the river in the breaking of dawn with nothing but the sky at his back.

Instead, he scooped her up into his arms and took a deliberate step into the water that meandered around his feet. The hobbled horses scattered.

Lacey recognized his intentions but could not dislodge herself from the corded grip of his arms. "Don't you dare, Morgan Caine!"

"This is what we do to prairie fires and little flirts who don't know any better."

He tossed her into the creek, and Lacey landed with a loud splash in icy water that drove the breath from her lungs. She came up gasping and sputtering, her eyes narrowed with sufficient rancor to burn Morgan to cinders.

"Next time, I won't be so gentle," he warned.

Lacey groaned inwardly. She'd thrown herself at the man's feet like a hussy, something no self-respecting woman would ever have done. Acted shamelessly. And she was in love with the arrogant, uncouth . . . barbarian!

He didn't deserve her.

They were drawing a crowd as Caleb and Jack ventured from the woods and set up a position beside the nearest tree to watch. Sitting in waist-high water, like a sodden puppy, Lacey glared at them all.

Grumbling, Morgan spun away. "Colin should have kept you in England. You don't belong out here, Lacey," he yelled over his shoulder, leaving Lacey to gape at his broad back as he whipped through the stand of bushes and disappeared.

"You think I can't do it?" She raised her voice in challenge, struggling to her feet. The icy water ran off her and left her drenched. "I'll wager I'm better at adapting to change than you are, *Mr.* Caine." She stumbled out of the water after him and opened her mouth to further vent her anger but a sudden loss of words ensued. In frustration, she kicked out at a stone and groaned aloud as her backside protested its abuse. She rubbed her painful derriere, reminded further of the sting of Morgan's words.

Caleb and Jack had not moved. They were watching her with stupid looks and did not seem inclined to leave her in peace.

Hot tears threatened. "He's surely the most exasperating man I've ever known," she snapped for wont of any other words to fill the space between them.

"A woman sometimes does that to a man," Jack observed casually.

"A ghastly affair," Caleb said, groaning. "Saw it happen to that marshal out of Boise City last year. Went and fell in love with this purdy gal. Could hardly see straight enough to shoot a gun. Had to retire that badge, he did."

Jack nodded. "Women tear a man up inside until they go to mush. Make useless creatures out of them."

"Seen it happen many times," Caleb agreed. "Though not to *that* man." He eyed Lacey speculatively. "What'd yuh do to 'im, anyway?"

"Me?" As if Morgan's rude behavior was her fault!

"Never seen him so taken by a bit of fluff," Jack continued, speaking to Caleb as if she wasn't standing right in front of them.

"Could be the breeches," Caleb surmised.

Lacey stomped past them both, the water in her boots squishing loudly in the stilted silence. Unable to bear their attitude a second longer, she spun and glared at them both equally. "Is there something about men that makes you *all* fools?"

Unaffected by her temper, they both chuckled. She turned around and stalked back to camp.

An hour later, dawn burst cheerfully across the mountain forest, greeting the sleepy-eyed world in a splash of glory. Lacey jerked her pants off the rock where they'd been drying and, shaking them of grit, shoved her legs into them. She tucked her precious but dwindling bar of soap into her breast pocket and braided her hair. She then made her way back to the camp, surprised that Hawk hadn't gotten impatient and come in search of her. Morgan certainly would have if he'd been in charge.

The cad. Her mind buzzed with retribution.

Lacey stopped short when she saw Hawk lounging negligently against a tree, evidently awaiting her approach. He pushed away and walked toward her. Behind him, the others were loading packs on the horses that once belonged to the men who'd ambushed them on the river.

Morgan's head tilted, and Lacey met his gaze over the saddle of his horse. She felt the annoying leap of her pulse before she schooled her emotions and shifted her complete attention to Hawk.

"Autumn Star," Hawk greeted her. Lacey found she liked the Indian name he'd taken upon himself to call her since last night. "All is ready for you to leave."

He took her elbow. With a backward glance at Morgan, she hesitantly followed, stopping in front of a beautiful horse. It was her golden horse. The one she'd befriended that morning. How had Hawk known? The mare's long, glamorous mane and tail were brushed to velvet. Its aristocratic beauty seemed out of place among the rugged trail breed that milled impatiently about.

"Palomino," Hawk said. "She's beautiful, like the Autumn Star."

Lacey raised questioning eyes to his. She was conscious of the others watching her. "You fancied her," Hawk explained. "I've groomed her. She is yours."

Her breath caught. Hawk must know that a gift of this magnitude was not acceptable. "This is a . . . beautiful horse," she said with admirable composure, considering her nearly speechless state.

"I have reassured John Caine that she is not stolen." He grinned, appearing unconcerned by Morgan's accusation. "He has explained the customary refusal you must give me on this matter."

"But you think otherwise."

Strong hands encircled her waist and lifted her onto the heavy western saddle. Before she could find a suitable response, he handed her the reins. And the horrible realization struck: She was astride this beautiful beast. Alone.

Hawk leaned closer. His whisper brushed her cheek. "It is a grave offense in our culture to refuse such a gift," he explained. "It could mean war between our people."

Her legs stretched the warm girth of the horse's midsection, and she watched stupidly as Hawk adjusted the stirrups to the length of her legs. "War?" Her voice was hoarse.

"I told John Caine that you would accept my gift."

"But Hawk . . ." she whispered frantically, "it's been too long since I was on a horse. I don't remember anything."

"A nudge of your heels will send her forward," Hawk instructed. "Pull back on the reins, and she will stop."

The others around her mounted. Joshua watched her expectantly. But it was Morgan's impassive expression that drew her up straight.

"He thinks that you cannot do this." Hawk's conspiratorial whisper further rallied her determination.

Bunching the reins in her hand, she regarded Hawk coolly. "How hard can it be?" she said with bravado, and didn't miss the amusement in Hawk's dark gaze. She had the sudden distinct impression that this was about more than riding a horse.

"Enjoy the pleasure of your gift, Lacey," he softly enjoined, and with a hint of triumph turned to face Morgan.

In the white man's tradition, he executed a brief masculine salute and mounted his own horse. Swinging the handsome appaloosa around, he led the group farther up the mountain toward his village.

The cruel pace tested the stamina of even the most seasoned rider. Alternately, walking and trotting, Hawk moved along the game trails as if the very devil rode his back. Lacey knew that until they reached the reservation, they were targets for Lawton's men. Hawk didn't want to be seen leading them anywhere. Her teeth rattled until she thought she'd chipped them all.

Periodically, Lacey would catch Morgan's eyes as he looked back to see her bouncing up and down like a rag doll. This alone gave her purpose. It amazed her that she kept the pace, and that Jack, who was behind her, didn't have to waste time prodding her.

That night they made a warm fire. Despite her fatigue, Lacey carried her burden. Watching the way the others tended to their mounts, she diligently copied their routine. It didn't matter that she was the last to reach camp. She'd rather be roasted on a spit than admit defeat. Barely able to stand, she curled up beside her saddle and immediately fell asleep.

By the third day Lacey couldn't walk. Every step the horse

took, she bit down on a groan of misery. The chafed areas of her legs burned. Her kid boots were not enough to protect her from the stirrups bruising her tender instep. While every muscle in her body cried out in agony, Lacey realized that no one else was suffering.

Somewhere after the fourth day, time ceased to matter. Slumped in the saddle, Lacey focused on the dusky sky. It looked so beautiful since coming out of the mountains a few hours back. All around her, the flat lands boasted green pastures, broken occasionally by grassy knolls and huge cottonwoods. Kingston was somewhere beyond the ridge, she thought dreamily. Tomorrow they would be at Hawk's camp.

"Lacey?" Her dazed mind registered that they had stopped, and she looked down to find Morgan standing beside her. She blinked, thinking he was some apparition of her imagination. It was only natural that she would want to touch it.

"When we get to Kingston, someone is going to have to teach you to ride." Before she registered his words, he lifted her off the horse. "I'm truly impressed you've stayed in the saddle this long."

"Put me down, Morgan." Frantic, she glanced around her to see if anyone else was watching. They were alone with the horses.

"Or what?" he scoffed. "You couldn't even fend off a flea at the moment. I'll take care of your horse tonight."

Lacey leaned her head against his shoulder, frustrated that he should remain so capable. "She's my responsibility."

"And you're my responsibility. Know when to quit, Lacey."

She could do nothing more than sigh her protest. Maybe it didn't matter. She'd been a fool to ever consider herself capable of being Morgan's equal in anything. Her only accomplishment was in convincing him he'd been right about her all along.

"You win, Morgan," she mumbled over her exhaustion when she felt him lay her in her bedroll beside the fire.

"Not by a long shot, sweetheart." Morgan's voice cracked oddly, but she was too worn out to care what strange mood drove him now.

Turning over in her blankets, sleep was on her before she took her next breath.

The next afternoon Hawk's village couldn't have been a more welcome sight. Lacey followed Hawk without comment to his lodge where she promptly tossed her blanket on the ground and collapsed in front of the fire. Tugging her boots, she jerked them off, furious to find her feet wrinkled from the abuse they were forced to endure.

"You are not happy with your treatment?" Hawk asked as he came to stand beside her.

"Of course I am." Her voice said she was not. After five days on the trail with Hawk, Lacey was no longer afraid that he would hurt her. His interaction with her seemed solely based on irritating Morgan, which he seemed to enjoy doing on a regular basis.

"You are content with your gift?"

"The horse is very beautiful."

Hawk grinned. "Perhaps it is John Caine who puts the shadows under your eyes," he observed lightly. "Would you like me to scalp him and be done with his foolishness?" Lacey's gaze shot to his face to see his faintly amused eyes trained on her. "Don't worry. I haven't beaten him in a fight since he was twelve."

"Yet, you still call him John Caine. I assumed—"

"Persistence is victory in itself. He merely got tired of fighting me."

Hawk walked past her to a chest that seemed out of place in a room inconspicuously absent of furnishings. Opening it, he revealed a stack of clothing, suspiciously feminine and of a fashion not in the least resembling the native attire she witnessed on the village women. Her brow lifted as she swept her gaze up to his.

"They're not stolen," he reassured her, drawing out a pair of denims and a faded red flannel from the trunk's contents. "The girl who wore these before you was about your size." A pair of slim moccasins followed. "I can do nothing for your boots, but you can wear these, for now."

Lacey climbed to her feet as Hawk approached and handed

her the clothes. "Where is the girl now?" Standing a head and shoulders above her, Hawk reminded her of Morgan.

He lifted a handful of her hair and palmed the silken strands in fascination. He seemed pleased that she was not afraid of him. "You have hair like the palomino," he said, "the color of warm meadow grass in autumn. You are like the Autumn Star high in the sky. Her light shines for all, guiding the traveler on his journey home."

Forgetting he had deftly sidetracked her from her question, Lacey's eyes widened. "That's very beautiful, Hawk. Where did you learn to speak English so eloquently?"

"I learned to speak English from John Caine. At one time he was anxious to teach a lost boy the words with which to share his language and his friendship. When we met, there was much we taught each other," he said, reading her curiosity. "We became brothers."

"Morgan doesn't seem to share your kinship."

A faint smile curved Hawk's mouth. "Through the years, I've missed the challenge of his company. But history marks us all with its passing. Time has changed us both."

"You would have shot him the other day."

"He is a dangerous man filled with much anger. One cannot always read the mind of such a man. If I had to, I would have killed him. . . . I would also die for him."

The revelation stunned her. "Why does he hate you?"

Hawk studied her, his expression passive. "He only thinks he hates me," was all he said.

Lacey found herself drawn to Hawk's honesty. Absently, she rubbed her neck. "You attacked me in the wagon the other night. Why?"

He observed her with a thin smile. "If you had screamed, you would have brought every man down upon me. You injured yourself because you would not cease your fight."

"You ride with outlaws, Hawk."

Hawk allowed her hair to slide through his hands. "I don't suffer the same conscience as your marshal," he mused. "Just as one white man is like another. Gold is the same no matter which hand feeds you."

"I don't believe you. If you fight the law, it is not for gold that you do it."

Hawk considered her with interest. He seemed to admire her frankness. "I don't fight the law," he said slowly. "I fight the men who raped and murdered my wife. When she died, she was pregnant with my son. The men who butchered her took them both. John Caine seeks revenge in justice. I don't care how they die."

Lacey's astonished gaze dropped to the clothes in her hands. "Shannon . . ." The name came out in a hoarse whisper. "She was your wife?"

Hawk said nothing more. Instead, he turned and strode from the lodge, leaving Lacey to shiver in the warmth.

Chapter Twelve

A dozen scrawny dogs, milling between the wikiups and pine-bough lodges, scattered as Morgan walked through the bunch. Stopping in front of the wikiup where the others in his party rested, Morgan hesitated. Lacey had gone in earlier, and he'd left, intent on avoiding her completely. Not that she spoke to him either, or pretended to be friendly. She was still furious with him since he'd thrown her into the creek, which she heartily deserved for making a pass at him. She didn't have the good sense to leave him the hell alone.

She may not have any sense, but she did have stamina, he conceded. He'd watched her ride that horse this past week. Even now, an unwelcome spark of admiration inserted itself into Morgan's thoughts.

He still didn't know how he felt assessing his sister's clothing on Lacey. Except the unpleasant turn of his stomach unnerved him.

Lacey possessed so much of Shannon's spirit. Shannon had also been full of life, and now she was dead.

The flap behind him lifted, and Jack ducked out of the

triangle-shaped opening. They both stood for a moment in silence.

"It's been a long time," Jack grunted, looking around him.

"I didn't think I'd ever be back here. For any reason."

Jack's tone was guarded. "You speak like a man plagued with regret."

"Regret is a nasty thing, Jack," Morgan said. "We all make our own choices. Hawk made his long ago. I made mine."

"It was never easy for either of you." Jack looked down at him over the stem of his pipe. "Though you've never been in need of a pa, you've been like my son, Morgan. I've done my best to let you make your own way. But perhaps it's time to make your peace with Hawk. Put down some roots here. Make a go of a life for yourself."

"Aren't you forgetting that nothing is over? Where can I go to run far enough from this badge or the men who continue to hunt me? Lawton may be dead. But he doesn't feel dead inside here." Morgan pressed a fist to his chest. "And there's still the matter of the man in Colin's camp who betrayed us."

Jack considered this. "There were more than a dozen men who helped us get out that night."

"Hawk must know who he is, but for some reason isn't saying. I intend to find out why."

"If Hawk hasn't told you, then he has a good reason."

The thought didn't comfort Morgan. Nor did the fact that Hawk continued to remain close to Lawton's men. "When I get to Kingston, I'm returning for Colin," Morgan said quietly. "I have a job to finish. I may not be back after that."

His gaze fixed on the magnificent sunset shimmering just beyond the mountains. Memories touched him in this place, sugarcoated dreams and, for the first time in his life, Morgan was unsure of himself.

Morgan left the village and skirted the grassy knoll until he came to a secluded copse of fledgling trees. The first breath of autumn had already changed their foliage to gold. In the fading sunset, the tranquil vision was out of place in a world that strangled itself on violence.

Expecting to find himself alone, Morgan stopped. A few

feet away, standing stiffly erect, with feet braced apart, Hawk stared down at Shannon's grave. Hawk's back was to Morgan. For a stunned moment, Morgan felt privy to something sacred.

Hawk lifted his head. "She would have given me a fine son, John Caine."

Silence remained fixed between them. Then Hawk turned, and for a brief moment, the years fell away.

"Let me finish this my way," Hawk said.

Morgan felt his chest tighten. Hawk was offering him a chance to escape the demons of the past, the hate that had been such a consuming force in his life. Could he? Just once, could he let something go?

"Always the lawman," Hawk grunted, when Morgan didn't reply. "Even Shannon believed in you."

The words cut into Morgan like a searing slash. "If I had taken her from here in the first place, she'd still be alive."

"You had no right."

"She was eighteen. What the hell does a child know of marriage. It was some romantic fantasy of hers being in love with an outlaw."

"She was no child."

"She was my *sister*."

"And my *wife!*" Hawk's eyes flickered skyward, and in the dying light of the day, they glittered behind a sheen of tears. It was the only emotion Morgan had ever seen the big renegade betray. "I loved her more than my own life."

"But you weren't the one to find her. You don't know what it was like, her throat cut. Everything she was . . . her life spilling around her. I couldn't save her. Christ, I tried. You didn't have to look into her eyes and watch her die." Morgan felt his stomach wrench as it always did when he remembered. He closed his eyes. Still she was there before him.

Brett Lawton had been there, too. Even now, Morgan could see the ice-water gaze directed at him over the barrel of a Colt .45. The shot flamed from the gun, hitting him in the head. He should have died, too, that day with his sister, but somehow fate had intervened. The bullet had only grazed his scalp, knocking him senseless. The mistake had been Lawton's fatal error, for Morgan then hunted the bastard down to pay with his life for every vile crime he'd ever committed.

"Where were you, Hawk? Where were you when she needed you?"

Hawk's proud demeanor shifted. "Lawton and his men rode into camp while I was gone. They were never supposed to come here. Never. They had just robbed the army payroll at Flat Springs. They needed me to guide them over the mountain, away from the blue coats chasing them. I was gone with most of the men in my village, hunting." Hawk's head dropped back as he glared at the sky. "No one knew she was my wife, John Caine. No one knew she carried my son."

"Why did Lawton want her dead? Why? He didn't know her."

"There was one among them . . ."

"Was it Brett Lawton?"

"His wasn't the knife that murdered her."

"Why haven't you told me this before? Who is he? The same man who betrayed us on the river?"

Hawk peered intently at Morgan. "I warned you about the danger to your Lacey Ashton. You owe me this one, John Caine."

Morgan's expression betrayed none of the anger rippling through him, but he knew Hawk could read it in his eyes.

Hawk's expression hardened. "Your justice is served to you as it is served to these people on this reservation. In a bowl riddled with the holes of greed. I do not trust your laws. I trust only myself to see this man brought down the same way he murdered my wife. You can fight me. But you will have to kill me if you do." Hawk turned, melding into the shadows.

The cool breeze bit into the fabric of Morgan's shirt, and his gaze dropped to the narrow mound of dirt at his feet. "Ah, Shannon," he whispered. "What am I to do?"

Something undeniable touched him. Vengeance had been an easy course to follow when emptiness filled every breath and space in his life. A week ago Morgan couldn't have cared less if Hawk paved the road to hell for his sins.

A week ago Morgan didn't know anything about hopes or dreams.

* * *

Lacey tied her palomino to a pine rail beside half a dozen other milling horses. Brushing the dust from Morgan's buckskin, she pulled it tighter around her body, wanting more than anything to go home, wherever that might be. All around her, buckboard wagons seemed to converge upon Kingston's main street as a crowd accumulated to greet the weary entourage. Neglected in the sweeping surge of gathering onlookers, she was content to remain anonymous. Night was descending on the town.

Stepping up on the boardwalk in front of the mercantile, Lacey leaned her head against the smooth wood-carved post. From beneath the edge of the roof overhang, she watched the proceedings.

She watched Morgan.

Leaning negligently with his arm braced against the door of the marshal's office, he appeared focused on conversation with those around him. His shirtsleeves were rolled up, exposing tanned forearms, his lean strength reminding her of more than she wanted to remember.

Absently, her fingers traced the sensitive curve of her lower lip. She knew she would never forget the feel of his mouth on hers.

Never forget the fluttering thrill of his touch.

Morgan's head lifted, drawing her gaze to the movement. His flat-crowned hat was cocked low over his eyes, and it took Lacey a moment to realize he was watching her.

She promptly cast her gaze in the opposite direction. Instantly, her attention diverted to a dark-haired woman rushing toward them from down the street. Wearing a white peasant blouse and a bright red skirt that flared around long legs as she ran toward Morgan, the woman's deep, throaty laughter reflected her obvious excitement. Aware of a sense of foreboding in the pit of her stomach, Lacey tracked the woman's harried progress as she jostled through the crowd . . . directly into Morgan's arms.

Jolene!

Tall, well-shaped, mature. Everything Lacey wasn't. She stared in disbelief.

Morgan kissed her. And Lacey's confidence shattered into

a thousand wretched pieces that rained over her head with an I-told-you-so brutality that almost made her weep. It was the last straw, the ballast that sank the ship. A slap! She stiffly turned her back on the wretched scene, too furious to take stock of her jealousy.

A hand latched firmly on to Lacey's, nearly yanking her off her feet. "Come on. They said Ma was at Jolene's."

Shoving Morgan from her thoughts, Lacey followed Joshua through the maze of alleys. "Is she all right?"

"Right as rain." His grin flashed bright. "She's done had the baby a week ago. A boy. We got a brother, Lacey."

A brother! This was a wonderful surprise.

On a quiet corner at the edge of town, shadowed by giant cottonwoods, stood a simple whitewashed house encircled by a white picket fence. Baskets of flowers swinging in the breeze hung from the porch, and the gardens surrounding the wooden porch all showed considerable care. Lacey hesitated.

"This way." Joshua didn't even slow, and Lacey stumbled up the stairs of the porch after him.

With familiar ease, he ran around to the back and threw open the door, bursting like a tornado into the kitchen. "Ma!" he yelled.

The kitchen smelled of fresh bread. Joshua breezed with purpose past the quaint living room into a hall. In a frenzy, he opened each door, coming to an abrupt halt inside the third room.

"Ma!" Dropping Lacey's hand, he flew across the room to the woman in the bed, struggling to lift herself up on her elbow even as Joshua flung into her arms.

Lacey watched from the doorway. With skin like the apricot porcelain of a fine china doll and hair the color of sunshine, Joshua's mother was beautiful. She looked to be in her late thirties. When she lifted her eyes past Joshua to settle anxiously on her, Lacey was startled by their green clarity, and the sheen of tears reflected in the woman's gaze. Lacey turned away to leave Joshua to his privacy.

"Please, don't go," the melodic voice called, the soft-spoken words drawing Lacey back. Somehow familiar. "I've been looking so forward to finally seeing you." The woman turned bright eyes toward her son. "Josh, bring your sister over here, please."

Joshua's mother struggled to sit up. Lacey rushed to her side. "It's all right," Lorraine hastily replied as Lacey fluffed the pillows behind her. "I'm not a *total* invalid." The warmth in her gaze touched Lacey. "Colin has spoken much of you."

"Of you, too," Lacey said. "I'm glad to finally meet you."

"We got a wire from Bodie two days ago. The wagon train will be here in a week. It's you we've been worried about."

"Ma, we had to take canoes up the river. Lacey's canoe got shot up, and she went over a waterfall. Then the Injuns got us." He leaned into his mother's arms, his vocal enthusiasm for the adventure waning beneath the reassuring presence of his mother. "I missed you."

"Morgan would never let anything happen to you," she said softly, holding her son. "You know that."

The underlying trust so evident in the tone of Lorraine's voice, struck Lacey. From where would such loyalty spring?

Lorraine's eyes settled on Lacey with a hint of pride. "Even coming here by way of the stage, it's never easy for a woman traveling in this territory. You made it."

Feeling less ambivalence toward the trip than she did toward a certain marshal at that moment, Lacey was unaware that she'd accomplished anything remarkable. The rustling sound of a baby saved her from answering. Her gaze fell on the ruffled bassinet behind her.

"He's beautiful, isn't he?" Lorraine said reverently. "He came early, but everything is going to be just fine now."

"Nothing a little bed rest won't cure," the sultry feminine voice interrupted from the doorway.

Lacey's gaze snapped to the dark-haired woman she'd last seen in Morgan's arms. Watching Lorraine with genuine concern, Jolene walked past Lacey to the bed.

"Lainey, I know you're excited to see everyone, but you need to rest. Joshua understands, don't you?" She tousled the boy's hair. He lowered his head and nodded. "Well, don't I even get a hug," she gently admonished, and Joshua went into her arms.

The reunion, though brief, further served to remind Lacey that she was an outsider.

Jolene turned her head; her expression shuttered as her dark eyes strayed over the buckskin Lacey was wearing. "You must be Lacey Ashton," she said quietly.

"Jolene is a good friend to our family," Lorraine replied.

"You both look like you could use some clean clothes," Jolene said. "Come, let's allow Lainey to sleep." She turned back to Lorraine and smiled. "These two will be fine. Morgan and Jack are still at the office. If they don't see you tonight, I'm sure they'll be by in the morning. You rest for now."

"Lacey—" Lorraine called. Lacey hesitantly took the hand stretching out to her from the covers. "I'm so happy that you're here." Lorraine's warm smile beckoned. A tremor shook Lacey's courage. Something about the older woman's soft-spoken strength embraced the need inside Lacey to be mothered.

"Now Lainey, you get your rest. We'll all feel better once you're on your feet again."

Jolene ushered Lacey and Joshua out of the room. Dusk had settled over the valley town, and shadows stretched into the corners of the house. Jolene hustled about lighting the living room lamps. It was a cozy house, Lacey thought as she scanned the simple decor.

Her appraisal ended abruptly as she slammed into Jolene's cool gaze. Lacey shoved her hands into her coat pockets and regarded the dark-haired woman passively.

Joshua swept past them to the front door. "When we get to the store, can I have some peppermints?"

Jolene smiled at Joshua. "Of course. As many as you want." Her cool glance returned to Lacey. "Shall we go?"

Lacey followed her out the door. Her body still ached, and no matter how hard she tried to hide it, her stiff walk reflected her pain. Jolene slowed to keep pace. They lost Joshua as he ran ahead.

"I know your other clothes won't be here for a few days," Jolene said, her tone kinder. "Maybe you can find something at the store."

"A simple dress would be nice," Lacey admitted, glancing

down at herself. "Men might find such attire practical, but I'm plain tired of having to bare my backside every time I perform a simple bodily function." She was ready to be a woman again.

Jolene's mouth tilted slightly. "We have one ready-made dress in stock at the moment. But I think it'll swallow you. You look to be about Lainey's build. Before she had the baby, that is," she amended. "I'm sure she won't mind if you wear something of hers."

"I'd appreciate that."

Jolene observed Lacey's stilted walk. Lacey smiled unhappily. "Morgan said it was because I didn't know how to ride."

"Does Morgan often offer such mindful comments?"

In all fairness to Morgan, Lacey didn't amplify her feelings on that remark. "He's right. I don't."

"Morgan is hard on people," Jolene said after a time.

"My father obviously puts a lot of trust in him," Lacey said. "That's all that matters, I suppose."

Jolene's dark eyes seemed to study her. "Morgan saved your father's life once." The words nearly stopped Lacey in her tracks. "You didn't know?" Jolene asked.

Expounding upon the past hadn't been a favorite topic of conversation, she thought grudgingly, but said instead, "My father hasn't had a lot of time to talk."

"Everyone knows what happened," Jolene said as if coming to a decision to answer the question in Lacey's eyes. "Five years ago in California, Morgan threw down on a man named Brett Lawton to defend Lorraine and to save Joshua from being kidnapped. Your father was shot trying to protect them. Lawton would have killed him, but for the lawman who stepped between your father and Lawton's gun. It was the only time any of us ever saw Brett Lawton beaten in a draw. Morgan didn't kill him, but the incident scarred Lawton's face forever."

Lacey ran a hand through the unruly strands of hair that had escaped the single thick braid down her back. These people had a history that stretched years in the past.

"Morgan and Jack were hell-bent on raising Shannon and doing a poor job of it. Though, it wasn't for lack of love. Shannon had a way with Morgan. She had spirit. Who couldn't help loving her? Lainey took Morgan's sister in as part of her family. Later when Morgan accepted the marshal's commission up here we moved."

"Why was this Lawton after Joshua?"

Jolene's voice grew quiet. "It doesn't matter now. Lawton is dead." She crossed her arms. "Though on nights like this, it doesn't feel that way."

Unease shivered over Lacey. In the damp, misty shadows, it seemed as if Brett Lawton came alive for her, too.

Jolene didn't talk anymore. They met Jack and Red coming out of the marshal's office. After a boisterous greeting, clearly between friends, Jolene slipped past Jack into the office. Lacey felt her pulse hitch.

A lantern burned in the office and, though the shades were half drawn, Lacey glimpsed Morgan inside leaning against the big desk near the back of the room. A rack of rifles lined the wall behind him and, to his right, Lacey could see the bars of a corner jail cell. He had changed into a clean shirt and now wore his badge on a black leather vest over the shirt, looking much as he did the first time she saw him in San Francisco. There were blue army regulars inside, and Caleb was standing beside them. Morgan appeared focused on the discussion.

Annoyed with herself, Lacey looked away. Stepping past the men conversing with Red and Jack, she looked toward the mountains, feeling nothing but a shaky determination to push on.

She didn't need Morgan. She had an intense longing to be free. To kick off her boots and walk barefoot in the grass. To run. To laugh. To belong. Especially to belong.

She ached to go home—not back to Jolene's house—but home!

Her horse still stood beside the hitching rail where Lacey had left her. A nervous surge of energy flooded her limbs, and she turned to find Jack watching her as if he'd read her thoughts and understood. Shrugging away from the wall where he'd been leaning, the barrel of his Sharps rifle gripped in his hand, he approached her. Conversation ceased as all eyes followed him.

"I'm taking Lacey home," he announced over his shoulder.

"Don't any of you go running to my nephew either. I don't want anyone stoppin' us." Tears sprang into Lacey's eyes. Jack knuckled her cheek and grinned. "Could I stop you even if I wanted to?"

"No," she said, sniffing. "But just the same, thank you." Wiping her eyes, she glanced across the street to the store where Joshua had entered. She wouldn't press for his company. His place was with his mother tonight.

Stepping back up on the boardwalk Lacey approached Red. "Thank you for everything these past couple of months," she said softly, kissing his cheek. "You've been a true friend."

Casting a sheepish glance around him, he blushed. "My pleasure, Miss Ashton."

"Tell Caleb thank you for me." Lacey felt no regret not saying good-bye to Morgan, and she certainly wasn't about to thank him for anything. He'd made his stance perfectly clear.

A few moments later, Lacey and Jack rode out of town.

In the darkness, Lacey couldn't grasp the feel of the land or the magnificence of the ranch that was to be her home. When they finally reached the rise overlooking the house, Jack explained to her that they'd already been on her father's land for more than a mile. The road wishboned off in two directions and Lacey glimpsed the field house where the ranch hands stayed. Nudging her horse forward, she followed the winding path to the barn down the hill from the house.

Biting back a groan, Lacey slid off the saddle. Watching Jack remove the saddle from her horse, she picked up a brush from the stall and, like she'd seen Morgan do a hundred times before, brushed the horse down. Jack lugged in a bucket of oats and after Lacey finished, closed the stall door.

Leading his horse behind them, Jack walked with Lacey to the house. "Have you named your horse, yet?"

"Star," she said brightly. "Not very original, but appropriate. Hawk should approve."

Jack stopped at the edge of the yard surrounding the house. Lacey stared up at the modest duo-level house, its whitewash exterior luminous in the breathtaking moonlight. Beneath the protected overhang of the roof, cascading vines climbed with unruly ease up trellises carved between posts on a porch that wrapped around the house. Two lone rocking chairs creaked in the chilly breeze, and the smell of pine filled the air. Excitement washed over her.

"It's magnificent."

Jack walked her up the stairs to the porch. "I'll tell the boys you're here at the house," he said.

Lacey stood on her toes and kissed his bearded cheek. Abruptly, she flung her arms around his barrel chest, clinging to his kindness, anchoring herself to his strength.

"It will be a good life for you here, Lacey," he said quietly.

"It's nothing like England."

"You're not English." Jack peered at her. "*This* is your land, Lacey. Learn everything there is to know so you can be anything you want."

He loped down the stairs to where he'd left his horse. With a half salute in her direction, he mounted and cantered off. Lacey had the sneaking suspicion that he left her in the dark on purpose. Unlike Morgan, who didn't believe in her, Jack expected her to learn to handle life on her own.

Chapter Thirteen

Lacey was out of bed sitting on the front porch steps before the first shimmering rays of dawn broke over the eastern mountain ridge. Her breath clouded on the frost-scented breeze. Snuggling deeper within the warmth of Morgan's buckskin, Lacey could only stare at the glorious sight presented her. A restless mind gave way to awe, clearing her head of troubling thoughts. This was home. And it was more magnificent than she ever dreamed.

After a sinfully huge breakfast of hotcakes smothered in maple syrup, Lacey made her rounds through the house. Dressed in one of Lorraine's suitably worn-out dresses, she explored every room with a child's curiosity. The house had been built with attention to detail but it was Lorraine's added touch, displayed in the ruffled curtains, demure wallpaper, and the essence of heliotrope wafting through every room, that made this house a home. The house smelled of warmth . . . and of love.

At the bottom of the stairway, Lacey had stopped in front of a framed sienna photo of her father and a little girl no older than five, her long, blond ringlets curled around a pert face brightened by a smile. Lacey slid her fingers past the familiar photo of herself to the drawings framed around the picture. Her gaze riveted on a self-portrait she'd mailed to her father when she was eleven. The work was comical but precious enough to be considered valuable to the one who'd received the gift and treasured it through the years.

Confused by an odd tangle of emotions, Lacey drew up. She'd spent years tucked away in England thinking she was satisfied with her lot in life. How little it compared to her feelings now.

The thought of it filled her with excitement.

Her lonely, sheltered world might have been adequate before, now she wondered how she'd stood it for so many years.

Maybe she hadn't, and that's what Clare had seen.

Lacey's gaze moved to the close-up of a woman and boy in the next photo. Wearing overalls, a straw hat, and his usual impish grin, Joshua sat beside his mother. Lacey glimpsed their resemblance.

Her eyes narrowed, focusing on the odd mark visible just below Joshua's collarbone—a birthmark—like hers.

Lacey felt herself pale.

A coincidence?

The idea that it could be anything else but a fluke was preposterous. Behind her, the muted ticking of a wagtail clock counted off the seconds. If Joshua truly *were* related to her in some way, what reason would anyone have to hide it from her? The notion was as far-fetched as the moon.

Still, the seed had been planted. It wouldn't be easy dismissing the identical birthmarks she and Joshua shared.

Brushing off her hands, Lacey stood and ventured to the stable. Having already made the rounds of the yard, met the men in the bunkhouse, and established her place in residence, she was now prepared to embark upon her first goal. Though her abused backside would get a temporary reprieve from the saddle today, Lacey was determined to learn everything she could about horses, even if it killed her, which she wasn't entirely positive wouldn't happen. She would learn to ride as well as Morgan or anyone.

He was leaving today to meet her father. . . .

Instantly, her emotions betrayed her. Not once all morning had she allowed herself to think of Morgan—or question where he'd spent the night. Now, he invaded every corner of her mind, fixing her with a headache. It was not an easy thing to be in love, she decided. Such passion was for the strong. She was definitely weak.

Running her hands through Star's golden mane, Lacey nuzzled her smooth jaw. "You'd never make such a fool of yourself over a male horse, would you?" she chided.

The wild odyssey of the past months granted Lacey no succor with which to wage any more battles fighting a lost cause. Morgan Caine was a hunter of men. She had fallen in love with a man who saw only black-and-white in a world bursting with color. A man tempered by vengeance and duty. For one exciting moment at Hawk's camp by the stream, she remembered his gentleness. Part of him had slipped into her world—and she had dared to hope. But he was too disciplined to deviate from his chosen path.

And he possessed not a bit of sense for what was good for him!

Lacey put a halter on Star and led the horse outside into the corral for a meal of grain. In the distance, cattle milled near a watering pond. Drawing in a deep, invigorating breath, she swung her gaze across the landscape, stopping briefly to admire her father's house.

A horse snorted, jolting Lacey from her thoughts. There was nothing friendly about the sound. She whirled toward the noise.

Paused on the crest of the hill overlooking the stable, Morgan watched her from the saddle of a restless steel-dust stallion. Fighting the bit, Morgan's horse pranced sideways, giving Lacey a glimpse of the raw power horse and rider shared. That Morgan finally rode his own horse was evident. The fire-breathing temper of that stallion was befitting the lean, dark man sitting astride him.

His mere presence shattered her confidence.

Snapping erect, Lacey scaled the corral fence. Her flight spurred Morgan down the hill after her, hastily closing the distance between them. He swung the horse in front of her, blocking her path of escape before she'd even reached halfway across the yard. Pounding the ground in a grand display of annoyance, the stallion looked every bit as ominous as a huge, black thunderhead.

Mesmerized by the predatory grace of Morgan's maneuver, Lacey forgot to move, or dared not for fear of being trampled. With her heart pounding, her gaze chased upward. Morgan's fierce eyes rooted her to the ground.

The sound of another horse approaching reached Lacey's thoughts. Tearing her gaze from Morgan, she spied Caleb casually trotting their way, evidently in less hurry to reach her than Morgan.

"I could have skinned Jack for bringing you out here last night." Morgan's voice cut in. "I had no idea you were gone until this morning. It's a damned foolish thing being out here alone."

Any momentary confusion Lacey felt vanished in a haze of red. Evidently, Morgan had been too blissfully occupied the night before to notice anything happening outside his office.

Despite the rebellious sweep of hair tumbling from the scarf on her head—a reminder that only moments ago, she'd run like a scared rabbit—Lacey now felt imperious in the face of his glower. "Life goes on, Morgan. And I'm finished with being coddled as if I was a child. I've already been cautioned about the dangers—"

Morgan's dark brows converged, and Lacey took an unconscious step out of his reach. "Cautioned?" he choked. "Lacey, there are men out here who eat innocent waifs like you for breakfast. They won't stop to ask your name, or care what kind of person you are. They'll use you, then kill you for the sport of it. They could be out here now."

Morgan's words ripped into Lacey. She knew such a thing was possible. Hadn't it happened to his sister? That act of violence tainted Morgan's whole life. But Lacey didn't want to view the world through Morgan's cynical eyes. This was her home. She finally belonged someplace, and he wanted to take it all away from her.

"Don't ask me to leave. I won't."

"Lacey, I know how you feel about being here. But this

isn't the time to be pigheaded about your independence. You need to stay in town with Lorraine where you'll be safe."

"I will *not* stay at your . . . at Jolene's house."

"You're *not* staying here."

Lacey marshaled her courage, surrendering not one square inch of ground. "Then you'll have to arrest me! I won't go any other way."

"Christ, I don't have time for this nonsense."

"Nonsense!"

"I owe your father the responsibility of seeing you safe until his return. After that, you're out of my hair."

Lacey was bloody exhausted of being someone's responsibility. Especially his! "Father doesn't own me . . . any more than you do. I relieve you of your obligations. You're fired. Now go—leave." Her attempt to swerve past him failed. His horse cut off her retreat.

"You can't fire me."

"Why not?"

"Because I don't work for you. Nor for your father."

"Really, Morgan. Then why are you here?"

"Dammit, Lacey." His voice turned as hard as flint. "What if I were someone bent on doing you harm? Then what?"

Lacey's hand swept down into the folds of her skirt. "Then I would *shoot* you, Mr. Caine." The gun was out of her pocket before she finished the sentence. A sense of satisfaction thrilled her at the look on Morgan's face. Swinging the gun up, Lacey discharged it harmlessly over his head.

A flurry of motion answered the shot, and all at once Morgan's attention broadened to the stable where a man emerged carrying a shotgun. At the bunk house two men ran from the doorway, guns drawn.

Triumph glittered in Lacey's eyes when Morgan's furious gaze again found its way back to her. "As you can see, I have prepared for trouble as best I could. They have orders to shoot anyone who is trespassing." She straightened in a further show of confidence. "Now, if you'll excuse my lack of hospitality." She didn't include Caleb in her glance. "I haven't any tea to invite you in for more chitchat. So . . . go away!" Lacey side-stepped Morgan's ornery horse and marched away like a seasoned warrior.

Yanking his hat brim lower, Morgan observed the indignant swing of Lacey's skirts. Damn contrary female. He didn't know if he should throttle her now for her stubbornness or drag her back to town and do the nasty deed there.

"Come down to talk some sense into her, did yuh?" Caleb laughed outright. "Don't know which one of yuh lost the argument."

The saddle creaked as Morgan twisted around, narrowing his glare on Caleb. "Don't you have something better to do?"

"And let yuh get shot chasin' after that gal? Someone has to watch yer back, explain yer intentions, *honorable* as they are."

Morgan turned away, his annoyed gaze falling on Lacey's approaching men-at-arms. "I'll deal with them."

"And after that, you best be prepared to make yer peace with that gal," Caleb casually commented, ignoring Morgan's dismissal. "She saw you an' Jolene last evening, right friendly actin'. Now I knowed you spent the night in yer office alone, 'cuz I borrowed the cot in that jail of yers and watched yuh sleep. But that girl up there don't. For someone what cottons to the notion of love, that's a mighty hard dish to swallow."

Morgan remembered the look on Lacey's face when Jolene kissed him yesterday. He'd never suffered from a conscience as much as he had these past months. Worse, he'd never felt the need to explain himself to anyone, and he'd almost done that very thing last night to Lacey. He wished now that he had. He would have found her and dragged her bottom back to town.

"The way I see it"—Caleb spit a streamer of brown juice—"a man in yer business don't have room for distractions. And yuh been mighty distracted as of late. Now when yuh finish here, yuh can join me on the trail."

On that parting sentiment, Caleb swung his shaggy mount around and trotted off. Morgan leaned into his saddle, peering steadily from beneath his hat at the wiry man. In all the years Morgan had known Caleb, the man had never given him advice on anything.

"Marshal Caine?" The nervous query drew Morgan's attention. Morgan recognized the speaker as Colin's top wrangler. Lowering his shotgun, the man stepped forward. "What's the trouble here?"

"Which one of you gave Miss Ashton that gun?" Morgan demanded.

"None of us . . . sir," the wrangler answered. "It belongs to her pa. She musta found it this morning. Come out after breakfast askin' how to use it. She's a game one fer sure. Wouldn't take no for an answer. Threatened to learn herself, right there in the bunkhouse, maybe even accidentally shoot the place up."

"I see." Morgan swung his gaze back toward the house. Lacey was standing just outside the picket fence watching the proceedings with wary interest. Probably thinking she was on safe ground. A misnomer, Morgan considered as he slid off his horse.

There was danger in his emotions. He felt the warning all the way to his boots. He could never belong to Lacey's world. They were too different. Like night and day. Winter and summer.

Morgan should have turned away then and there. Followed Caleb.

"Jack probably told you the town sheriff is still up north handling a mine-jumping claim," he said without removing his gaze from Lacey. "Because of the possibility that we might still be dealing with the Lawton gang, Jack will be standing in for me until I get back at the end of the week."

"Mr. Kipp said he'd be out every day to check on the girl and find some excuse to take her into town."

Maybe Jack wasn't as negligent as Morgan contended. Apparently, recognizing a losing battle when he saw it, Jack evidently resorted to other auspicious tactics to manage the ever-stubborn Lacey Ashton.

"Now if you'll excuse me"—he handed the reins of his horse to the wrangler—"I have personal business to attend to before I leave."

Morgan started up the incline toward the house. He was close enough to see Lacey's pretty little mouth open in shock before the realization that he was coming after her spurred her to action. Whirling in a tangle of petticoats, she promptly set off in a run. Morgan was impressed by her speed.

He caught up to her just as she slammed the door in his face. He heard the bolt slide home with a finality that blistered his ears.

"Go away!" she shouted. "I told you I'm not leaving!"

Narrowing his gaze on the door, Morgan considered busting the blasted thing down. Wisdom rescued him from the rash decision. "I have something to say to you, Lacey."

"Oh, really, Morgan. There aren't any creeks around here. What if I should get excited?"

He braced his arms against the door frame and glared at the portal. "I didn't lie to you that day by the river," he finally said. "When you asked if there was someone else."

"Morgan, I have no des—"

"There *is* no one else in my life," he finished.

"Why should that matter to me?" Lacey answered stiffly.

"Jolene and I go way back, Lacey. It's not what you think."

"Like you and Caitlyn Madigan?"

"No, not like me and Caitlyn. Cat is—" Hell, he wasn't about to explain Caitlyn Madigan. "Jolene . . . has been a friend. She and Lorraine ran the boardinghouse in California where Jack and Shannon stayed. Her husband was my deputy. He died when a stray bullet hit him during a shoot-out. I owe her my protection."

No answer.

Morgan glowered his impatience. "Will you open this door?"

"You were talking about what you said at the river," she quietly reminded him.

"Yes, the river." He paced on the porch, feeling a tinge of lunacy carrying on this intimate conversation with a door. He couldn't think of another thing to say. For someone who'd never deviated from any course, his confidence certainly betrayed him now. He felt ridiculous that a scrap of a girl should reduce him to a blithering idiot.

A long pause ensued. With a mental curse, Morgan turned away, then back again. "Lacey! Open this goddamned door!"

Silence answered him. Then the door clicked and swung open. Morgan dropped his arm from the door frame.

"Why tell me anything?" Her soft voice beckoned his gaze.

Morgan considered his answer for a space, realizing his words were an impoverished attempt to measure that which he couldn't explain. He didn't possess Jared's inane charisma, or Jack's humor. Only a self-disciplined logic that warned him he was treading on dangerous ground. She looked up at him, her magnificent eyes wide and as unsure as he felt. Morgan tilted her chin, his passion now banked by a strange possessive tenderness that enveloped him. It wasn't the world shifting beneath his feet. It was something in him. Something undeniable. A part of the darkness had been chipped away revealing a small point of light.

Gently, he cupped her face within his palm. "I didn't want to leave here today having you thinking I lied." He saw the tears in her eyes and tipped her chin. "Lacey . . ."

She jerked from his grip. Turning back into the house, she gave him her back. "You could learn much from Jack's manners, Morgan Caine," she snapped when he made no effort to leave her in peace. "At least *he* has the grace to leave a woman alone while she cries."

He closed the door. The intrusive click pulled her around. "You should leave," she said.

Morgan threw the bolt. "Do you often share such intimacies with my uncle?" Unstrapping his gun belt, he laid it on the table beside the door.

Her tongue skipped across her raspberry mouth. "Enough to know he's far better at acting the gentleman than you are." He walked toward her, his spurs marking each step. "So is Joshua for that matter. And Hawk. Even Hawk's nasty . . . horse." Her voice faded to a wary murmur.

He could smell her soap. With her wind-tousled hair; full, expressive lips; and flushed face, she resembled nothing of the lovesick, virtuous daughter of his friend.

Lovesick? He should laugh. She had rendered him incapable of logic since the moment he'd met her.

Now she was rendering him incapable of reason as well. He was half crazed from wanting her. Where was that famous self-control he possessed? If there were a shred of decency in him, he'd leave.

He reached out and pulled the scarf from her head, and her hair tumbled over her shoulders like silken moonlight.

"What right do you have to paw me?" Her voice was a whisper.

"None whatsoever."

"You're the one who threw me in the creek, remember?"

"I have regretted that rash decision many times since."

"You don't seem like a man who makes mistakes."

"Autumn Star." Taking up a handful of hair in his hand, Morgan regarded her dolefully. "Hawk chose your name well. It's one of the few things he's ever done that I totally approve of."

"He must be ecstatic," she said, sniffing indelicately.

"Lacey"—his mouth hovered near her temple—"you're tearing me up inside."

"I . . . am?"

"A man in my business can't be sidetracked."

"And I do not wish to be a side attraction." An impish tilt to her chin dared him to argue. "I want to be the main attraction. The only attraction."

She made him laugh. She made him so damn hard, he couldn't think of anything else. His eyes hidden beneath half-closed lids, Morgan bent his mouth over hers. "Christ . . . I want you."

"I want you, too."

"This is so wr—"

Lacey placed a finger on his lips. She'd spent her whole life being someone's burden: running from the unseen force hovering over her existence like a dark cloud. Her other hand splayed his chest. He smelled of sandalwood and pine, of all things outdoors. For the first time in so long, she tasted the sunshine on her face. The vision of what life could be.

"No, Morgan." She could not still the pounding in her chest, or the rush of blood in her ears. Her veins sang with the rhythm of her heartbeat. "This is so right."

Pulling herself flush against his unyielding body, Lacey sealed her mouth to his. She felt his struggle. His need to pull away. His want for her. She deepened the kiss, edging closer to the precipice. He was dark and dangerous. She should not be doing these things. His name broke over her lips, a dark mantra against the light.

Then his arms wrapped around her and crushed her to him. With a deep groan, he slid his mouth over the arched column of her neck, lingering on the frantic beat of her pulse. Sliding lower, he laved her breasts through the thin barrier of her dress until his mouth claimed hers again, drinking deeply of her passion.

Towering above her, Morgan backed her against the wall. He dragged her skirts up her thighs. Somehow he'd removed his gloves and, his hands cupped her bottom, pressing her intimately against him. He sucked her into a vortex. She couldn't breathe. She could do naught but groan beneath the emotional onslaught.

He edged her thighs apart. Not even her pantalets separated her from his touch. Her hands fisted in his shirt. She wanted him to touch her there. Harder. Deeper.

"Sweet mercy." Her ragged whisper scraped her throat. She'd wanted him for so long, she could barely breathe to have him touching her now, wanting her back with the same passion.

Her body was ablaze.

"Lacey . . ." He beckoned her to open her eyes. Her bodice was unbuttoned to her waist. "Stop me now"—his voice was feral against her lips—"or it's too damn late."

Lacey blinked up at him in wanton confusion. Her body wept over his hand, her breath came in short gasps, shuddering with frustration. She felt his restraint, his muscles coiling beneath her touch as she pushed into him, wanting so much more of that intrusive bliss. "Morgan Caine"—she gripped his shirt in two hands and edged him toward the stairs—"you talk too much."

Without hesitation, she melded her mouth to his, pressing him backward. The hot whisper of his response mingled with her rasp. His heel hit the stairs, and he sat abruptly. Grinning down at him with a giddiness that made her dizzy, she straddled his hips. Her fingers unfastened the buttons on his vest, then his shirt. "It's only fair that I get to see you, too, Mr. Marshal. All of you."

His eyes glittered. He still wore his hat. She snapped his shirt open to her gaze. He was magnificent, she realized, sculpted in perfection. His wide shoulders narrowed to a taut waist. Tentatively she lifted fingers and fanned her hand against his furred skin above his heart. It beat strongly beneath her touch. Promising . . . and thrilling all at once.

His hand wrapped around the back of her head, bringing her mouth down on his. A low sound came from deep in his chest. Bracing her bottom, he lifted her until she straddled his waist. They stumbled up the stairs and still the kiss went on, recklessly consuming her with each wet flick of his tongue against hers. Their clothes littered the stairs.

On the landing, they hit the wall. She slid down the half-naked length of him. His mouth caressed her breasts, suckling each nipple through her chemise with the hot promise of that elemental, carnal touch of his lips. Morgan removed her pantalets, and she kicked them aside, helping him work the buttons of his pants, his impatience nearly tearing them from their moorings. Lacey followed the glide of his hands as he slid the pants over his hips.

Boldly, she slid her hands over the tempered length of him, greedy to share a carnal world she knew nothing about, except that she burned for want of him.

A shuddering groan escaped him, rippling through his body. He filled both her palms, and she savored the astonishing feel of him. A single cloudy drop formed at its silky tip.

She suddenly found her hands seized in his. He lifted her.

"Don't tempt fate, sweetheart."

"You are my fate, Morgan."

He shouldered against the nearest door.

"No," she rasped, kissing him. "Not that room." She pointed to the one across the narrow hallway. The room she'd taken for her own. The brass bed had been a reminder of San Francisco. Morgan yanked the white down comforter from the bed. His body covered hers.

She felt his questing probe between her thighs, searching; then he was pushing inside her.

The pain was unexpected. Stunning her.

Morgan muffled a groan in her hair. "It hurts. I know."

"Don't . . . stop."

"Hell, I couldn't . . . if I tried." His mouth took hers. Then he was sliding deeper into her body.

She arched up. Her body could not fit all of him. With one swift motion, Morgan rolled her on top. She straddled his hips. Her hair fell around them in skeins of gold. His fingers laced with hers, drawing her hands behind her to her bottom, and slowly she settled on top of him until her body covered the whole length of him. Sensations curled in and out of her belly.

"You . . . feel incredible." His ragged voice broke. "So damned . . . incredible."

Slowly, he began to move her back and forth, thrusting deeper. Then her hands were free as he settled his palms against her hips, tightly kneading her skin, measuring her hungry response. Reality ceased to matter. She braced her palms on his shoulders, her own cries filling her senses. Her heart pounded. Morgan made an anguished sound. She tangled her hands in his hair, drinking in the sound of her name on his lips. And Lacey surrendered herself completely to the brilliant heat radiating through every inch of her being. Her own release convulsed through her shivering body. Like nothing she'd ever felt before. It filled her body and drained her very soul.

For a moment, the thudding of her heart filled the opulent glow surrounding her, and she could do naught but sprawl on top of him, drugged with her own pleasure. Her head rested on his shoulder.

Slowly the sounds of birds outside intruded. She heard someone chopping wood. A horse whinnied. "I never knew . . ." She traced a finger around his mouth. "Is it like this for everyone?"

"I wouldn't know." A rueful smile seemed to touch his words, and something else, something more formidable, as reality settled over them. She followed his eyes to the smiling photos that marched up and down the walls of this room, and felt her heart stop.

Abruptly, turning her over, he touched her face with his blue summer gaze. "I should have Jack shoot me now and just get it over with."

"You haven't failed my father."

Morgan vigorously pumped cold water into the sink. Water spilled into a porcelain bowl. He bent and washed his face. Bracing both palms on the sink rim, he looked sick.

She would not let Morgan make her the yoke around his neck: the mistake he made during a moment of uncontrolled lust.

"I know my own mind," Lacey said to his back. Her fingers found solace in the thin folds of her skirt. She sounded more like a diplomat than a woman on the verge of an emotional collapse. "It's not as if I'm going to make you marry me. Not if you don't want to," she said quietly. Then upped her chin. "I won't marry a man for any reason less than love. The kind that lasts forever."

"How noble."

"I guess that counts you out."

"After today?" He snorted. "I guess you're right."

Lacey tried to swallow the silly surge of tears. Brushing futilely at her cheeks, she crossed her arms.

Morgan dried his face on a towel. Little blue posies dotted the rag. "I'm a territorial marshal, Lacey. And ten kinds of fool."

"Only one kind." She smiled, beckoning him to look at her. "But when you decide that we're good for each other, you'll be perfect."

He lifted his face from the towel. His hair was wet. "You're plum loco, Lacey. Loco." He tossed down the towel, and snatching up his hat from the counter, walked past her out of the kitchen. "I've never known anyone like you in my whole life."

"Is that good or bad?"

Her words swung him around, and he stared at her wedged in a sliver of sunlight. It was the only warmth left in the room, and she stayed cradled within its embrace.

"Lacey." She thought his eyes softened in the shadow beneath his hat. "I can't promise you a future."

Clasping her hands behind her back, she studied her boot as it traced a scratch on the floor. "Can you promise that I'll see you tomorrow?"

He bent to retrieve his gloves from the table beside the door. Crystal tinkled as the lamp vibrated. "I have to go."

Just like that, he was going to walk out of her life. "Maybe you would like me better if I were a French strumpet." She slapped a hand on her waist and sashayed around him. "Is that what you want me to be? Then you can bed me with a clear conscience."

Sliding on one glove, he settled his gaze on her breasts, making his point clear. He no longer had a conscience.

"Oh, you . . ." Swear words failed her. "Never come back then."

His gloved hand moved behind her to the door. Suddenly, as if caught by a vague sense of uncertainty, he hesitated. She blinked up into his face. His breath was a whisper's touch from her lips. For a pair of heartbeats, neither moved.

"I *will* be back."

"You will?"

His free hand curled around her cheek. "As soon as I can."

Then his mouth moved over hers, a flutter, more powerful than light. When she opened her eyes again, he was gone.

Chapter Fourteen

"Are you and Marshal Caine gonna get hitched?"

Lacey choked on the apple she was chewing. "Wherever did you hear that?" She eyed her errant brother. The sun had begun to set more than an hour ago. A chill was in the air.

"Everyone in town is talking. Ma calls it gossip, and said I ain't supposed to listen. But heck fire, sis, I can't be covering my ears every time someone talks. I'll be rubbing them clean off."

"There are no marriage plans for me, Joshua."

Water splashed as Lacey readjusted her backside on the edge of the horse trough where she sat. She'd rolled her breeches to her knees and now found bliss in dunking her sore feet. An afternoon of horseback riding lessons showed readily in her hair and posterior. Dust and straw littered the water.

"Besides"—she sat straighter—"who'd want me? I'm about as green as they come for this country. Practically worthless. I have to make myself useful to be any good to anyone."

"You have pretty hair. And you make good apple pies."

Lacey snorted. Tossing the apple core away, she leaned over

and picked another apple from the basket. The movement made her groan.

"And you're riding real good, too," Joshua cheerfully added. "Jack told Ma so. I'm not even embarrassed to be seen with you now."

Biting into the apple, Lacey eyed her horse. Jack was bent over the back of one hoof talking to her father's wrangler. "Jack is good with horses."

He'd been so patient teaching her to ride, too. Never once saying that she couldn't do what she set her mind on, believing in her even when doubts plagued her so.

"Has Jack never married at all?"

Joshua wiggled a toe in the water. "He had him a wife once, and a little girl," he quietly said, his tone reminding Lacey that it was impolite to gossip. But he told her anyway. "Ma said they died a long time ago when they came west on the wagon train."

Lacey looked at the hills. This land swallowed the weak.

"Is it true that you applied for Ma's old teaching spot?"

"Having me at school can't be any worse than having your mother as a teacher, can it?" She finished the apple and dropped it beside the other three cores. "That is, if I get the job. The town council asked me questions about ranching, farming, and even gold mining. They were all pretty astonished that someone could grow up in this world and know so little about so much."

"Maybe you can learn us all how to dance and curtsy."

She kicked water on him. "And maybe I'll just dunk you in this trough and teach you to swim. I do know how to read and write."

"Lacey?" Josh asked after a moment. "Aren't you lonely out here at night with no one to talk to? Afraid?"

Her heart squeezed when she found Joshua watching her as if he were the one afraid. She handed him a towel, and together they walked back to the house. There was something to be said when her only companion in this world was a ten-year-old boy. One that might even be her half brother if their shared birthmarks meant anything.

"I love this place." She sighed, feeling completely secure.

Nestled in a valley at the hilly base of a mountain range that stretched into British Columbia, Kingston's simplistic charm blended with the surrounding knolls and forested hills. The town boasted seven dusty streets hopscotching the majority of the small valley with makeshift shelters, false-front wooden buildings, and two-story structures that made an attempt at modern architecture. In the weeks since she'd been here, she'd explored the town and the hills beyond.

And there was something of Lorraine that touched deep into Lacey's core, going beyond the internal struggles in her life.

Later, Lacey sat on the porch and watched Jack and Joshua ride away. Listening to the wagon rattle over the hill, she curled her arms around her knees and, drawing in her breath, took in this new world. Distant lightning illuminated the faraway mountains but overhead a dome of stars glittered against the indigo, velvet sky. The middle of October signaled the change of seasons in the surrounding mountains. In daylight, the colors of fall painted the hills in a sunburst of reds and golds. Lacey had never known such beauty. She pulled it inside her where it warmed her, especially at night when the sheltered valley yielded to the brisk chill sweeping down from the mountains. When she'd curl in bed with her pillow, watching the sky, and wonder if Morgan did the same.

Colin pulled his gaze from Morgan's back. "How long has he been up there?" Settling deeper into his jacket, Colin spread his hands out to the fire. Morgan had been on the hill smoking those damn cheroots and staring at the sky since they set camp two hours ago.

"Friend"—Caleb spat a wad of brown juice—"he's been a lawman most all his life. I'm of a mind that he's thinking about things he's never considered before."

Colin considered this with a frown. For days now, there'd been no sign of those outlaws dogging their trail since Waylen Springs.

Twice Colin had thwarted their efforts to rob the wagon train during the past weeks, even killing three outlaws in the process. Now, as Colin approached Kingston, the gang had disappeared without a trace. He'd expected Morgan to take up their trail once he'd arrived two days ago.

"Lovesick." Caleb grinned. "That's what he is. Ain't actin' normal at all. Sayin' thank you and please. Ain't even had to tear him off Jared, neither. Not once. That girl of yers did a fine job of getting beneath his skin."

"Morgan told you this?"

"Didn't have to. A man with eyes can see fer hisself what those two feel fer each other."

Crossing his arms, Colin sat back against the rock where his saddle lay. A sudden gnawing worry took hold. Life had come full circle in twenty years, and Colin was no longer the hunted man who'd run from Virginia. He'd carved a life out of this wilderness. He had a family. A brand-new son. A future.

He valued Morgan's friendship as he valued the air he breathed. Lacey and Morgan were so ill-suited personally that he'd never thought twice about asking Morgan to protect her.

"Can a man truly bury his past, Caleb?"

"Is it his past you're worryin' on, or yers?"

Colin lifted his gaze and met Caleb's squarely.

"Like the fact that yer girl looks more like yer wife than she should, or that yer not her real pa." Caleb spat tobacco into the fire. "I seen that mark on her shoulder. The same brand that Joshua has. And me bein' the finest tracker in this territory, I'd be remiss if I didn't put together all the pieces. Now, if yer askin' my opinion if you should walk up there and tell that man the truth . . . what do you think? Let the past lie, friend, and maybe time will bury it fer both of you."

The sound of riders approaching stirred the camp. Men roused from their bedrolls. Jared, who was standing guard, walked into the flickering circle of firelight. Two soldiers thundered into camp, their horses lathered and sawing hard.

The younger man slid off the saddle and stumbled. Breathing hard, he faced Colin. "Is Marshal Caine still riding with you?"

Colin turned to see Morgan approaching. The shadows hid his face beneath his hat.

"Marshal"—the young corporal handed Morgan a missive—

"this just came in from Flat Springs. I was told to find you at once."

Morgan read the missive. His fist closed around the paper. "When did this happen?"

"A few hours ago. They killed the deputy and two other men. They're headed to Kingston. We've telegraphed the marshal's office."

"Christ." Morgan's gaze lifted, and fear pummeled Colin. "Your spread is between Flat Springs and the town."

Colin caught his sleeve. "What, man? What is it?"

Morgan jammed the crushed missive into his hand. "Brett Lawton is alive."

Lacey lifted her baby brother from his bassinet to bring him to Lorraine. At once, he stopped his squalling, and Lacey stared in awe as their eyes connected. All his fingers and toes wiggled. She touched his soft downy scalp, reverently awed at the precious miracle of life, wondering suddenly what Morgan's child would look like.

Lacey's effort to dismiss the coincidence of Joshua's birthmark was not hampered by the disappointing discovery that her new brother didn't possess one.

"I would like to think of Joshua's mark as a kiss from an angel." Lorraine answered Lacey's previous query as she tucked the baby against her breast. "But some folks claim birthmarks are inherited."

Such an idea illuminated the possibility of Colin passing down the birthmark. She realized that this was what her father most likely wanted to discuss with her once they were together again as a family.

"Hello."

Lacey's head came up at the tone of Jolene's voice. Feeling the older woman's eyes boring into her, Lacey remained composed as she turned. Jolene's dark eyes went over her. Today Lacey wore a white blouse and split-wool riding skirt. Undoubtedly, Jolene always expected her to make an appearance in flounces, and could never quite contain her surprise when she showed up looking markedly dull.

"I found this letter in my box outside," Jolene said. "It's

from the mayor's office. I don't know why they sent it here."

Jolene handed her the letter. Lacey's heart raced in anticipation. Trying not to show her excitement, she stared at the letter. What if the council didn't want her?

"Open it," Lorraine encouraged.

Carefully, Lacey tore open the crisp white envelope, aware that everyone was waiting. Lacey scanned the letter.

"Well, hurry, child. Don't keep us waiting."

Swallowing over the sudden lump, she met Lorraine's hopeful gaze. "I'm not hired."

Lorraine laughed. "But of course you are. Why wouldn't . . . they're fools that's what they are. Why not?"

"They said I was too young." Her attempt to sound unaffected failed dismally, and she cast her gaze out the window rather than face Lorraine or Jolene.

Outside, it was nearing dusk, and she turned away, suddenly anxious to leave. Her feelings were horribly reminiscent of England where she'd been a complete social outcast.

Her throat felt tight. Lacey hurried into the drawing room and removed Morgan's buckskin off a peg on the wall.

Jolene followed her into the room. "I'm sorry."

Lacey shrugged into Morgan's buckskin. "You don't seem surprised," she said without turning.

"Everything about you surprises me," Jolene answered dryly, and Lacey turned. "But I know how much you wanted that job."

Lacey didn't want Jolene to be her foe. Under different circumstances, she would have tried to cultivate a friendship with this woman. Jolene was strong, independent, a successful entrepreneur in a man's world, and beautiful. Morgan's equal in everything.

"Despite that"—she pointed toward the letter still clutched in her hand—"the people here are pretty fair. And nice." Jolene walked to the window and fingered the yellow curtains. "Have you met my brother, Jared, yet?" The question startled Lacey. "But of course you have. You both traveled on the same wagon train together for weeks."

"He spoke of you often."

"After Shannon, I was hoping to see him find a new lady love," Jolene said absently.

"Shannon?" Lacey's curiosity drew Jolene around.

"Morgan's half sister," she said. "Jared was smitten with her, but she wouldn't give my poor brother the time of day. Spent most of her time camped on that reservation with her Indian relatives." Jolene sighed. "Jared would make a fine beau."

"Why are you telling me this?"

"Maybe because I want to like you, and I'm not sure that I do. But I care for Jared, and I think he would want to know you." Jolene's composure suddenly deserted her, and she turned to stare outside. "I'm not in love with Morgan, if that's what you're thinking this is about. I quit trying a long time ago. And when I did, we became friends. He's never behaved any less than a gentleman around me."

Clutching the crumpled letter to her chest, Lacey felt something inside her lift. They were merely . . . friends. Not lovers.

Jolene opened the door. "Jack is good at cheering people up. Maybe you can ask him to tell you one of his tall tales. I just left him at the office. The telegraph is down, and he's waiting for word from the man he sent out earlier to check."

"Is that normal? The telegraph, I mean?"

She shrugged. "It happens mostly in winter with the ice."

Lacey hesitated at the door. Then without another word, she walked out the door and down the steps. A cold breeze nipped her face. Distant storm clouds gathered. Star was tied to the hitching post across from the marshal's office where Lacey had left her earlier. Stopping to smell a lilac vine, she dawdled, and told herself again that the teaching job didn't matter. But she knew it was a lie.

Lacey kicked at a pebble. And exhaled her disappointment, determined to stay optimistic. Her lungs froze.

In the distance a bilge of heavy black smoke spewed into the sky, spreading like a disease over the tops of the pine trees.

"My God!" The words closed her throat.

Her father's house was on fire!

Heart pounding, Lacey shoved past the people filling the streets and ran toward Jack's office.

Above the chaos, her panicked mind registered the sound of approaching riders. All around Lacey, people screamed and scattered in terror, leaving her standing rooted to the street.

A solid rank of men drew rein at the end of the street, their foam-flecked horses blowing and stomping in a fierce show of force, as certain as the hard breed that casually sat their saddles.

A hand clamped on her arm, yanking her over the board-walk and into the marshal's office. The door slammed. Jack swept past her to the desk. Jolene stood by the desk. "He's supposed to be dead, Jack! What happened!" Panic laced her voice. "How did he escape?"

"I don't know." Jack thumbed bullets into a gun. His eyes lifted. Fierce. So like Morgan's. He asked Lacey, "You still got that shooter in your pocket?"

Was he asking if she could kill someone? There was no time to ask him to explain what was happening. "Get out, both of you. And for God's sake make sure Joshua and Lorraine stay hidden."

Jack grabbed his Spencer. "They're probably going for the bank."

Jolene stopped him. "Brett Lawton will kill yo—"

The door crashed open, and smashed against the wall.

Lacey whirled—and froze.

Guns drawn, four men fanned out in the room, their heavy spurs jangling on the hardwood floor, the only sound in the stunned silence. The tall one drew a bead on Jack, cocking the trigger as Jack swung his own gun up, meeting him equally from across the room. Glaring at each other down the sights of their barrels, neither man moved. Then the gun in the other man's hand shifted imperceptibly to Lacey—and she found herself staring into the black emptiness of the steel barrel. Her knees almost folded. A faint cloying nausea rose in her throat. Even the sound of her ragged breathing stilled.

Eyes as cold as lake water narrowed. "Drop the gun, Kipp, or this doll will have a hole in her face the size of your fist."

Lacey's heart froze. Her eyes slid past the barrel to the man who held the gun. The lean planes of his tanned face boasted a hint of southern aristocracy. At one time, he might have been considered handsome before the scar running from his mouth to his eye ravaged his appearance. Beneath the dusty brim of his confederate-gray hat, his hair was fair. Lacey had never seen a man more confident in his deadly arrogance to put the fear of God in his victims' faces.

Instinct told her this man was Brett Lawton. And she'd looked once before into that face of death. In her nightmares.

Jack's gun seemed to dip slightly. Lacey felt his struggle as he considered the futility of his stand. She wanted to scream at him to keep his gun, but this man's eyes paralyzed her.

Hesitantly, the gun lowered, then finally slammed against the desk. A savage oath followed, and Jack raised his hands. Spurs rattled. Lawton stepped to the desk. He handed Jack's gun over his shoulder. Someone jumped forward to retrieve it. The Spencer followed. He leaned into the desk, his face dark with anger. "Where the hell is that bastard who calls himself a federal marshal?"

"Obviously it's your lucky day, Lawton."

"Ah, the faithful Uncle Jack." Lawton backhanded him.

The office grew ominously still. Lawton's assessing gaze fell first on Jolene then Lacey. A ball of ice formed in her gut. She wanted to curl into the corner and make herself as tiny as possible. Anything to escape the touch of those eyes.

"How'd you do it, Lawton?" Lacey heard Jack ask, but Lawton's eyes remained fixed on her.

Spurs jangling in the heavy silence, Lawton came to stand before her. "A good woman and fifty thousand in gold buys a man a lot of justice in this country. A poorer man hanged in my place."

With horror, Lacey remembered the man who had fought and struggled on the gallows that wretched day. All the prisoners had worn black hoods.

"If it makes you feel better, sweet"—Lawton tipped her chin—"the man would have hanged anyway."

One hand wrapped around the braided coil of her hair while the other gripped her chin, forcing her to look directly into Lawton's cold eyes. She tried to turn away. His fingers dug into the soft flesh of her face compelling her to look at him.

Lacey hated that her fear showed so readily. It trembled through her like a quaking aspen.

He looked over his shoulder at his men. "Get back to me after the men finish cleaning out the bank." Lawton grinned malevolently at Jack. "We figure this town owes us big for all the trouble we've been through. We're going to settle with the bank for that. The other debt is with Caine. I figure what I take today is just a down payment for all the trouble he's put me through."

"For God's sake, don't do it, Lawton," Jack hissed.

The door swung open. "Horses comin', Cap'n, from Ashton's place. They're comin' at a run." The man stomped in from the street, and Lacey stared into the eyes of Sam Gressett.

Surprise and shock were simultaneous for them both. Her hands clenched, and instantly she felt the gun in her pocket.

"Cap'n, that's *her*!"

"I know who she is." Lawton grinned. "You've grown since I last saw you."

"Impossible." Lacey took a step back, stopping as the desk hit her legs. "I don't . . . know you."

"But I know *you*, Lacey." Lawton raised his gun. "And now, what am I to do with all of you? I can't be having anyone following, now can I?" He turned his gun on Jack.

"No!" Lacey pulled out her gun before she could breathe, or question her ability to kill. This was not the same as shooting at the sky, or bottles. She cocked the hammer on the gun, and it almost slipped from her moist grasp. "I swear . . . I'll shoot!"

Lawton's slow smile crept through Lacey. "Get out, boys. She looks just terrified enough to accidentally pull that trigger."

When the office was empty, Lawton casually turned his gun on Lacey. Her own gun visibly shook in her hands. Outside she could hear screaming. Glass shattered as Lawton's men shot up the street.

"They call this a Mexican standoff where I come from, girl." Lawton chuckled. "Or is it a Virginia wallbanger?"

"Just get out, Lawton," Jack whispered. "Leave her alone."

Lawton held her gaze. "You know I can't do that. But to

be fair . . ." The gun muzzle raked Jolene, then Jack. Mocking. Taunting.

Pull the trigger! the voice screamed in her head.

Lawton cocked the gun. "You always were in the way, Jack." He shrugged eloquently and fired.

Lacey screamed. Flame stabbed from his gun, exploding in the enclosed room. The bullet slammed Jack backward against the wall. Lawton fired again. Jack crumpled headlong into the floor.

A strangled sob broke. Lacey's breath came too hard. Too fast. Her gasps filled the space around her, enclosing her in a vise, choking her. Tugging his battered gray hat down on his head, Lawton assessed the gun in her hands. Hot tears streamed from her eyes. He walked toward her until the barrel touched his heart.

"Give Ashton a message for me." His whisper moved the hair on her temple. "I want my son. And I want Caine to deliver him. Will you tell him that?"

Lacey tried to nod, tried to respond. She couldn't breathe.

A contemptuous smile spread across his scarred features. "Until next time, Lacey." Dipping with eloquent flair, he bowed out the door and with harried grace, swept onto the saddle of a waiting horse. The last to leave, the horse did a prancing circle, before Lawton spurred him hard and disappeared in a thunder of hooves.

The acrid smell of gunpowder lingered in the air, pressing against her. Her hands remained frozen on the trigger. Through the tangle of her hair, her gaze fell on Jack.

There was so much blood.

She struggled to think. Her legs wouldn't move. Her mind was frozen. Her eyes locked on Jolene's horrified face. At any moment, people would burst into the room.

With a cry, Jolene dropped beside Jack and began to tear at her petticoat, ripping it to shreds. The action spurred Lacey, and she jammed the gun back into her pocket, missing twice. Her legs gave out, and she dropped beside Jack. His heavy buckskin had become soaked. She wasn't wearing a petticoat beneath her riding skirt and had no way to stem the lifeblood pooling over the floor, around her knees and into her skirt. In desperation, she pushed her hands against the wounds. Blood seeped through her fingers.

"You should have killed that bastard," Jolene hissed.

Lord, there was so much blood.

Somewhere Lacey could hear raised voices. Her head lifted, and she peered blankly out the open doorway. The breeze had shifted into the room and the door knocked against the wall. Outside the sky had darkened to a prophetic gray. All this she absorbed in a brace of seconds as nothing more significant than the shadows on the wall reached into her mind. Boots thudded on the walkway. Then Morgan was standing in the doorway with his gun drawn. Lacey heard her own gasp, unable to keep the anguish from her voice.

Days of trail dirt coated his clothes a dusty gray. Blue eyes, stark against the black stubble on his face, dropped to her in cold alarm. She felt the jolt of fear in his eyes.

Then the door filled with people. Her father and Jared squeezed into the room. Colin took in the situation at a glance and immediately called for a doctor.

Jared pulled Jolene away from Jack. Lacey watched helplessly as Morgan and her father moved Jack to a wagon outside. Lacey shut her eyes. Voices were everywhere, like angry wasps in her head. A man returned with news of Joshua and Lorraine. The bank had been robbed.

"Lacey?" Morgan's voice was a command. She opened her eyes.

He pulled her to her feet. Someone handed him a wet rag. He wiped the blood from her hands. She watched his gloved fingers work over hers. Slowly, his eyes lifted to hers and held. She eased her hands away and clasped them behind her back unable to bear it that he should see their ugliness.

"Lacey . . ."

She leaned slightly in to his body, needing desperately to feel his heartbeat. He cupped her face between hands that trembled and kissed the corner of her eyes. "I have to go to Jack."

She nodded. His place was beside his uncle. Not her.

"Go with your father, Lacey."

Again, she nodded, because she didn't know what else to

do. Then he was gone, and her father took her in his arms. "Let me get you out of this place."

"Who is Lawton's son?" she choked out in a hushed whisper.

Lacey didn't miss the startled flash in his eyes. A sudden fear stabbed through Lacey. The realization of whom he was protecting stole into her. Her eyes widened in horror and as her control slipped away like icy rivulets of water running through her fingers, she backed away from him.

What Brett Lawton was. What he did to Jack. His threats to Morgan. To her.

His son was Joshua!

"Lacey"—her father took her by the shoulders—"for God's sake . . . Joshua is just a young boy. He doesn't know. It was supposed to be over for all of us."

"And no one thought to tell me? No one at all?"

"Listen to me!" Her father wrestled her wrists.

Irrational rage, white-hot, shot through her. "What other lies have you told me? What haven't you told me? Who are you, Daddy? Who are you that you would let this happen?"

No longer controlled, his eyes bore into hers. He cupped her chin, compelling her to look at him. But Lacey resisted his embrace. It was too late. Her fury was mixed with so many incomprehensible emotions, she could no longer think. "I know how you feel," he whispered against her hair. The same place Lawton had touched.

"You don't know anything about me!"

With all her strength, she swung her fist and hit him across the face. Before anyone could grab her, she ran out the door.

She had to get away, flee the brutality and the insanity that had suddenly taken hold of her—and the whole world.

She wanted to go home. Back to England.

Home. To Clare.

People were gathered in a half-circle around the office, their ghost-white faces a fragile barrier to the painful reality that was swallowing Lacey. She slowed, and her hand lifted against her mouth to still the sob. Then she bolted and ran.

Behind her, the crowd surged forward, cutting Colin off as they fired questions at him from all directions. Lacey was on her horse before her father reached her. The mare reared and leaped forward, tearing up the street with a distance-eating gait.

She didn't stop until the town was a pale glimmer in the valley behind her.

Chapter Fifteen

Nothing remained of the moon when Lacey drew rein at the forest edge overlooking the smoldering remnants of her father's beautiful house. Her home. Trees swayed like wild banshees. The wind whipped against her face, tearing her hair from the remains of a braid. The air smelled of smoke. The stench of burned wood and ruined dreams.

The encroaching storm agitated her horse, and Lacey tightened her grip on the reins. Wiping the moisture from her face, she stared over the rocky edge of the hill. Desolate cedar scrub blocked her descent. She could bear to go no farther.

Lightning sluiced against the surrounding hills. The first splatter of raindrops heralded the tempest's arrival.

Lacey lifted her face, offering herself to the powerful cleansing of the torrential rainfall. Jack's lifeblood stained her clothes and body. She reeked of death.

The horror of Brett Lawton's brutality crashed down on her with a vengeance. When she should have been strong, she'd proved only that she was weak. Her hands trembled on the reins. She lifted her chin, letting the rain pummel her face unmercifully. Lacey couldn't find the strength to fight the terrible rage inside.

She felt betrayed by the secrets. By her own cowardice and a past she didn't understand. Brett Lawton had known her as a child. She'd been a child in Virginia.

Joshua was his son.

Lacey's heart shriveled at the very image of her gentle stepmother's association with Lawton. The relationship was inconceivable. Repugnant. It made sense now why Morgan had taken Brett Lawton to San Francisco—far away from Washington—to be tried for other heinous crimes. Crimes horrible enough to see the man hang, without bringing Lorraine and Joshua into the public eye. He'd been protecting them from scandal. He'd been protecting Joshua.

"Morgan," she whispered. What price had he paid for his loyalty to Colin? The murder of his beloved sister. Now, after everything, Lawton still lived.

She could have killed him. If she had pulled the trigger, Jack would still be alive.

Star nickered.

Drawing in a shuddering breath, Lacey opened her eyes and wiped the hair from her face. The rain had stopped. Nothing moved but the restless wind through the trees. Star had wandered during the storm.

Forcing herself to remain within the cover of the woods, Lacey studied the night. She didn't know where she was. She ran her hand beneath the golden mane plastered to Star's neck. Nudging her horse, Lacey let Star find her own way over the rocks. The valley opened before her.

Suddenly, her mare's head snapped up. A shadow came out of the night. Jared's stallion whinnied, and her mare answered.

Lacey's heart beat in relief. She urged Star out of hiding. "You found me."

Jared caught the bridle of her horse, swinging her mare alongside his bigger stallion.

Neither horse liked the proximity to the other. "What are you doing?" Alarmed, she gripped the reins on her skittish mare.

"Everyone is out looking for you. I just now found your tracks. Frankly, I thought you possessed more sense than to run off."

Lacey's fingers bit into his, trying to make him release Star's bridle. "Let go, Jared. You're hurting her."

"I have to know something before . . . everyone else gets here."

She looked past him. "Before my father. Why?"

"Was there ever a chance for us?"

"Jared, this is hardly the time—" His grip on her mare tightened. "No," she said carefully. "There was never a chance."

Lacey watched in confusion as Jared dropped his hand and pulled a silver flask from beneath his slicker. "Was it him?" His voice was flat. "Caine?"

Lacey shrank from his gaze. Something was terribly wrong. She gripped the reins, edging Star away.

Uncapping the flask, Jared looked over at Lacey, regarding her stunned expression with amusement. "Should I offer you some?"

"I'm leaving now."

"And begrudge a wounded man your company?" he mocked, swigging from the flask. "I've had one hell of a couple of weeks, Lacey. And frankly, I'm just not in the mood anymore to be honorable."

Lacey was too shocked to feel anything beyond disbelief. The whole world had gone mad. "You were the one who gave us away after we left the wagon train?" The smile remained fixed on Jared's face. "My father . . . all those people who trusted you? Why?"

"For money."

"Money!" The notion was inconceivable. "How much money could be enough to make someone commit murder and thievery?"

"The only thing I did for *pleasure* was poison that damn cat of yours. It belonged to Morgan. I hated the pathetic thing."

Her insides gave. "She was a little kitten, Jared."

Lightning shattered the black sky overhead, and time froze in that one blinding flash. At least a dozen riders fanned out across the valley, were advancing toward her. Reality struck. She swung her gaze back to Jared and knew he saw the look of terror in her eyes.

Jared was going to hand her over to the Lawton gang!

"Your marshal isn't going to have anything to do with you after Lawton finishes with you," he sneered. "No man will."

His confidence was his undoing. He barely reined back as the gun flashed in her hand. Disbelief still registered on his face when she fired. Though in her heart she wanted to put a bullet between his miserable double-crossing eyes, Lacey aimed at the ground beneath his horse instead. The gunshot cracked into the night.

Black arched and bucked, tossing Jared out of the saddle. Lacey's horse reared. Pulling hard on the reins, Lacey swung around, vaulting forward into a full run. She lost the gun. She didn't have time to react. It was enough staying in the saddle at a dead run in the dark of night.

The field swept by Lacey in a shadowed blur echoed by the thunder of Star's hooves. Stretching low against the mare's neck, Lacey's braid slapped behind her like a tattered rope. Panic and exhaustion sent her heart racing. She wiped her eyes, keeping them focused on the ground. She dared not risk a glance behind her.

The gully came out of the darkness. Fear tore a gasp from her lungs. Clutching the reins, she braced her weight against the stirrups, praying she had the skill to stay in the saddle. The horse jumped—and she was in the air. Behind her, she could hear shouting and running horses. Hitting the other side with pantherlike grace, the palomino crashed into a line of trees. She was lost.

Branches slapped her. The horse stumbled. She knew she would have to slow her pace or seriously injure her mare.

But fear of falling into Brett Lawton's hands paralyzed her reasoning. Lacey broke free from the trees into an open meadow. Her blouse was hot with the mare's sweat. She stifled her tears. The horse hurdled a fallen log, slamming her against the saddle with enough force to knock her teeth together. Unable to negotiate the treacherous path, the horse stumbled and went down to its knees.

Lacey screamed. The ground hit her, smashing the wind from her lungs. She rolled onto her belly and lay panting in the grass. Through the rush in her ears, she made out the sound of riders crashing through the woods. Struggling to push herself up on one elbow, she sucked in huge gulps of air. Whipping her gaze frantically around her surroundings, she gasped at the sight of her horse lying against a fallen log, its attempts to stand useless on a lame leg.

"Star!"

Something moved in the darkness, taking the shape of a pony as it approached. A spotted pony. An Appaloosa. Before Lacey could register this new threat, she was looking dazedly up at a familiar face. His frown masked the concern in his dark eyes as he stared down at her from atop his horse.

"Autumn Star," the deep voice came out of the darkness, "I am truly sorry to meet you again under these circumstances."

Lacey gasped at Hawk. She pushed herself to her feet and grimaced at the pain in her ribs. "Run—"

"You will do exactly as I say, Autumn Star," he said, cutting her off. The sound of pursuit grew more ominous. "Or you and I both will be dead."

"I . . . don't understand."

He leaned and, gripping her arm, lifted her up onto the horse. She cried out against the pain that wrapped around her chest as he pulled her against him. "Remember. Fear." She heard his harsh command against her cheek.

The ground trembled. A dozen lathered horses crashed through the trees, and Lacey felt the muscles in Hawk's chest bunch with the effort to bring the horse under control. All around them, horses snorted and pawed, blowing steam from lungs weak with exertion. When Lacey faced Lawton again, a rifle was steady in Hawk's grip.

"Just so you do not get the impression that I am here because I have a fondness for your company," Hawk remarked, training his rifle on Brett Lawton.

With the battered confederate-gray hat slanted over his eyes, Lawton leaned negligently against the pommel of his saddle and said nothing.

"You gotta lot a nerve, breed!" Gressett sneered, flagging

his own gun threateningly. "Didn't think to see you again after you ran out on Frank an' the boys at the river."

"I am not here to trade insults with you, Gressett." His gun never wavered past Lawton. "I have been tracking this girl."

"And here she is," Lawton said, his insolent appraisal never wavering from Lacey.

"Her foolishness is gold in my pocket," Hawk said.

Lawton's eyes sliced back to Hawk. "Where is my kid?"

"Kipp has had him too well guarded. But this one—" Hawk lifted the cold edge of his rifle and ran it along the length of Lacey's arm. "This one has a penchant for folly."

Lawton nudged his horse alongside Hawk's. A gloved hand cupped Lacey's chin, forcing her eyes to his. His gaze slid down her wet blouse, and she knew with a shrinking horror he could see through the rain-soaked cloth beneath the opened buckskin. She was conscious of the smirking grins of the others. Lawton lowered his hand to her thigh, testing the folds of her skirt.

"No gun?" he mocked.

Lacey could barely breathe.

"Put your hardware away, boys. We wouldn't want to maim our prize catch, now would we?" He grinned malevolently. "Considering the years I've been waiting for this. No, indeed."

"What do you want from me?" Lacey's faint question drew a new round of crude remarks.

"What do I want from you?" Lawton repeated with dismay. "Why, everything, my dear."

"But . . . I have nothing."

"My son. Your father's wealth. Caine's life. Revenge—" He waved his hand casually. "You're a veritable treasure with many possibilities. And I'm collecting them all."

Lightning shattered the stillness around them. Lacey's eyes strayed beyond Lawton and narrowed on Jared. "How could you? Jolene is your sister. This man could have killed her tonight."

Jared turned his gaze on Lawton. Lawton laughed. "Jared knows business is business. Shannon found that out the hard way, didn't she, son?" The statement came out of nowhere, and Jared froze.

Lacey couldn't remove her eyes from Jared's face. She was sick. Behind her, Hawk felt like stone.

"You murdered Shannon?" she rasped.

"Some of the boys had sportin' fun with that one," Lawton continued. "Unfortunately, I couldn't join in the festivities personally, but Jared here is very good at tying up loose ends. Aren't you, son?"

"Shut your mouth, Brett."

Lawton twisted in the saddle. "Don't get cocky on me, you little bastard. Now get back to town. When they find out we've taken the girl, all hell's going to break loose."

"It already has, Brett," Jared blandly reminded him. "You didn't exactly leave the town any gentle reminders of your passing."

"The posse should rival the occasion." Lawton fixed Lacey with a cold stare. "When we finish with them, they'll rue the day they ever crossed my path. Ashton will have to trade the son he stole from me, if he wants to save your neck. Caine will come because I have you. Among other things, it's his job to lead that posse."

Lacey felt her throat constrict. Fear waged with desperation. She felt Hawk's grip tighten around her waist, warning her against acting impulsively. She wanted to rip his arm from its hold.

Thunder erupted overhead, spooking the horses.

"Back trail the girl," Lawton instructed the two men wearing dark slickers on his left. "Make sure she was alone up there on that hill." He looked pointedly at Jared. "We wouldn't want anything to happen to our informant because of his arrogance."

The men swung their horses away and galloped off. The force of Lawton's attention returned to Lacey. After a moment his gaze slid up to Hawk's. "You look intent on keeping the girl yourself."

"I do not trust you," Hawk said stoically. "After I get my gold, you can do what you want with her."

Lawton leaned against the saddle horn. "No honor among thieves?"

"There is not enough honor among the lot of us to fill a spoon."

"I could kill you now and be done with you."

"You will need me to guide you over the mountains after this is over. Who among you knows the way?" Hawk challenged.

"Where did you go after leaving the river?" Lawton suddenly asked.

Hawk's gaze impaled Jared. "Back to the village. My men are not outlaws and tired easily of that man's game." His voice was mild.

"You're the incompetent, Hawk," Jared hissed.

Tension penetrated Lacey's numbed senses. Lawton just kept staring as if he had the power to dive into her mind, or Hawk's. Maybe he did. "The girl will ride with you until we reach camp." She barely heard Lawton reply. "Then you'll turn her over to the watchful eye of my woman."

Hawk nodded. Lawton lifted the gun hidden between his gloved hands on the saddle. He swung his horse around to Lacey's palomino, his intentions all too clear.

"What are you doing?" Lacey cried.

"She's lame," he informed her. "Useless things are destroyed."

Lacey screamed as Lawton fired. The single bullet slammed into her beautiful Star. She watched in horror as her horse thrashed, finally succumbing to death. Hawk swung his mount around. Lawton's men turned and fell in beside them.

Lightning streaked across the sky barely ahead of the thunder rolling with the devil's fury across the valley. They were heading toward the distant mountains.

"Why are you doing this, Hawk?" She could not stop the tears.

"Fear me," he whispered savagely against her ear. "I am one of them."

"I don't believe you!" she cried.

He didn't reply.

"You're letting Morgan walk into a trap."

"I'm counting on it."

Lacey stared into the bleak coldness of the night and, knew with certainty that she was riding with them all into hell.

Morgan came awake with a start. His head rested on his hands. Scraping his fingers through his hair, he sat up. On the table beside him, the flickering light from the lamp cast a pale halo around the bed. Jack's labored breathing could be heard over the patter of rain.

Jolene was at the window looking out. Dawn crept over the mountains to the east.

"Listen," Jolene whispered; then he heard it, too.

At once, he joined her at the window. The sound registered ominously in the bleak stillness of the room: the sound of approaching riders. The horses were walking with a weary, almost clumsy gait in the muddy street, evidently coming far through the storm and the night.

Colin was out there. Twice, last night, Morgan's restless pacing had taken him to the door to join the search for Lacey. But he couldn't leave Jolene or Jack unprotected. Not with Lawton on the prod. Lacey had needed him. And he hadn't been there for her, anymore than he had for Shannon or Jack. Brett Lawton still lived because he didn't do his job.

"You couldn't have known he was alive," he heard Jolene say.

Morgan braced his hands against the windowsill and glared out the rain-splattered glass. For the first time in his life, he was vulnerable to his emotions. Feelings he hadn't experienced since his father died, and he and his mother were dragged kicking and screaming into captivity. Even after Shannon had died, his hate overwhelmed every volatile feeling. Now he felt it all. Pain. Fear. Helplessness.

The sound of horses grew louder. Moving Jolene out of sight, Morgan watched the street and waited for some clue to the identity of the riders. He didn't wait long. Snapping out an oath, he was out the door before Caleb drew rein in the yard.

A pair of dead men bobbed across the saddles of the two horses plodding behind him. A glimpse of each sagging profile was all Morgan needed to recognize them both. One, a petty thief; the other, a cold-blooded murderer. Caleb's steady gray eyes held Morgan's.

"Reckon Lawton's gonna be two men short," Caleb said shortly, sliding out of the saddle. "Met 'em on that knoll south of Colin's spread. Not too friendly, neither."

Jolene greeted Caleb on the porch with a hot cup of coffee. Behind her, the doctor and his sleepy-eyed wife emerged from their bedroom. After informing the doctor of the two dead men, Caleb followed the wife into a small firelit office. He plunked down in a leather chair.

"Back-trailed the buzzards." Warming his hands around the cup of hot coffee, Caleb's eyes remained steadfastly fixed to the black, steaming brew.

Closing the door behind the doctor's wife, Morgan didn't move as his gaze fixed on the silver-haired man hunkered in the chair. There was a quiet warning in Caleb's expression. Morgan felt nausea stick in his gut.

"Found Miss Ashton's horse. Dead. Looked like the girl met trouble an' tried to make a run fer it . . . before they got her." Caleb's eyes shifted to Jolene's and narrowed. "Jared's with 'em. At least wise that black of his is."

Jolene gasped. "That's impossible."

"Who else would be riding that black stud of his?"

"But how can you be so sure it was Jared's horse?"

"Now that black wears a real particular T shoe on his left hind foot that any half-blind dog could track. Seen it at the wagon train 'fore we left. Surprised that stud ain't already throwed the shoe."

"It couldn't have been Jared." Jolene was desperate as she stood before him. "Please, let him at least explain."

"Explain?" The cold fury in Morgan's voice settled like ice water over the room. "Explain why he was riding with Lawton?"

"Morgan . . . not like this. You'll kill him!" Jolene twisted back to face Caleb. "It was dark. Couldn't you have been mistaken?"

Caleb didn't reply. A body didn't question Caleb's skill, and Jolene looked stricken enough to realize the futility of her hopes. Morgan had heard enough.

Jolene swept around him before he could open the door. "Let me talk to Jared first," she pleaded.

Exhaustion ringed her dark eyes. Morgan saw the fear in her face as she looked up at him. Fear of him.

"He could have ridden out there before everything happened. He went to look for Lacey the same as everyone else."

Her pain drove into Morgan like a fist, and he reined in his own anger. "Trust me to handle this, Jolene."

Morgan heard the words, but the voice belonged to someone else. Another man who was in control of himself. Who knew the dangers of emotions. Who had worked his whole life to develop the hard-edged persona to survive in a world unforgiving of mistakes.

"You won't . . . kill him?"

"I don't kill my prisoners, Jolene," he snapped out savagely. But the narrow line he tread was as thin as it had ever been.

Morgan went once more to Jack's room. He stood over his last living family, and knew he might never see the big man alive again.

Morgan had failed everyone.

For the first time in his life, he questioned his beliefs. Questioned upholding laws that justice could not serve. A system where money bought freedom for the damned and allowed the guilty to dance over their victim's graves. There was something to be said about Hawk's methods of justice—and Morgan, who had never killed except out of self-defense—now contemplated cold-blooded murder.

An hour later, Morgan rode into town. The drizzle changed to a fine mist by the time Morgan neared his office to collect his gear. The day promised to be cold beneath a dreary dome of gray sky. Morgan filled his mind with everything—and nothing at all. His fingers ached against the hard grip he held on the reins of his steel dust.

Morgan suddenly pulled back on the reins.

Jared's black languished at the hitching rail in front of the Fool's Gold Saloon up the street. It wasn't a sight Morgan had expected to see. Marking its lathered state and mud-splattered hocks, Morgan lifted his head and considered the swinging bat wings of the saloon. His searching glance registered no other movement on the street.

Dismounting, he tied his own horse away from the saloon and crossed the muddy street with slow, careful strides. He stepped up on the boardwalk, hesitating in front of the batwing doors. Scanning the shadows within, his gaze stopped on Jared sitting in the far corner of the room hunkered over a glass of rye. Jared's hat was on the table beside a half-emptied bottle of whiskey. His dirt-caked black duster and disheveled appearance clearly belonged to the man who rode that black into town. Morgan felt something primeval stir in his gut.

The barkeeper, who was diligently polishing a score of mugs, glanced up, his hand pausing mid-motion as Morgan pushed through the swinging doors. The spurs on the back of Morgan's boots chinked dully on the wooden floor as he walked past.

Lifting his head from a dazed stupor, Jared's bleary gaze focused first on Morgan's belt buckle, before traveling disdainfully past the badge, to the cold eyes that measured him with dark promise.

"If it isn't our own famous marshal." He grinned, drunkenly. "And what brings you to this social den of impropriety so early in the morning?"

"You're usually more selective in your taste for the local rotgut," Morgan said carefully.

Returning his attention to the bottle, Jared sloshed whiskey over his glass. "Is there some reason why that should matter to you, *Marshal?*" He slurred this last word.

"It'll never hide a conscience, Jared. If you have one to hide."

Jared started to come to his feet but Morgan slammed him back down in the chair. "Where have you been, Jared?"

"What business is it of yours?"

"Now that all depends on your whereabouts the past few hours."

Jared wiped his chin with the back of his hand. "I've been out looking for your English Rose, if you must know." He eyed Morgan with a smirk. "Which is obviously more than you've been doing—"

"You didn't leave town with the search party," Morgan interrupted, his voice a savage echo of his eyes. "Where did you go?"

Jared pushed past Morgan, but the viselike grip on his shoulder kept him from leaving. "Get your hands off me, Caine."

"Answer my question."

Jared stabbed down for his gun but Morgan, already prepared for the movement, slammed him backward against the wall and ripped the weapon furiously from his hand. "You throw down on me, Jared, and so help me I'll kill you." Morgan caught Jared by the shirt and, pinning him to the wall, sent the gun skidding across the floor out of his reach. "To hell with my promise to your sister. Now," he said through clenched teeth, "I'll ask again. Where did you go after you left town?"

"I told you . . ." Jared's eyes shifted nervously, and the glaze in his focus seemed to vanish. "What do you mean . . . what promise to my sister?"

Morgan dampened down his fury and dropped his hands. "That black of yours was shod in Waylen Springs for a contracted heel."

"So what if he was?"

"Any damn fool knows a T shoe leaves a signature an idiot could recognize. Would you like to tell me what that black stud of yours was doing riding with Lawton last night?"

Jared's eyes darkened. Fear flickered across his face. Morgan knew the look. It was the panic of a cornered animal—a damned rat. Jared was guilty as sin. He had betrayed Lacey. Betrayed her to the likes of Lawton and his men.

"You son of a bitch. I should kill you for what you've done."

"I swear . . . it wasn't me!" Jared came around a spindle-backed chair. "She got away from me. I swear. She got away. It was Hawk. *He's* the one who turned her over."

The measure of emotion that swept through Morgan stopped him cold. "Believe it," Jared sneered. "She would have gotten away if not for him. He's taking her to Lawton's camp himself."

Morgan was too late seeing the fist that came up and smashed him in the jaw, sending him reeling backward over the chair.

"Do you know what Lawton's men do to women?" Jared railed wildly, snatching up a bottle. It sailed over Morgan's head, shattering on the floor. "There won't be anything left of her." He launched himself over the chair hammering blindly at Morgan's face, but Morgan dumped him back on the table, sidestepping a booted toe.

Grasping Jared's shirtfront with both his fists, Morgan hauled him against the wall. "Like Shannon, Jared? Were you a part of that as well? Were you?"

Jared swung and missed. Morgan didn't. "Where have they taken Lacey?"

"Don't . . . don't know."

"Where is she?" Morgan flung Jared across a table filled with stacked chips and cards, spilling everything to the floor. "You know where they are!" He dragged Jared back by the collar across the floor, jerking him to his feet. Morgan found his hands around Jared's throat. "Where is she?"

"It's . . . too late," he gasped. "Lawton will kill her . . . if he doesn't get Joshua."

Morgan's grip tightened on Jared's throat. Rage surged unchecked through every thought, every taut muscle. Lacey would face the same horror as Shannon, and Morgan couldn't help her any more than he could help his sister. He could tear Jared's heart from his chest, and it wouldn't release the fury consuming him.

Jared's eyes flew to a spot past Morgan.

Morgan knew an instant too late that he'd just made a fatal error in judgment. Someone had come up behind him. He spun, but his swollen hands made it impossible to draw his gun.

"You're killing him!" Jolene shoved past him to her brother, crumpled on the floor. Caleb stepped in front of Morgan.

Morgan stumbled back, attempting to wrest from his furious mind any coherent thought. Colin stood just inside the batwing doors. Mud stiffened his clothes. The sense of urgency just beyond the fog in his head took focus. Despair glared back at him.

Colin gaped from Jared to Morgan. "I'm forming a posse," Colin rasped. "We're going after Lawton."

"He'll cut you to ribbons before he lets you within miles of where they're hiding."

"For the love of God, he'll kill her, Morgan, if I don't hand over Joshua. I have to do something."

"No posse." His eyes fell on his scraped knuckles. He flexed his fingers and found them sore. "Where's Joshua now?"

"Lainey and the kids are staying with Red's family. I've got men with them." Colin's gaze leveled on Morgan. "Lainey's health isn't good. She's very upset."

"There can be no trade for Joshua," Morgan said. "It's an impossible request. You know it."

"Hell, don't you think I've considered that? But Lacey . . ."

"I know where they took her," Jared interrupted. His voice was hoarse, barely audible over his swollen mouth.

In the dull lamplight of the room, the silence roared in Morgan's ears. He met Jolene's dark, uncertain gaze with a frown that didn't nearly express the full measure of his fury.

She shook her head, eyes misting with tears. "No matter what you think, Jared is still my brother. He's all I've got in this world. You need him. He's agreed to help."

Jared spat blood. "I want to walk when this is over."

Walk straight to hell. Then Morgan would tear Hawk in two.

"He ain't countin' on you livin', is all," Caleb replied.

"I'm all you got, Caine!"

"Take him with you," Jolene's voice broke. "Give him a chance."

How could Morgan explain to her the monster that her brother was? He turned away from her. He had a lot of work to do before he left. He'd lost too much precious time already. He didn't think about whether he'd see Lacey alive again. He had to believe that she would survive until he found her.

He fought a surge of pain. Christ, his head throbbed.

"Morgan." Colin gripped his sleeve. "I love her."

"Then you should have told her the truth about Joshua, Colin."

And I should have put the rope around Lawton's neck myself.

He would not make the same mistake twice.

Morgan stepped out of the saloon and peered toward the mountains. Pushed by the northerly wind that swept down from Canada, the clouds gathered ominously over the peaks. It looked like winter had already started in the high country.

Cold eyes measured the time before sunset.

For the space of a heartbeat, Morgan felt the tension twist inside him—then he felt nothing. Like a great cat, he crossed the street to the jail.

He was now the hunter.

Chapter Sixteen

For three days Lacey's path climbed higher into the mountains. Cold and hungry, her body ached. Her hair tangled in a makeshift braid down her back. When she slept, it was on a horse with Hawk at her back. Lacey realized Hawk would be unable to stop the inevitable once they reached camp. No one could. Except maybe Brett Lawton.

By the fourth day, Lacey barely managed to lift her head when they finally rode into camp. "Take her to the tent," she heard Lawton direct Hawk. "I want her out of those stinking rags."

Lacey ran bleak eyes down her bloodstained blouse and skirt. She stared back at Lawton. "The clothes suit me fine." Her throat ached. "They serve as a reminder of the kind of man you are."

The grin on Lawton's face didn't reach his ice-water eyes. "I'm actually more interested in your health than anything you got, girl." He raked her crudely with his eyes. "I wouldn't offer you to my worst enemy at the moment."

"Change, Lacey," Hawk interceded. "You'll freeze to death up here in these mountains without warmer clothes."

"Yes. Change, *dearest* Lacey." The familiar voice snapped Lacey around. She looked straight into Caitlyn Madigan's eyes. "Why, Lacey, dear. Your sense of fashion hasn't improved since the last time we met," Caitlyn sneered wrapping her arms around Lawton.

They were anything but chaste in their public display of affection. With avid attention everyone watched every detail of their kiss, including Lacey, who was unable to turn away.

"My woman," Lawton said when he finally lifted his head. Lacey felt dizzy. "A fine one she is, too. Keeps me on the straight and narrow, if you know what I mean. Very useful, too." Lawton looked down at Caitlyn, snuggled suggestively in his arms. "Thanks to her efforts and Caine's taste in women, I'm a free man today. Cat, fetch our guest the nice riding habit we took off that eastern lady outside Bodie," he instructed. "She was a little thing, but I'm sure it will fit nicely."

Lacey leaned in Hawk's arms and shuddered.

"Oh, she wasn't wearing it when she died," Lawton reassured her. "Was she, boys?"

Their jeering response made Lacey cringe. She felt Hawk's grip tighten. "I'm wearing what I have on," she whispered.

Lawton dragged her off the horse. She hit the ground on her knees and felt the pain stab up her body. Grabbing what was left of the pathetic braid on her head, he pulled her to her feet.

"You'll change." His voice struck the fear of God in every stiff muscle. "And you'll do it in front of us all. The boys want to see what you got to offer for all their troubles."

Lacey was appalled that she was looking at Lawton through a wall of tears. She loathed the thought of surrendering her pride to him. But the grueling hours of her journey had worn her down.

"Lacey!" Lawton's voice reached her.

Tilting her chin, her defiant gaze remained fixed on his scarred face. That Morgan had been responsible for the disfigurement lent her a small spark of satisfaction.

Enough to give her strength.

She removed Morgan's buckskin. Her fingers trembled over the buttons on her blouse—one slow button at a time. The tattered remnant of what once had been Lorraine's shirt, shivered to the ground in a puddle at her feet. Brett Lawton's heartless gaze drilled her. Willing her to crumble.

Stretching deeper into herself for the courage to look him straight in the eye, her fingers released the buttons on her skirt. It slid down her body. The cold air lifted bumps on her skin. She stood before them all in her shift and pantalets, her eyes never wavering from Lawton's face.

"Gotta a lot of spunk, girl." His voice was almost quiet as his gaze held hers. "Didn't think you had it in you."

She loathed him.

Caitlyn returned with the riding habit, a heavy royal-blue velvet creation with a petticoat sewed into the skirt. A hand firmly attached to her hip, she demanded, "You will pass her to the men?"

"Your claws are showing, Cat."

"She's Morgan's whore and deserves no better."

Lawton's gaze swept over her with new interest. Lord, they were going to use her against Morgan.

"What about you and Caine? Is he in love with you?"

"No." It was no lie. "If he comes, it will be to hunt you down."

"She's lying," Caitlyn scoffed. "A blind idiot could see the way he looked at her in Waylen Springs."

"It could prove entertaining if you are indeed Caine's Achilles' heel." He raised a hand to tip Lacey's chin, only to find it snatched from its purpose.

"Give her to the men," Caitlyn snapped, wrapping Lacey's braid around her other hand. "And when they're finished . . ." Caitlyn jerked so hard on the braid it brought stinging tears to Lacey's eyes. "I want a piece of her myself. Her hair would make a nice trophy. I imagine Morgan found it beautiful at one time."

Lacey's eyes dropped to the knife on Lawton's belt. She was barely aware that she'd moved. Instinct to survive drove her against Caitlyn, the same instant she launched for the knife. The weapon was in her hand before she registered the feel of the bone handle in her grasp. Sweeping the knife around in a half circle, she listened as the guffawing voices dimmed until only the whispering branches of pine stalked her sanity.

"Give me the knife, girl," Lawton warned, setting Caitlyn aside.

Lacey swung a hysterical gaze over them all. Hawk had pulled his rifle from the scabbard. Lacey realized he would shoot the first man who dared attack her. He would die for her; she couldn't allow it. She turned the knife in on herself.

"Put the knife away, girl."

Brett Lawton worried that she would somehow deprive him of the pleasure of revenge. Ruin his plans. But Lacey possessed no such courage to end her own life. She swung the length of her braid over her shoulder, sawing at it swiftly until it came off in her hands. Astonishment registered on every man's face.

"A gift for your wife." Lacey flung the heavy flaxen rope. Lawton snatched it furiously from the air. "I wouldn't give her the satisfaction of *taking* anything from me!"

Caitlyn screeched. Lawton yanked her from Lacey. Ignoring Caitlyn's fury, his eyes narrowed on the tiny heart-shaped birthmark on Lacey's collarbone, no longer hidden beneath a wealth of tangled hair. Lacey thought she saw him pale. Her pitiful attempt at bravado lasted no longer than the time it took for his gaze to travel the short distance from her shoulder to her eyes. Dawning recognition of his discovery chilled inside lungs that no longer worked. She took a terrified step backward. Away from the knowing look in his eyes.

This man was Joshua's father. Joshua possessed the same birthmark she did. Brett Lawton couldn't be . . .

The very thought nearly drove Lacey to her knees.

This vile man would take everything from her. Everything, including the last vestige of her past. Leaving her with nothing but a shattered body and an identity that was no longer hers.

She cringed when Lawton touched what was left of her hair. "I wouldn't have allowed Cat to cut it so short," he said mildly, moving his palm over the knife in her hand. Lacey was silent. She would test fate no further by bearding him with defiance. She couldn't kill him anymore now than she could in town.

Flinging the riding habit in Lacey's face, Caitlyn severed their contact. "I will not do your bidding again, princess," she sneered. "Brett may want you alive, but I don't."

Lacey had no doubt of the woman's lack of conscience; she would stick a knife in her back at the first opportunity. Clutching the garment, she measured her own fate in Lawton's gaze and tried not to consider the girl who had worn the outfit before her. But in that moment, for whatever reason she wouldn't consider, Brett Lawton spared her the horror of throwing her to his men. Hesitantly, Lacey shrugged the habit over her head. When she popped out of the top, Lawton still watched her.

"Our hostage needs a guard, even from my trusting woman, it seems. How about it . . . Gressett?" He called over his shoulder, obviously intent on riling some response from Hawk. "How'd you like to be in charge of our hostage?"

Lacey finished the last button up the length of her bodice in time to glimpse the look on Gressett's face. He wiped his stubbled chin, admiring her with frank lust.

"Keep the men off her. When this is over, I'll consider how you should be rewarded." Lawton's gaze narrowed on Hawk. "We wouldn't want you sidetracked from your business at hand. Would we?"

Hawk's brow lifted. "If you live after Caine finds you, I will be only too happy to take you over these mountains."

"Sarcasm is unbecoming, Hawk," Lawton said. "Every man has his usefulness here. Without it—" He shrugged, and Lacey remembered her horse. Her eyes flew to Hawk, pleading with him not to do anything.

She was beyond his meager protection now.

She was beyond Morgan. He would not trade Joshua.

Clenching her eyes shut, she felt the tattered remnants of her courage shatter. Cold reality shuddered through her veins. If she didn't do something, she would die.

Floating on an invisible current of air, a falcon drifted listlessly over the bright canopy of firs banked against the steep slopes of the mountain. A lone ferret passed across the trail, and Morgan's horse shied before gloved hands tightened on the reins to steady him. He stopped where the trail forked, and Jared watched him tug the collar of his shearling coat together.

"It's your choice, Marshal," Jared insolently called.

Shackled as he was, Jared's only function was to guide Morgan through the mountain pass to Lawton. The responsibility did not weigh heavily on his conscience—no matter what their agreement had been.

"You don't talk much, do you, Caine?" Jared sneered, detesting Morgan's silence and the impervious edge of control that needled away at Jared's nerves.

Without a word, Morgan nudged the steel dust. The tether connecting his horse to Jared's snapped taut, jerking Jared backward, nearly unseating him. His hate-filled eyes hesitated on Morgan, before he swept an unsteady gaze across the steep, rocky incline where his horse picked its way up the trail.

"What I still don't understand is why you'd ruin that sterling reputation you have as a lawman just to let me go when this is all over. That is what you're still planning, isn't it, Caine?"

Morgan ignored him.

Branches creaked in the cold, settling like frost in Jared's veins. He jerked his jacket collar closer to keep the brisk wind at bay. The chains on his wrists rattled. Glaring at their restricting presence, he swore he'd kill Morgan.

"A man would have to be a monk not to want a piece of Lacey Ashton," Jared taunted. "Did she share some with you, Caine? Was it so good you're willing to die for her now? Is that it?"

The cold wind flapped Jared's hat brim, and he tugged it lower on his head as he'd seen Morgan do. Burying his chin into his coat, Jared glowered at Morgan's back.

For another hour, they climbed steadily. Then suddenly they left the sheltering canopy of the forest and found themselves on a rocky plateau. The descending cloud bank had snatched a portion of the sky and the chill of a winter zephyr began to settle in for the night.

Morgan twisted in his saddle.

"I told you I wasn't sure which camp they'd ride to," Jared hedged.

Morgan swung his horse nose to nose with Jared's. "Take

an educated guess," he suggested, speaking for the first time that day. "Try earning some of that freedom I promised you."

"It seems to me, you've been doing a fine job trailing them all by your lonesome, without my help. *You* choose the way."

Morgan's eyes flashed. "You know as well as I, they've set false trails all over this mountainside. I don't have the time to follow every ghost lead."

Jared's breath steamed out of his mouth, reminding him that it was cold, and Morgan was waiting for him to answer—patiently waiting—just like he'd been doing for days with a violence kept tightly in check. So tight, Jared waited for it to snap.

When it did, he would make his move.

Jared pointed to the southern ridge in the distance. "There are some caves in that mountain. A lot of gold used to be stashed there from that government payroll robbery last year." His grin was sly. "Before it bought Lawton's freedom."

Morgan's gloved hand tightened around the reins. He pulled his eyes from Jared's face and scanned their back trail. Night shadows had crept in. Only a pale magenta dusk remained of the day.

Jared glimpsed the faint change in Morgan's expression and scanned the rock ledges around them with renewed interest. "You're not worried, are you?"

Morgan slid the rifle from its scabbard.

"How many men you got following behind us?" Jared asked. "Didn't really think you'd come alone."

Morgan shifted his attention back to Jared. "Maybe you're not as dumb as you act."

Jared's face reddened. "Always the tough marshal, aren't you?" he sneered. "You're going to make a mistake, Caine . . . like you did when you left Lawton in the trust of that greedy magistrate."

Something betrayed itself in Morgan's face. Like a piranha, Jared smelled blood. "A mistake, Marshal Caine. And now, Lawton has your precious Lacey. She's been with him for three days. Three days with the likes of Gressett and that bunch of—"

"Don't say it, Jared."

"Remember Shannon? I wasn't the only one who enjoyed—"

Morgan swung the butt of his rifle, hitting Jared in the jaw. He toppled over the back of the horse and smashed to the ground. Jared felt his lungs explode.

"You're lucky I've let you live this long, you bastard." Morgan hauled him to his feet, dragging him toward a brace of trees. "So help me, you're a dead man." Morgan slammed him against a tree.

Dazed, Jared slid down its trunk. Morgan chained his cuffs around a limb above his head.

"Someone's going to put a bullet in you," Jared gasped.

"I know one thing"—Morgan stood back, breathing hard in the higher altitude—"it won't be you."

Jared jerked violently at his restraint, struggling to his feet. "Lacey was supposed to be mine, Caine. You took her from me. As you took everything that belonged to me. I was never good enough for that high'n mighty sister of yours. Jolene never listened to me. Colin amused himself thinking I was a grown-up version of some brat of his." Fury snapped at every nerve. "Lacey would have fallen in love with me, if not for you. She was supposed to be mine!"

"She was *never* yours."

"She would have loved me, but for you. God's truth if Lawton hadn't come on her that night, she'd still be safe."

"Like hell, Jared. You don't know the meaning of truth. You betrayed her as you betrayed every other person in your life."

"You always did think you were smart. Well, not this time."

"Let me guess." Morgan's voice was sarcastic, jolting some of the smugness from Jared's face. "Those men of yours who've been doggin' our trail for the past two hours are finally behind me."

"You're half right," Jared sneered. "Only *she* isn't a man."

"Howdy, Morgan." At the sound of Caitlyn's voice, Morgan straightened as if struck. "Keep those hands high, honey, or I'll blow that handsome head of yours clean off your shoulders."

Slowly raising his arms, Morgan turned. Face-to-face with

Caitlyn Madigan, his half-smile belied his insolent gaze as he crudely raked his eyes over her. "Caitlyn Madigan. I should have known," he said flatly, his eyes never leaving hers as she knelt to pick up the rifle he'd dropped when he went off the horse with Jared. "No wonder the whole friggin' frontier knew about the shipment to Bodie. You took the missive from your brother's office."

"My brother is a trusting fool. There wasn't a thing that came through this whole territory I didn't know about first." Caitlyn's smile boasted her arrogance. "Unfortunately"—her glare pierced Jared—"certain people lack the competence to follow orders."

"Marshal, meet Caitlyn," Jared announced. "Brett Lawton's beloved whore for two years now."

"Shut up, Jared," Cat snarled. "I haven't spent the last few hours in that saddle to be insulted by scum like you."

"If you'd done your job right in the first place, dear heart, I wouldn't be here." Jared turned to Morgan who shifted subtly. "You weren't *supposed* to make it out of Portland, or Waylen Springs. You have more lives than that stupid cat you gave Lacey."

"It wasn't me who failed," Caitlyn announced. "It was that moron, Gressett—"

"Who else is with you?" Jared cut in. He didn't trust Morgan.

Warily, Caitlyn circled Morgan. Intense blue eyes followed her every movement, silent testimony to Morgan's restraint. "Bud and Joe are on the hill. I wanted to do this personally," she said succinctly, handing the shotgun to Jared, while transferring Morgan's rifle to her other hand. "We've been waiting for the posse. I like what I've caught much better."

"Don't, Cat," Jared said, "unless you want me to shoot through you if he should try something."

Caitlyn stiffened. Deciding not to argue his warning, she walked a wide path around Morgan to the saddlebags on his steel dust.

"No, you idiot, on him. The key is somewhere on him." Jared had been practically unconscious when Morgan chained him to the tree. Yet, the key had to be on him. But where? "I have him covered, Cat."

Caitlyn's dubious gaze settled on the shotgun in Jared's hands. Morgan appeared quietly amused by her dilemma.

Jared felt like shooting them both and being done with it. "Where is it, Caine?"

"He always keeps that key in his hat, son," a voice cracked from behind Jared. A double-barrel shotgun pressed directly against Jared's back. At that range there would be nothing of Jared to salvage should Caleb's finger slip on the trigger.

Jared's glare narrowed on Caitlyn. Damn her. Caleb reached around him and lifted the gun from his grasp.

Morgan stalked the short distance from Caitlyn. "I've never hit a woman." He ripped the rifle from her hands. "But I'm just in the mood to do you damage. Watch her," he warned Caleb.

"Don't have to," Caleb reassured him. "Red has her under his sights right now."

Replacing the rifle in its scabbard on the horse, Morgan dug through his bags and removed a pair of cuffs.

"Where are my men?" she demanded, her glare on Caleb as Morgan clipped the cuffs on her wrists.

"Oh, they're in restful repose, ma'am, for the night, anyway. Not to worry. The posse will pick 'em up in a few hours, if no hungry mountain cat finds 'em first."

Jared swung around. "So help me, I'm not taking you any farther, Caine!"

"No need to, boy," Caleb reassured him. "The camp's 'bout a mile's ride southeast. You was mostly right when yuh pointed to that ridge yonder."

Jared's eyes swung to Morgan. "If you knew where they were all the time, then why'd you need me?"

"I didn't know where they were," Morgan said. "But with you along, someone was bound to get worried."

"Back-trailed yer little group, ma'am." Caleb grinned, clearly admiring the flush that crept over Caitlyn. "It was easy enough."

"You'll never get into that camp," Jared warned.

"Maybe," Morgan said, drawing the key for Jared's cuff

from inside his hat. "But with more than half their men out looking for that posse, this is as good a time as any to try."

"I didn't agree to walk into that camp. Brett will kill us."

"The hazards of my profession. The consequences of yours. It's the price we both pay for what we do."

Chapter Seventeen

Lacey woke first to the bone-chilling cold, then to the gnawing ache of hunger. She moved deeper within the coat Lawton had given her. Her riding habit was barely adequate for mountain temperatures. Even Morgan's buckskin beneath the coat didn't ward off the chill.

Listening to the rumble of voices around her, Lacey opened her eyes a tiny slit and from beneath her lashes made a quick scan of the camp. Six men gathered around the fire. The bonds on her hands chaffed against wrists made raw by the constant abuse of the rope.

". . . don't understand what could've happened to them."

"No offense, Brett," Gressett scoffed, "but considerin' Caine's reputation, yuh shoulda sent someone else. Caine's no tenderfoot."

Lawton uncoiled from his seat beside the hot fire. "You don't want me to take offense, then keep your mouth shut." He whipped his gaze across the faces around the fire. "She's as good as the lot of you put together. When we get word of the posse, we'll know where to go. Just be ready."

"We're ready," a large man in a stained leather coat grumbled as he glared into the fire over the rim of a coffee cup. "But I agree with Gressett. If Caine's out there—"

"He's only a man, Johns," Lawton said.

"And you took somethin' that belongs to him," the big outlaw said, looking across the fire and directly into Lacey's eyes. "I'd be rightly pissed myself."

Lawton's eyes swung around, hesitating on Lacey. His mouth drew back into a smile, pulling at the scar on his cheek. With the firelight dancing over his face, he looked diabolical.

"Your marshal is making my men nervous," he said conversationally. "But he's just an ordinary man, isn't he, Lacey?"

Giving up her pretense of sleep, Lacey sat up. "I understand you've been acquainted with Marshal Caine for many years," she managed even as he came to squat before her. "*You* can answer that question far better than I."

"Such bravery," he said, surveying her butchered hair. "A pity that you marred such perfection."

Lacey's courage faltered when a wicked knife appeared in his hand. Clearly amused by the look of terror that sprang into her eyes, he lifted her hands and sliced the rope.

"Sam," he called over his shoulder, "bring this girl some food. We can't have her starving on us."

"I'm not hungry."

"I'll only offer once, Lacey." Lawton's voice whispered over her. "After that, you'll starve."

The food arrived, and despite Lacey's resolve, she took the plate. Gressett hovered around her, the smell of his unwashed body settling distastefully over her meal. He had pawed and groped her all day, watching her, even during her most private ablutions. The food clogged her throat, but still she forced herself to eat.

"Not the toity lady no more, are yuh?" Gressett observed, flicking a filthy hand over her hair.

Lacey's gaze passed over his hand, before settling on his face. "It's a pity my aim wasn't a little lower in Portland." Her expression was serene. "But I suppose even a bullet would have trouble negotiating a path through that thick skull of yours."

Gressett jumped to his feet. "And what's that 'spose to mean?"

Lacey returned her attention to the plate. "It means you're too dim-witted to know you haven't got the brains God gave a jackass."

"Yuh just remember them words when I got yuh squirmin' beneath me, missy," he sneered. "I ain't a fergetten type of man, and I been doin' my share of lookin' lately. Maybe tonight I'll jest finally take what yuh owe me from San Francisco."

"Don't count on it." Lawton's voice came from behind him, and Gressett spun, nearly toppling the dinner plate from Lacey's lap.

Heart pounding, Lacey's gaze settled uneasily on Lawton.

"Get her a blanket, Gressett," he directed. "Can't you see our hostage is cold?"

The clip of a fast-approaching horse distracted both men. Lacey found herself dismissed when Lawton left to meet the incoming rider.

She dropped the dinner plate and tried not to throw up.

Somewhere in the forest an owl hooted. She surveyed the darkness around her. Abruptly her eyes swung back to the men in camp. They sounded edgy, all but ignoring her as they argued. She'd already determined that there was nowhere to run behind her but a slate cliff. Her departure would make enough noise to wake the dead. Coming slowly to her feet, she darted a glance to the trees on her left.

Without a backward glance, Lacey plunged into the bushes.

Blindly, she forged ahead. Over her thundering heartbeat, she heard signs of pursuit behind her. Legs, powerful and faster than hers, were gaining. Caught in a blinding panic, she ran through the trees, heedless of the danger that came with the darkness.

Lacey gave a half sob as someone plunged into her, sending her crashing into the underbrush. Flailing her arms and wrists, she struggled to wrench free, screaming and bucking until exhaustion claimed her. Glaring up into Lawton's savage face, she tried to spit.

"A little wildcat," he hissed. "You're a fool to waste your

strength running away. Especially since we've been so hospitable."

"Like you were in town when you shot Jack?"

"You weren't such a tough sprite back there, were you? Still, when I looked down your gun, it was enough to make any papa proud. You couldn't kill me."

Lacey turned her face away, hating his leer. Lawton chuckled. "If you only knew, English. You wouldn't be worried about anything I might have in mind."

"Yank," Lacey snapped, her eyes flashing with contempt. "I'm not English," she spat.

Lawton pulled back and looked down at her with curious detachment. Even with tangled hair and tattered clothes, she couldn't help but wonder whom he was seeing at that moment. The emotion was fleeting and almost immediately, he shut it away from her.

"No, you certainly are not English," he agreed. "Born January ninth, 1853, in Roanoke, Virginia, to one Lorraine Cranston Lawton . . . my wife. In every way, you're like your mother. Did you know that?"

Lorraine? *Her* Lorraine? Lawton cheerfully smiled at her shock. This was safe ground for him, and in her fear and anger, he clearly knew his place.

"My own daughter," he added less gently. "But then you already suspected, didn't you?"

"No! You're lying!"

"I have no qualms about lying," he admitted. "But in this matter, it does me no good to lie. You have thrown a wrench into my well-laid plans. What kind of hostage is my own daughter?"

"No . . . this is impossible. Lorraine would never—"

"Lorraine loved me before that good-for-nothing Ashton came along. A penniless pauper, and she dared bed the man." Lawton's rage spiked through Lacey. Any relapse of conscience he might have experienced was now gone in the face of his fury.

"Her father married that conniving whore quick enough to me before anyone ever knew what she'd done. But *I* knew." Eyes dark with rage caressed Lacey's face. "To think, you were mine after all, princess," he whispered harshly against her cheek. "I thought you were Colin's bast—"

"Stop it!" Lacey closed her eyes. He was telling her too much.

"I would have killed you without ever knowing the truth. Lorraine hid you with Ashton. I looked years to find you." He glared down at her with hate-filled eyes, gently stroking her hair and face. "And here you are—after twenty years. The very vision of your deceitful mother." His finger traced the soft contour of her cheek. "It would have been such poignant justice, had you been Colin's brat. Now, what do I do, when the weapon of my choice turns out to be the very thing I covet? Even I have my principles."

"Principles!" Lacey swung her arms, but they were easily captured. The pain snapped her eyes back to his. Reality was all too harsh, and she couldn't stop the well of tears. "You're insane!"

"On the other hand, dearest," Lawton replied, his eyes probing hers. "If you run from me again, I'll hunt you down. I have no moral restrictions in killing you if you betray me." He lightly kissed her nose in a fatherly peck. "And I *will* find you," he promised, pulling back to assess her stricken gaze. "Ask Lorraine and Colin how many years they've been running. They'd be dead now, if it weren't for that bastard, Caine."

Lawton dislodged himself from Lacey, yanking her to her feet. She stumbled forward against him, her hands tore the collar of his shirt, ripping it away before he could stop her.

The birthmark! Tears burned behind her lids.

Lawton only laughed. "A kiss for Daddy?"

Branded by the fires of hell, Lacey jerked away. "I hate you!" She slapped him, clearly surprising him with the full import of her strength. He allowed her the indiscretion, perhaps because fatherly pride tainted his temperament.

"I'll let you follow me back to camp on your own accord." His eyes were cool. "I'm sure you'd like to use this time constructively to take care of any private needs you might wish to deal with. If you're not back, say within five minutes of my return, I'll assume you've run. Do I make myself clear?"

Lawton kept his eyes securely pinned on hers. He had no idea what it cost her to concede him his victory. He had stripped her of her life. Stolen her dreams. He was a monster.

And he was her father!

"Now if you don't mind? Caitlyn is out there somewhere, and I do have more pressing business than to coddle you, dear heart." Lawton spun on his heel. Only the sound of his spurs marked the path through the darkness back toward camp.

Pressed flat on the rocky knoll a hundred feet above the camp, Morgan had his field glasses trained on the camp when Lawton stepped through the trees. Bringing the glasses around, Morgan watched the outlaw swing a quick glance about the camp then walk to a large tree, where he turned and waited in arrogant repose. Morgan hesitated. A movement to Lawton's right drew his glasses.

Lacey walked into the clearing. Despite himself, Morgan felt his heart slam violently. He was lost in her vision. He watched her face for a space of one breath, two . . . he waited. Christ, her hair was chopped unevenly to a point just above her shoulders. Her eyes looked huge in a face too thin and strained. She was standing at the edge of camp—just standing as if someone had crushed the life from her. Morgan swung his glasses back to Lawton.

Something had happened. Morgan went cold inside.

Lacey walked over to Lawton. With a defiance he recognized even from where he was lying, Morgan saw her lift her hands, seething as Lawton tied them.

"Yuh gonna trust Jared?" He barely heard Caleb ask beside him. "Shame 'bout him. Never figured." Morgan heard him spit. "Fog's coming in thick," Caleb observed a moment later. "It's a mean one, too. Full of ice."

Morgan finally lowered the glasses. His head sagged to the soft pine needles.

"By the looks of this weather closin' in on us, we ain't got much time," Caleb continued. "Hate to be caught down there when that stuff settles thick on this mountain."

"I'm not leaving her with them another night."

Caleb spat a wad of brown juice, looking ponderously toward the camp below. "I 'spose if she was my woman, I'd feel the same," he mumbled. "But that still don't make it right to go down and get all shot fulla holes."

Morgan lifted his glasses to resume his search for one in particular—he wasn't there.

The cold barrel of a rifle pressed against his ear. Morgan lowered his glasses. Beside him Caleb didn't move.

"I would not want to be mistaken for one of Lawton's men and shot," Hawk said carefully. "You look in just the mood to be careless."

Silence.

"What?" Hawk inquired. "No words?"

"You wouldn't like what I have to say." Morgan's voice was close to savage.

The rifle lowered. Morgan was on his feet before Hawk stepped away. Each man equaled the other in height, formidable foes should they come to blows.

Hawk's brow raised subtly above dark eyes. "Your fight is with Lawton," he reminded him. "And so is mine."

"Maybe yuh should consider what he has to say," Caleb offered.

"I did not bargain for your woman to be a part of this," Hawk said quietly. "But I was there when they chased her horse into the ground. I didn't have a choice."

"Why didn't you warn me that Brett Lawton didn't hang?"

"You would have chased after him, and probably gotten yourself killed this time. The hunt is mine."

"And you're doing a real job of it, too, Hawk." Some of the tension uncoiled inside Morgan. "Is she all right?"

"That one has courage. I have protected her as much as I could."

And Morgan believed him.

For a moment, the years fell away. They were friends again—closer than friends. Hawk was at his side, guiding him, watching over him, teaching a younger boy the skills to survive in a harsh world unforgiving of ignorance and youth.

They owed each other their lives tenfold.

For a brief moment, his eyes glanced off Hawk, and he read the unspoken question in his dark eyes.

Would there ever be forgiveness between them?

Morgan opened his jacket, and drawing his gun, he checked the load as he led the way back to their horses. "We don't have much time. What's the status of Lawton's guard?"

"Lawton's man on watch is . . . no longer a threat," Hawk said. "There are six men still in camp. The others are combing these mountains for any sign of the posse. I think the fog will keep them separated from us at least for the night. Brett Lawton's woman is missing, and he's distracted by her absence."

"Colin's posse is a decoy. He's somewhere behind me," Morgan said. "I have to get Lacey out before Lawton's men spot that posse and return. There will be no bargaining with this group."

"Lawton will not be looking for you to walk into his camp," Hawk said flatly, a note of approval in his voice. "You are a fool."

They reached their horses, and Hawk abruptly stopped. Jared, who was sitting morosely against a rock chewing on jerky, blanched at Hawk's unexpected appearance. Beside Jared, Caitlyn seemed content to play the captive, clearly enjoying Jared's sudden discomfiture. Behind them, shotgun poised, Red nodded.

"I will have the pleasure of taking care of this one personally," Hawk said, planting his feet in front of Jared.

"You two-faced breed," Jared sneered. "You won't live long enough to shave."

Caitlyn laughed. "Look on the bright side, Jared," she said. "It wasn't your incompetence after all that lost us the money on that wagon train . . ."

Hawk silenced her with a frozen look.

"He's warning you to shut up, Cat. I would think real hard about taking his advice." Morgan kicked Jared's boots. "Let's go. It's time to make yourself useful."

"Yea"—Jared kicked back—"don't do me any favors, Caine."

Morgan gripped Jared's collar and pulled him to his feet. "Let me explain something to you, Jared. I *am* doing you a favor, because I need you in that camp standing between me and anyone who gets it in his head to shoot before I finish what I came to do. You see, Hawk feels the same as I do about you, but he's not bound by any word."

"Yea, well I never did anything to him."

"Tell that to Saint Pete on your way to hell." Morgan shoved him forward, away from Hawk. "Shannon was his wife."

Jared registered the horror of Morgan's words.

"Caleb, take Caitlyn below with you." Swinging his gaze around the wooded copse, Morgan tried not to notice the thin, white tendrils creeping down from the sky, settling with eerie indifference over the mountainside. In less than an hour, Lacey's fate would no longer rest in his hands.

If his plan failed, they would all be dead.

"So how'd yuh like the cap'n, lady," the taunting voice carried to Lacey. The smell of charred beans filled the air and made her stomach churn.

"This weather is spooky," someone complained. "Gives me the creeps-like, bein' all socked in this way."

"Ain't afraid, are yuh?"

"Poke fun, Johns. But I don't see you out there waitin'. Seein' as how yer so all-fired brave and all."

The man called Johns shifted his attention away from Lacey, and the yellow-haired speaker paled nervously. "Lyon, you yellow belly. Thought it would be real easy snatching that kid of Ashton's, didn't yuh. Now we got a little work cut out for us, and yuh grovel like a snivelin' coward."

"Why all the fuss over some brat?" Lyon demanded.

Johns tossed his dinner tin onto the jutting boulder at his feet. "That kid belongs to Lawton." His hard-edged voice penetrated the cold. He moved behind Lacey and, leaning against the tree, casually pulled out the makings to roll a smoke. "But this one?" His mouth twisted in a leer, and Lacey met his shark-like eyes. "This one is a special kind of bonus for all our sufferin' of late. I imagine now that she's been broke in proper, we'll all have a taste."

Johns rolled his cigarette and put it between his lips. A slight grin tugged at the corners of his mouth as he nudged

Lacey with the toe of his boot. "You that Redskin's whore, too?"

Lacey shoved at the intruding boot, scooting as far away as the tethered rope bound to her hands allowed. Gressett planted himself behind her. "That tongue of yours broke, missy?"

Lacey lifted her chin, her silence her only weapon against them.

"Why don't yuh find out," Johns taunted. "I bet she tastes real fine."

Gressett tangled a dirty hand in Lacey's hair. "Maybe I will."

Lawton stepped out of the tent, silencing the group with a look. His predatory gaze raked Gressett, stilling on Lacey. She watched his approach as one watches a wolf.

He crouched in front of her. "So you think you're man enough to handle this one without help," he said to Gressett.

"Or man enough to even try," Lyon said, snorting.

Johns chuckled. A match flared. Cupping the flame, he brought it up to light the cigarette. His hand froze midair.

As one, they all turned and stared straight into the blazing eyes of Morgan Caine. Lacey's cry caught in her throat. The gun butt of his colt was in his right hand. His shearling coat was open. But for his eyes and the flash of metal on the brass cartridges in his gun belt, he would have been nearly invisible beneath the huge canopy of pine just outside the ring of firelight. A savage curse sounded in the dead silence that followed, and Johns dropped the match that burned his hand.

Making no more noise than a shadow, he walked into camp, shoving Jared ahead of him. A look over Morgan's shoulder confirmed he wasn't alone as Caleb fanned out to cover the edge of camp to his right.

Morgan's gaze hesitated on her face. Tears swam in her eyes.

Their contact was too brief, and Lacey almost cried out in pain when his gaze shifted. "Hello, Lawton," he said. In the firelight, Morgan's eyes glittered black. "Sort of reminds me of old times. You leave a trail a mile wide. One would think you wanted to be found."

The last to rise to his feet, Lawton looked with casual interest at the gun in Morgan's hand. "I didn't think you had it in you, Caine," he mused, glancing in the shadows around the camp, then back at Morgan. "I'm impressed."

"That's why you're always so easy to catch, Lawton."

Lawton's mouth flattened. "How did you get past my men?"

"Which ones? The fools in the hills waiting to ambush the posse, or the one asleep at the edge of your camp?"

"Asleep? Or dead?"

"Same difference to you, Lawton." Morgan looked over at Gressett, hovering over Lacey. "Get away from her."

"Real sociable tonight, ain't yuh, Caine?" Gressett said.

Struggling to dislodge Sam Gressett's hand from her hair, Lacey climbed to her feet, her eyes fixed on Morgan. His pulse slammed. For a brief, dangerous heartbeat, he swam in that liquid gaze more brilliant than the firelight that surrounded her.

Stepping beside Lacey, Lawton ran a finger along her jaw. "Tell him, sweetheart, how well you've been cared for. When he tries to kill us, I want it to be for crimes we've committed."

Morgan divided his attention equally between the two men. "Are you all right, Lacey?" he asked, without looking at her.

"They haven't hurt me," he heard her whisper.

"He looks fit to string you up, Sam," Lawton said mildly. "Perhaps you'd like to argue the marshal's claim on the girl, now that he's here to take her back."

"Maybe I just will," Gressett swaggered.

"And maybe you can finish what we went to town to do a few days ago. Then you can have the girl all to yourself." Gressett's gaze flickered sideways to Brett. "Now I know the man can fork a gun mighty fast," Brett continued. "But he's outnumbered here. He won't dare move his gun from me. You could take him, Sam." Brett urged, clearly enjoying Gressett's discomfiture.

"Now, Sam here has been champin' for a taste of that girl. He's been real helpful and all in her care." Brett chuckled. "Right, Sam?"

Sam glanced nervously at Lawton.

Brett looked dispassionately at Jared. "I can't lie, son. I'm not exactly happy to see you here tonight. This is unexpected."

"He traded the end of a rope for your neck," Morgan said.

"Like hell," Jared protested. "I didn't lead them here, Lawton. They figured out already. Hawk is with them."

Lawton's expression darkened. "So how many are up there?"

"Enough to do the job I came in to do," Morgan said.

"Which is?"

"To take Lacey out of here. I'm not interested in any of you."

"And you want me to believe that?"

"Ashton and the posse are behind me. We figured you'd be tracking them. Among other things, Lawton, you're predictable."

A noticeable tick took up residence in Lawton's jaw. "So you came to take the girl before my men spotted the posse and returned to warn us? How terribly heroic."

Lawton stepped sideways, drawing Lacey from Morgan's line of vision. "Even if you escape, my men are combing these hills."

Lawton walked to the edge of the light, surveying the densely shrouded trees. Morgan recognized Cherokee Johns and Mike Lyon as they moved behind him, army deserters who were wanted in Montana Territory. Of the two, Johns was the more dangerous and had a price on his head for murder. A side-glance told him that Caleb had Johns covered.

Lawton's eyes lifted with casual interest to assess the rocky ledge above the camp. A gray canopy revealed nothing beyond its murky shadows. The fog was upon them, and Lawton's calculating leer flaunted the boast that the strategic advantage would soon be his.

Morgan took a step backward in an attempt to keep Lawton in his sights, as well as Gressett who seemed about as jumpy as a coyote. Jared also watched both men.

"We've been playing this game for too long, Caine." Lawton's voice filled with quiet menace. "Tonight it ends . . . for everyone."

"It ended a long time ago," Morgan said, taking a step back. "This time justice won't be bought."

Lawton's mouth curved into a grim smile. "Kill the girl,

Gressett," he said, without taking his eyes off Morgan. "If I can't have her, no one can."

Gressett's eyes bulged. His arrogance fled. Evidently, it was one thing to molest a woman and an entirely different matter to murder one in cold blood.

"Sorry, Lacey child," Lawton tenderly mocked. "It's you or the marshal here. I'll let him make the choice. Him or you."

Morgan felt a prickle of fear pushing past his icy calm. It wedged itself in his chest. If Lawton killed him, Lacey wouldn't last the night. There would be no negotiations when the posse arrived. Lawton would butcher her when he realized Joshua wasn't with Colin.

"Now! Gressett." Lawton's voice was hard.

Gressett brought his gun up on Lacey.

A wild almost soundless groan of rage tore from Morgan's throat. He swung his gun around. And at once, a shrill, feminine cry pierced the darkness behind him. Someone had propelled Caitlyn down the rocky ledge directly into camp. A diversion.

Morgan fired twice at Gressett, hitting him in the chest and between the eyes. All around him, lead ricocheted between the stone cliffs that walled in two sides of the camp. The deadly barrage of fire came simultaneously from the shadows around the camp.

Hitting the ground in a roll, Morgan landed on his knees, swinging his gun on Lawton. But even as Morgan fired from the hip, he glimpsed the flame of Lawton's gun. A bullet hit Morgan, knocking him backward. He slammed against the filth-strewn ground. His vision tunneled. Fire snaked through his whole body.

Gasping, he rolled over onto his belly, and glimpsed Caitlyn folding into the dirt. She'd been cut down in the crossfire. Jared was gone. His vision blurred.

He pressed his hand to his side. Blood oozed from between his fingers. Bullets spattered dust into his face. A few feet away, his gun glimmered in the fading firelight. Out of reach.

"Morgan!" He heard Lacey's choked scream.

Gressett lay sprawled over the tether that bound her wrists, imprisoning her within a few inches of his prostrate form. The sight of her violent effort to tear herself free and reach him gave strength to his legs. He stumbled to her side.

She saw the blood on his hands. "You're shot!"

Morgan slid a knife from his boot, severing the thick rope around her wrists. Bullets clipped the tree beside them. "Run!"

He grabbed her arm, propelling her toward the rocky embankment rolling away into a shroud of darkness. Half-falling and stumbling, they hit the incline with careless speed. An avalanche of shale rattled behind them marking the path of their desperate flight deeper into the black abyss. Lacey had the shocking sense of flying, as the steep ground seemed to give away beneath their feet.

The staccato of gunfire drilled the rocks around them, tearing Morgan's grip from her arm. Unable to slow, they both continued their treacherous orbit down. And then the ground came up to meet them. Morgan's hand fumbled clumsily, catching hers in the darkness. Evergreen branches slapped at them until they reached an animal trail leading farther down the hill.

Morgan's labored breathing sounded loud in the stillness. When they finally stopped, no sound but theirs whispered back at them from the shadows. Wrapped in a thin cocoon of mist, the forest waited.

Braced against a tree, Morgan pulled Lacey against him. "Your hair . . ."

Her pride and glory was gone. But unlike the rest of her life, her hair would grow back to its former beauty.

He cupped her face, and kissed her. "I couldn't save . . . Shannon. I didn't know if I would reach you in time." Morgan's head lolled against the tree. "Did they . . . hurt you?"

Lacey felt the stickiness of blood against her cheek. "Morgan"—she probed his shoulders and face—"how many places are you hit?"

"Your father is on his way." He slackened against the tree for support. "He probably heard the shooting. You have to leave—"

"Understand me now, Morgan Caine," she said against his mouth. "You just walked through hell for me. I won't leave you out here to die. I won't."

He fell to his knees. She swung her gaze around the clearing. The fog had yet to penetrate completely. They needed to hide.

The sound of hoofbeats rattled the silence.

"Lacey," Morgan whispered raggedly. "Get out of here. Now!"

Scant moonlight illuminated the foggy shroud. Lacey recognized the man riding Morgan's horse. Wearing his black duster and hat, only the pale oval of his face revealed him in the darkness.

The steel dust walked a path straight for Morgan.

Jared thumbed his hat back on his head, turning the barrel of his rifle to cover their movements. "The smell of marshal stinks like a polecat. As easy to track as a cockroach through slop." He glared at Lacey. "You followed the wrong man."

"Let us go, Jared," she pleaded.

"Is that what you want, Caine? This woman to beg for your miserable life?"

"Go . . . to hell, Jared," Morgan rasped.

Jared deferred back to Lacey with a shrug. "See Lacey, he doesn't want your help. I, on the other hand, would have treated you with more respect."

Lacey hastened to reply but could think of nothing. Panic infused every muscle in her body. She had to protect Morgan.

"I'm going to kill her first, Caine," Jared said flatly. "Helpless as you are, it looks like I won't even have to waste a bullet on you. You don't even have a gun."

"Run . . . damn you."

Lacey heard Morgan's gasp; then he tumbled into the ground. She cried out, dropping beside him.

"You could have had it all," Jared said regretfully.

Slowly, Lacey lifted her head. Cold-blooded fury eclipsed her fear. If she were going to die, it wouldn't be on her knees in front of a bastard like Jared Coyle.

"I did have it all," she said, climbing to her feet. "You could work at it a hundred years and still never equal the man Morgan is."

Jared's eyes seemed to widen at the strength behind her voice. She imagined it didn't fit the pitiful image of the woman standing in tatters before him. He raised the rifle.

A knife whispered through the trees and slammed into Jared's back, jerking him upright. Lacey crammed a fist in her mouth, muffling her cry. Staring with horror-filled eyes, Jared watched the gun slide from his hands. It hit the ground with a dull, metallic thud.

Lacey didn't waste time questioning her reprieve. Her only thought was to recover the rifle. Jared tumbled from the saddle, nearly on top of her. Snaking out his hand, he grasped the rifle barrel as she pounced on it. Fingers gripping the cold metal in a tangled frenzy, she tried to rip the rifle away from him.

"Do you have the guts to murder me, Lacey?" Jared hissed, groping for the gun in his belt with his other hand.

"For God's sake, Jared!"

A crunch of stone, and Hawk was beside her, kicking the gun from Jared's grip. It landed at her feet. Taking the reins of the skittish horse, Hawk pulled the rifle out of her hands and uncocked it.

"They are all around you." Taking her arm, he pulled her back to Morgan's side. Blinded by a wall of tears, Lacey nodded. "These are very bad men. Especially the one over there. You must take John Caine and leave, now."

"Hawk, he's so badly hurt."

"I know, but he will die if you do not get him away."

Hawk handed her the rifle and reached under Morgan's shoulder, pulling him to his feet. The movement drove Morgan to consciousness. The vile word he uttered sounded beautiful to Lacey's ears. Somehow, Hawk managed to get Morgan into the saddle. Sliding the rifle into the boot, he then picked up Jared's revolver and shoved it into Morgan's empty holster.

She didn't see another horse. "What about you?"

He looked down at her. "There are two men up on that mountain who are Caine's friends," he said. "If they are still alive, they will need my help. I cannot leave them until I know for sure."

Understanding the sacrifice he was making made it no easier to accept. Hawk cupped her chin. For a long moment he didn't speak.

"Perhaps by helping save your life, I can in some small way repay John Caine for the other one he loved and lost because of me." His black eyes encompassed Lacey's face. "I am not doing this out of sacrifice. I have no intention of dying."

Lacey's voice faltered. His grip on her chin loosened, and two firm hands lifted her onto the saddle in front of Morgan.

"It will be hard to keep him on the horse," he said.

Morgan stirred. "I'll . . . manage," he rasped. "Especially . . . after you've gone to so much trouble to get me up here."

Hawk's gaze lingered on Morgan. Then relinquishing the reins of the horse to Lacey, he stepped back. "Go far away," he whispered fiercely. "There are twelve men down below us hunting you both like a pack of wolves. Tomorrow, you must follow the path of the sun across the sky. The mountain pass is your only hope of escape."

A movement on the ground startled Lacey, and she twisted in the saddle to see Jared. His eyes were wide and very much alive as he stared up at her. Her gaze swung back to Hawk.

"Tonight will finish it for me," he said past her to Morgan, who was peering down at him through half-opened eyes. "And for Shannon."

Morgan reached around her, fumbling for the reins.

"Don't . . . leave me, Lacey," Jared begged. "For God's sake, don't leave me."

"I'm sorry." Morgan's whisper touched Lacey's cheek.

She squeezed her eyes shut. The horse vaulted forward.

And as the stallion carried them deeper into the darkness, all that remained of Jared's life was the final echo of his scream carrying her name into eternity.

Chapter Eighteen

The trail climbed higher into the mountains. Morgan's steady loss of blood stripped him of his strength. He was badly hurt. Three times, Lacey stopped for water. The canteen was now empty. Twice Morgan blacked out, only to come to at the sound of Lacey's terrified voice as she sensed him slipping from the saddle.

And she was cold. Freezing.

Morning came with barely a hint of light penetrating the fog. All around them an ice-encrusted forest wept with the weight of crystal flakes and icicles dripping in artistic pinnacles from every tree and granite overhang. A white wonderland muted their world, its very beauty a dichotomy, for in the icy castle of this mountain fortress, life was frozen. Neither dead nor alive, it hung in precarious limbo that chilled Lacey to her soul.

She lost all track of time. Sometime during the day, the steel dust began to stumble. Desperately afraid of losing both Morgan and the horse, Lacey finally stopped. She slid from the saddle. Shards of pain shot up her legs.

Frozen, she thought. Everything about her was frozen.

Clutching the horse's mane for support, she grasped the reins before the stallion sidled away. Morgan swayed, catching himself on the saddle horn. Lacey could see the trail of blood down the side of the horse. Beneath the sleeves of his sheepskin coat, blood caked his right wrist. She needed to tend to his wounds with more than the superficial effort she'd already made.

"Don't . . . stop." Morgan's ragged whisper snapped up her head.

"The horse won't make it. And neither will you."

"Must . . . go on."

Lacey gritted her teeth. Faint rifle fire pocked the unearthly stillness behind them. If Lawton caught them, Morgan was as good as dead. Digging beneath Morgan's jacket, Lacey traced the cartridges over his belt until she found the small knife she knew he kept there. Her hand came back wet with his blood.

Shaking herself free, Lacey cut a slice of rope from the ragged hemp looped through a cinch ring on the back of the saddle. "Then I'm walking the horse and tying you to the saddle." She sawed on the rope. "If you fall off, I'll never get you back on again."

Morgan's mouth lifted on one corner. Thick lashes veiled the pain in his eyes as his gaze held hers. "Take my gloves," he whispered. "You need . . . them."

The blanket Lacey unrolled from the saddlebag and the gloves helped ward off the bone-chilling cold. Covering Morgan's hands with his coat sleeves, Lacey wrapped the rope around his wrists, securing him the best she could to the saddle.

Throughout the day, she climbed the trail until even the faraway sound of gunfire vanished in the vast stillness. Lacey stopped looking over her shoulder to check on Morgan. It was enough that the horse followed and that she had the strength to hold its reins. She clung to the bright orb of light hanging suspended in the white mist, lighting her path, beckoning her to follow.

As the forest thinned to scraggy cedar and pine scrub, a rocky trail opened between two granite escarpments. Wind shrieked through the pass, fanning Lacey's imagination and fears with images of screaming spirits. The stallion balked, tugging at the lead, and Lacey swung on the horse.

"Don't even think it," she rasped furiously. She knew she was pulling hard on the bit. "I'll shoot your bloody miserable hide myself, if you try to run off now." The horse snorted. One swift blow from its massive head would send her sprawling.

Lacey's gaze lifted heavenward, following the dark, glistening walls ascending into the thinning cloud bank. She fumbled with her footing on the broken rocky slips that tiptoed like steps up the trail. Tugging the stallion's reins, Lacey forced the big horse to follow.

For a mile, the trail leveled out and only the sound of her heavy breathing mingled with the horse's steady clip against stone. The walls narrowed so much in places, Lacey could not have walked abreast with another human being. Many times she stopped for breath and let the horse blow. When the trail began to climb steeply again, the mountain wall to her left gave way to the clouds, and Lacey felt her legs stop. The world in front of her had vanished.

"Holy Mary," she whispered, using an expletive she'd never uttered in her life. Clinging to the face of the cliff, a wisp of a trail disappeared into the mist.

Lacey stood on the ledge overlooking the empty precipice for what seemed an eternity, the strain on her heart intolerable. Testing the sheer drop of the cliff, she tossed a rock into the empty air. She didn't hear it hit bottom. Tears of panic swam in her eyes. The horse stomped. Terror seized Lacey. The trail behind her was too narrow to turn around on. To do so might cause the horse to slip. Her gaze reached out to Morgan, slumped in the saddle. She ached for guidance.

For the first time in her life, she was truly on her own.

Think! Morgan's life depended on making the right choice.

Lacey tested the strength in her fingers. She tied the reins to her wrist because it was the only way to keep them in her hand.

Then she stepped onto the trail.

The wind hit her, plucking at her hair and the fastenings on her coat. The steel dust didn't like the path. But when Lacey spoke, the horse followed, each tentative step reminding her that Morgan's life no longer rested in her hands. Fifty feet out, the funneled wind died to a breeze. The mist licked her feet.

With infinite care, Lacey walked, never moving her eyes from the rocky footing. Talus crumbled, and every once in awhile she could hear it hitting somewhere just below her. Most of the time she never heard it hit at all. Somewhere a river roared down a gorge, echoing up through the mist. A misstep would send them tumbling over the edge into the abysmal crevice below.

The minutes bled into an hour. Time became insignificant. Every step was an effort of concentration, until suddenly she felt the sun on her face.

Lacey stepped from the bowels of the granite pass into a mountain meadow, where a braided stream forked across the grassy plateau. Where autumn warmed the earth, burning away the fog. A pair of red-tailed hawks floated over the distant treetops against a pleasant blue sky. In the vast hollow of silence, the world stretched out before them. Tears glittered in Lacey's eyes. With a cry, she twisted to face Morgan—and her heart stopped.

Leaning over his bound wrists, his head hung listlessly against the sweaty neck of the steel dust. His hat had tumbled to the meadow floor, and dark hair fanned over his face. Lacey's world reeled. She sought the spot on Morgan's neck that pulsed with life, and for a brace of seconds, she waited, crying aloud when she finally felt his heartbeat. She scooped up his hat, and clutching it protectively to her chest, swung her gaze around the meadow.

Which direction?

Follow the sun. The words came out of the stillness.

A stream whispered in the breeze, and Lacey turned west, tugging the reins of the stallion. A hundred yards later she found a sheltered hollow burrowed by mountain elements from a rock chimney.

"Morgan, you have to wake up." Lacey saw his eyes open and close, then slowly open again. He tried moving his hands toward her, not realizing they were still tied.

"Morgan, you have to help me get you off this horse."

His sluggish gaze rested on her face, and then his thoughts seemed to assemble. "Cut the rope."

Lacey cut the rope, bracing a shoulder against him as he slid from the horse. He managed to take a few steps before going to his knees on the blanket Lacey spread over the ground.

"Hobble . . . the horse," he rasped.

"Morgan—"

"If . . . horse runs off . . . we're stranded."

Lacey glanced anxiously at the steel dust, its head hanging between the reins trailing on the ground. It worried Lacey more that the horse would collapse.

"I have to get you fixed."

Morgan opened his eyes, clearly struggling for consciousness. He pushed her hands away. "Go . . . I'll take care of this."

Reluctantly Lacey stood. Dizziness unbalanced her. There was a roaring in her ears she could not shut out. She knew hunger weakened her, and worried over ways to find food. Anything to sustain them.

Hobbling the stallion nearby in the grass, Lacey managed to pull the saddle and all the gear off its back. Steam rolled off its sweat-soaked body. The horse wasted no time rolling in the grass. Despite its ornery disposition, Lacey wanted to hug the huge beast. She knew enough about horses to realize they would never have made it that day had he been less resilient. This one possessed stamina.

Like its master.

Lacey swung the saddlebags over her shoulders and dragged everything else back to the camp. When she reached Morgan, he was no longer conscious.

Lacey had never seen a bullet wound. A small hole the size of her thumbnail marked its entry just above Morgan's hip, exiting out the back, leaving a jagged wound. His upper arm suffered a gash just below the shoulder. It was his gun arm.

Despite the danger of being discovered, Lacey struggled to build a fire with matches she found in the saddlebags. She racked her memory for every detail that she'd learned from Jack.

Jack. She wouldn't think of him right now. She couldn't.

To her disbelief, the fire took hold, licking hungrily at the wood and grass. She heated water from the creek to cleanse Morgan's wounds and wash the blood from his body. Her knuckles grazed hot skin. She worked over him, no longer thinking or remembering what it was that had happened, or why they were running. His body was bathed in shadows and firelight, marking his corded strength, vulnerable now to her touch. Tenderly, she traced his heart.

"Don't cry, Lacey."

The whisper brushed her cheek. Her gaze swung to Morgan's face. "I'm sorry," she managed, swiping at the twin trails creeping down her cheeks. She loved him with a longing as fierce as life itself, and she questioned her ability to keep him alive.

He tried to touch her hair. She pulled back. "Don't," she whispered, taking his hand and pressing it to her mouth.

He frowned incoherently. Blue eyes lifted from her face to the sky. A lone buzzard floated above them. A premonition. Lacey wanted to throw a rock at it.

"Be dark soon. Cold. Keep rifle with you. Can't protect you."

Lacey glared down at Morgan with frustrated rage. "Stop worrying about me and think about yourself. How can I help you? I don't know what to do."

His blue eyes flared before his hand moved over hers. "I . . . have never depended on anyone . . . in my whole life, Lacey. If Lawton finds us . . ."

Not trusting her voice to speak, Lacey squeezed his hand. It was so cold between hers.

He grinned, a boyish lopsided grin that trembled through her. "Don't . . . look so worried. Makes . . . me nervous."

She tried to smile, but her attempt to reassure him failed miserably. His eyes closed. "You won't like what you must do," he murmured distantly.

"Tell me, Morgan."

"Find the knife . . . the saddlebags. Look in the saddlebags." She started to argue Morgan's sanity when he silenced her. "It's the only thing I have . . . that will work. Heat it. Must be hot."

He was delirious. Lacey sat up. Above her the wind roamed

restlessly through the treetops. The partial cave protected them from the worst of the cold. Struggling to her feet, Lacey followed Morgan's instructions. She dumped the saddlebags out, strewing cartridges, a comb, a whiskey bottle, scissors in every direction. She found field glasses, set them aside, and finally pulled out the knife. Sheathed in a leather thong the length of her forearm, the lethal blade flashed demonic against the firelight.

"Make sure . . . gloves on."

Again, Lacey followed Morgan's directions.

"The wound on my side . . . must be cauterized, Lacey."

It became clear what he was going to make her do. "I can't!" How could she deliberately burn him? "Morgan, don't make me do it."

"For Christ's sake—do it!"

Don't think, Lacey, she pleaded to herself. She gripped the knife handle, sliding the heated blade from the fire. *Oh, God, don't think.*

Squeezing her eyes shut, she sucked in a deep breath, and laid the blade against his flesh. Morgan's head thrashed back. Lacey dropped the knife.

Morgan lay still as death. The wound bubbled black. Bidding herself not to think, she bound his waist and shoulder with what once had been the middle tier of her petticoat. She covered him with the blanket, then stood and walked out of camp.

Wolves howled in the distance, hunting their meal. When she reached the creek, she fell to her knees and retched.

Awareness came at once, crushing her. The horse wickered restlessly. Lacey sat up and pushed the hair out of her eyes.

Lord! She'd slept. She was still beside the creek. Her whole body shivered in the damp cold.

Stumbling back to camp, Lacey dropped beside Morgan. He was alive. Willing herself to calm, Lacey put more wood on the fire, teasing the flame into a warm blaze. A shimmering mist hung over the moonlit meadow like eerie trails of smoke.

Something was out there.

She bent slightly, her arm reaching toward the saddle at her feet. The metal of the rifle felt cold in her hand. She lifted it, gripping it to her breast.

Could she shoot Lawton if he were out there? Could she kill her own father?

Sensing Morgan's attention, Lacey looked down to find him staring up at her. Firelight rippled over his face. Even wounded as he was, his uncompromisingly masculine regard made her feel safer.

"Bear," he rasped. "Listen."

Lacey heard the sounds, far away at first, then closer as the bear lumbered with little stealth or grace through the woods behind them. Her breath caught as the bear broke from the trees and moved with purpose to the creek.

"It's all right." She heard Morgan's whisper.

With only a hurried glance in their direction, the bear meandered on, ignoring them as it made its way across the meadow. Lacey was still gaping when she heard Morgan speak again.

"He's gone . . . Lacey."

She sank to her knees beside Morgan, desperate to share the strength that seemed so much a part of him.

"They usually won't . . . eat you."

With a half-laugh, half-sob, she ran her hands over his stubbled cheek. His handsome face was terribly hot beneath her probing touch. "How are you feeling?"

"Like hell chewed me up and spat me out again." He looked at her once and tried to lift his hand as if to touch her face, but didn't have the strength. "Stay . . . alert," he rasped.

Gripping his hands, she nodded.

"I love you," he said and closed his eyes.

The darkness fell around Lacey. Powerful and suffocating. She couldn't breathe.

He loved her. He'd walked through hell for her, and now he might die because of her. Hot tears surfaced. She swung her gaze to the sky.

Cast in sharp relief against pale moonlight, the black pinnacles of a distant mountain range looked like sharp teeth against the mottled sky. Around her, nothing moved. Not even the wind.

A strangled sob caught in her throat. Lawton was somewhere in these mountains. Her father.

He would follow, for he was a man to whom hate was a driving force. It justified his very existence for living.

Fury swam through her. "I will not let you have him!"

She climbed to her feet and, scraping up a handful of rocks, she ran into the pasture.

"You will not win, you bastard." She threw a rock at the moon. She hated them all. Her father and mother. Her life.

Her labored breathing sent steam into the air. She cursed. Daring God to take her instead of Morgan. The only innocent person in this whole tragedy. The one who had suffered the most.

She threw one rock after another and shouted obscenities. When she ran out of rocks, she threw sticks and grass, until her arms were shaking and she stumbled to the wet ground in defeat, drawing in huge gulps of frigid air.

A creek gurgled through the meadow and took away the silence. Her gaze suddenly fell on one of Morgan's saddlebags. Embraced by a wispy frame of moonlight, it stared back at her in the darkness. Her heart lurched. A tin of peaches had rolled from the flap. She must have dropped the bag when she pulled the saddle off the steel dust.

With a sob, Lacey snatched up the can. She slid the small knife from her coat pocket and raked the blade along the can's rim. Tears blurred her vision. She stabbed the tin again and again until sobs wracked her body. The can would not open.

Lacey dropped the knife. She fell back and buried her face into hands so filthy she should have been abhorred by their state. She smelled of smoke and sweat. Her hair clumped in a snarled mass. Clare would have taken a scrubbing brush to her until she was pink.

"Oh, Clare." Lacey curled against the wet ground and wept.

She was not even distantly related to the woman who'd raised her for thirteen years.

Her life had been a lie.

Her dreams laughable fancies.

She wrapped her arms around her body and cried until there was nothing else left inside to bury. She shivered in the cold.

Morgan needed her. If she should die up here, who would

care for him? When she finally lifted her head, the last of her tears gave way as a new surge of determination lent strength to her limbs.

Brett Lawton would not win. She would find a way to keep him separated from Morgan.

She shoved at the insipid tin of peaches, watching with satisfaction as it rolled into the stream.

Dark shadows, just barely visible in the moonlight, scattered beneath the water's clear surface. In disbelief, Lacey crawled to the water's edge.

Fish! Huge fish! She laughed.

Tearing off her boots and stockings, Lacey lifted her skirts and boldly sloshed in after them. Madness had surely touched her. For the icy cold made her feel alive again.

Hell hadn't claimed him. He hurt, but whatever had been burning inside him no longer tore at his head. Opening his eyes, his gaze fell first on the fire. The smell of food cooking permeated the air, sifting past the cotton webbed across Morgan's mind, forcing him to awaken.

A quick scan around the clearing found Lacey, and she became the subject of his regard, his eyes measuring her as if she were some angel conjured up in his delirium.

His angel was bent over a fire, engaged in battle with a string of blackened fish impaled on a wooden spit.

He frowned. Fractured images assailed his memory. Visions of their flight through the forest: Lacey walking the horse, the bitter cold . . . her voice.

Morgan raised on his elbow. His head was muddled. He noted uneasily that she looked far younger than her twenty years. Too young to have endured Lawton's abuse . . . or his own sensuous regard. Her cropped hair was wet and tied in a queue. She must have found the scissors stowed in his bags. Her hair was no longer uneven.

Laid over the rocks beside Lacey, their clothes dried in the sunshine. She wore nothing underneath the blanket draped around her shoulders but her camisole and pantalets. Every feminine curve of her body was revealed to his lingering gaze. The thin cotton batiste strained across breasts belonging to no child.

The overpowering urge to take this angel in his arms snapped his restraint. He must have made a noise, because her head lifted in alarm. Relief flooded her face. His gaze probed hers as she dropped beside him. "You're alive. And coherent. You're talking."

He allowed her her brief unsteady ministrations over his body. Her hands felt good against his face.

"You're still feverish." She sat back on her knees. "How do you feel?"

"Like I've lost a lot of blood." His throat hurt to talk. "Hungry as hell."

"Finding something to eat on this mountain hasn't been easy. I tried to catch fish the first night with my hands. Can you believe that? I was slightly deranged, I think, that night. It was right after we saw that bear—"

"Lacey," he stopped her. His head ached.

"Then I remembered when I caught that salmon Red used a net. I rigged a net out of my petticoat—" The fire popped, claiming her attention, and she rushed to readjust the spit. "Catching fish isn't nearly so difficult as cooking up the slimy buggers. They don't like to stay on the spit. And they crumb—"

"How long have I been out?" He swigged out of the canteen set next to him.

"Three days . . . on and off."

Three days!

The import of her revelation stunned him.

Her eyes warmed over his face. "I told you I wouldn't let anything happen to you," she whispered.

Morgan shoved the hair out of his eyes. He was mesmerized. His heart beat in a silly pattern against his ribs. It came to him suddenly that he had not expected this manner of independence from her. Her ability to keep them both alive. And where were they that Lawton or the posse hadn't found them?

She knelt beside him again. "You must be terribly weak."

Not weak enough, he mused, enjoying the sound of her voice, even if she was babbling like a nervous cat. He tried to sit up.

"Not by yourself, you don't."

"Lacey, for Christ's sake. I need to get up."

"Morgan Caine, I've just had the worst week of my life, and I don't intend to suffer through your mulishness and watch you tear open your wound. You'll do as I say or I'll bloody well sit on you."

The blanket slipped off her shoulders. With her flashing green eyes, all she needed was a lightning bolt clutched in her fist.

Following the line of his gaze, Lacey stood. "Are you enjoying yourself?"

"Do you feel safe?" he taunted, reckless for a man who lacked the ability to stand on his own. Some of Lacey's spunk vanished. "Even a wounded man has needs, Lacey," he amended. "But mine takes me to the woods at this moment. Would you help me up?"

Lacey helped him to his feet. Waiting for the dizziness to subside, he secured the blanket around his flannel-clad hips. He didn't remember undressing. The crimson-stained wrap around his shoulder and waist reminded him that he was lucky to be alive. That this woman had been responsible for saving his life humbled him.

Hands made clumsy by a combination of pain and emotion reached up to cup her face. He had a need to touch her. To feel her light and know that she belonged to him.

"Don't." She stepped out of his reach.

Her action caught him off guard. A jolt of fear stabbed him. What had happened to her at Lawton's camp?

"It's just that I don't want you to hurt yourself," she said. Lacey grew uncomfortable beneath his penetrating gaze.

"Are you all right?" he asked.

"Really, Morgan. I'm not the one who was shot." She waved a hand, turning away from him. "Hurry. You need to eat."

In the solitude that followed his departure, Lacey dressed and attended to their small meal, all the while keeping an anxious eye on his beautiful shadow near the creek.

So unlike the awful one near her heart.

"No, Morgan," she whispered. "I'm not all right. Nothing will ever be all right again."

Chapter Nineteen

Morgan's mood darkened with each passing minute that clicked off in his head. He pulled a cheroot from his coat pocket, noting that it was almost his last one. Clamping it between his teeth, he lit a match against his boot heel and scanned the meadow, listening for any sign that unwelcome trespassers had violated their sanctuary. He listened for Lacey's presence.

He hadn't expected to wake up and find her gone. Though the devil only knew she'd acted strangely around him all week.

The cheroot caught flame, and Morgan dropped the match, grinding it into the damp earth with the toe of his boot. He could see the steel dust picketed near the creek contentedly munching the grass. The restless whisper of pines warned of approaching weather. In the mountains, such a threat loomed more fiercely over their lives than Brett Lawton.

He buckled his gun belt on with stiff precision. His arm was useless if it came to a showdown with Lawton any time soon.

Slapping his hat on, he took off in search of Lacey.

Morgan discovered her trail easily. The cold nipped at his

face. The niggling fear that Lacey might be lost fueled his pace.

His steps soon became more pronounced, his temper noticeably shorter every time he stopped to rest.

Hell, he'd been shot before. He knew the sooner he worked through the pain, the less it would cripple him.

A quarter of an hour passed before Morgan found Lacey, belly-flat against a talus overhang banking the edge of a huge chasm. The breathtaking emptiness stretching out before him stopped him cold. His gaze first took in the surrounding mountain peaks cast in sharp relief against a somber sky, before narrowing on the granite wall some eight hundred yards away rising from the bowels of the gorge. Even from this distance, Morgan could make out scraggily pine trees rooted precariously to the ancient trail hugging the rock.

Why would Lacey be watching such a pass? No man in his right mind would attempt to cross that killer trail.

A sudden coldness seized him, and he took a moment to study the land. Where was the route Lacey took into this mountain meadow?

"Enjoying the scenery?"

Lacey twisted, her eyes chasing up his body to land squarely on his face. Shadows smudged her eyes. She sat up. "Morgan, what are you doing here?"

Her bleak look disintegrated his anger at finding her gone from camp. "I should ask you that question."

"I always come up here after sunrise. It's the best place to keep watch."

Easing himself down beside Lacey, he pressed his back against a boulder for support. "Lacey," he said carefully, "what exactly are you watching?"

"Morgan, let me take you back to camp."

"Lacey, I want to carry on a conversation without constantly being coddled."

"Hah!" Her eyes flashed. "When you can beat me down with more than your tongue then I'll consider it."

Plopping a huge blackberry in her mouth, she raised the glasses back to her eyes and dismissed him, leaving him to stare at her backside as she wiggled back into position.

In a soundless exhale, Morgan frowned. A flickering glance around the clearing revealed a blackberry bramble thick with berries. Ignoring him, Lacey seemed intent, studying the trees on the other side of the gorge. He decided to move beside her. Stretching out in the grass next to the pile of berries, he helped himself to a handful.

"Do you want to tell me what we're watching?" he asked after awhile.

"Someone is over there in those trees."

Morgan stopped chewing, her words riveting his attention on the forest across the canyon. Lacey handed him the glasses.

"I don't know who it is," she said. "But I saw a flash earlier, like a glare. So, I suspect someone has been watching me with similar glasses. He's probably trying to figure out how I got over here."

Morgan scanned the woods and finally asked the inevitable. "How *did* you get here, Lacey?"

"I didn't know there was more than one way."

Morgan lowered the glasses, giving her his full attention.

"I followed that trail." She pointed to the cliff.

Morgan didn't bother looking at the trail again. He'd already seen more than enough. His head drooped into his hands.

"It was foggy," he heard her say. "It didn't look nearly that bad. At least I don't think it did."

Morgan made a pained sound, muffled against the grass. "Foggy?"

"There had been an ice fog that day. We walked through it."

Morgan's head lifted. "Ice?"

"And rain," she added. "I don't remember everything. I was too exhausted—"

"You're nuts."

Clearly indignant, Lacey sat up. "I most certainly am not!"

"How the hell did you get that ornery stallion to follow? Carry him?"

"With you on its back? Really, Morgan. What do you take me for?"

He looked at her in pure, unadulterated awe. "Don't mistake my shock for lack of gratitude, sweetheart. In truth . . ." He was sick. "I'm speechless."

Lacey nodded toward the distant trees. "What about the person over there?"

"If anyone is out there, he's probably trying to get up the nerve to travel that pass. Obviously, he's handicapped with a sense of self-preservation, which probably makes him one of Lawton's men. Or Lawton himself." He swung the glasses to the shadowed wall opening out onto the trail. Three hundred yards away, a talus overhang with the weight of tons of rock dipped treacherously over the trail. Again, his stomach turned queasy at the idea of Lacey on that precarious trail.

"Have you ever shot a rifle?" he asked, lowering the glasses. It was obvious by the look on her face, she hadn't. "You're about to have your first lesson. Come on."

Morgan climbed slowly to his feet. Lacey picked up the rifle and followed him to the boulder. Sitting beside him, she fingered the cold metal of the rifle barrel, gripping it tight.

"If there's someone over there, we're about to end his hopes of following us. The only other way to get over here is about a two-week ride around that mountain."

Her eyes found his. "Do you know this place?"

"I have an idea where we are. This meadow leads into a valley that arrows straight into Kingston."

"Then we're not lost?"

"No, sweet."

Morgan stepped behind Lacey, pressing her back into his chest as he raised the rifle in her arms. He could feel the rapid beat of her pulse in her wrist. That pleased him, as did the familiar scent of his shaving soap in her hair. The top of her head barely reached beneath his chin.

Feeling strangely possessive, Morgan brought the rifle against Lacey's shoulder and chambered a bullet into the breech.

"Won't this make a lot of noise?" she asked.

"Not as much as what's about to follow." Morgan adjusted the sights of the rifle, accommodating the weapon for the distance. "See that overhang?" Lacey followed his hand and nodded. "When the dust clears, let's hope we won't see it anymore."

Morgan snuggled Lacey against his chest, far closer than necessary. "Pull the trigger, Lacey."

Her muscles tensed. Morgan's steady grip on the rifle kept the weapon level in her hands. It fired, kicking back into her shoulder. Making no sound, she triggered the rifle as he had done and fired again. Together, they did this ten more times. Morgan was impressed by her fortitude. He thought she would complain of the pain and insist on putting the rifle down. Instead, she seemed determined to rain destruction on the granite cliff.

Morgan heard her bullets whine and ricochet in the pass, like angry bees darting furiously. And above the din, Morgan heard the slight vibration of moving earth. It grew, building in strength. A rolling thunder of shale and boulders began to break away, followed by the whole ledge. The granite overhang crumbled in on itself. Dirt and dust exploded, belching out in a mushrooming cloud of debris, cascading into the gorge. In its wake was absolute silence.

When the dust cleared, the passage was sealed.

"Thank you for the lesson," Lacey said abruptly. "Now I'd like to know how we're going to get out of here."

She turned in Morgan's arms, her movements somehow unfastening his coat. She looked directly at his bare chest. His bloodstained shirt was unbuttoned and hanging loosely over his bandages. He'd been in too much of a hurry earlier to see himself properly attired.

She shoved the rifle at him. "Especially since you have no respect for your health. You may have an aversion to heights, but I came across that trail . . . just fine. Mostly fine anyway," she amended. "What am I supposed to do when you succumb to the chill? How can you take everything else in life so seriously and mock your own health?"

"It's been awhile since anyone has cared—"

"And that's your own fault, too, Morgan Caine," she said right over his words. "If you weren't so bullheaded, you'd be surprised how many people might actually grow to like you. Though I'm hardly a sterling example of Miss Popularity . . ."

She kept talking about bullies and offensive outlaws, all who compared favorably to him.

Her inane words. Her courage. Everything she was humbled him. His passion now banked by a strange possessive tenderness that enveloped him, Morgan looked down into her beautiful face, flushed pink from the cold, and did the only thing he could do to shut her up.

He kissed her, swallowing her protests, and groan all at one time. She tasted sweet as berries, and Morgan parted her lips to thrust his tongue deeply into her mouth.

He felt her suddenly stiffen. "No . . ."

Morgan lifted his head. His gaze delved into eyes made bright green with emotion. Reaching behind the thick fall of her cropped hair, his hand cupped her head. "What are you running from, Lacey?" His voice was a husky whisper against the corner of her expressive lips. "Me?"

Her wet gaze encompassed him. "Let me go, Morgan."

Something smashed the boulder wall behind him, shattering rock over his head. A faraway pop rippled across the canyon, followed by another shot.

"Christ!"

Morgan dropped with Lacey and pinned her to the frigid ground. His wound tore, and he gritted his teeth. The firing stopped.

Trying to conceal his outline in the grass, he edged Lacey behind the cluster of boulders. Struggling to sit, he leaned against a rock to test his flesh, assess the damage.

Lacey knelt beside him. "Are you shot?"

"That was a goddamn Sharps," he hissed. "Jack's rifle."

"How can you tell?"

"I'd recognize the sound anywhere. That buffalo gun can take off a man's arm at a thousand yards."

"Brett Lawton has Jack's rifle," she whispered. "He took it . . . that day in town."

"How could I have been so blind, careless, stupid!" Morgan studied Lacey's pale face and waited for the residue of fear inside him to subside. "Hell, you've been in his sights all morning."

She paled so white he thought she might faint. She leaned

into him, holding him tightly, resting her head against his chest. A bitter winter breeze swept across the meadow, lifting the dead autumn leaves around them into a swirling mass. Raising his head, Morgan contemplated the pewter-tinted sky. The pressure of her body was protective as if she were the one trying to shield him. His gaze lowered, and he followed the stroke of his gloved hands over the moonlight softness of her hair.

Why hadn't Lawton shot sooner? He could have killed either one of them at any time.

"He knows where we are, Morgan. We have to leave. Now."

Huge snowflakes floated to the ground. The air thickened with white. Morgan hadn't said a word as he watched Lacey swing her gaze over the campsite she'd worked so hard to build. In the hushed silence, he could almost hear her heart pounding against her ribs. Clearly, she didn't know where to start packing. Only that they must leave. He could feel the terror inside her.

Water boiled on the fire. She grabbed a stick and scooped the rag out of the water letting the steam rise over her. Her hands trembled.

"Talk to me, Lacey."

His voice made her lurch. "I have been talking to you." She snapped the thin cloth taut and dabbed it carefully on his wound before reapplying his bandage. "You're in no condition to fight anyone. We need to get you to shelter."

One gloved hand tangled gently in her hair, stopping just at its length below the nape of her neck. She'd washed with his shaving soap, and he smelled the scent of sandalwood on her hair. His presence was all over her. She belonged to him. He wanted her to talk to him. Christ, he wanted her trust.

"Look at me, Lacey."

"I told you nothing happened to me at Lawton's camp."

"To hell with that."

Lacey tried to extricate his fingers, but he only tightened his grip, preventing her from moving away. Her eyes snapped to his face. "He could have killed you on that cliff. Why didn't he?"

"He's playing with your mind . . . for Christ's sake!" She winced at the expletive. "Listen to me"—he gripped her shoulders to shake sense into her—"Lawton has never shown mercy to another living soul. He would have had Gressett kill you just to get to me. You could be his sainted mother, and he'd let nothing stand in his way of what he wants."

"I don't care what he wants. It has nothing to do with me. Do you understand? Nothing!" She threw the rag at him. He caught it easily. "You think you're invulnerable. That bullets can just pass through you, and everything will return to normal. You're selfish . . . and inconsiderate, Morgan Caine. You're a gunslinger just like Lawton. You'll die just like him, too. And I hate you for that!"

His fingers worked the buttons on his shirt. "I'll check the snares," he said crisply, shoving his shirt inside his pants. His side hurt, but he couldn't dwell on that. "While I'm gone, start packing."

He buckled his gun belt around his waist. Slapping his hat on, he started to turn when his eyes caught her watching him. Bundled beneath her coat, she didn't move. Firelight played on her bleak face. He made a living reading people. Their expressions. The shine in her eyes warned Morgan how close she was to losing control.

"I'm . . . sorry." Her voice cracked.

His gloved hand went to the Winchester perched against the rock beside him. "You know how to use this. Keep it near you."

She took the rifle. Her fingertips brushed his, and slowly her chin lifted.

Morgan bent and kissed her deeply. There was no gentleness in the act, only a ruthless, hungry need to reclaim her. When he raised his head again, his eyes bore in the emerald depths of her uncertain gaze. "This isn't finished between us, Lacey."

Lacey shifted in the saddle. Morgan looped the reins around his wrist, locking his gloved hands beneath the blanket near her belly. She drew in her breath and could not hide the nervous puff of steam that rolled from her lips.

"Do you know where we're going?" she asked finally.

He hadn't spoken to her since they left camp. When he still ignored her, she turned her face to look up at him. Stubble covered his jaw. Beneath his hat, his eyes were as stark as the winter sky as they went over her. Despite herself, her heart fluttered, and she remembered his kiss.

Imprisoned by her imagination, and the manner of unfinished business between them, Lacey suffered through a profound stretch of dread. Morgan frightened her. Not because she worried that he would hurt her, but he read inside her. Touched her in places she no longer wanted to be touched. She didn't want him to see the coward she was.

"The weather didn't turn out so bad," she said.

"As usual, you underestimate the enemy, Lacey."

She snapped her mouth shut. Morgan was right, of course. He was always right, and before noon the snowstorm slammed into the mountainside.

Chased by a bitter chill that chafed Lacey's hands and face, huge white flakes stuck to her lashes as she squinted through the narrow slats that separated the blankets she'd wrapped around her head and torso. By nightfall, wind moaned through the treetops.

They'd been riding most of the day, stopping only to eat some of the cooked rabbit she'd saved from dinner the previous night.

Morgan had no business on a horse this long. But he'd been intent on reaching a lower elevation. Lacey tightened her arms around him, wrapping him in her warmth. He'd put her behind him after their last stop. Head down, he took the brunt of the wind and ice. They forded a stream that looked like frozen obsidian in the gray light of dusk. Morgan slowed the horse.

"We're getting off." She heard him over the wind.

Abandoned by his warmth, she leaned forward to grip the horn. Cold battered her. The hem of her heavy skirts was sodden with snow. Morgan's strong hands wrapped around her waist and drew her off the saddle. She slumped against the length of his body, ashamed that she wasn't stronger.

Holding the reins of the horse, Morgan wrapped his other arm around her shoulders. His heat encompassed her. Made her feel safe in a world barren of warmth. "Follow me," he said against her ear. "There's a grove of trees over here."

She held his torso and, bracing each other, they both plodded up the incline. While Morgan picketed the horse in a safe shelter of trees nearby, Lacey rushed to prepare the camp. Shaking life back into her frozen hands and feet, she took Morgan's big battle knife from his bags and chopped at pine branches. Blinded by the blowing snow, she sliced and cut, severing the boughs, creating more than a windbreak or simple shelter. She'd built castles out of rocks and trees when she was a child in England. Knights and princesses had occupied her imaginary world, a world that seemed so trite now. She could not have guessed at the reality of life. Her very existence depended on a tall and dangerous gunfighter who made her ache with hunger.

The irony of it clawed a hole in her gut. Morgan had nearly died to rescue the daughter of his most hated enemy. Badge or not. Would he have walked into Lawton's camp had he known the truth about her? She was too cold to cry, but the hot tears were there anyway.

"Come . . . you're cold," Morgan beckoned, wrapping an arm around her. He'd built a fire, and took her down with him to a bed of pine. "You need warmth as much as I."

A dull pain throbbed behind her eyes. *Tell him,* her conscience shouted. Tell him that if she stayed with him, she would surely get him killed. Instead, she forced out between chattering teeth; "I'll hurt you."

"Lacey?" He gripped her sleeve, keeping her from moving away. "Why don't you let me be the judge of that?"

The ground was cold, and more than anything Lacey wanted to share his warmth. The need to touch him was tearing her apart.

Tell him, the voice demanded. *Tell him the vicious killer he's going to hunt down is your own father. That Lawton's blood runs through your veins. Tell him.*

Would he still want to touch her then?

It seemed as if she'd only just fallen asleep when a hand pressed over her mouth. A lone howl splintered the ghostly stillness of the sleeping forest. Flailing out, Lacey started to scream.

"Easy, Lacey." Morgan's hot breath touched her ear. Heart racing, she sensed danger in those words. The horse was making sounds of distress. "Wolves," Morgan rasped, throwing the blankets off. Snow fluttered over her. "Get up. We're leaving."

In the predawn light, she glimpsed two of the shaggy creatures thirty yards to her left. Standing in wary repose beneath the weeping branches of a pine, they merely watched her. Though Lacey had spent many a night these past weeks listening to the mournful, often hungry howl of roving wolves, she had never actually seen a real wolf before. The scrawny, gray shapes hardly looked fearsome. "They look like dogs," she remarked, curiously unimpressed.

"Just don't try to pet one, sweetheart." He was already rolling the blankets, his movements slow with cold and obvious pain.

Lacey dropped to her knees and helped him. Together they swept through the camp with clean efficiency.

Noting four more shapes slinking just at the edge of the trail ahead, Lacey said, "They don't look too vicious."

Handing her the rifle, Morgan's breath steamed over her cheek. The unexpected caress against her temple made Lacey's breath break.

"Be ready to shoot if you have to." He saddled and packed the horse. "Precious here isn't likely to stay around much longer if they get too much closer."

"Precious?" she asked. "This stallion's name is *Precious?*"

"My sister had a sick sense of humor."

"Precious?" Lacey laughed, and Morgan turned to look down at her. In the predawn light, his blue eyes glittered over her face with startling warmth that killed the laughter in her throat.

"Let's go," he said lightly, and climbed into the saddle.

Lacey would never be able to get up there on her own. The steel dust shied, leaving her standing in the center of the camp.

"Morgan . . ." Panic laced her cry before she crammed a fist in her mouth to keep silent.

He steadied the horse with a skill that could only come from years of practice. When his eyes found hers again they were furious. "Give me the rifle."

She eagerly complied and, taking his good arm, she pulled herself up behind him.

"Christ, did you think I was going to leave you?"

Lacey struggled with her shame. The horse leaped into a full gallop, and her heart didn't still its mad flight until they reached the open meadow.

Morgan stopped periodically to eat and walk the horse. The tension between them had not changed. He didn't speak to her, nor did he touch her, except to wrap the blanket securely over her shoulders.

By midmorning, a hushed stillness fell over the forest. Snow continued to fall. Movement in the trees told Lacey that they still had not lost the wolves. All day their shadows skipped like loping dogs in and out of the distant trees. They hardly appeared to be a threat. But Morgan had drawn out the rifle, and it rested across his lap.

Lacey closed her eyes. She listened to the steady squeak of the horse's feet on the pristine snow. Morgan was doing an admirable job seeing them down the mountain with far more skill and efficiency than she'd gotten them up the other side. Buried beneath the blankets, she pressed to his back. Her fingers dug into his jacket. She did not let him go. Since he'd left her momentarily alone in the glade with the wolves, she had not relinquished her hold.

"Wake up, Lacey." Morgan's voice came out of the darkness. Lacey blinked the sleep from her eyes. Her heart beat unsteadily.

"We're home."

The strange words jolted her with their intimacy.

She almost missed seeing the cabin in the darkness. Barely discernible for what it was against the woodsy backdrop of pine trees, its moonlit shadow welcomed her. Morgan was already guiding the stallion down the shallow ravine.

A wolf suddenly ran out from behind a tree.

"Morgan—"

He slid from the saddle. She heard his muffled curse when he hit the ground. The trail of reins in his hand snapped taut, swinging the horse around. He grabbed the bridle, soothing the agitated stallion.

"Take him to the lean-to," he said. She edged off the horse. "I'm right behind you." He then released the bridle and drew his gun from his holster, walking backward following Lacey.

Swinging open the heavy door, Lacey pulled the stallion inside the wooden shelter. It smelled of aged wood and wet earth. She could barely see in the darkness and worked her frozen fingers over the saddle by touch alone. Outside a staccato of gunfire erupted, shattering her nerves. Wasting no time, Lacey stripped the saddle off, and it crashed to the ground at her feet. Morgan came to stand in front of the door. She saw his gaze sweep the interior of the narrow building. Someone at one time had taken great care with the construction of the animal shelter. Obviously satisfied that their horse would not become fodder for a pack of hungry wolves, Morgan moved out of the doorway. Lacey found a tin bucket beside the door and hurried just outside to fill it with snow.

"He has no food," she said.

"He'll go hungry the same as us for the time being," Morgan replied. "It can't be helped. Now hurry."

At least the snow would melt to water. She heaved the blankets and saddlebags off the ground, keeping near Morgan as he shoved the stall door shut, sealing the stallion safely inside. The ankle-deep snow crunched beneath their quickened steps as Morgan pulled her toward the cabin.

The door opened easily. Morgan hauled Lacey inside, and slammed the portal shut behind her. Their staggered breathing filled the darkness.

Outside the wolves set up howling.

Lacey calmed her pounding heart until there was nothing left but the silence inside the cabin. And Morgan.

Chapter Twenty

Lacey dropped the load she carried. Collapsing beside the bags, she tore around in the darkness for the matches.

"Looking for these?" Morgan's voice followed a scraping sound, and a wooden match fired to life in his hand.

Their eyes met over the tiny flame. Lacey could see the white of Morgan's teeth against the dark contour of his jaw. The clarity of his gaze unnerved her.

He stepped past her into the cabin, his spurs clinking in the heavy silence. Lacey breathed in the damp pine aroma and coughed through the grainy air stirred up by their movements. With the exception of an old wooden table, a stove, and a chair put together with rawhide strips, the small frost-ridden room was as empty as it was cold. The chill seeped up from the floorboards into Lacey's wet boots. But one sweep of their minuscule light revealed a hearth stacked with wood and sturdy log-hewn walls that would hold the wind and wolves at bay.

"Won't someone be upset to find us here?"

The light flickered out. A match scraped again followed by the brighter light of an oil lamp. "I don't think he'll mind," he said as if it was the most natural thing to be invading someone else's house.

"You know who owns this place?"

"I do."

A hundred questions jumped to her mind, but when he put the lamp on the table and turned into her gaze, every thought skidded to an abrupt halt. In the pool of flickering light, his eyes held hers and set her heart racing. She stood fixed to the floor.

A treacherous edge clung to him. Not quite anger, yet his eyes raked her with a strange sort of fire that made her wary. A beard darkened his jaw. When he was ill, it had been simpler to hide her attraction for him and bend herself to sacrificial standards because of her no-good father. Now Morgan was not helpless. His male presence dominated the room. She'd been a fool to ever think herself capable of pursuing this man on her terms. She knew now with absolute certainty, she'd always been way out of her element. How had he stood her presence for so long?

"We'll need to heat water," Morgan said.

A cauldron still hanging on its stoop in the fireplace became the welcome object of her focus. Morgan was holding it out to her, watching her with an odd mixture of curiosity and something else that sent a fluttering thrill through her veins. She struggled to cling to some small portion of her honor and not to stare or invite him to stare back. She possessed a dizzying wont to flee. To tame the palsied tremble in her hands. With rifle in hand, Morgan took her outside, standing over her as she filled the cooking pot with snow.

While Morgan worked at building a fire, Lacey spread their coats and blankets over the floor. Far more skilled than she at such things, he had the flames licking greedily at the dry kindling within minutes. The room filled with seductive golden warmth.

Morgan unbuttoned his bloodstained shirt. He didn't ask for her help when he eased the bandage away from his wounds. Lacey averted her gaze. Retrieving scraps she'd saved from her petticoat for his bandage, Lacey approached him. He took them from her, his eyes touching her face before turning away.

"Get me the whiskey," he said, easing out of his tattered shirt.

Lacey watched anxiously as he uncorked the bottle and took a healthy swig. Then another. "Hell, I hate this stuff," he said, grimacing, and proceeding to dribble the bottle's contents over the wound above his hip.

Lacey's stomach turned. "Morgan, let me help—"

His eyes flashed. "Get out of those wet clothes. I can handle this without having to worry about you fainting."

"Has it occurred to you that I've dealt with far worse?"

A dark brow lifted. But it was the intent in his eyes as they held hers that made her mouth go dry. "Don't argue with me, Lacey. Go change."

Lacey turned away. Argue with him, indeed. She was near to falling down at his feet. What was wrong with her?

Lacey dug through Morgan's saddlebags for his black wool shirt. Glancing surreptitiously in his direction, she struggled beneath the drape of his shirt while she stripped out of the hated riding habit. The uncooperative shirt was wont to slide in all directions, threatening her modesty. After much struggling, Lacey finally pulled free of her damp clothes. Digging through the pockets of her coat, she retrieved her comb and sat near the fire. Tucking the blanket around her legs, Lacey started to work the tangles out of her hair. Even short, it was a painful task. She tackled it with sufficient rancor to take the edge off her mood. The tension in the room could be cut with a knife.

Morgan propped his foot on the hearth. One hand squeezed into a fist. He swigged the whiskey, letting his gaze roam all over Lacey. She hunched over her lap unsnagging her hair, oblivious to his carnal interest. He'd contemplated her disrobing with no conscience for privacy or formality. He was finished denying himself what he wanted most.

Noting that Lacey's hand had suddenly stilled, he caught his breath and waited as her face lifted slowly to his.

Time stood still. Paused. In the firelight, her eyes shimmered, entangling him within their jeweled grasp. A flood of color heightened her cheeks. The swell of her breasts rose and fell in ragged crescendo. Framed between shadow and light, she was a vision. His vision.

He wanted to take her face between his hands and shake the ghosts from her head, to burn Lawton from her mind, exorcise the memory.

"Did you really believe I would leave you to those wolves, Lacey?"

He could see the comb trembling slightly in her hand. He set the bottle down and straightened. He was finished with patience and dogging her reticence. He wanted her. Christ, he wanted her body and soul.

"Morgan . . ." Panic laced her voice.

She climbed to her feet, the blanket falling unheeded to the ground. His shirt did nothing to hide the feminine taper of her hips or the silken curve of her thighs.

"Look at me and tell me I would have left you out there, Lacey."

"I didn't . . . know."

"Why," he asked, advancing on her, "since the moment I woke, have you run scared every time I glance in your direction?"

"I don't know what you're talking about."

"Of course you don't."

"But you've been ill," she protested.

"You've caught our food, found shelter, tended my wounds—"

"I've done nothing—"

"—kept watch. Washed my clothes. Fed the horse."

Her bottom hit the table. "You saved my life, Morgan."

"Saved your life?" His voice gentled, and he reached up to touch her hair. "Talk to me, Lacey . . . Autumn Star—"

"Don't call me that!"

"Why?"

"You need to ask?"

"Because of your hair? Do you think this matters to me?" He laced his hand through her hair. "It'll grow back, Lacey."

"It's not that simple anymore."

"It isn't simple. I know that."

"Morgan . . . please—"

"You used to look at me with eyes I could read to your soul. Did Lawton steal that from you?"

She averted her gaze, her breath coming swiftly, betraying every ounce of her facade.

"Tell me what we have isn't worth fighting for. Christ"—he breathed in the spicy scent of her hair—"tell me he didn't take that away."

Tears glistened in her eyes. His fingers curled in her hair tilting her face upward. "Is that why you turn away when I touch you?"

Still clutching the comb in her hand, she gripped it to her breast as if it were a shield.

"Oh, please, Morgan—"

He bent his lips to her hair. "Are you afraid of me?"

"No."

"Then why are you running?"

"I'm not running."

Morgan trapped her between the powerful brace of his arms. "You're not afraid . . . and you're not running."

Tears swam in her eyes and spiked her dark lashes. "It's just that, that . . . when I was in Lawton's camp, I prayed that you wouldn't come after me. And then you were there beside the fire like some avenging angel. I knew I loved you more than life itself. When you took that bullet to save me, I promised . . . I promised that I would never let him ever hurt you again."

Her courage. Her words took his voice. "Is that what this is about?" he rasped. "You're afraid for me?"

"I failed to protect you."

"Because of what happened at the cliff?"

"I would never have him hurt you again, Morgan. Never."

He looked into her face, into her eyes. His throat tightened. "I would die for you, Lacey, if that's what it took to keep you safe."

A strangled sob broke from her lips. The comb fell unheeded to her feet. "Oh, Mor—"

His mouth moved hers. He kissed her deeply, swallowing her groan, tasting the wet salt on her lips. He touched her nowhere else but her lips, drinking in her sigh with a restless ache to end his banishment from her life. He feared his hunger for her. It stripped him of his strength and lent new meaning to vulnerability.

He needed her.

And Morgan had never needed anyone.

She lifted on her toes. Her tongue slid against his, seeking, melding to his completely. Their breathing filled the small, sensual space of the cabin and mixed with the potent heat of the fire. Still he did not touch her and let the kiss go on and on.

He felt Lacey's knees slacken. "I . . . can't breathe, Morgan."

His lips brushed across her temple, down the column of her neck. She filled his senses. She filled his life. Made the blood hum in his veins.

"We must talk," she rasped.

Morgan began to work the buttons on her shirt. "Why?"

"It . . . hurts . . . you see."

"Where does it hurt?"

Each button slipped through its mooring with hands no longer steady. His fingers brushed the bare skin of her collarbone, lingering over the frantic beat of her pulse.

For an immeasurable moment, time remained suspended. "Here?" he whispered haltingly.

The small sound of her whimper sliced huge pieces out of his self-restraint.

Slowly he opened the shirt, reverently exposing her to his hungry gaze. He marveled at the perfect beauty of each breast, the apricot hue of her skin. His hungry gaze swept over her tapered waist, to the ethereal curls that beckoned his thorough exploration. The glide of his hands over her breasts sent the blood thundering in his ears. Her nipples hardened in hands that ached with need for her.

"Open your eyes, Lacey," he commanded, wanting to see all of her. Desire consumed him. Staggering him. He would see its equal reflected in her molten gaze. He had a profound need to know that what he was about to do, she wanted, too. To hell with tomorrow. To hell with the rest of the world.

Sweeping the hair from her face, he beckoned her to open her eyes. "Look at me, Lacey," he whispered again.

Lacey's eyes opened in wonder. There was no retreat from the dark, sensuous promise in Morgan's gaze.

In the firelight, his skin glowed bronze against the stark-white bandage. His wide shoulders narrowed to a taut waist, though covered with a bandage, which failed to hide the sleek muscles that wrapped his torso.

Morgan brushed his hands over her shoulders, pushing the shirt from her body. It billowed to the table. Lacey felt devoured by the dark measure in his eyes. Eaten alive. Consumed.

His fingers tangled in her hair. "I'm in pain just looking at you." He laughed, a deep, throaty sound, resembling more a growl, as his mouth hovered over hers. It had been so long since she'd seen him smile, much less heard his laugh. He took her breath, her very soul.

He dropped to his knees, taking her with him to the soft cushion of blankets. She twined around his body, basking in his strength.

Morgan rose above her, his eyes sweeping her body. "I've waited too long for this." His husky whisper burned against her mouth. "I've waited forever." He bent over her. "Let me love you, Lacey." His fingers grazed the silky triangle of curls between her legs. "All of you."

"Morgan?" She stopped him with the spread of her hand against his firm chest.

His eyes hidden beneath half-closed lids, Morgan bent his mouth over hers, seizing her lips, pushing her back down into the blankets. The fire at her back had made them hot, and she cooked deliciously. His stubble tenderly scraped a silken trail down the flat plain of her belly, helplessly distracting her, taunting her. Her fingers wrapped into his hair.

His hands dropped to her bottom, lifting her, and he parted her thighs to his sensual gaze. "Oh, God . . . Morgan!"

His grin was purely wicked, possessive, a flaming brand so totally consuming he burned her to ashes. He brushed his mouth against the silken triangle of curls.

Lacey's head dropped back, a cry tearing itself from her lungs. Reality ceased to matter. She clung to him. He was the center of her world. Her pleasure. The very air she breathed. Outside, the wolves howled mournfully with hunger, inside a hunger of a different, more savage bent, spread through her limbs. She heard her breath break over his name. Then his mouth reclaimed hers, recklessly consuming her, giving her a taste of her own seductive desire.

Somewhere along the way, he'd shed his pants. He entered her. Tears fell unheeded. And while he loved her, he kissed the tears from her face. He mastered her body as easily as he mastered her heart. She would give him more if she could. He had said that he would die for her; she knew in that moment that no power on earth would hurt him again. It was time that someone watched over him.

Morgan plundered her mouth, beckoning her response with every powerful thrust of his body. The world surrendered to her cries.

And then she was laughing in reckless abandon, loving him, taking this precious gift and giving back all that she had in life.

When their hearts had stilled, and Lacey opened her eyes, he was watching her with a tenderly fierce expression that swelled her heart. For now, she could pretend that she belonged solely to him. Then he rolled off her taking her against him, holding her as if to keep the world at bay. She laid her head on his shoulder and closed her eyes.

"Marry me, Lacey," his quiet voice whispered over her.

Lacey's heart pounded to a stop. The world was in those words. His world. A part of her withered and died in the awful silence that followed. She could not bear to tell him the truth.

When she didn't answer, his breathing grew quiet.

The fire popped as wood crumbled in on itself. Morgan merely watched the play of firelight on the ceiling.

And said nothing.

Morgan propped a leg on the weathered pole fence and rested the Winchester across his thigh. The land to the west of the meadow dropped steeply and, with the army field glasses, he scanned the pristine crevasses for any movement or sign of tracks. Sunrise blossomed like the first blush of spring, its beauty overshadowing the threat that loomed over his life.

The stallion tossed his head and snorted, prancing about in the corral as if on parade. Morgan had awakened early and, after setting the snares, he'd moved the horse to the sturdy corral. Stiff blades of grass poked through the melting snow, and the steel dust had feasted. This was tall-grass country. A man could make a living here. If he had a reason to stay.

His mood darkened. He'd never thought of the future, and now, he could think of little else. But the life of a lawman was so ingrained in him; he didn't quite know how to let it go. Even with Lacey.

Something had happened between her and Lawton. And it wasn't rape. The bastard had crawled inside her head somehow.

He was there now.

Slowly killing her.

Morgan rubbed the smooth rifle stock, then flexed his fingers until the wound on his arm began to burn. A whisper of movement turned him toward the cabin.

Lacey stood on the porch watching him, her gaze wide in her pale face, as if she feared he'd left her. It was the same frightened look she'd given him that morning when they'd run from the wolves. The cool breeze tousled her short hair and fluttered her skirt.

Pulling the last cheroot from his coat pocket, Morgan lit it and flicked the match into the snow. If it were the last thing on earth he ever did, he would hunt Lawton down and, this time, he'd put a bullet between the man's eyes himself.

Lacey remained standing on the porch, watching Morgan smoke. Her breath misted. He'd set his rifle against the huge oak that laid a broken shadow over the corral. Leaning with his arms crossed against the tree, he watched her back with a masculine vigilance that set her on edge. The mere touch of those blue eyes elevated her temperature. She could not conceal the blush that stole into her face as she vividly remembered their shared passion last night.

He was remembering it, too.

His marriage proffer hung in the air between them.

Wrapping her arms tightly against her body, she considered retreating. Instead, she stepped off the porch and approached the corral. The steel dust raised his head and nickered, strutting in a high-stepping gait as she settled herself against the fence post where Morgan rested his boot.

Lacey compared the unbridled spirit of the stallion to the man beside her. Morgan belonged to the rugged grandeur of this country. It was a part of him as it could never be a part of her.

"Precious," she mused. "I would have liked your sister."

The words were out before she could take them back. Her throat tightened. Brett Lawton had destroyed so many lives.

Including hers.

Lacey understood revenge in a way she'd never fathomed before, and the knowledge terrified her. But despite what Brett Lawton was, she couldn't bear the thought of his blood on Morgan's hands.

Her thigh pressed against Morgan's calf. Though he was careful not to blow smoke in her direction, the air smelled of sweet tobacco. His continued silence as he watched her was unnerving.

With a fortifying breath, she turned to face him. "Do you remember when you told me how hard it would be here? That I should marry someone who would take me to Portland or San Francisco?"

He squinted down at her from beneath his hat, clearly waiting for her to get to the point.

"You've taken nothing from me that I haven't freely given," she said softly. "No promises, remember?"

"It's not that simple anymore, and you know it."

"You still see me as Colin's daughter. And now you don't quite know what to do with me. You're only being honorable."

He dropped the cheroot and ground it beneath the toe of his boot. "You think so?"

"I have something to tell you." She clasped her hands in front of her, and suddenly her voice faltered, and her heart raced in panic. She couldn't do this. Not now.

"I'm asking . . ." She curled her hands into her skirt. "I'm asking that you let someone else hunt down Brett Lawton."

His eyes narrowed slightly. "I can't do that, and you of all people know it."

"You can."

"I won't."

"There can never be anything between us if you don't walk away from this."

He straightened. And she came flush up against the fence post. "Christ, what's he done to you, Lacey?"

Tears surfaced but sheer will kept them in check. "He's my father, Morgan! I don't know how. Or why. I only know that he is!"

Silence fell around them. Ugly, cruel silence that told her in more than words that he was suddenly appalled.

"What the hell are you talking about?"

She clasped her hands tightly to keep them from twisting. "I don't know the story. Or how I came to be under Colin's care. But I'm not his daughter."

"You're mad. That's what you are."

"It's the truth."

His eyes went over her face and she watched his expression transform into something she didn't want to understand. Somewhere a wolf howled. A hollow sound filled with loneliness.

"I tried to tell you sooner, Morgan. I swear."

He tipped her chin, turning her face into the sunlight. "You're Lorraine's daughter." His voice was like ice. "I should have seen the resemblance."

But he hadn't, and his eyes narrowed on her now. Cold shivered up Lacey's spine. He valued trust and loyalty, and she hadn't trusted him enough to tell him the truth earlier.

Before last night.

Before he'd asked her to be his wife.

Morgan looked away. His mouth tightened. "Colin sent me into those mountains knowing Lawton would never hurt his own daughter."

"You don't understand—"

His glare froze her. "I nearly got myself killed."

"Please . . . Morgan."

"Christ!" He slammed a fist against the tree. "I applaud your ability to act. You let me say all those things about Lawton. When all this time . . . were you worried for him? Is that why you don't want me going after him?"

"For him? Never! I know I should have told you."

Morgan's unblinking stare tore into her. "Damn right, lady! You would be having my children. Didn't you think I had a right to know who their grandfather would be?"

"I wanted to be so important to you that nothing could ever come between us. Not your badge. Not Lawton. Not your vengeance. Nothing." Her words echoed her misery. "But you won't change. And I can't change who I am."

"You should have let me decide for myself what *I* wanted."

"You don't want me anymore. Is that what you're trying to say?"

His hand wrapped in her hair, pressing her backward into the fence. "I want you more than I've ever wanted another woman. I want you so damn much I can't think straight." His voice was a hot whisper against her hair. "And I'm pissed as hell that Lawton can claim any part of you. That he owns more of you than I do." His hand cradled her face. "That it's his damn daughter I've been—"

"Don't you say it, Morgan Caine!" She shoved his hand away. With an oath, he braced his fist against the tree. Taut. Ready to explode. Lacey shoved a finger against his chest. "And what about *my* life? Will you ever be able to look at me again and not see him?"

The truth flickered in his eyes before he looked away. He hated Brett Lawton too much to ever look at her the same way again. Somewhere in the tumult of her cascading thoughts, Lacey felt the ground swell and drop beneath her. She whirled away and made a straight path for the cabin.

Saying nothing to stop her retreat, Morgan raked a closed fist over the tree, gritting back the urge to beat its unyielding mass.

As unyielding as his heart.

He was an idiot.

She had judged him with such flawless accuracy, and he'd made no effort to prove her wrong.

Morgan could accept what fate had dealt because it had

saved Lacey's life, a deuced paradox. Whom was he kidding? He'd been willing to sell his soul to the devil in trade for Lacey's life; it now looked as if he'd done just that.

The door slammed, echoing in the mountain silence like a gunshot to his heart. For a long time, he listened to the sound of his heartbeat, and the wind in the trees.

Then he snatched up his rifle and went to check the snares.

Lacey carried the tin plates outside to the creek and dumped them in the grass. Her breath steamed from her frigid lips. Kneeling near the water, she cared little that the snow dampened her dress. She scrubbed the plates vigorously. Morgan stood on the porch, rifle in hand, watching her. They'd said very little all day. He'd complimented her on dinner, as if shocked that she could cook.

How quickly he'd forgotten that she knew how to do anything except lie and keep awful secrets about her parentage.

Gathering the utensils, Lacey walked back to the cabin. Her feet squeaked in the snow, and her skirts swished with each stride, tangling with her feet. Morgan opened the door for her. She swept past him to go inside, pulling aside her skirts, careful not to touch any part of his body. He was too dangerous to her state of mind.

After she realized he wasn't going to follow her, she opened the front door and found him on the porch, leaning against one of the wooden poles that held up the roof. The rifle was crooked across his arms. When she stepped outside on to the wooden planking, he turned his head, and she was looking into his eyes. His hat brim shadowed their expression, but she felt their heat all the way to her toes.

Silence emptied the space between them, and suddenly, Lacey felt more than his gaze. His presence surrounded her, making her warm all over, when she preferred the chill. Abruptly, she turned to look out at the rolling meadow sloping away from the cabin. The creek shimmered oily black in the indigo twilight, meandering for miles through the grass and narrow patches of melting snow.

"Where are we?" Her voice trembled, and she braced her spine against the weakness.

"Kingston is north of here."

Lacey hoped she was looking in the right direction. She didn't want to look stupid, so instead she looked at the sky. Stars filled the velvet dome, and all at once, she hated the way her throat tightened. Suddenly she felt vulnerable, incapable of even the slightest bit of courage.

"It's beautiful here," she whispered.

The silver jingle of spurs told her Morgan had moved behind her. His shearling coat was a hot whisper against her back. He'd shaved and smelled of soap. She could neither step to his right nor left without falling off the porch.

"There's a view from that south ridge where you can see clear through the whole territory."

A fine layer of mist hovered over the ground. But the night was alive with the sounds of life. Somewhere faraway the shrill of a cougar echoed against the high walls of the distant cliffs. A raccoon waddled through the high grass. Morgan stood so close she could almost hear his heart beat.

"You know this place well."

"Jack's land begins about five miles west of here, the other side of those trees," he said, pointing beyond the distant tract of forest. "Your father's land borders this meadow." His voice had softened, "And the rest belongs to me."

Her jaw dropped open. "This whole valley is yours?"

Morgan's gaze embraced the land with a strange longing she'd never seen in his eyes. A look she'd give her heart and soul to possess. "Enough to make a living."

Lacey let her daunted gaze fall on the rough-hewed logs that made the cabin. Hard work and dreams had gone into building this place. The corral was sturdy. The yard had wasted away with neglect, but beneath it all, was a man's pride. Dreams to build a life on.

She touched the newel post. "This is the house you mentioned when we were in Waylen Springs?"

"At one time I wondered what it would be like to settle down and live here. Raise a family."

"With . . . Jolene?"

He lowered his gaze and looked at her. Moonlight played

over his features, so ruggedly handsome, she felt him with every fiber in her being. "Things changed."

"Then she's been up here?"

"No, Lacey. Only you've been here."

Her boot traced a knothole on the porch. "And now you don't want me anymore." Her voice was a whisper.

"Wanting?" He laughed at the absurdity. "Hell, lady. Wanting you is the whole damn problem. You're a part of me. You have been since the first moment I saw you in San Francisco. There was something in your eyes . . . like an angel's."

A slow ache tightened her chest. "An angel?" she scoffed at the ridiculous parody. "But you thought I was a prostitute."

"I saw you earlier that day in a carriage. Christ, but I couldn't forget you. Even when you stole my money all I could think about was that you'd gotten away, and I didn't even know your name." Searching his coat pocket, he withdrew the blue satin choker she'd thought forever lost to her. "It's never left my person."

Lacey blinked back the hot rush of tears. That she had somehow always been in his thoughts. A man like him . . . Morgan Caine. She could hardly breathe for the swell of her heart.

"Then why can't you forgive me?"

"This isn't about forgiveness." She looked away but his finger beneath her chin compelled her full attention. "What makes you so all-fired rational about everything?" he demanded.

"Isn't that a switch?"

"You're asking something from me that I don't know how to give." He hit a fist against his chest. "There's a hurt inside that I can't make go away in a day. And a lifetime of reality that will never go away. I can only be what I am, Lacey. Nothing more."

Lacey's wet eyes embraced Morgan with longing. It came to him suddenly that the rewards of traveling a shared path with her would prove to be a pliable mix of pleasure and challenge.

If he would let it happen.

Her eyes lost a little of their sadness: a verdant splash of hope replaced the emptiness. Doubts swept down into thoughts more programmed to fight outlaws than deal with matters of the heart. He raised a gloved hand to her shorn hair and stopped just short of touching her.

He wanted to back her against the wall and bury himself inside her until he drowned in her body.

But it wouldn't replace the truth.

Or the fact that she'd betrayed him with her silence. And that he'd nearly been killed rescuing Lawton's own daughter.

She'd destroyed the balance of his life and expected a kiss-me patch to conceal the damage.

He wanted to rip Brett Lawton from her soul.

"He'll come for you," Morgan said quietly. Her eyes widened with more than fear. "But then you already knew that. Didn't you, sweet?"

"I . . . don't want you to kill him. I don't want you to die."

"It's a little too late to be thinking about that."

Morgan swept up his rifle and started down the porch stairs. The pine creaked beneath his heavy step. He had to stable his horse for the night. Hesitating, he turned. Lacey remained standing where he'd left her. From beneath the low brim of his hat, he held her gaze.

"The choice to fight is no longer mine. It never was. Not since the moment I took you from Lawton's camp."

Chapter Twenty-one

Morgan opened his eyes to the fractured wedge of sunlight slicing across the shadowed interior of the cabin. The door creaked slightly, and a vibrant breeze washed over him. This was the first morning since his arrival more than a week before that he hadn't awakened with the inkling of a persistent fever.

Awareness hit him at the same time his hand reached for the gun near his blankets. Then he heard Lacey outside splashing in the creek. His body relaxed. But only for a moment.

Morgan strapped on his gun belt and hauled open the door. He'd fallen asleep after checking the snares at dawn, and still wore his boots. His heels clicked on the wooden floor, sounding impatient in the silence of the cabin. A red squirrel jaunted across the porch rail. The fickle autumn temperature had risen, lifting the wooded grove from the grasping breath of a premature winter. He found Lacey down the hill, bent over the creek. Her coat lay beside her. His gaze cut past the corral, over the mix of evergreen trees, back to the hollow where the stream ran.

With his shirt unbuttoned and the white bandage stretching across his shoulder and around his waist, Morgan braced one hand against the frame. Makeshift net in her hands, Lacey huddled over the icy water. Her bountiful catch flopped in the grass beside her, promising to provide them a hearty breakfast. Dressed in her camisole and damp pantalets, which shaped against her backside, she hadn't a lick of sense parading around him like some carnal wood sprite.

Morgan slapped on his hat and loped off the porch stairs. He buttoned his shirt on the way down the hill, then stuffed the length in his pants. Already, as he closed the distance and reached the bank where she fished, the constriction in his chest began to change to something far more formidable.

Capturing her seventh fish, Lacey tossed the slimy thing behind her, where it nearly slapped him in the face. Morgan barely ducked the missile, averting disaster as his boot slipped precariously close to her catch and down the grassy slope. He could not evade the icy wash of water over his boots as he skated into the creek.

"Morgan!" Lacey's shocked eyes skipped up to his. One slender eyebrow arched. "You should be more careful. The grass is slippery."

He stalked out of the water. "I'll remember that next time."

Corn-silk hair cupped her delicate face and a rush of heat swept through him. God, she was more beautiful than moonlight.

A fish flopped over his boots.

"Perhaps you should go back to bed, Marshal." Gathering her fish, she dumped them in a wooden bucket. "You could hurt yourself out here. This creek is dangerous."

Morgan intercepted her hands. "I told you never to leave the cabin without me, Lacey."

Her eyebrows shot up like a flag of war. "You were asleep, Morgan. Would you have us starve?"

"I would have checked the snares—"

"I checked the snares already. They're empty."

"You . . ." He was incredulous. "Dammit, Lacey."

"In case you haven't noticed, you're still recovering from wounds, Morgan."

She reached for her coat, only to find her wrist firmly captured in his. He yanked her to her feet. "In case *you* haven't noticed, we're in the middle of nowhere. Lawton might be out there—and I don't care if you are the bastard's daughter, I don't want you within a hundred miles of him. Not counting the fact that there are wolves and mountain lions out here that would think you're downright interesting enough to eat—"

"Am I?"

His voice fumbled, and he blinked. "Are you what?"

"Interesting enough to eat?"

Morgan frowned. Christ, could she change the subject.

"But in case you haven't noticed, Mr. Marshal, which I'm sure you haven't, because you don't even look at me anymore"—her slim hand fluttered against her forehead—"me and my helpless self have survived thus far."

"You think I don't look at you?"

"I could flaunt my naked bosoms"—her provocative shimmy dropped his jaw—"and you wouldn't notice!"

He took a threatening step toward the brassy imp. His mood was ornery enough to throw her in the grass and have done with his want of her. "Hell, I look at you too much. You're so damn distracting, I'm exhausted looking at you." It was a blatant lie. His eyes strafed her body with a mercenary precision that left him wanting more than just this visual fantasy.

A subtle shift in her breathing occurred. The narrow space between filled with the scent of her, heating his veins like expensive whiskey, smooth, and all fire going down. She tasted like that. And he remembered the way she'd melted in his mouth.

He remembered more.

So did she. The pink tip of her tongue skimmed her lips. A primitive thrill, almost savage, shot through him. The breeze pulled at the strands of his collar-length hair. Slowly, his gaze lifted and found her watching him, wary vigilance in her eyes.

She'd made a shambles of his will.

And the irony of his complete and utter surrender when it came to dealing with his feelings for her left him bereft of thought.

His hand trembled with the wild tempo inside, and the need just to touch her. But at the moment, all he felt was contempt for himself, for acting like an ass when she'd needed him to be strong. But he didn't know how to let it go.

Or if he should.

Movement behind him suddenly pulled her gaze past his shoulder. Morgan saw her expression change. He went cold.

Before she could say a word, he'd drawn his gun and spun.

"Hawk!" He heard Lacey laugh. "You're alive!"

"Shit . . ." Morgan's thumb let up on the hammer, and he forced his pulse to slow.

"You'll have to be faster than that if you wish to take on Lawton," Hawk said, ignoring the harassed look Morgan threw at him as he holstered his gun.

Lacey scrambled up the grassy bank and into Hawk's arms as if they were long-lost cousins. "Isn't it wonderful"—Morgan watched her slim hands crawl all over Hawk's arms and face—"You're safe! Isn't it wonderful, Morgan?"

Hawk's dark gaze assessed him with mild amusement. A pair of birds darted in and out of the trees overhead. "I would have made my presence known sooner, but you both looked . . . busy. And here I'd been worried overmuch for your injuries."

Finally, snatching up her coat from the grass, Morgan stalked up the hill and wrapped it around Lacey's wet form. He glared up into Hawk's sobering visage. "Where the hell have you been?"

"Trying to find your ass all over these mountains." He looked at Lacey. Despite the chill, her face flushed. "I have something that might interest you, Autumn Star." Hawk reached into the saddlebags at his feet and pulled out a pair of boy's pants and a woolen shirt.

Lacey gasped at the treasure and snatched them from his hands. "Clothes! Oh, Hawk. Where did you get these?"

He grinned. "At the small farmhouse about a day's ride from these foothills. A very nice family, once I convinced them I wasn't out to scalp them."

Morgan yanked his hat lower. "I can well imagine."

Hawk looked keenly at Lacey. "You found Granite Pass. Or what's left of it. Very few people have the courage to follow that trail. I was impressed." Dark eyes lifted to encompass Morgan. "You're very lucky to have such a loyal woman."

"Yes, we've talked about that very subject."

"Are you the only one here?" Lacey asked, clearly anxious to change the subject. "We haven't seen signs of another soul."

"There were injured to care for." Hawk shifted his gaze to Morgan. "Red still lives, but Caleb was dead when I reached him. I'm sorry. I know the white-haired man was a friend of yours."

Lacey pressed her hand to her mouth.

"And the posse?" Morgan quietly asked.

"They weren't prepared for the winter storm that came down on us all. They returned to town for supplies. Jack Kipp is on his feet." Hawk looked at Lacey. "Your father will not give up on either of you. He's already back in these hills. Not far behind me."

"Go inside, Lacey." Morgan's voice was hard. "Get dressed."

Her eyes snapped to his. "But I want to hear everything."

"She's right." Hawk jaunted down the shallow bank and scooped up the wooden bucket of fish. Lacey's trout flopped about. "I'm hungry and wish to invite myself to dine with you while we talk."

"No."

Both pairs of eyes moved over Morgan. Hawk read him more clearly. His obsidian gaze flickered over Lacey. Then, setting down the bucket, walked up the bank, and took up a stance beside the thick trunk of an aging chestnut. Sunlight passed through the gnarly branches in a burst of amber warmth.

Arms akimbo, Lacey faced him. "He's our friend, Morgan Caine."

"Go inside," Morgan said without taking his eyes off her face. Stubborn lines bracketed her mouth. "Please?"

"Odious man." She cast a wary look at Hawk. Then without another word, she turned and fled up the grassy bank. A few moments later, the door shut.

Leaning indolently against the tree, Hawk crossed his arms over his chest and casually considered Morgan. "Have you ever wondered by what fate fools are made?"

"I don't need your introspection into my life."

"That is precisely why you are still alone, brother."

Morgan lifted a brow. "Are you finished?"

"Are you?"

"Where's Lawton?" Scarcely were the words out when Hawk's mouth tilted in disgust. Morgan swore. Hands on his hips, he shook his head. "The bastard got past you. Then he's probably already here."

"I see she's told you about him."

"I don't make it a habit of getting involved with family members of men I've tried to hang. Or the daughter of a cold-blooded murderer. I can't say that I handled the news very well."

Hawk's eyes narrowed.

"Don't say it." But Morgan may as well have been talking to a knothole for all the good it did.

"You're a fool for hurting her."

"Don't you think I know that?"

Hawk readjusted himself. "Brett Lawton didn't know that she was his daughter."

The comment grabbed Morgan's full attention.

"She has a birthmark. Here." Hawk palmed his collarbone. "You are probably acquainted with it."

Intimately, Morgan realized before he sought to question how Hawk would know of it. Or anyone for that matter.

"You may hate the blood that flows through her veins, but it saved her life . . . I could not have spared her the horror of what would have happened otherwise."

Morgan lifted his gaze, and let the sunlight warm his face. "I couldn't have saved her back at Lawton's camp without your help. No one had ever beaten me before. I owe you more than . . ."

"I didn't do this for you." Hawk's voice held an odd rasp as he lost the stoic inflection of his speech. He was no longer wild or savage but simply a man, a soldier, who battled with the tragic whispers of his own past. "I did this for myself."

"You never could lie to save your butt."

"You have wounded me, John Caine." Hawk walked down the bank.

"And quit calling me that . . . *Chase Hawken.*"

Hawk lifted the bucket of fish. "It must be nice to have so many people waiting on you, *Morgan.*"

His gaze shifted to the cabin. Smoke from the stone chimney lifted gracefully toward the sky. Lacey stood on the porch. And all that was left of his anger vanished as he met her eyes.

"I could get used to it."

Lacey walked the length of the corral, watching Precious as he tossed his head and pranced beside her. She tightened her arms across her chest. Hawk had left earlier. She'd enjoyed his company all day. Then he just vanished, and Lacey was left alone with Morgan.

A distant roar that sounded too close to a woman's scream snapped her chin up. Heart racing, Lacey swung her gaze around.

Morgan stood a few feet away, Winchester in hand, his heavy coat unfastened and opened to the chill. Beneath his dark hat brim, blue eyes smiled.

"How long have you been there?" she demanded.

"Not nearly long enough." He nodded toward the hills. "It's a mountain lion. A cougar. That's all. They live in these hills."

She sagged against the fence. "Tell me they don't eat people."

"Not normally." It was in his eyes to tease her but obviously, he could tell that she was genuinely terrified. "You'll get used to all the sounds of the night in time."

Her eyes lifted to his. But he'd stepped beside her. She startled when his hand touched her hair. "My whole life I've looked toward the sunset. I didn't know what I wanted," he whispered, "except a deep-down sense of purpose against the world for committing murder against my life. Shannon and I never knew your kind of world. Whatever the reason you ended up in Colin's care, I'm glad."

She blinked back tears.

"I know so little of love, Lacey." His roughened hand curved the soft skin of her cheek. "I only know that I hope I haven't destroyed ours."

"Oh, Morgan." It seemed as if all the wind left her lungs. "You haven't destroyed anything."

As if sensing her distress, he wrapped his arms around her, pulling her against him.

"Don't," she protested.

"Will you just be quiet and let me hold you?"

He did, and she cried. His arms tightened. Hot tears wet his shirt. Saying nothing, he let her weep. Finally, she felt the tension leave her body, and a few minutes later only her sniffles remained.

"I'm . . . sorry," she said.

"And quit saying you're sorry."

Lacey sniffed indelicately. "I've lost my mind."

"It happens."

"Not to you."

"No, Lacey," he said quietly. "I've been just as afraid."

"You?" She lifted her eyes to his.

"I've been afraid most of my life." He combed his fingers through her silken hair. "Until I met you."

Morgan's mouth slanted across hers. She gripped his thick jacket collar and, lifting high on her tiptoes, opened her lips to his probing tongue. Lacey felt the kiss all the way to her soul. Her heart pounded, her blood rushed like a raging river in her ears.

"We can go away." Her breath mingled with his. "Someplace else. Far away."

"Where, Lacey?" His whisper caressed her hair, her neck, the pulse at her throat. She could feel the dark premonition of his mood hovering between them. As if he were leaving. That no matter what she said, it would never be enough to make him flee this fight. A hot, treacherous lump rose in her throat. Morgan pulled back.

One hand still clutched the rifle; the other tilted her chin. His eyes searched her face. Then he was kissing her fiercely. Caught by the intensity of his possession, she could think of naught save the strength of his arms and the feel of his mouth on hers.

Walking her backward to the cabin, Morgan reached around

behind her and opened the door. Her hands worked the fastenings of his pants as he dropped his coat beside the hearth. His mouth sought hers. She deepened the kiss. When no clothes separated them, he lay her back against the blankets warmed by the fire.

There could be no running. No escape from the noose her sire had placed around her neck. But Brett Lawton didn't know that she would never let Morgan be the one to face him. Morgan had taught her that much about courage when he came after her. She would not let him die now. "I love you," she whispered, for the words were in his eyes. "I will always love you."

Morgan covered her with his body. She wrapped her arms around his back, absorbing the power of his movements, his raspy breath breaking against her ear. He no longer wore his bandage, and Lacey's hands reveled in the feel of his taut, smooth skin rippling beneath her palms. Sweat glistened on his skin. She wondered if it would always be like this between them.

If they would have a future after tomorrow.

Then she ceased wondering anything at all.

Lacey moved beneath him, dragging her pleasure from him, swallowing every groan as he melded his mouth to hers. When it came, the explosion shattered them both. Morgan gripped her hair in fists that trembled with his release. Lacey felt him sag against her.

The wild tattoo of her heart turned into the sound of a dozen approaching horses. The horses drummed closer.

For a moment neither one of them moved.

"Damn!" Morgan's rasp shattered the warm silence. He shoved his legs into his underwear. "Get dressed." Yanking on his pants, he reached for the gun, never far from his side.

Lacey barely had her camisole buttoned and had just tied her pantalets when voices outside raised in shouts. The trespassers had recognized Morgan's steel dust in the corral. Looking like a wild man, half-naked with one boot on, Morgan was in front of her, feet braced to fire his gun. The door crashed against the wall. Lacey screamed as three men spilled into the room. Colin was at the front, his eyes raking in the situation at a glance. The gun in his hand drooped a moment after Morgan lowered his.

"Get out!" Colin snapped over his shoulder to the speechless men at his back. They obeyed as if their very lives depended on their haste.

Colin slammed the door behind them. With parental violence sizzling in his eyes, he settled his glare on Morgan. "God blast it, Caine!" Colin advanced a step. "I scour these mountains for nearly four weeks worried to death over the both of you. What the hell do you think you're doing with my daughter?" He smashed Morgan on the jaw, sending him stumbling backward. Morgan didn't even try to defend himself. "Four weeks, Caine!"

"Stop it!" Lacey leaped forward.

Morgan grabbed her arm, preventing her from springing past him to his defense. "Stay out of this," he warned, meeting Colin's menacing glare with nothing more violent than a frown.

Lacey glared at Colin. As ragged as he looked, Lacey felt only a twinge of guilt lasting all of a pair of heartbeats before she regained her composure. "Morgan has been hurt—"

Morgan's glower silenced her. His wounds blared their presence without an explanation from her.

Colin's eyes lifted back to Morgan's face before he shifted the full import of his gaze on Lacey. "I've been worried sick over you." He reached out to stroke her hair. "We followed tracks into this valley three days ago. Tonight when we smelled your fire . . . I didn't know what to expect." Colin swallowed. "For God's sake. I've been out of my mind not knowing where you two were."

"I'm all right," she said.

"By the time we got to Lawton's camp his men were scattered, we couldn't find you. Hawk said Morgan was injured." Colin's gaze sliced back to Morgan. "I can see that you've fully recovered."

Walking to the fireplace, Morgan shrugged into his black shirt. The one Lacey wore to sleep in. He tossed her a blanket to cover herself. "I'm sorry you had to come in on us, Colin," he said sharply. "But what's done is done."

"The hell it is."

"I have every intention of marrying her. There is no issue here to settle."

Lacey gripped the blanket around her shoulders, and said nothing. Morgan turned toward her, his shirt unbuttoned, forgotten for the moment. They stared at each other across the short distance separating them, the fire in the hearth crackling in the silence.

When he spoke, it was to Colin. "Do you mind if I have a word with your daughter? Alone?"

Lacey thought Colin would refuse the request.

"I suppose it won't make a lot of difference now." He spun on his heel, announcing his exit with the slam of the door.

The room wavered before Lacey's eyes, and she dropped to her knees. The sound of Colin's harsh voice outside mixed with at least a dozen others who were breaking out their bedrolls for camp. Already she could smell their cooking fire. Weariness seeped into her. She felt a strange sense of acceptance. Resignation. And with it blossomed courage.

Morgan knelt beside her on the blankets. The firelight reflected in his eyes, a flicker of amber amidst the sky-blue depths. He'd pinned on his badge. "Brett Lawton is someplace in this valley, isn't he?" she asked.

"I want you to return to town with . . . your father. Lacey—" He caught her mouth in a deep kiss, then pressed his lips against her hair. He smelled of his shaving spice. "Tomorrow it ends. I swear."

Lacey dressed in the pants and flannel shirt Hawk had brought to her only that morning. She put more wood on the fire, stirring the embers until they sparked to life. Still, she shivered. Wrapping her arms tightly over her chest, she stepped away from the flames and ran her gaze along the floor. Morgan's place in the blankets was cold and empty. Like death.

Lacey rolled up the blankets and tied them with a leather thong. She set them beside the saddlebags. Her gaze fell on the gun she'd pulled from Morgan's gear, and she wrapped her hand around the walnut grip. It felt smooth and cold in her palm. Releasing the chamber, she emptied each bullet from the gun. With a swing of her arm, she threw the brass casing against the wall.

She needed one more gun.

Lacey stood. She yanked her coat from the table and shoved each arm into the sleeves. Her fingers worked the buttons on the coat. The crisp chill wrapped around her. It would not go away.

Bracing her shoulders, Lacey slung the saddlebags over her shoulders and, lifting the blanket roll, stepped outside. In the darkness, she hoped to pass for one of the posse. At least long enough to steal Morgan's horse.

She stepped out of the cabin into the night. A fire burned just outside. One man sat beside the flames, attempting to work some grounds into a coffeepot. And her heart slowed two beats.

Colin looked so alone. Without conscious thought, she lowered her gear to the porch and approached.

He peered at her from beneath the ocher rim of his hat. "Good evening." His uncertain greeting sounded as stark as the frost-laden ground.

The late-evening moonlight framed his face. Hesitantly, she lifted her eyes past him, relieved to see Morgan's steel dust among the line of horses in the corral.

"Morgan was just here," Colin said, drawing her eyes back to his.

Gathering her courage, Lacey sat beside him. The fire, though warm, did not radiate enough heat to thaw the icy dread building inside. "He's leaving now, isn't he?"

"He's taking Hawk with him."

"How does Morgan even know where Lawton is?"

"We've been on the man's trail for more than a week. We followed him into this valley a few days ago. It's over for him, Lacey."

Her heart jolted. He'd confirmed her suspicions. And a horrible part of her despised that she would mourn Lawton's passing even a fraction.

But it wasn't Lawton she mourned. It was the loss of her

childhood, and a whole lifetime of wanting a family that shattered like so much fragile glass with the discovery of her past.

Lacey glanced up, blinking away the expression on her face. Her gaze swept the woods, stretching past the skeletal branches of majestic trees, once robed in beautiful autumn foliage. Clusters of pine carpeted the distant hills like plush velvet in the darkness.

"I don't think I told you how glad I was to find you both alive." Colin seemed to be focused on the mechanics of the coffeepot.

Lacey watched him fumble with the contraption, finally taking it herself. "Coffee's not half bad, once you get use to it," she stated, firmly attaching the stubborn lid to the pot. "Especially on cold days."

Her father hadn't replied. She looked up to find him watching her. "I apologize for my temper tonight," he said.

"Why? Did you overreact?"

Half-amused, he broke into the kind of smile that warmed Lacey's heart. He took the coffeepot from her hands, setting it on a rock heated by the flame. "Morgan is a good man, Lacey. He has paid dearly for that badge he wears. I couldn't ask for a better man to be your husband."

Questioning her silence, Colin's eyes met hers over the fire. He removed his hat and ran a hand through his hair. "You know, don't you?"

She glanced away sharply. "That Lorraine is my mother?" The next words stuck in her throat. "That Lawton's my father?" she finally answered.

Colin slumped, burying his head into his hands. "Lawton never believed Lainey before. Why now?"

"I have a birthmark."

"Like Joshua."

It was the first time that Lacey realized Joshua was her real brother. If any good could be wrung from Lawton's revelation, she knew it was that sweet bit of knowledge.

"It cost Lorraine twenty years to see you safe. Safe from Lawton and the knowledge that he was your father. Your disappearance from town nearly killed her."

"You should have told me the truth long ago."

"How could I tell you your father was a man like Lawton? That he'd hunted us both because he thought you were mine. He would have killed you when you were just a little girl. Eventually he would have found us again."

Colin was right, of course.

It would have been better had she never known the truth.

"You let me think all those years in England that you'd abandoned me. I hated you for that."

"I know."

"How could Lorraine ever have married a man like Brett Lawton?"

Colin sighed. "When I met Lainey, she was engaged to a wealthy southern slick from a very powerful family. Her father considered it a disgrace . . . beneath the family that any daughter of his should love some no-account immigrant. Her father had me arrested, and forced her to marry Lawton before I would ever see the light of day. I rotted in that stinkin' jail for almost a year. By the grace of God, your mother found me and somehow got me out. She brought you to me, with the promise that I would take you and never try to see her again. Lawton thought you were mine, you see."

"You took me in, knowing my father was Lawton?"

"I loved her enough to do anything she asked." He swallowed a ragged breath and said bleakly, "Somehow we made it, you and I, for seven years. And they were wonderful years, Lacey."

They'd sustained her in England, until time had eroded the hope that she'd ever see Colin again. "I remember the night we ran," Lacey said quietly.

"You were just a little girl. You were very brave."

The terror of that night was vivid.

"I knew then you wouldn't be safe until I found a place to hide you where he would never think to look," Colin said. "When I left England, I went back for Lainey. By then, a war was raging in Virginia. Lawton had found his forte killing the Yanks and had forgotten about you and me. I escaped with Lainey to California where Joshua was later born. We thought we were finally free. Through the years, Lawton made his name with a ruthless band of killers who rode under a man named Quantril. Then the war ended. And it seems we've been running from Lawton ever since. If it hadn't been for Morgan, Lawton would have killed Lainey and me years ago."

Lacey's heart skipped painfully. How often in the past had she wanted parents and brothers and sisters? She liked her stake in life. Belonging to a family. Lawton threatened everything in life she held dear.

He threatened Morgan.

There was only one way to set things right. And she'd known for a long time that it had to be this way.

"Daddy." She used the term lovingly. "You're my father, not Lawton. It will never be Lawton."

He took her into his arms and, for a long time beside the fire, they said nothing. When she pulled away, his gun was hidden beneath her jacket. "I just wanted you to know that."

Then Lacey kissed his weathered cheek, and said good-bye.

Chapter Twenty-two

Morgan hunched on the south rim of the rocky escarpment that overlooked his land. The night was black. Fires dotted the pasture. Bracing an elbow on his knee, he watched the house. Earlier he'd seen Lacey moving around inside. He'd had a clear glimpse of her blond head through the back window. He listened to the wind. And knew that Lawton was somewhere out there doing the same.

"He is probably watching the valley now. And amused." Hawk lay half-hidden near a cluster of boulders, hands clasped behind his neck, studying the sky. "Do you think your friend might have been a little less subtle about his arrival?"

"Let him light up the whole valley," Morgan said. "I want that ranch house visible at all times." He leaned back against a rock and began building a smoke.

"We are too many men," Hawk said.

"Tomorrow I'm sending the posse east." He struck a match and put it to his cigarette. "We're heading west. Better get some sleep."

Hawk reached for his moccasins. "I'm going to scout around."

Morgan watched him melt into the darkness. The faint smell of tobacco smoke mingled with the breeze. To his left, there was a trail, barely visible in the dim moonlight. Morgan crushed the cigarette beneath the toe of his boot and headed down. He could not eliminate the uneasiness.

At the bottom of the hill, Morgan leaned a shoulder against the big chestnut tree and watched the cabin. He hadn't seen Lacey moving inside for a while. Then he closed his eyes. The breeze picked through the wind-worried trees.

Morgan slipped the colt from his holster to test an arm that still lacked the strength and lethal swiftness he once possessed. His hand remained unsteady.

"You'll never beat him."

Hawk's voice came from behind Morgan. A dark mosaic green-and-red poncho separated him from the shadows. He wore a black low-brim hat. His long hair hung loose and fell forward over his shoulders as he hunched beside Morgan.

"Are you dogging my heels, Hawk?" Laying the gun sideways against his elbow, Morgan sighted down the seven-inch barrel. "What do you want?"

"I thought that you might enjoy my company."

"Like hell."

A long knife appeared in Hawk's hand. He worked the blade over a stick. "You haven't smoked one of those cigarettes in years."

Morgan's hand tightened on the gun. He listened to the steady click-click of the ratchet as he slid the metal cylinder down the length of his forearm. His gut knotted.

Lawton had the edge. No matter the crimes he'd committed against Morgan, he was Lacey's father. A split second—barely a heartbeat—was all a man had between living and dying. And suddenly, with a cold certainty Morgan knew he would die if he faced the outlaw tomorrow.

The thought shivered through him, cleaving his rapidly crumbling restraint. Then he closed his eyes, and Lacey was there, in his head and his heart. She'd invaded him, conquering his jaded soul.

She reached so deep into him it ached. He didn't understand

it. Maybe he didn't want to. He only knew that he could never go back to being the man he was.

Moments crawled past. Reason slowly stripped Morgan's choices away, save the only one that mattered.

"I won't let Lawton destroy us," he said finally, holstering his gun. "If I find him, and he kills me. He wins. If I kill him. He wins. I don't ever want this to come back to haunt Lacey and me."

Hawk chuckled. The big knife kept whittling. "I am relieved that you have saved me the trouble of having to beat sense into you."

Morgan met Hawk's gaze directly.

"I've already planned to leave at first light without you," Hawk said. "You can lead the posse."

"There is a substantial reward out for him—if he makes it back to San Francisco."

The knife in Hawk's hands stilled. His hat tilted, and he looked up at Morgan, a dark glitter in his eyes. "I'll remember that."

The slap of running boots drew Morgan around. Hawk came slowly to his feet.

"Marshal!" A young man barely Lacey's age sloshed through the creek toward them. "We've been looking everywhere for you."

Something about the boy's manner sent a vague uneasiness over Morgan. "What is it?"

"Your horse . . ." Morgan's dark brows furrowed. "Miss Ashton is saddling it—"

The kid whirled after Morgan, his shorter legs no match for Morgan's long stride. "We tried to tell her about the tracks. That big cat we spotted this morning is close," he called after Morgan. "We couldn't stop her. That stallion wouldn't let no one else near."

"Get Colin," Morgan yelled over his shoulder.

Three distant shots sent every man in camp to ground. The horses along the picket line scattered. Someone had run the others out of the corral. Lacey arced the steel dust around in a graceful sweep, firing the colt once more. His thoughts froze. Somewhere amidst his disbelief, he wondered where the hell she'd learned to execute such a maneuver. And on his horse.

His eyes narrowed furiously. They saw each other at the same time across the distance separating them. Without hesitation, Lacey swung the steel dust away and leaped the corral fence.

Morgan swore savagely. "Get those damn horses!"

He cut across the yard to the edge of the cabin, leaping a lightning-felled tree. She was a pale blur in the distant moonlight when he stopped running. A tremor raked his body. He bent at the waist, sucking air into his lungs. His side burned.

"Dammit, Lacey."

He knew instinctively, she was going after Lawton.

Lacey gritted her teeth against the useless chatter in her mind, the ripple of regret. And panic. Four hours ago, she was staunchly prepared to commit cold-blooded murder. She must have been mad.

Shaking off the cloying fear, Lacey bent her head beneath low-hanging branches. It served no purpose to question whether she was doing the right thing. Using every trick Morgan had inadvertently taught her about concealing her sign, she hoped to delay being caught long enough to accomplish her task. By the time they'd recaptured the horses, she'd traveled down the creek bed at least two miles before veering off on bedrock into the dark forest of pine and birch. They wouldn't pick up her trail until daylight. By then . . . she let the thought fade.

Tugging Morgan's buckskin tighter around the exposed areas of her neck, she regretted not grabbing the warmer coat when she ran out of the cabin. Unable to see, she couldn't go much farther in the pitch darkness. If Lawton was somewhere close, it was her plan that he would find her . . . before Morgan did.

Lacey pulled the steel dust beneath a canopy of pine. She listened for any signs of pursuit. Her breath came out in huge puffs of steam against the mountain chill. She dismounted near a creek and let the steel dust drink. Then made camp. Huddled near a tree, she waited out the darkness and the night. Lacey couldn't think of facing Morgan or Colin with an explanation of her motives.

She didn't want to face Morgan ever again.

Dawn came over the forest in a musical chorus of sunshine and cheer. Lacey rolled out of her blankets. Without eating, she was riding again. Deeper into the dense forest.

What if the tracks Colin described didn't belong to Lawton? By noon, she was exhausted and starved. She reined in beneath a tree. Her hands ached. The reality of failure hit her.

Suddenly, the steel dust shied, jerking the reins from her grip.

"Whoa, boy," Lacey whispered, searching the shadows ahead for what was agitating the horse. Her lungs filled with the tangy scent of pine. Bending over his neck, Lacey stretched for a handhold on the reins. They dragged on the ground. The stallion grumbled again, and Lacey realized she was about to lose control of the horse.

Slipping off his back, she made a last attempt for the reins when the horse reared violently. She caught the bit, but didn't have the strength to hold on. The steel dust threw her backward. She slammed against the ground, barely rolling out from beneath the stallion's pawing hooves.

From somewhere ahead, a high-pitched roar rent the air. Frozen in terror, Lacey listened. She'd heard the same wail only last night.

The horse shied and, before Lacey could grip the reins, he thundered away in a drumroll of hooves, leaving her alone in the quelling silence to face whatever creature made that horrible sound.

"Cougar," the still voice came at Lacey, and she gasped, clawing back to her feet. Lawton nudged his horse closer, extending his gloved hand. His expression lacked the customary arrogance as he looked impassively down at her. "Unless you intend on being that big cat's dinner, I suggest you take my hand."

The shrill scream came again. Lacey jumped forward. The horrible sound even dimmed her terror of Lawton.

"First, your gun," he said. "I wouldn't want you to get it into your head to shoot me in the back."

Lacey blinked, trying to separate his words from her panic. She envisioned the sharp claws of the cat ripping into her back. Lawton's horse stomped impatiently. Only moments away from being unseated, Brett Lawton gripped the reins in a tight fist.

"Why else would you go to such a deliberate attempt to find me?" he casually queried, mocking her fright. "I've been following you since last night."

Without a word, Lacey withdrew the colt from her coat pocket, tossing it up to him with little regard to safety. She watched uneasily as he holstered the gun into a belt lacking the sign of any other weapon. He had no gun. Before she could respond, he latched on to her arm, swinging her easily behind him.

Lacey barely grabbed him before he spurred the horse into a run.

"Never waste an opportunity, my dear," he said over his shoulder. "You'll find that's your first lesson on survival."

"Dare I ask your second?" The wind took the words, but Lawton had heard enough to laugh.

"Always have a plan. Did you think I was stupid enough to let you just walk up to me?"

Lacey didn't answer. "What happened to your gun?"

"That posse shot it off me. Count it as a blessing though, my dear," he said grimacing. "I've known where you and Caine were for some time. That bastard Hawk's been watching over you like a loyal hound. I didn't expect you to make my job so easy. If you came to plead for Caine's life or Ashton's, don't waste your breath. I hate them both more than I could ever love you, daughter."

The words were knife-edged reminders of the kind of man Lawton was. The horse stumbled, drawing Lawton's attention. He slowed the gelding to a walk.

"My name is Lacey," she said into the silence.

Lawton snorted. "That was Lainey's mother's name. A flighty woman. Not at all practical like my Lainey."

Lacey realized sadly that this man knew more about her family than she did. "It doesn't bother you to have missed what might have been between any of us as a family, does it?"

"Are you questioning whether I would have enjoyed being a father?" He chuckled. Then his humor seemed to slide away. "I have a bad temper, girl. Could you have abided having me for a father?"

"No," she said flatly. "It was better to have had no one."

"Bright girl. I wish I'd been given the same choice in my lifetime. Lainey couldn't even stomach my skills as a husband. I must admit, my own father didn't teach me much on tenderness. Caitlyn never seemed to mind . . ." His voice faded. "Caine and Ashton ruined everything. It'll take me months to round up everyone who's scattered in these mountains. Recruit some more . . . Cat will be much harder to replace."

On that account, Lacey felt no grief and told him so.

Lawton stopped. Twisting in the saddle, he pulled her off the horse, following closely behind her descent.

"What are you doing?" She looked around the open clearing. "Aren't we still close to the cougar?"

Without answering, Lawton frisked her, digging beneath her coat to pat her waist and thighs. With narrowed eyes, he probed her mind. She could tell he suspected the ease of his conquest. It worried him, she thought with a tinge of satisfaction.

"I should be asking you that question."

"I came to kill you," she said bluntly.

He presented his back to her as he inspected the horse's front hoof. "Did your plan fail . . . or are you merely a coward."

Her back stiffened. "I wanted to see you first."

"Then I'm afraid you'll have to stand in line, my dear." He dug around the shoe of the horse. "We'll have to put off our chat for another time. This horse is lame, and Caine and Hawk are behind us." He eyed Lacey keenly. "Don't be fooled into thinking I won't kill you if you try to do something heroic."

Lacey felt the fear and hate for him flow back into her veins. It was insane to think she had the power to barter with him. It was in her best interest to run. Looking in the direction where they had come, Lacey pondered the shadows.

"And if you run, I'll shoot you," he said, cutting in to her thoughts.

Lacey's eyes snapped back to his. His bearded countenance cracked into a mocking grin. "I wouldn't want you to think I'd grown soft since our last encounter, daughter. Nothing about me has changed."

"Why did you bother helping me when you could have let the cougar do your job?"

"Have you ever seen what an animal like that does to its victims? On an enemy I wouldn't blink an eye." Lawton gripped her chin, compelling her to look at him. "You're not my enemy."

She *was* his enemy.

"No, you're not," he said, reading her thoughts, disarming her completely. "You're my daughter. What's mine, I take."

The horse snorted, showing signs of distress. Lawton jerked around. Only the wind whisking through the pines answered his silent query. Lacey saw nothing, either.

"We're being stalked," Lawton said slowly, easing the revolver out of his holster.

"What do you mean?"

"It's not the two-legged beast out there right now, dear."

Lawton walked the horse to a nearby tree. Lacey's uneasy gaze followed the gun at his side. The one he'd taken from her. She watched while he dug through the bags behind the saddle, pulling out hobble straps. She could make a run and escape. If he looked too closely at the weapon . . . if they really were being stalked.

What remained of her good sense warned her to run.

The horse jerked his head back. He yanked at his bit, drawing Lawton's full wrath, then reared, tearing free.

"Goddamm, miserable . . ." Lawton threw the hobble straps after the fleeing animal. He swung on Lacey. "Sit down, girl."

Lacey lowered herself uneasily to the ground. "We should leave."

"We're staying."

"Why?"

"Because it suits me," he said furiously.

"Is this one of your games?"

"With you as bait?" Lawton chuckled as if the idea bore considering. "Caine might be real particular about that cat reaching you first. You better hope they get here real soon then, daughter."

"You're . . . insane," Lacey whispered, realizing too late that she'd spoken her thoughts aloud.

Lawton pounced on her. "I forgave you the first time you called me that." He dragged her back to her feet. "Maybe I *will* make you bait. Should I tie you to a tree?"

Lacey glared at him, blinking back the tears stinging her eyes. Lawton would have them torn to shreds by some forest beast, just for arrogant spite.

Fury tangled her emotions. This madman was her father. How had Lorraine ever endured him? Even from the short time Lawton had spent with her, Lacey was already teetering on the verge of hysteria.

"Cat got your tongue?" Lawton's smooth taunt crippled her.

"Bastard!" Swinging with all her strength, she launched herself against him. "Why did you have to tell me the truth? You didn't have the right to ruin my life!"

Lawton stumbled backward before he could wrestle her hands from his face. Lacey shoved against him. He threw her sideways. She landed hard on the ground, rolling to face him again. She stared over the barrel of the gun into Lawton's cold eyes.

Wiping his mouth, Lawton admired the blood on his hand. "I respect violence, dear," he said casually. "A little bit of work, and we could be partners, you and I and Joshua."

Lacey's anguish seared her. Shame gripped her. Her fingers knotted at her sides. "You and I are nothing alike. You don't even know who I am."

"Lorraine and Colin stole my chance to ever know my children."

"They saved my life and my brother's. I would do no less for them now."

Lawton laughed, clearly pleased with her spirit. It was not Lacey's intention to win his approval. Yet, nothing she did seemed to affect him.

"You came out to kill me today," Lawton pointed out. "I'm

curious to see how you're going to accomplish—"

The shriek of the cougar shuddered through the trees, spinning Lacey around, her throat closing against a scream. The sleek cat crouched on the huge branches of a knobby pine. Feral eyes gleamed.

"Oh, God." She shuddered. "OhGodohGodohGod."

The huge, sleek beast growled, a long, rolling sound deep in its throat, its tail flicking methodically. Lacey remained paralyzed.

Lawton faced the big cat. Only the faint tic in his jaw betrayed any emotion. "Keep your voice calm, girl. No sudden movements." He took a step backward, drawing the cat's golden glare.

"Don't . . ." Lacey whispered. "Don't move."

"One of us has to, girl."

Lacey choked on a gasp. "Don't move," she pleaded.

The cat shifted its attention completely to Lawton. Tension gripped Lacey's lungs like a fist. She couldn't breathe. Couldn't talk.

Lawton took another step back and brought up the weapon in his hand. "Keeping you alive is purely selfish, my dear."

Lacey stared at the gun in horror. The memory of her plan hit her with the cold fury of a broadside.

Lawton fired.

The weapon clicked on an empty chamber and clicked again.

Brett's expression emptied of shock. He remained like granite, his gaze riveted to the naked branches above their head. Lacey watched behind her tears as he lowered the useless weapon.

"Very clever, daughter," he said quietly.

Fumbling in her boot for the loaded gun she had stowed, Lacey watched in a panic as the cat crouched. "Run," she whispered. "Oh, please. Run."

A black shuddering silence followed. Then a feral shriek rent the air. In the empty space of Brett Lawton's last heartbeat, the big cat leaped, slamming into his body, tearing flesh and bone. Lacey screamed and screamed. She fired the gun.

She kept firing. The explosions deafened her. A rifle barked from somewhere behind her.

Were those her screams? Lacey heard Morgan yell her name. A swirling eddy of blackness crushed her. Her vision narrowed to a pinpoint, barely discernible as the earth tilted, and she crumbled to her knees. The gun lowered, still clicking on each spent chamber as she continued to rake the trigger. Strong arms seized her, tugging the gun from her hand. A tremor built in her chest, catching in her throat as Morgan's mouth melted over hers.

"You brave little fool." She heard the faint words break against her lips. His voice was shaking. His other words were lost as he crushed her to him.

He held her as if she somehow might turn to dust and blow away. "It's over, Lacey. It's over."

A hollow sensation crept outward from her gut, plunging her into oblivion. Violence had answered violence, measuring out in death what had been lived in life.

Justice had been rendered with a horrible vengeance.

Chapter Twenty-three

Lacey arrived in Kingston three days later. Beneath a pewter-colored sky, the snow began to fall an hour before the first welcome lights in the valley came in sight. Hawk vanished as simply as he had appeared. He'd been by her side during the last few days, watching over her as protectively as Colin did. Lacey wished she'd had a chance to say good-bye.

She hadn't even told Morgan good-bye.

Lacey remembered little after Lawton fell beneath the cougar. She'd lived suspended somewhere between the twilight and consciousness, aware of neither state. Morgan had held her as if frightened of ever letting her go.

Yet, he had.

He left without saying good-bye. Even now, she couldn't believe he was gone.

Lacey rode into town beside her father at the head of the ragtag posse. The muffled *clip-clop* of a dozen exhausted horses sounded hushed in the stillness around them. At first, their presence in town went undetected; then slowly people began to crowd into the street. The gathering throng pulled along the horses in much the same way as the very first day

Lacey had arrived in Kingston. When she'd been with Morgan . . . and Jack . . . and Caleb. A lifetime ago.

Lacey clasped the reins of her horse. Her hands trembled.

The windows of the mercantile were boarded against the winter elements. It would be spring before a new pane of glass arrived to replace the one Lawton's gang had shot out. Her horse stopped. Strong hands lifted Lacey off the saddle.

"Jack!" she cried, flinging her arms around him. "Look at you! I'm glad to see you're alive . . . looking so fit."

"As a fiddle, my dear. Better than I can say for all of you." He glanced between Lacey and Colin. "You've been gone more than a month."

Jack's gaze riveted on Lacey's hair, before he turned to Colin. "Lainey will be mighty glad to see the lot of you. Morgan's been to town twice already lookin' for you."

"Morgan?" Lacey repeated, unable to hide the tenseness in her voice. "Here?"

"Come ridin' in day before yesterday, like a bat out of . . . in a real hurry."

"Is he all right?"

Jack's big smile flashed. "No sense worryin' about him, Lacey. He doesn't do anything except with reason, and he's not a man that comes to terms real easy with reason. I reckon he's been tendin' to business."

"How's Jolene?" Colin asked.

"Morgan talked to her yesterday. Jared was her only kin. To know that he had turned was doubly hard as his death has been."

"We'll head on over to the livery. I want to see the family as soon as possible," Colin replied. "Can you walk?" he asked Jack.

"It'll be a lot easier than if you try to carry me."

Lacey walked between Jack and Colin, following behind everyone else who had already reached the livery. Jack's moccasin-clad feet made no sound in the snow, and Lacey felt as ponderous as the noisy horses behind them. It was the first time in more than a month that she had not lived in constant fear, whether of Lawton or of Morgan's life.

Focusing on her steps in the snow, Lacey found herself

leaning into her father. Colin would be nothing less in her heart than her true father. She knew by his manner, he had never assumed otherwise.

Lacey glimpsed the warm glow of light emanating from within the livery. It lay in a half circle outside the stable, inviting the weary group inside. She remained just inside the door, listening to the dull drone of voices. The pungent smell of hay irritated her nose. The horses were fed and curried. Jack prepared the buckboard to transport them to . . . Lacey realized she had no home. Where were they going?

The voices inside the stable mingled with the sound of a wagon and the hushed footfalls of an approaching crowd. Someone called her name, and Lacey turned; then she was in her mother's arms, hearing but understanding little of the unintelligible words mumbled through the maze of confusion. Joshua wrapped Lacey in an enthusiastic embrace, and through the tears gathering in her eyes, she looked over Lorraine's shoulders into Morgan's handsome face.

He was standing behind Lorraine, his face shadowed by the brim of his flat crown hat. In his high-heeled star boots, he towered over her. His expression was inscrutable, but his eyes said he loved her.

"Morgan told me you know everything," Lacey heard her mother whisper. "I've waited a lifetime for this."

Tearing her gaze from Morgan, Lacey closed her eyes, a surge of euphoria lifting her heavenward. She hugged her mother with an intensity that reflected more than the joy in her heart.

For a long time no one spoke. Then Lorraine released her, and Morgan pulled her into his arms, moving her outside into the snow away from prying eyes.

Lacey's heart thumped against her chest. "You're here. I didn't know if—"

"I have something for you," Morgan said quietly, stilling the hushed words and questions that flowed unbidden between them. "Open it," he prompted when Lacey merely stared at the paper he gave her.

Slowly she unfolded the parchment. A gold seal stared back

at her, stamped over a deed. She lifted her gaze, questioning his.

"Our ranch," he supplied. "It's not much, I know—"

"I . . . don't understand," she whispered shakily. If she fainted now, she would never forgive herself.

"Did you think I would marry you and have nowhere to go with our life? No dreams?" he softly queried. "This is our cabin hideaway and another five hundred acres around it to raise cattle."

Lacey choked out a feeble reply.

"I told you, I'm not totally destitute." He grinned down at her. "What I didn't have, I borrowed. We'll have the loan paid back as soon as we run our first herd of cattle across to the mining camps in British Columbia."

Lacey blinked back her tears. "I didn't know if I'd ever see you again."

"I came back to take care of things before you got here," he chided. A single crystal droplet rolled down her cheek captured by Morgan's thumb. "Will you marry me?" His mouth splayed hungrily over hers. "Or does love require that I go down on bended knee?"

He kissed her soundly, paying no heed to their public display. Her lips parted beneath his. Their kiss was long and languorous. She felt the heat of his breath against her mouth. "The simple fact is, I want you by my side. Forever. I want green-eyed children. I want laughter. I want a life I can be proud of."

Lacey swallowed, blinking away her tears. "If you go down on your knee, Mr. Caine, it won't be your talk that interests me."

Lacey wrapped her arms around his waist. She knew she was crying, but couldn't help it. Morgan gathered her within the comforting strength of his embrace, holding her tight against his chest. His heart beat in tandem to hers. She loved him. Somehow, life had blessed her. When she thought she'd lost everything, fate had given it all back and so much more.

"We're getting married now."

"Now?" Lacey blotted her nose indelicately on a sleeve. *"Now?"*

She turned to find a happy crowd gathered outside the stable watching them. Lacey blushed that they should have an audience. And one so clearly enjoying the show.

Lorraine was the first to step forward. Pinning her golden locket around Lacey's neck, Lorraine snapped it open. "I've worn this close to my heart for fourteen years."

Lacey looked down at the locket. It was a picture of Lacey, taken before she'd left for England when she was six, a miniature version of the photo that had burned in the fire at Colin's house.

"You can fill it with the faces of your own beautiful children. This is my wedding gift. Something old."

Around them people began to shuffle, making way for Joshua who excitedly waved a ragged neckerchief that had seen better days. "Ma said I should give this to you. It's my favorite. And it's blue," he pointed out. "Ma said it had to be blue."

"Thank you, Joshua." Lacey leaned over to kiss her brother.

"It's my favorite," he said again. "My only one."

"I shall take very good care of it." To prove her point, Lacey tied it around her neck.

Jolene stepped forward. Securing a lovely bonnet over Lacey's mussed hair, her eyes glimmered with tears. "I never did get your dress with feminine frippery," she said softly. "I hope this will do for a start. It doesn't match your wedding attire, but it *is* something new." Jolene hugged her. "We'll have to do something about your wardrobe," she whispered, a profound observation, Lacey realized, feeling ridiculous but wonderfully happy in the feminine bonnet.

She'd never wear pants again.

Morgan tightened his arm around Lacey's shoulders and turned to Colin. "I hope you don't mind, but I stole your wagon," he said as he moved Lacey through the parting crowd toward a sturdy canvas-draped wagon.

Lacey gaped at the beautiful brass bedframe peeking from beneath the canvas covering. A cast-iron stove and her trunks filled the back end.

Morgan lifted Lacey onto the seat.

"I . . ." Colin looked dumbly at his wife, then spun back on

Morgan, his mouth open. "Of course, I mind. Where the hell do you think you're going, leaving the rest of us here?"

"Home."

"With my daughter?"

"After we're married, of course."

"Someone's tryin' to find the preacher now," Red piped in. "He's not at the church."

Jack stepped forward, taking the bridle of the horse in his big hands. "Miller!" he bellowed into the shadow of faces behind Colin.

"Aren't you a parson?"

A straw-haired man eagerly stepped forward. "Been that a time or two," he agreed.

"Ever married anyone?" Colin suspiciously demanded.

"Reckon I done that a time or two also."

"Then do it again," Jack snapped. "These two want to be on their way. No sense in wasting time in this snow trying to track down the preacher man. Hear he has the chicken pox anyway."

Miller looked up importantly into Morgan's amused countenance, clearing his throat as he hastily tried to remember proper wedding etiquette.

"Well, get on with it," Jack said impatiently.

"I'm thinking," he protested. "You don't expect everything to come back, just like that, do you?"

"How hard can a weddin' be, Miller," someone said from behind him, and the small newly appointed parson raked a glower across the eager crowd. He shook himself and looked back up at Morgan and Lacey.

"Do you, Marshal, want this woman?" He cleared his throat. "To be your wife, that is?"

"Yes," came the deep reply. Immensely pleased with himself, the parson turned to Lacey.

"And you, ma'am?" Miller politely inquired.

"I do," she replied.

"Well hell, parson." Jack grinned, slapping him on the back with unaccustomed gusto. The poor man stumbled forward nearly falling facedown in the straw. "That's just about the finest weddin' I ever attended."

"But I ain't finished." Miller complained.

"What else is there?" Jack asked. "You said all the important stuff already."

"I have to pronounce them husband and wife."

And the words rang out like music in the hushed silence of the falling snow. Morgan leaned over and kissed his bride, his whispered words soft and gentle against her lips, promising all he had in life, all he could give. Lacey smiled back at him, her eyes bright with hope. He shoved his hand beneath his jacket and took the badge from his vest. The star he followed was no longer the one he wore. Without tearing his gaze from Lacey's beautiful face, he flicked it over his shoulder where Colin easily caught it.

He'd found an angel and all of heaven at his feet. He'd found his Autumn Star.